I'm an Irish author who is addicted to writing romances featuring damaged, moody, book boyfriends searching for their happily ever after.

Visit K.A. Finn online:

www.kafinn.com
(trailers, excerpts, artwork, playlists etc)

Facebook: kafinnauthor

Instagram: kafinnauthor

Twitter @K_A_Finn

Also by K.A. Finn

Nomad Series (Space Opera)

Ares

Nemesis

Perses

Chaos

Mania

Cronus

Talos (TBA)

Blackjacks Series (Paranormal Romance)

Breaking Phoenix

Reviving Davyn

Defying Shep

Defending Rhain (TBA)

Broken Chords (Rockstar Romance)

Broken Rock (Tate)

Fractured Rock (Gregg)

Split Rock (Tate # 2)

Crushed Rock (Luke)

Shattered Rock (Dillon)

Twisted Legends (Folklore Retelling/Romance)

North Bound (Nick/Santa)

Shadow Bound (Damon/The Boogeyman

Broken Chords #3

SPLIT *Rock*

K.A. FINN

Cover design by Deranged Doctor Design
www.derangeddoctordesign.com

Photographer: Kruse Images & Photography
www.kruseimagesandphotography.com
Model: Jonny James

Published by Cooper Publishing
www.cooperbookservices.com

ISBN: 978-1-914177-46-0

Coming next

Split Rock Playlist

Although I haven't mentioned any song lyrics in this book, that doesn't mean music didn't play a MASSIVE part in its creation.

This playlist was on every time I wrote, edited, or just read the book.

The bands, the songs, or the lyrics remind me of Tate, Gregg, Luke, or Dillon in some way. It's still a playlist I listen to regularly and it always reminds me of the band.

If you want to check out the playlist that I had blaring in the background while I was writing *Split Rock,* you can find it on my website (www.kafinn.com/splitrock), by scanning the QR code below, or by searching the following songs.

Just make sure to play it LOUD!

Last Dance– Camera Can't Lie
I'll Fight – Daughtry
Call On Me – Smash Into Pieces
Here For You – Devin Williams
Used To Be – Lansdowne
I'm Not Alright – Sanctus Reel
Fears – Twin Wild
Enemy Reimagined – Designer Disguise
Monsters – Shinedown
Best I Ever Had – State Of Shock
State Of My Mind – Shinedown
Call You Mine – Daughtry
Without You – Breaking Benjamin
A Reason to Fight – Disturbed
Waiting on the Sun – Citizen Soldier
If I Surrender– Citizen Soldier
Paranoia – Nathan Wagner
Getting Sober – Nathan Wagner
15 Minutes of Fame – Citizen Soldier
Can't Help Me Now – Rob Thomas

Bring Mr Back To Life – HT Bristol
Better Half Of Me – Dash Berlin
U – Gareth Emery
If You Love Her – Forest Blakk
Forgive Me Friend – Smith & Snell
Lose You Now – Lindsey Sterling
Acoustic #3 – Goo Goo Dolls
I Am Human – Escape The Fate
Break Away – Artist Vs Poet
Daylight – Shindeown
Hole In My Heart – Luke Friend
Ashes – Bobina/Gid Sedgwick
Try Again – Walking On Cars
Lost Without You – Kygo/ Dean Lewis
What About Us – Davina Michelle
Higher – Creed
Bad Life – Sigrid/Bring Me The Horizon
Legends Are Made – Sam Tinnesz
Limit – Citizen Soldier
Gone Too Soon – Daughtry

Well, enough from me. I'll leave you in the band's more than capable hands – have fun!

Intro

This series is based in the Republic of Ireland. The timescales, procedures, and context are reflective of local practices and policy.

Content Information

This book contains strong subject matter that may not be suitable for all readers, including scenes that may depict, mention, or discuss:

- abduction
- abusive relationship
- alcohol and drug use
- anxiety
- assault
- emotional abuse
- kidnapping
- physical abuse
- rape
- sexual abuse
- sexual assault
- suicide
- violence

This one is for Tate, Gregg, Luke, and Dillon.
Thank you for being so much fun to write about, and for pushing me further than I thought I could go.

Tate Archer stands at the edge of the magnificent ballroom and watches his friend and fellow band mate, Luke, dance with his new wife. The wedding has gone exactly as he thought it would. Luke's wife, Pippa, was all about the attention, endless spotlights, and anything else her husband's celebrity status brings. She lapped it up like a drug, and their wedding was no exception. No expense had been spared. Her new husband was worth a fair bit, so that's no surprise.

Tate smiles as his beautiful girlfriend, Chloe, emerges from the crowd of guests and walks over to him. They've been together less than a year, but he can't imagine ever being without her. She's worked her way into his life, and he loves her deeply.

She reaches up and kisses him. 'Hey gorgeous. Are you surviving?'

He puts on an exaggerated grin, and she playfully hits him on the chest.

'Oh knock it off. I promise I'll make it up to you later.'

He wraps his arms around her and holds her against his chest. 'You're really going to have to do something epic, to make up for this.'

'It's a wedding, Tate. It's kind of a normal thing.'

'Nothing about this fiasco is normal. She must have spent six figures on it. It's ridiculous!'

'My goodness, you are in a grumpy mood today.' Her face softens and she rubs his back. 'Are you doing okay though?'

Tate nods, even though he's far from okay. Being a recovering drug addict and a borderline alcoholic, this wedding isn't his idea of fun. He's stressed and on edge. Not sleeping last night is also adding exhaustion to the list. The sooner he can get out of here, the better.

He catches his sister, Bria, waving at them from across the room, then pointing at Chloe. 'I think someone wants you.'

'Are you okay to be left alone?'

'I promise I won't go on a rampage and destroy the place... no matter how tempting.'

'Behave. I'll be back in a few minutes.'

He watches her disappear around the corner with his sister, then looks around the stuffy, over decorated room. A lot of the guests are celebrities he recognises, but a few must be Pippa's school or college friends. And those are the ones giving him a little too much attention.

He makes his way over to the toilets, politely smiling at everyone as he passes, before eventually reaching safety. He's well used to the whole polite smiling thing with his job, but he's not in the mood for it tonight. Far from it.

After using the facilities, he washes his hands and faces his reflection. He looks tired. He thought he got rid of the black rings while he was away. Seems he'd only dodged them for a few weeks. The mess with Bria and Gregg has been on his mind since he got back which isn't helping his less than regular sleeping patterns.

Tate dries his hands, then glances over his shoulder as the bathroom door shuts and locks. He freezes as he stares over at the door and the person he's now apparently trapped with. 'Astrid? What the fuck are you doing here?'

'I'm friends with Pippa. Of course I'd be invited to her wedding. You look well.'

'Thanks. Now open the fucking door and get out of my way.'

'Oh now, don't be like that. I haven't seen you for well over a year. We have a lot to catch up on.'

'No we don't.'

'How are you?'

'I'm seriously not doing this with you. Get out of my way!'

'Why are you being like this?'

'Are you fucking serious? You threw me under the bus. Pouring your heart and soul out to any reporter who'd give you five minutes in the spotlight. You near on called me a junkie. Said I'd been using heavily for years. You stuck a knife in my back to get yourself some publicity. That's why I'm being like this.'

'You know what the press is like. My comments were exaggerated by the reporters who spoke to me.'

Tate crosses his arms so she can't see him clenching his fists. The comments had come from Astrid. The reporters just ran with what she fed them. 'That must be one hell of a lawsuit.'

Her forehead scrunches at his words. 'Excuse me?'

'You suing the papers for misquoting you.'

It takes a few seconds for what he's saying to sink in. She shrugs and smiles at him. 'It's done now. There's no point going over old news. So, you look well.'

'You said that already. Move.'

She takes a step closer to him and he straightens his shoulders. He'd pretty much trust anyone and anything over Astrid. 'So, how are things with the band?'

'Grand.'

She steps closer and he backs away, bumping in to the sink. If this was a guy he'd shove them aside and be on his way. But Astrid is a whole other entity. There's no way he's going to even sidestep around her, in case he bumps into her. 'And Chloe? Things are still going well with her?'

He's not going there with her. Not now. Not ever. After a long wait, she realises she's not going to get an answer. She smiles and holds out a piece of paper. 'Just in case you lost it.'

'Lost what?'

'My number of course.' She reaches out to touch his chest, but he jumps back and shouts. 'Don't you fucking touch me!'

'Very well.' She places the paper on the edge of the sink and smiles up at him. 'Give me a shout. I've missed you.'

Astrid waves and turns around, unlocks the door, then goes back to the reception party. Tate waits another minute to make sure she's gone, then slumps back against the sink.

What the fuck just happened? That was weird, even for her. He looks down at the number resting on the sink, then angrily tears it into pieces, and drops it in the bin before he turns away and heads back to Gregg. He drops down in the seat beside him and takes a long drink of coke, briefly wishing it was something stronger.

'What the fuck happened to you? You're as white as a sheet.'

'Astrid.'

Gregg looks over his shoulder to the toilet. 'I thought you went for a piss?'

'She made an appearance and locked the two of us in the room.'

'She's here?'

'Mates with Pippa apparently. Nice of her to give me the heads up that Astrid would be here.'

'I'd say the same about Luke, but I doubt he knew. Shit. That's not at all creepy. You okay?'

Tate nods then takes a drink. He's not okay and that's pissing him off. Seeing her like that out of the blue, had completely thrown him.

The woman hadn't been a major part of his life for the six weeks they were together. It was sex. Nothing more. Unfortunately, she hadn't seen their relationship the same way. She'd imagined this big romance between them, and when he dumped her, she'd taken it badly.

Telling everyone who would listen, that he's a junkie, had been a great way to get back at him. 'Just threw me a little. Wasn't expecting to run into her in the toilet like that.'

'Too right. What did she want?'

'Me.'

Gregg grimaces. 'Are you serious?'

'Left me her number in case I forgot it. I tore it up and threw it in the bin, before you ask.'

'Didn't think you'd do different, buddy. You manage to extract yourself without losing any limbs?'

'Just about.' He drums his fingers on the bar top, as he glances around the room. Everywhere he looks there are people with cameras, or waiters with drink. It's suffocating. He needs to get out of here. 'Where's Chloe?'

Gregg shakes his head. 'Went off somewhere with Bria. Bit of a girly chat. Probably comparing their studly boyfriends. Hey, you okay?'

'No. I need to go.'

Gregg stops joking around and squeezes his arm. 'Come on. Let's get you to the car and then I'll track down Chloe.'

'Thanks. Sorry about this.'

'Never apologise, Tate. I'd prefer you go, than stay and struggle.'

Dillon

In his thirty-eight fucked up years on the planet, Dillon has had

5

his fair share of heartache. Time and time again, he was hurt by people he thought had his back. He learned his lesson a long time ago. Built a wall around his heart to protect himself from the pain.

He's had enough of that to last him a lifetime.

Sitting in a posh hotel room, best man at his friend's wedding, he realises all his wall-building came to nothing.

His heart has yet again been torn apart, but this time it's entirely his fault.

No one did this to him. No one betrayed him or walked away from him.

He takes another drink from the bottle of whiskey, not feeling the effects of the alcohol. His body is used to it at this stage. Which is probably something he should be worried about.

He keeps his alcohol and drug use off the radar for the most part. The guys aren't idiots. They know he uses, but he's got a handle on it. He's not addicted to any one drug. He'll take whatever he can get.

That's also probably something he should be worried about.

Right now he's not. Right now, he couldn't give a fuck what he takes. As long as it stops the pain he'll take it all.

The coke he got from a friend of Luke's seemed like a good idea at the time. He doesn't usually go for coke, but it was all he could get his hands on. And fuck knows he needed something.

He tears off the suit jacket, rolling it in a ball and throwing it across the room, followed by the tie. Damn thing is suffocating him. He should be downstairs. He should be making sure Luke is being looked after. Should be making sure he's having the best day of his fucking life.

But he can't.

He spends most of his life pretending to be someone else. It's easier than dealing with the shit that's in his head. But he can't pretend about this. The thought of going downstairs, smiling and chatting to people with a gaping wound in his chest is far from appealing.

He rubs his chest, a little surprised there isn't a fucking massive hole there. That's what it feels like. He curses himself and gets up, nervous energy forcing him to pace at the foot of the bed.

He loves Luke.

He's completely, totally, and stupidly in love with his best friend. Has been for years.

But now Luke is married. Not that it makes a difference. He could never have anything with Luke.

That didn't stop him wishing for it.

He takes another drink, the agitation building with every step. What the fuck is he supposed to do now? How is he expected to carry on like nothing has happened?

Nothing did happen. This is affecting him and him alone.

As always.

God he's so sick of being alone.

He stumbles into a nest of tables, knocking the lamp onto the floor, breaking the glass shade. The mix of coke and whiskey is fucking with his balance.

He looks down at the broken lamp for a long time, just staring at it like the damn thing is going to put itself back together again.

But it's fucked. No putting that back together. Some things can't be put back together once they're broken.

For some reason, he finds that funny. He must be wasted if he's comparing himself to a fucking lamp.

He turns and looks around the room, catching his reflection in the mirror over the vast bed.

The laughter fades as he stares at himself. He takes another drink from the bottle, watching his reflection do the same.

'You're a right fuck up you know that.' He points to himself, taking an unsteady step closer to the mirror. 'No wonder no one wants you. Fucking pathetic waste of space.'

He picks up the remains of the lamp from the ground and launches it at the mirror, taking out his reflection. The mirror drops from the wall, landing against the wooden headboard, shattering into pieces.

Before the mirror has settled on the bed, he picks up the chair by the desk and throws it against the wardrobe door, splitting the wood.

With hot angry tears pouring down his face, Dillon unleashes his temper that he usually keeps a hold on. But there's no holding it back now. His world has just collapsed and he hasn't got a fucking clue what to do about it.

He knows he's gone too far when the TV flies out the window, landing in the flowerbed under his room, shattered glass falling on the perfectly pruned flowers. But there's no point holding back at this stage. He's already fucked himself again.

Might as well go out in style.

2

Tate

Tate leans against the wall surrounding the patio, listening to Gregg on the phone with Bria. He hates that he's dragging them away from the wedding like this, but he needs to leave before he does something stupid. And right now he has no idea what that stupid will be.

He pulls out his own phone, answering it when he sees Dillon's bodyguard, Jason's, name on the screen. 'What's up?'

'We need you and Gregg upstairs now. Room fifteen on the second floor.'

Tate gestures to Gregg and they hurry over to the elevator. 'On the way up. What's the problem?'

Tate curses when he hears shouting and a loud crash. 'Dillon... well he's upset. We've tried talking him down, but it's not working. He's drunk and we reckon he's taken something. No idea what though.'

Tate hangs up and shoves his phone into his pocket. 'Dillon is off his head. Sounds like he's destroying his room. They can't calm him down.'

Gregg rubs his face. 'Well isn't that just the perfect end to a shitty day.'

Tate's security, Liam, is waiting for them when the elevator doors open, and he brings them to Dillon's room. Not that there was any doubt where it was. You could hear Dillon shouting from down the corridor. Tate takes off his jacket and passes it to Liam, before he steps into the room.

Dillon is standing in the centre of the room braced for a fight. Not a great start. The rest of their bodyguards are fanned out in front of him with Jason, Dillon's security trying to talk to him.

Tate's only been in the room a few seconds, but he knows Jason is wasting his breath. Dillon's green eyes are wild, thanks in part to whatever he's taken. The bottle of whiskey in his hand won't be helping the situation either.

'Hey Dillon. What's going on?'

Dillon laughs and points his bottle at Tate. 'Called in the big guns, did they.'

'What the hell are you doing, Dillon? You want to get yourself in trouble again?'

'What the fuck does it matter? It's a party isn't it. I'm having fun.'

Tate slowly approaches him, gesturing for the bodyguards to take a step back. Out of the corner of his eye, he sees Gregg moving towards Dillon from the other side. 'It matters to us. To Gregg and me. Put the bottle down, okay. I could really do with some proper food. Want to call for room service?'

Instead of handing over the bottle, Dillon takes a long drink. Tate scratches the inside of his left arm before he realises what he's doing.

He hasn't scratched his track scars for ages. It was a habit he developed in rehab to deal with the stress, and is absolutely the last thing he needs to start doing again.

'I don't want food.'

'Okay, so what do you want?' He takes another step closer. He's within arm's reach of Dillon, but doesn't want to make a grab for the bottle. Not yet. 'Tell us what you want mate, and we'll try to help you.'

Dillon laughs to himself.

'What did you take?'

'It's all gone.' Dillon points the bottle at Tate again. 'You need to stay clean. For Chloe.'

'I know and I am. I'm asking about you. Do you remember what you took?'

Dillon shakes his head and takes another drink. 'Doesn't matter. Not anymore.'

Tate glances over at Gregg. His friend is as freaked out by this as Tate is. He's never seen Dillon like this before. He can't seem to focus on any of them for longer than a few seconds, his eyes darting around the room as he mutters incoherently to himself. 'Why not, Dillon?'

Dillon seems to run out of steam at that point and stumbles backwards, crashing into a lamp, knocking it to the ground. He hits the wall and slumps to the ground. Tate turns to the bodyguards. 'Give us a minute. We'll be fine.'

They leave the room, closing the door behind them. Tate and Gregg sit on the ground opposite Dillon, but he doesn't seem to notice they're there. His head is buried under his hand, while the other clutches the neck of the bottle.

'It's Luke, isn't it?' Gregg says softly. 'This is because he's married now.'

Tate glances over at Gregg and mouths, *'What?'*

Gregg leans over and whispers in his ear. 'I think he has feelings for Luke.'

11

Tate curses to himself. He'd never thought about that before, but now it's been pointed out, it makes perfect sense. They both look back at Dillon as he curses and drops the bottle. He wraps both arms over his head and pulls his knees up to his chest. Gregg is right. He's falling apart because the man he loves has just got married. 'I'm sorry, Dillon. I had no idea.'

Dillon laughs and lifts his head, resting it back against the wall. Tate has known Dillon for decades, but he's never seen him cry. Not until that moment.

'Will I tell you what I want, Tate? I want Luke.' He wipes his face and takes a long breath, then laughs. 'There. I've said it. Fucking tragic, right? I'm in love with my best mate, but he's just married that *cow*. So, I thought I'd have a drink to celebrate. Do some drugs to make me forget. Guess I'm all out of luck there too. Didn't take enough.' He laughs again and reaches for the bottle before Tate can grab it. 'Can't even do that right.'

Tate looks at Gregg briefly. 'Do what right, Dillon? What are you talking about?'

He swallows the last of the whiskey, wiping his mouth on his arm when he's done. 'Add it to the list of things I've fucked up.' He laughs harshly. 'And here was me wondering why they hate me? I'm a fucking embarrassment.' Dillon points at Gregg. 'Your psycho bitch, Angel, said as much. She told me I was an embarrassment, just before she stabbed me. Said no one would want to be with me. That I kept fucking up.'

'Yeah well, she said a lot of stuff,' Gregg mutters. 'None of it was worth listening to.'

Then they hear the sirens. Tate curses and gets to his feet. He peers out the window behind Dillon, and sees the flashing lights approaching the building. 'Fuck.'

'Pippa must have called the cops,' Dillon mutters from the floor. 'She's been threatening to call the cops on me for years. Best wedding present I could have given her.'

Tate crouches down in front of him. 'This is serious. They're going to arrest you, Dillon.'

Dillon nods, as the tears trail down his face. 'I know. It's all grand.'

'It's not grand you idiot. You have a record.' Tate looks around the room at the broken mirror, overturned furniture, and smashed glasses. 'You could get time for this.'

'It's where I belong.'

'No it's not. Dillon...' Tate runs out of things to say. The cars have stopped outside and it's only a matter of minutes before they get to Dillon's room. 'You belong with us, Dillon. Always have.'

Dillon shakes his head. 'I'm tired of it all, Tate.'

'Tired of what?'

But Tate doesn't get his answer. The hotel room door opens and Max steps inside. He looks at the damage, then over at Gregg, Dillon, and Tate.

'I persuaded them to let me talk to you first.' Max moves closer and sits on the end of the couch. 'First wedding I've been to where I've had to work. But, it's also the first wedding I've been to with you lot as guests. What's going on, Dillon?'

Dillon looks over at Max with unfocused eyes and shrugs. 'Boring party, so decided to spice things up, rock star style.'

Max nods and clasps his hands on his knees, as he looks around the room again. 'This is criminal damage, you know that, right?'

Dillon nods. 'I hope so. I put a lot of effort into it.'

'I have to take you in, Dillon. I don't want to, but you've left me no choice. I gave you fair warning, after the whole Angel fiasco. I told you to keep your nose clean or that would be it. What the hell were you thinking?'

Dillon shrugs, and Tate wants to throttle him.

Max nods and stands up. 'Fine. I'll get them in. Please say you're at least going to go willingly?'

Dillon smirks, and pushes to his feet. 'Where would be the fun in that?'

This time Gregg actually steps in to stop Tate from throttling him. 'Fuck's sake, Dillon. Stop this. Just walk out yourself.'

But Dillon clearly is ready for a fight, squaring up to Max instead of backing off.

Max shakes his head and mutters under his breath. 'You really want to add resisting arrest to your list?'

'Looks that way,' Dillon replies.

'Perfect. You're a real pain in the ass, Dillon. Get in here!'

Tate and Gregg are ushered from the room as a team of Garda come in to arrest Dillon. Tate leans against the wall with Gregg, listening to the shouting from Dillon's room.

Dillon could have just walked out. Could have made things easier, and maybe even a little better for himself, but Dillon was all about extremes. If he's being arrested, he's going to make it loud.

'Don't know if I feel more sorry for Max or Dillon right now,' Gregg says, peering over at the door.

'This is a fucking nightmare. Any sign of Luke?'

Gregg shakes his head. 'Probably busy with the guests.'

'His best mate is being arrested. Fuck the guests!'

The door opens again, and Dillon is led out in handcuffs, as Luke finally makes an appearance. He stares in shock when he sees what's going on. 'Dillon! What the hell?'

Dillon is dragged past him and pushed into the elevator, while Luke stares after him. He races over to Tate and Gregg. 'What happened to him? What's going on?'

'Thrashed the hotel room. He's been arrested,' Gregg explains.

'He did what? Why?'

Gregg glances over at Tate, but they already know what Dillon said in the room has to stay between them. 'He was drunk. He said he'd taken drugs too, but we don't know what.'

Luke scrubs his hand over his hair as he stares after Dillon. When he suddenly runs down the corridor, Tate and Gregg follow him downstairs. They get to the front steps of the venue, as Dillon is being put into a Garda car, under the flash of far too many cameras. Pippa steps up beside her husband, and wraps her arms around his waist.

Tate's anger boils in his gut when he sees Pippa. 'Bitch is smiling.'

Gregg looks over at Pippa and discretely holds Tate's arm, keeping him back. 'Yeah, I see it. Not now though, buddy. It's bad enough Dillon has just been arrested. Having you taken away too won't help anyone. Come on. We gotta find the girls and regroup. I don't know about you, but I've had more than enough of this wedding.'

Tate scrubs his hand over his face and looks at the fire in front of him. The hotel management had given the band access to a small private living room, so they could get themselves together. Waste of time. Dillon had just been led away in handcuffs. It's a fucking disaster. No amount of time would help them get themselves together after this.

Gregg is slouched in the armchair opposite him, playing with the strap on his medic alert cuff.

He looks at the door as Chloe and Bria come in, closing it behind them. 'Well?'

'No sign of Luke,' Chloe answers, taking a seat beside him. 'Even Andy hasn't got a clue where he is. He's probably with guests somewhere. Have you seen the size of this place?'

'Fucking perfect. Whatever. We need to get out of here.' And that's an understatement. He's wound up, and fucked off. All he wants to do is get the hell away from this place and go home. 'Is Liam still outside?'

Chloe nods. 'They all are. Do you want me to get them?'

'Yeah. Time to go. We're not doing anything here.'

'What about Luke?' Gregg asks, as Chloe opens the door and gestures for their bodyguards to come in. 'We can't blow off his wedding without saying something. What?' Gregg continues as Tate glowers at him. 'I know, okay. He should be here, but he's in a shite position, buddy. It is his wedding day after all. Cut him some slack.'

Gregg may have a point, but he's not about to concede.

Liam, Andy, Jason, and Ciaran stand in front of the door, all business as usual. Tate was completely against the idea of a bodyguard from the second Ellen mentioned it. Being babysat every time he left his house, didn't appeal in the slightest. But, the decision was taken out of his hands. And he gets why.

Dara kidnapping him had scared the hell out of everyone. And after Angel got to Gregg, the need for their protection detail was more obvious than ever. And Liam actually wasn't too bad. He didn't say much, which suits Tate just fine.

'It's time you guys thought about heading,' Ciaran says. 'The vultures are swarming.'

'Vultures?' Bria asks.

'The press,' he explains. 'Dillon's less than quiet exit has attracted attention. More reporters have shown up.'

'Fuck.' This shite day is going from bad, to really fucking bad.

'Don't worry. We've got a plan,' Liam says as he leans against the wall. 'There's an entrance around the back of the kitchens. We can bring you out there.'

'Sounds good, but I've got my truck with me.'

Jason nods at him. 'I've got that covered. It's not like I have anything else to do at the moment, while Dillon is preoccupied. I'll drop it back to yours.'

'Thanks.'

He nods and leaves the room. 'I'll sort out transport to sneak you out,' Liam offers, following after Jason.

'What about Luke?' he asks Andy. 'Has he shown up?'

'Bridal suite. He'll give me a shout when he's ready to come down again.'

Gregg grimaces and shifts uncomfortably in his seat. 'For the love of God, please don't tell me he was consummating his marriage?'

'No, Gregg. I probably shouldn't say, but it sounded like they were arguing, not getting up close and personal.'

'Thank God for that. Not that I mean it's a good thing they were arguing. It's not. I'm just glad—'

'We get it, Gregg!' Tate didn't mean to snap, but his head is fucking killing him, and he just wants his bed.

Liam sticks his head around the door and nods. 'Transport will be here in ten. Let's get you out of here.'

He pushes to his feet, exhaustion spinning his head. Chloe takes his hand and squeezes it. 'Are you okay?' she asks quietly.

'Yeah. Just tired.'

They follow Liam from the room, along the corridor to the lobby. And a horde of reporters.

Liam shoves Tate aside, as the group gravitate towards them, cameras flashing and microphones out in front of them. Tate hears his name being shouted by too many people, mixing with the headache that's been a permanent fucking fixture for the last few days.

Chloe tugs on his arm, but he's trapped in the noise, in the lights.

Liam steps in front of him, blocking his view of the cameras and the reporters. He manhandles Tate back, forcefully pushing him around the corner. 'Hey. You okay?'

Tate takes a few seconds to register what Liam said. 'Eh, yeah. I'm fine.'

Liam looks less than convinced, but doesn't comment as he points to the door in front of them. 'Through there.'

Chloe grabs his hand and leads him along the corridor and into the kitchen where Gregg, Bria, and the others are waiting for him.

'You okay?'

Tate nods at Gregg. He doesn't know what the fuck just happened out there, but it's seriously freaking him out. 'Has Jason left with my truck?'

Ciaran nods as he checks his mobile. 'He's clear. And the van has just pulled up outside. Let's get you out of here and home.'

Chloe

Chloe unlocks the front door and turns off the alarm. As weddings go, that will go down as the most dramatic of her life. She hasn't even begun to process the result of the pregnancy test yet. As soon as she got the positive result, Gregg called Bria to tell her about Dillon.

She can't get her head around that either.

As she turns on the kettle, she discretely looks over at Tate, leaning against the counter with his arms crossed. He hasn't said much since he froze in the hotel lobby. Rounding the corner and running into all those reporters knocked her too, but his reaction worries her. It was like he had been dragged back into his own head by the intrusion and couldn't deal with it.

She hasn't seen him like that for months. All the drama with Gregg, Angel, and Bria had knocked him off course. Now Dillon is in custody, and Luke appears to be pulling back from the group. In the space of a few hours, the future of the band had gone from secure, to uncertain.

That can't be helping his head-space at all.

Chloe walks over to him and rubs his arms. 'Why don't you go up to bed? I'll bring you a drink in a few minutes.'

He shakes his head. 'No point trying to crash. I'm too wound up to sleep. I'll grab an hour in the gym first, then give it a shot.'

Chloe doesn't believe that for a second. He's had about four hours sleep in the last two days. He needs sleep, not a workout. Usually she wouldn't interfere when he wants to exercise instead of sleep, but not this time. She'll lock the door to his gym if she has to, until he gets a few hours at least.

'How about we get into bed and watch a movie. Your choice. I'll even make some popcorn if you want.'

'I'm seriously not in the mood, Chloe. I'm not good company right now.'

'It's a movie. All you have to do is sit beside me.'

'What if Dillon gets time?' he asks, his mind clearly too preoccupied on tonight's events. 'Why did Luke leave without saying goodbye to us?'

'Don't hold that against him. He was going on honeymoon, Tate. He just got married.'

'Do you think he knows Dillon is in love with him? And how the hell did I miss that? Did you know? Was I so wound up in my own head the last few months that I didn't see it?'

Chloe takes a minute to let the words sink in. 'Dillon is in love with Luke? Are you sure?'

'Said it up in the room. Dillon had just watched the man he's in love with, marry someone else. No wonder he was all over the place today.'

'I had no idea he felt that way. Poor Dillon. How long has he had feelings for Luke?'

'Who knows. As usual, Dillon kept it to himself. People have a go at me about opening up and sharing shit. He needs to do the same.' Tate suddenly shouts and kicks the wall. 'Fuck!'

'Hey! Calm down. Look at me, Tate. Tate?'

He lifts his head and turns his bloodshot blue eyes towards her. Chloe holds out her hand and waits for him to either ignore it and go to his gym, or to take it. She smiles when he finally does the latter.

She leads him up the stairs to the bedroom then unfastens his waistcoat and shirt. He stands where he is, as she undresses him, either too tired, or too worn out to argue with her. She takes a minute to straighten the griffin pendant he always wears around his neck. 'Sorry about kicking the wall.'

Chloe rises to her tiptoes and kisses him. 'You're worried about your friends. I get that. I am too. But getting angry at the kitchen wall won't help anyone. Sleep will.'

He nods and kisses her forehead, then disappears into the bathroom.

Chloe slips out of her dress and hangs it up, while she waits to clean her teeth. As she passes the mirror she looks at her stomach in the reflection in the mirror.

She's pregnant.

She's going to have Tate's son or daughter.

While it's terrifying, a small part of her likes the thought of having Tate's child. They may not have discussed children at any stage, but she knows it's something she wants. The timing could have been better, a lot better, but it's happening, and there's no hiding from that.

As much as she wants to tell Tate, now isn't the time. Until they know what's happening with Dillon, she needs to keep this to herself.

When Tate comes out of the bathroom, she knows her decision to keep the pregnancy a secret for now, was the right one. He looks beaten. His broad shoulders are slouched, his face is pale, and the black rings under his eyes that had faded while they were away, are back.

She quickly cleans her teeth, then climbs into bed beside Tate and cuddles up against him. Tate wraps his arms around her and kisses her head. 'You looked beautiful today.'

She smiles against his chest. 'Thanks. You too. You know I can never get enough of you in a suit.'

He laughs but it's not his usual laugh. It's forced. 'Good night, Chloe. Love you.'

'Love you too.'

He releases her from his arms and turns onto his front, facing away from her. He's not doing it to hurt her, she knows that. He's upset and is doing his usual *bottling it up* thing he's so good at. She'll leave him for now. Sleep is more important. Hopefully he'll talk to her in the morning.

Tate

The nightmare starts the same every time. He's hiding, either in the cupboard, or under his bed. He can hear shouting, crying, furniture breaking or being knocked over.

Then silence, followed by heavy footsteps on the bare wooden floor of the flat.

He's looking for Tate.

Tate peers out from under the bed and meets his father's eyes. Then his father smiles, his grin terrifying.

Tate scrambles away from him, squeezing himself under the bed as far as he can. He buries his head under his arms, trying to protect himself from what he knows is coming. He never manages to get away for long. His father always finds him, no matter how well he hides. He's always dragged out and beaten every single time.

And this time is no different. A heavy hand wraps around his wrist, dragging him out from under the bed. It won't do any good, but instinct kicks in, and Tate shoves his father away as hard as he can. It buys him another few seconds but it's better than nothing.

Then his father pins him to the bed, laughing at his feeble attempts to escape. The stench of stale alcohol is everywhere. Tate struggles to get out from under him, but he's too small, too weak, to dislodge his father. He's crying, begging to be let go, but as usual, his father doesn't pay him any attention.

Over the sound of his father's heavy breathing, he hears a zipper and his struggles increase. He knows what's coming next.

Tate bucks, desperate to get away. And this time it works. He lands on the ground with a thud and scrambles over to the corner of the room.

'Tate!'

He hears his name but it doesn't sound right. He wasn't called Tate back then.

'Look at me, Tate.'

He opens his eyes and sees Chloe crouching on the floor in front of him. He's back in his own room. 'Fuck. Sorry. I'm sorry.'

'It's okay. Let's get you back to the bed.'

'Why am I on the floor?'

'You fell out of the bed. C'mon. Back on the bed and get yourself together.'

Tate nods and wipes his shaking hands over his face, as he attempts to separate himself from the remnants of the nightmare. He sits beside Chloe and notices something that makes him feel sick. There's a red mark on the side of her face. 'What happened to you?'

'It's nothing. Would you like a drink?'

Tate pushes to his feet and crouches down in front of her. He glances down at his hand then back at her face. 'Oh God. I did that.' She tries to take his hand, but he pulls it back. 'I just hit you.'

'You lashed out in your sleep. It's an entirely different thing.'

'I'm so sorry, Chloe. I'll get you some ice.'

'Tate. I don't need—'

But he doesn't hear anything else she says. He's already on his way downstairs. Tate stands in the middle of his kitchen and can't remember why he's there in the first place. The only thing on his mind is that he hit Chloe. Who gives a fuck if he was awake or asleep. He still hit her. He hit the women he loves, and nothing he ever does will be able to erase that.

He's lashed out in his sleep before, but never like that. At least he doesn't think so. The moments between the nightmare ending, and him waking up, were always blurred. The dream and reality merge and he struggles to tell the difference. And this had been a nasty nightmare. Not that any of them were a bundle of laughs, but the memories of what his father did to him were getting more vivid. He's had countless dreams about being hit. This one was different. This one was more about the other abuse his father inflicted on him. Abuse he's still unable to talk about, no matter how hard he tries.

His therapist is helping him deal with a lot of shit. Witnessing his father beat his mother to death, after years of abuse, had left its mark deep inside him. He talked about the beatings. He talked about his dependency on drugs and drink to cope with it. He can't talk about the sexual stuff.

He'd sat the band down a few months ago and told them what his father did to him. He hadn't directly said he'd been sexually assaulted. He'd hinted at it, but couldn't say the words out loud. Since then he's pushed all that to the back of his mind.

Or at least tried to.

Not talking about it, not facing up to it isn't helping and he knows it, but his head puts up a block every time he's asked about it. His father was a first class sadistic bastard. He always knew that. It's the level of sadistic bastard he's having trouble getting his head around.

Tate lifts his hand and looks at his palm as the realisation sinks in. He's just like him. Just like his father. His father hit his mother and hit him. It's how it all started. Then he got more inventive with his punishments. But it started with a slap.

He leans against the counter and grips the edge to support himself. Then he lunges for the sink and vomits repeatedly, until there's nothing left in his stomach. Tate washes his mouth and the sink.

'It was a bad one, wasn't it,' Chloe says, placing a bottle of juice on the counter beside him.

Her cheek is far more noticeable in the light. He reaches out to touch her face, but pulls his hand back. 'I'm so, so, sorry. I'd never hurt you. I mean intentionally. Not that it makes a difference.'

'It was an accident, Tate. I know that, and so do you. Now are you going to come back to bed?'

'Chloe—'

'Tate. Please, I don't want you to blame yourself for this. It was an accident. End of story.' She holds out her hand, but he can't bring himself to take it.

'I might just workout for a bit first. Do you mind?'

She shakes her head, but her smile falters. 'Of course not. Don't overdo it though. You need to get some sleep.'

He nods, and watches her go back upstairs, then walks through the living room to the back of the house. He turns on the light in the gym, and looks around the well equipped room. Working out usually helped him deal with the nightmares, but this is different. Nothing is going to help him deal with the fact that he had hit the woman he loves more than anything.

The gym is far away from the bedrooms, so he turns the music up loud and lifts some weights from the rack, sliding them onto the barbell.

Chloe

Chloe wakes up in an empty bed. It's becoming the norm, and that's not what she wants. She knows Tate worries about keeping her awake, but sleeping on the couch, or in one of the spare rooms, isn't doing their relationship any good.

And it's certainly not going to improve things when she tells him she's pregnant. Trying to find the right time is going to be nearly impossible.

She groans as the alarm on her phone rings. Leaving Tate home alone while he's like this, isn't something she's keen on, but having a month off work was pushing it. If she told them she couldn't come back today, she could very well be risking her job.

Chloe drags herself out of bed and goes downstairs, but there's no sign of Tate. She tries the gym, coming to a stop when she finds him on the treadmill. That isn't anything new. It's the fact he's leaning heavily on the machine and barely dragging his feet along, that's worrying her the most.

'How long have you been on that?'

Tate ignores her, so she moves closer. He's probably zoned out, which usually happens when he's thinking. 'Tate?'

He blinks and looks over at her. 'What?'

'Can you get off that, please. Have you been walking all night?'

'I think so.'

He sits on the edge of the track and Chloe doesn't miss the fact he hangs onto the handles to stop himself falling. She opens the small fridge and takes out a bottle of water. 'Drink this. You're probably dehydrated.'

He smiles and takes the bottle. 'Sorry. Just kind of got carried away.'

'You think? This isn't good for you, Tate. Can you make it into the living room?'

'Yeah.'

She helps him next door and he flops back on the couch. Tate peers over at her, his eyes focused on her face. 'How is it?'

'It's fine, really.'

'I'm sorry—'

She takes his hand, squeezing it before he can get a chance to pull it away. 'I told you to stop apologising. Are you hungry? I need to head into work in a bit, but I can make you something before I go.'

'You're going into work?'

'I kind of have to. I've been off for weeks. I need to show my face before they permanently replace me.'

His eyes move back to her face and she knows what he's worried about.

'There's nothing there, Tate.'

He leans forward and buries his face in his hands. 'Fuck! I'm not like him, Chloe. I swear.'

Chloe kneels down in front of him and pulls his hands from his face. 'I know you're not. I have never thought that for one second, do you hear me?'

He nods but it's half-hearted.

'Do you think it's worth giving Billy a call? Talk it over with him? That's what a sponsor is for.'

'You really think I want anyone else to know about this? I'll be fine. I just need a shower and some food. I have to go check on Dillon too.'

Chloe doesn't push him. She knows by now there's no point. That doesn't mean she's happy with his response. Billy is there for Tate if he's struggling. And he's clearly struggling. 'I'll get breakfast ready. Why don't you have a shower.'

He trudges up the stairs and Chloe turns on the kettle. She had been so looking forward to getting back to work. The month off with Tate had been incredible, but she loved work and missed her pupils. Now she's going to be worrying about Tate for the day. She thought they were over this. That she wouldn't have any more sleepless nights.

She looks down at her stomach. Sleepless nights. That's something they could have a lot of, soon enough. She needs to tell him. Whatever else is going on with him, he deserves to know. They need to figure this out as a couple. Maybe later. She'll let him find out what's happening with Dillon first. Hopefully after that he'll be in a slightly better place.

Ten minutes later he makes an appearance, just as she's putting together his bacon sandwich. He thanks her and sits on the stool next to hers. While he eats, she hurries upstairs and gets ready for work.

A part of her doesn't want to go anywhere near the school with everything that happened yesterday. But she needs to. She needs to get back to the normal non-rock star part of her life. The part she feels like she actually has control over. Because, if she's learned nothing else the last year with Tate, it's that his life is chaotic and unpredictable.

'So do you have anything else planned for today?' she asks as she comes back downstairs. Tate is frowning into his coffee, but he'd eaten at least, so that's a good start.

'Nothing band related. Gregg will probably come over. Ellen just sent a text. Dillon will be let out in a few hours.'

'That's brilliant.'

'On bail.'

'Oh. So he's been charged?'

Tate shrugs. 'I guess so. We'll find out the details when we see her and Dillon.'

'Keep me posted, okay?'

'Of course.'

She checks the time. 'Shoot. I better go. Are you sure you'll—'

He peers up at her and smiles. 'I'm fine. Really. Go and have fun. I know you missed the kids.'

'I have actually. I can't wait to see them again.' She kisses him, then grabs her bags from the couch. 'See you later.'

He nods and Chloe goes through the utility room and into the garage. She unlocks her pristine, shiny, red, classic Mini, and drops her bags on to the passenger seat. She doesn't want to leave Tate while he's gloomy, but she can't babysit him just in case he might do something...

She scolds herself as she starts the engine, and hits the remote to lift the garage door. He's not going to do something stupid. He's been clean for six months. Six months of hard work. There's no way he'd jeopardise his recovery.

As she pulls out of the driveway, she glances over her shoulder at the impressive house. Who is she kidding. He's an addict and always will be. There's no telling what events or situations will push him too far.

But she has to trust him. There's no future for them otherwise. He's the lead singer in a well-known band. Part of that means he has to leave her to go on tour for months at a time. She has to trust him.

Tate

Tate stifles a yawn and takes his coffee from the centre console of Gregg's car. He's exhausted and his legs are aching. Fucking stupid idea to get on the treadmill when he's like that. He's damn lucky he didn't fall on his face and do some serious damage to himself.

'Late one?'

Tate nods as another yawn hits. 'Yeah. Sorry.'

'Nightmare?'

'Yeah.'

Gregg glances over at him. 'Fancy talking about it?'

'They're getting worse, Gregg. More vivid you know.'

Gregg nods, but doesn't take his eyes off the road. He's never once said the words *sexual abuse* or *rape*, out loud. His brain shuts down, blocking him from admitting out loud what his father did to him. The guys, Chloe, and his parents know, but that's it. And they only know because of an old medical report. But he hasn't told them he's started remembering the details. Hasn't told them about the new and vivid nightmares which now include his father forcing himself...

'Fuck.'

'You what?'

'Nothing.'

Gregg glances over at him. 'What's up, buddy? I know that face. You're brooding.'

Tate rests his forehead against the window, watching the landscape race by, as Gregg drives through Wicklow town.

He spent all his summers here after the Archer's adopted him. He used to love this place. Always had. But ever since Dara drugged and kidnapped him from the harbour, he's not feeling all warm and fuzzy about it anymore. Fucking Dara had ruined those memories for him. Just like he did when he dragged him back to his grandparents' old farmhouse. Waking up chained to a bed in that house hadn't helped.

'Tate?'

'What?'

'Talk to me.'

'I did something really bad, Gregg.'

Gregg indicates, before veering off the road, stopping on the hard shoulder. He turns on his hazard lights and faces Tate. 'Go on.'

'When I was...' he trails off, not sure he can admit what he did to Chloe, out loud.

'When you were what, buddy? You know there's no judgement. You can tell me anything.'

'You know I get confused when I'm waking up. It's like the dream is still going on. It takes a minute or so to get my head clear.'

Gregg nods. 'Oh I remember. Best not to get too close to you when you're like that.' Tate looks over at him, and Gregg winces when he figures it out for himself. 'Oh no. Chloe?'

'I lashed out and hit her, Gregg.'

Gregg takes a minute before he responds. 'Okay, so that's shite. But it was an accident, right. I mean she knows that, doesn't she?'

'You sound just like her. She keeps making excuses for me. What I did, it's unforgivable.'

'Ah come on now, Tate. It was an accident. You'd never hit her.'

'I hit you. Twice.'

Gregg rubs his jaw, then grins. 'Well, technically you hit me more than twice. You went a little nuts in the garage after you had the fight with Chloe. I vaguely remember having to pin you to the driveway.'

'Yeah. Thanks for clearing that up for me. I've got form. Is that what you're saying?'

'Jesus, no. I was just making sure the details were correct. I wasn't having a go. I mean it. Anyway, we're getting off topic here.'

'Are we? I don't think so. What if I do it again? What if I really hurt her next time?'

'Now you hang on there one minute, Tate. You had a nightmare. You lashed out. Chloe got in the way. That's it. Don't go reading anything in to what happened. When you hit her, was it a punch, or was it a tap?'

'It wasn't a punch. More like a forceful shove, but I must have slapped her face too. I don't know. I just wanted to get my father away from me. I didn't know it was her.'

'Did you hurt her?'

'She had a red mark on her cheek.'

'Okay, so I get why you're upset about it, but it was a freak accident and we all know it. Well, everyone except you. Seriously, stop beating yourself up about it. You're going to drive yourself crazy. Talk to your therapist. Talk to your sponsor. Talk to me as much as you want. Just talk about it, get it straight in your head, and move on.'

'I don't want to lose her, Gregg.'

'Hey now, don't even go there. Chloe knows it was an accident.'

Tate nods, no more convinced than he was when he first got into the car. 'I know. I just... what if this is just the beginning?'

Gregg takes a second to get what he's saying. Then his eyebrows shoot up and he shakes his head. 'No way. Stop.'

'Gregg—'

'Nope. You are not like him. Not even close. You're blowing this way out of proportion. Like epic style, out of proportion. You had a nightmare. You pushed her and accidentally hit her. That's it. It doesn't mean anything. You can't control where your head goes when you're asleep. I know how it can go off on a tangent,' he adds, his voice dropping, as he looks down at his lap.

'Are you having nightmares?'

Gregg does something between a nod and a shrug. 'Every now and again. Being kidnapped by a psycho gets into your head.'

'How bad?'

Gregg grins at him, but it's a feeble attempt. 'Bad enough. I don't know if it's the same with you. Angel did a lot of messed up stuff while she had me, but it's only the one scene that plays out in the nightmares every single time.'

Tate nods, but doesn't say anything. He had no idea his friend was still struggling. He should have. It was only a few weeks since Angel had tried to kill Gregg, whereas Tate's nightmares are from memories that are thirty odd years old. Some friend he is. He should have known, or even guessed, that Gregg needed support.

'I'm in the sea, chained to the jetty, with Angel quietly watching as I slowly drown, over, and over, and over again. I can't even take a damn shower without having music blaring to block out the sound of the water. I even kind of freaked out giving myself my insulin shot this morning. I have to keep checking the dose to make sure I'm not giving myself too much. She's seriously messed with my head, Tate. Great fun,' he adds with a laugh.

'Why didn't you say anything?'

'We're all dealing with our own problems, buddy.'

'And are you okay? Medically I mean.'

'My diabetes? Yeah. That's all back to normal now. Her overdose didn't do me any long term damage. Life isn't exactly a bundle of laughs at the moment, is it?' He rests his head against the back of the seat and turns to look at him. 'Kind of miss when life was more fun.'

'Yeah. Couldn't agree more. This is getting boring.'

Gregg sighs dramatically. 'So boring. But at least we've got our looks, right?'

They both laugh, easing some of the tension in the car.

Tate looks out the window again. 'God, we're a mess.'

'True, but a damn good looking mess.'

No laugh from his mate this time. Tate just shakes his head. 'I suppose we'd better go.'

The rest of the drive to Dillon's seaside cottage takes place in comfortable silence. He's still upset about what happened with Chloe, but maybe Gregg is right. Maybe he's reading too much into what happened. Maybe.

Gregg pulls down the overgrown track leading to the unassuming house and stops outside. Dillon's cottage isn't somewhere you'd imagine a rock star with a healthy bank balance would live, but that's the point.

The driveway is overgrown, the paint peeling from the walls, and moss is spilling down from the roof. But just like a lot of things when it comes to Dillon, the outside is a ruse to keep people from discovering the truth.

They get out of the car and Tate pulls the spare keys from his pocket. He turns off the alarm and wanders into the main living area. The inside bears no resemblance to the outside. The clean white walls and highly polished floor compliment the exposed beams and impressive wood-burner set into the far wall.

Tate loves this house. It's hard not to. Especially when you see the view out of the patio windows. The Irish Sea stretches out to the horizon, the unspoiled beach a stone's throw from the back door, empty in both directions. It's the perfect retreat for someone who leads a hectic life and needs space.

Unfortunately, it's not looking its best.

Gregg whistles as he walks around the living room. 'He's not usually this messy, is he?'

Tate shakes his head. From the look of the living room and the kitchen, Dillon hasn't been in a tidying mood for quite some time. The kitchen counter is covered in dirty plates and empty whiskey bottles. Pizza and takeaway boxes are scattered over the couches and coffee table, and he's strewn clothes on the two armchairs and the floor. This isn't Dillon. He's not untidy in any way. 'He loves this place. I've never seen it like this.'

'Clearly he's had other things on his mind. I know me and cleaning don't see eye to eye, but this is even making me uncomfortable. Should we tidy it before he gets back?'

'It's fine. Leave it.'

They turn to find Dillon glaring at them from the open front door. 'Hey. You're back,' Gregg says with a huge grin on his face.

'Yeah. Seems so. Why don't you make yourselves at home?' he

says, his voice loaded with sarcasm. 'What are you doing here?'

'Ellen contacted me and Tate to say you got out and she was going to pick you up.'

Dillon dumps his suit jacket on the couch, on top of all the other clothes he's thrown there over the last few weeks. He goes over to the cupboard and takes out a bottle of whiskey.

'No you don't,' Ellen says, as she walks inside and closes the front door.

He doesn't bother looking at Ellen as he unscrews the cap off the bottle. 'None of you have to be here, so why don't you go and let me drink in peace.'

She grabs the bottle from his hand and points to the couch. 'Sit.'

Tate holds his breath waiting for the retaliation. Dillon never took well to being told what to do, but he surprises both Tate and Gregg by doing as he's told.

Ellen nods towards the other couch and Tate shoves a pizza box aside before himself and Gregg sit down.

'Now, I'll make this quick. I'm sure you could do with some sleep, Dillon.'

He barely looks at her, as she sits on the armchair facing them.

'Have you been charged?' Tate asks, earning a glare from Dillon.

'Yes.' Ellen answers for him. 'He's only with us today, because his lawyer pretty much got down on her knees and begged. The court case is scheduled for a week's time.'

'Any idea what you'll get?'

'A month. Maybe longer.' Dillon scrubs a hand over his face and laughs. 'Guess I'll be missing the next tour.'

'This isn't funny, Dillon,' Ellen scolds.

'Hey, I know it's not funny. Believe me. But not much I can do about it now.'

Ellen sits back in the chair and crosses her legs. 'No, there isn't. All we can do is wait for the court case and go from there. In the meantime he's been strongly advised to behave. As in, no drinking, no drugs, and ideally, no leaving this house.

'If you even so much as look at someone the wrong way, you're going to be back inside before you can blink. Your lawyer went to a lot of trouble to get you out. The least you can do is abide by the rules.'

She walks over to the kitchen and empties the alcohol down the sink.

'Fuck, Ellen! Do you have any idea how much that cost?'

'I'll reimburse you if it's that important.' She opens the cupboard and takes out all the alcohol, filling a few shopping bags with the bottles. 'I'll be taking these with me. Now, I don't know about you, but I'm exhausted. I'll grab a few hours sleep and head into the office to see where we go from here.'

'If I'm out of the band you can just tell me.'

'Out of the band? Why would you say something like that?'

'Angel said next hit, I'm out.'

Ellen rests her hands on her hips. 'Angel? You're seriously taking anything she said seriously? Yes, Vox would prefer you didn't rub people up the wrong way as often as you do, but there's been no talk of removing you from Broken. I can promise you that. Now, I need my bed. It's been a long night. I'll be in touch.'

Tate waits until Ellen has left, before he turns to Dillon again. 'You seriously okay? You look fucked.'

Dillon nods at Tate. 'Yeah. Wasn't the best night of my life. I've got one hell of a headache.'

'Wow. That's a shock!' Gregg says. 'You remember yesterday at all?'

'Bits of it. Well, too much of it. I fucked up.'

'Yeah, buddy. You did.'

Tate knows why Gregg is so pissed off. He's feeling the same way. 'What the fuck were you playing at?'

'I don't know, okay! I feel shite enough about the whole situation without you two getting on my back. I can't undo what I did, and I reckon the possibility of heading inside for a month is enough of a kick in the balls, thanks all the same.' He pauses and rubs the back of his neck. 'I don't suppose you've heard from Luke at all? I don't blame him for being pissed with me after what I did at his wedding, but I thought he'd at least text and lay in to me.'

Tate glances over at Gregg. 'Yeah, he went on honeymoon. None of us have heard from him.'

Dillon looks like he's been stabbed in the gut, but as usual, he tries to hide it. 'Right. That's fair enough I guess. I think I'll grab some sleep in a comfortable bed while I still can. You can stay or go. Whatever.'

He gets up and leaves Tate and Gregg in his living room, as he slams his bedroom door behind him.

'Well,' Gregg says. 'He's certainly cheerier than usual.'

'We might as well head. Leave him to it for a bit.'

They close his front door and climb back into Gregg's car. 'Where to?'

Tate fastens his seat belt and shrugs. 'Home I guess. I'll see if I can meet up with Chloe for lunch. Apologise some more.'

Gregg glances over at him. 'You're seriously beating yourself up over this, aren't you?'

'Of course I fucking am!'

'Knowing you, I'm wasting my time trying to talk you out of *said* beating up. That's Chloe's job. But I will say one thing, as your most valued friend.'

'Most valued friend?'

'Shut up. Let it go, Tate. It was a stupid accident. Don't let it ruin what you have with Chloe.'

Tate nods but can't even manage a smile. Gregg is probably right, but that doesn't take away any of the guilt.

5

Chloe

Chloe leaves the school with her sandwiches, and crosses the road to sit on the bench overlooking the sea. The morning had gone well enough. There was loads of catching up to do after a month away, and seeing the kids again was amazing.

She pulls her phone out of her bag. No messages from Tate. Hopefully he's still with Gregg. There's no way he should be alone after what happened last night.

She thought he'd moved on from his nightmares. While they were away, he'd had a handful but not nearly as many as before. But they're back, and they seem to be worse than ever. More intense and certainly darker.

It's entirely her fault for getting in his way. He was a scared kid, lashing out at the man who was hurting him in his dreams. She was just unfortunate enough to get in the way. Chloe knew better than that by now. What she should have done is keep away from him, until he woke up properly.

She had planned on telling him about the baby tonight, but now she's not so sure. She suddenly gets the urge to hear his voice, to make sure he's okay.

Chloe taps on Tate's number, but cancels the call, lowering the phone when a motorbike pulls up behind her. The matte black and red Kawasaki is one she recognises instantly. The rider takes off his helmet and sits beside her on the bench, stretching his long legs out in front of him. 'Spooky.'

Tate peers across at her. 'Sorry?'

'I was just about to text you,' she says, holding up her phone. 'You beat me to it.'

'I wanted to see you in person.' Tate nods towards the school. 'Good to be back?'

'Yeah. It's great to get back into some sort of a routine. Well, as much of a routine I can have being with you,' she adds with a grin.

'Yeah. I don't make things easy, do I?'

'I wouldn't be dating Tate Archer if I wanted an easy life.'

Chloe looks over his shoulder at a group of girls from her school. They're staring at Tate and quietly talking to each other. Chloe puts on her best teacher glare and shakes her head. This isn't the time for a photo or an autograph. The girls wander away but keep staring back at them.

Tate smiles. 'Yeah. I guess not. So, I rang and left a message for Billy. He'll call me back when he's free.'

'That's good. This isn't as big a deal as you're making it, Tate. We're good, okay.'

Tate turns around to face her. 'I deserve a pretty decent bollocking.'

'I'd prefer to give you a hug.' Tate pulls her closer to him and wraps his arm around her. He kisses her hair as he holds her against him. 'I love you.'

'I love you too, you grumpy git.'

He laughs and it almost sounds genuine. 'Thank you.'

'For what?'

'Understanding. You have to put up with a lot of shit from me.'

'I think you're worth it. How about we get a proper lunch before I have to head back and deal with rowdy eight year olds.'

'You got time?'

'Of course. Besides, I think we could do with getting away from all these people. I'm getting a complex.'

Tate glances around them and grimaces. 'Yeah. Got it. Sorry. I forgot my fool proof disguise.'

'Oh you mean your cap and glasses. Yeah. That always works!'

He gets up and takes her hand. 'I'll grab some toasties from the van in town and meet you on the beach.'

'No way! I'll grab the toasties and you go to the beach. I've only half an hour for lunch. If you go anywhere near the town you'll get mobbed, and I'll be hungry for the rest of the day.'

Tate wipes his hands on a napkin and throws it in the empty sandwich box. 'That hit the spot. I was hungry.'

'You're always hungry.'

'I'm a big guy. It takes a lot to fill me. How long you got left?'

'A little longer. So, I forgot to ask. Did you get to see Dillon?' His face drops so she knows he did. 'Oh dear. Not good?'

'No. He's a fucking mess. It's looking like he'll get a month or two.'

That surprises her. She knows he's had a few run-ins over the years with the press and hotel room doors, but didn't think it would result in actual prison time. 'Oh no! How is he?'

'Quiet. I'm seriously worried about him. Dillon's always been…'

'In your face,' Chloe finishes for him.

'Yeah. But the guy we saw this morning is bordering on withdrawn. He's in bits, and I have no idea how to help him. His cottage is always pristine. He loves that house and now he's destroyed it. The place is a mess. It's like he's giving up. The only thing he seems to be interested in, is getting drunk and knocking himself out with drugs.'

'It can't be easy for him. If he is in love with Luke, it must have been heart-breaking to be best man at his wedding to someone else. I really feel for him.' She thinks for a minute. 'How about his sisters. He's close to them, isn't he? Is it worth talking to them?'

Tate leans back on his elbows and shakes his head. 'No way. I'm not even going there. He's unbelievably protective of Clara and Eva. If I talk to them and upset them, he'll deck me. And that's if I'm lucky. No, I think the only person he needs to talk to, is the one person who's ignoring everyone.'

'Luke.'

'Yep. I know he's on honeymoon and all, but Dillon is like his brother. I don't get why he's cut him off like he has. Luke doesn't hold grudges. Never has. There's no way he'd just turn his back on Dillon like this. I mean you saw him when Dillon was being arrested. He was devastated. I know for a fact Luke would want to get in touch with him.'

Chloe wipes her hands and packs the rubbish into the sandwich box. 'I'd imagine Pippa is playing a part in his lack of contact. Dillon did kind of cause an embarrassing scene at their wedding. If she didn't like him before, she certainly won't like him after that. I think you have to accept you won't hear from Luke until he gets back.'

'Yeah, and by then Dillon will be sentenced. Broken will be well and truly broken. There's no way we can do anything without Dillon. Wouldn't want to either.'

She checks her watch and grimaces. 'Shoot. I have to go. Listen, try not to worry about Dillon too much. Knowing him, he's gone all out on the lawyer and he has Ellen backing him too. I think you just might have to accept there's nothing you can do to help him right now. Until he gets this mess out of the way, he's going to be dwelling on it.'

'Yeah. It's just hard seeing him like that.'

She reaches across and kisses him. 'I know. I really better go. See you later.'

'Yeah. I might even get dinner ready for you.'

She stands up and dusts the sand from her trousers. 'Oh order a take away you mean.'

'Nope. I might actually cook you something.'

'Bacon butty or spaghetti bolognese?' Tate was useless in the kitchen apart from his two signature dishes which, she has to admit, are pretty tasty.

'You'll have to wait and see.' He takes her hand as they walk back to the school. Chloe watches as he climbs on his bike, and safely leaves without causing too much of a scene. No doubt someone will have taken a picture of them having toasties on the beach, but she doesn't care. It's part of being with someone like Tate. Besides, it may have taken some time, but she's finally getting used to the attention her boyfriend gets.

Bria is waiting for Chloe when she pulls into the car park. Bria walks over to her car, a drink in each hand so Chloe opens the door for her. 'Hey, thanks for meeting with me.'

Bria hands her a smoothie and closes the door again. 'No problem. So, what's up? Did you tell him?'

'No. I couldn't, Bria. I don't think the timing could have been any worse. He was devastated about Dillon and, as usual, he didn't deal with it in the best way.'

'Working out in his gym until he collapsed?'

'Yeah.

'How do you feel about it all? We didn't get any chance to talk, after you got the results.'

Chloe shrugs. 'I don't know, if I'm honest. I mean, I love Tate. What we have is great. But it's still so new. We haven't been together a year yet. And it's not like that time together was what you'd call typical.'

Bria snorts loudly. 'Yeah, that's putting it mildly. I think you can be fairly confident there are no more crazy cousins plotting to kidnap Tate. That was a one off.'

Chloe nods, but doesn't share Bria's enthusiasm. The time with Tate had been the most intense of her life. Leaving aside Dara emotionally tormenting Tate for months, then kidnapping him and giving him drugs, that time with Tate had been incredible. She finally thought things were heading in the right direction for him the last few weeks.

He hadn't touched a drop of alcohol since his slip in July, and no drugs since Dara took him in August. It's not as long as either of them would have liked, but there was no point going over what happened with Dara. It wouldn't change anything.

'Hey,' Bria says as she squeezes Chloe's leg. 'You worried how he'll take it?'

'How can I not be? He's better, but he's... I think he still struggles every now and again.'

Bria nods. 'Yeah. I see it too, but he's talking about it and Gregg and the guys have his back. You can't let all that take away from what's going on here.'

'Okay, so something else happened.'

Bria turns around to face her. 'What is it?'

'Tate had a nightmare last night. He sometimes thrashes around in the bed when it's a particularly upsetting one. Unfortunately I got in the way.'

Bria frowns and is quiet for a minute. 'Are you saying Tate hit you?'

'No! Well, yes, indirectly. He was asleep, Bria. I mean that. He'd never hurt me.'

Bria stares over at her, but eventually nods. 'Yeah. I know. Are you okay though?'

'I'm fine. It was a little scary at the time, but as soon as he woke up, he was in bits about it. He's being really hard on himself.'

'Of course he is. He loves you. It wouldn't matter to him that he was asleep. It's still going to kill him what he did. Wow. I can see why you held off telling him you're pregnant. Is he around tonight?'

She nods. 'He's cooking me dinner tonight. I might tell him, depending on how his mood is.'

Bria raises her eyebrows and takes a long drink from her smoothie. 'What's that look for?'

'Just thinking about how many conversations I've put off, because of Tate's mood. When he goes into one of his deep, brooding moods, he barely hears what you're saying to him. Total waste of time talking to him.'

'Thanks. That makes me feel so much better. Did Gregg tell you about Dillon?'

Bria nods. 'I really feel for him. He doesn't deserve this. I actually got closer to him while you were in Canada. He's a difficult one to get to know, but I saw a side of him I didn't know was there. He's a genuinely decent guy. He was super supportive the last few weeks.'

'I heard. I know what Dillon did was stupid, but he was—' Chloe stops herself in time. She doesn't know if it's common knowledge about Dillon's feelings for Luke.

'You were going to say he's heartbroken, right? I guessed that he had feelings for Luke a while ago.'

'It's such a mess. I don't suppose Gregg heard from Luke at all?'

'Nope. His phone is off too. Maybe he's pissed off that Dillon pulled a stunt like that at his wedding? It's all over social today, obviously. Having one of the band arrested, while at the wedding of another band member, is kind of big news.'

Chloe grimaces and takes a sip of her drink. That's putting it mildly. She's skimmed some of the headlines and none were painting Dillon in a favourable light. 'I guess all we can do is wait and see what happens with Dillon.' She glances at her watch. 'Shoot. I'd better go. Tate is expecting me. But thanks for the chat. I needed it.'

Bria hugs her before opening the car door. 'Any time. And good luck with Tate. I don't mean that the way it sounds. Really. I just mean good luck finding a suitable time, at the moment. But maybe this is something you both need. A bit of normal life, instead of celebrity nonsense.'

'Yeah. Maybe.'

Chloe reverses out of the parking spot, waves at Bria, then goes back towards Blackrock and Tate. Bria is right. She needs to tell him - sooner rather than later.

Chloe opens the front door of Tate's house and smiles when the mouth-watering smell of bolognese hits her. She hangs up her coat and bag, then opens the door into the main living area.

The sight that greets her, is one she'd never get tired of. Her stunning rock star boyfriend is dressed in his usual jeans and black t-shirt, stirring dinner on the stove. She'd quite happily stare at him for the next hour and not get bored.

'Quit staring and get your ass over here.'

Chloe smiles and breathes him in, as he hugs her to his chest. The welcoming scent of leather and sandalwood instantly makes her feel at home. 'Dinner smells amazing.'

'I hope so. I've been working on it for ages.'

'So what's the special occasion?'

'It's an apology dinner, but not for last night,' he adds quickly. 'I still feel shitty about it, but I was asleep so...' he shrugs and smiles tightly at her. 'I guess I have to accept it was an accident, and not anything else.'

She kisses him and moves around the counter to sit on one of the stools. 'I'm glad to hear it. Now I don't want you to mention it again, okay. It's done.'

'Fair enough.'

'So, what did you do that you need to apologise for?'

'Being a moody dick the last few days.'

She laughs and pours herself a glass of juice. 'That I will take and accept the apology for. You have been particularly moody, but I understand why. It's been a crazy few weeks.'

He dishes out their dinner and sits beside her. 'It's been a crazy fucking year.'

'Have you heard anything else from Dillon?'

Tate takes a drink before he answers. 'I rang him about an hour ago. Didn't get much out of him. He's pulling back from us.'

'I can't imagine what's going through his head right now. I'm sure he's scared.' Chloe has no doubt Dillon's scared. He comes across as a hard ass through and through, but she's seen glimpses of what he's hiding underneath.

'We'll all be there for him as much as we can. And you were right about Luke. I was being a dick to the guy. He's on honeymoon. I just got wrapped up in the fact he should be here for this, but... yeah... I was a bit...'

'Unreasonable,' she adds with a grin.

He shrugs. 'Maybe. Your choice of words, not mine.'

'He'll be home in a few weeks and will have to face everything then. So, I know this probably isn't the right time to ask but, what happens with your performances? You're booked to do a few soon.'

'We have musicians who can fill in for one of the guys if they're not up to performing. When you're travelling all over the world, you can pick up dodgy stomachs, colds, and stuff like that. If that happens, we have options so we don't have to cancel.'

She smiles and points her fork towards him. 'Options for you too?'

He grins and shakes his head. 'Nope. No back up for me. If the lead singer gets sick, it's a cancelled show.'

'That adds a bit of pressure to you.'

'We don't like going on unless the four of us are there. People come to see the band, not some members of the band and a stand in. Unfortunately, if Dillon goes down we won't have a choice. At least if we keep performing he'll have something to come back to.'

Chloe tidies away the dishes and grabs a tub of ice cream from the freezer. 'Why don't you get comfy. We can watch a movie. Just relax together.'

'That sounds fucking amazing. Are you okay though, you didn't eat much. Was the food good?'

'It was delicious. I'm just not overly hungry. Go and sit in the living room. I'll get the ice-cream.'

She can feel Tate watching her as he sits back on the couch. He knows something is up with her. He's twirling the ring on his thumb, something he only does when he's anxious, or thinking too much.

She takes the lid off the tub and grabs two spoons from the drawer before joining him on the couch. She passes him the tub then cuddles up next to him. Tate drapes his arm across the back of the couch behind her, twirling a lock of her hair around his fingers. 'Are you sure you're okay? I know you didn't get much sleep, but you look tired. And I don't mean that in a dick way. I'm just worried.'

He's given her an opening. One she can't, and shouldn't ignore. With Dillon facing prison in the coming weeks, there isn't going to be a right time.

He pushes back from her and tilts her head back. 'Hey? What's wrong?'

'Okay, I need to tell you something.'

His eyes narrow slightly. 'Okay...'

'So you know I wasn't feeling well when we were in Canada.'

'Yeah. You still feeling sick? Why didn't you tell me?'

'No, well, yes a little.' She pauses and looks away from him.

'Hey. You can tell me anything. You know that. What's up?'

'I didn't realise what it could be until I spoke to Bria at Luke's wedding. Tate, I'm pregnant.'

Gregg parks his car in his driveway and peers up at his house. He used to love this place. It wasn't anything near as grand or expensive as Tate or Luke's places, but it was his. Well, his and the bank's, but that was part of life. Or was, until the guys helped him pay off his mortgage. Something he'll never be able to thank them enough for.

After what Angel did to him though, his house feels wrong. He can't explain it. Ciaran and the other security guys had picked through the house, finding all her hidden cameras. Everything is locked up tight. New locks. New alarm system. New security lights.

So why is he still hesitant about going inside?

He's being stupid. Deep down he knows he is. His parents, Bria, the guys, they'd all tried to convince him to sell up when he got out of hospital. But he'd stood firm. He didn't want Angel to win, by driving him out of the first house he's ever owned. He wasn't going to let her win like that.

But she kind of is.

He turns and looks through the trees at the house next door. Her old house. He can only see the top of the chimney from his driveway, but it's her chimney and that freaks him out.

'Are you okay?'

He jumps and places his hand over his racing heart when he sees his neighbour, Mrs. Rafferty, beside him. 'Don't sneak up on me like that. You scared the life out of me.'

'Oh I'm sorry dear.'

'It's grand. I reckon my heart is back where it belongs now. Is everything all right?'

'Oh yes. I noticed you were standing out here looking a little lost.'

'Me? Lost? Yeah, I probably usually am,' he admits with a grin.

She smiles kindly at him, as she wraps her cardigan around her thin frame. 'You may have a point there.' She peers over the trees at the other house. 'I wonder what will happen to the house now?'

He shrugs. 'Who knows? The landlord got in touch a few weeks ago to apologise. Like it was his fault he rented his house to a psycho. I worked with her and didn't see it, so how was he supposed to know?'

'Can I ask you something?'

'Go for it.'

'Why are you still here?'

Gregg frowns and looks around his driveway. 'What? You mean like on the planet, or here specifically?'

'Why are you still living in this house, Gregg?'

'You trying to get rid of me, Mrs. R.?'

'No, you silly boy. You know we love having you as our neighbour. You help bring a little excitement to our otherwise predictable life. After knowing me for so long, you know I always speak my mind.'

'It's part of your charm,' he replies, grinning at her to lighten the mood. This conversation is heading towards somewhere serious, and he's not sure he wants to go there.

'Indeed. Gregg, you look tired. Now, I know I am out of the loop when it comes to your job, and that it can be stressful and tiring at times. But I think this is something more.'

Yep. Definitely not where he wants to go with his neighbour. She's a sweet lady and takes care of both him and his house. But opening up about his nightmares and crippling fears is only going to worry her. 'There's just a lot on with the band. No doubt you heard about Dillon being arrested?'

She nods, her face turning serious. 'Yes. How is he?'

'Not good.' God he's going to hell for this. Using Dillon's situation to take the spotlight off himself is low.

'Is Bria coming over tonight?'

'Should be.'

'Good.' She nods to herself and looks at Angel's old house again. 'You went through a horrific ordeal, Gregg. You deserve to be able to move from it and enjoy the rest of your life. If that means moving from here, then that's what you have to do. It's not letting her win.'

She smiles again, before turning and disappearing around the corner.

That woman is nearly as intuitive as his mother. She'd said pretty much the same thing to him, when he woke up in hospital. No doubt she's still thinking the same thing.

He unlocks his front door, turns off the alarm, and walks down the corridor to the kitchen, passing the downstairs spare room on his way.

The floorplan is the same as her house next door, and that's the room he was kept in in her house. It doesn't matter that it's a different house. He can't walk by the damn door without thinking about Angel and what she did.

'Jesus Gregg, would you stop with the pity party.' After putting on the kettle, he leans back against the sink and looks around the room. He really does like living here. But does he love it?

Honestly? No. Not anymore.

He's on edge here. They'd been staying over in Bria's flat more than here and that was ridiculous. They're using a small flat she shares with her roommate, over an empty house. It makes no sense.

He has no problem staying with her as much as she wants, but it's not ideal. Her flatmate is great, but they need their own place. He needs somewhere he feels safe.

A few weeks ago, Dillon had offered him his cottage to use as long as he wants. Maybe he should take him up on that. He makes himself a cup of coffee. He knows now how Tate feels when the nightmares hit him, robbing him of sleep. The last full night of sleep he had, was before that cow took him. Must be starting to show too, if even Mrs. Rafferty had noticed.

With his extra strong coffee in hand, he trudges upstairs and into his bedroom. Gregg places the cup on the bedside table and glances up at the ceiling before he can stop himself. He can't get undressed without checking. The camera Angel had installed in the light fitting was removed while he was in hospital, but he still has to make sure it's not there.

Every. Damn. Time.

He takes a mouthful of coffee, hoping the caffeine hit will work in. He needs the extra boost. He hadn't slept well last night and promised Bria he'd take her out tonight for a few hours. Then what? Bringing her back here isn't going to end in a hot and steamy night. They might have to go back to her flat again.

After cranking up the music as loud as it goes, he turns on the shower, standing outside the stall with his eyes closed for a few minutes. 'Come on, Gregg. No one has drowned in a shower.'

Well, maybe they had, but he's not about to Google it to find out for sure. That would be a sure-fire way of really screwing himself up.

The music helps to mask the sound of running water, but he still has to force himself to step in to the cubicle, leaving the door open.

Gregg washes himself in record time, shuts off the water and wraps a towel around his waist. He survived the ordeal, but his damn heart is racing again. His watch buzzes angrily, startling him. This is getting ridiculous. He's a nervous wreck. His watch keeps screaming at him so he checks the screen, cursing himself when he sees the problem. He forgot to take his shot. Idiot!

He never forgets. Shows where his head is. He hurries downstairs and grabs a pen from the fridge, then sits on the couch.

After checking the dose is correct, then checking again, just to be sure. And once more for good luck, he injects the insulin into his stomach.

No wonder he's a nervous wreck. Angel had infiltrated so many aspects of his life. Things he took for granted before he was kidnapped, are suddenly suspicions or might kill him. Like water, his shots, spare rooms, food he hasn't prepared himself. That last one is really screwing with him. He doesn't cook. Can't cook at all. He survived on takeaways, or Bria's cooking when he stayed with her.

He doesn't think for one second that the local pizzeria would want to drug his food, but that doesn't stop the irrational, scared part of his brain from heading off on a tangent. One that ends with him dying. Not the best thoughts for someone in his mid-thirties, but it's where the bitch left him.

Scared and second guessing everything.

Gregg lies back on the couch, still wet from the shower. He closes his eyes and tries the deep breathing exercises his therapist gave him.

He can get over this. It'll take time, but he'll have to feel like his old self again soon. One day he'll wake up and won't be looking over his shoulder, won't jump at every unknown sound, won't be scared of water. It has to be okay, because if this is what his life is going to be like... he shakes his head, squeezing his eyes shut.

No. It will be okay.

Tate

Tate hears every single word she says to him, but that's as far as the reaction goes. He should say something. Anything. He knows that, but his mind has gone blank. There's nothing there. Then it flips on him and royally fucks him. 'But how?'

'I'm sure I don't need to draw you a diagram.'

Tate curses himself and the ridiculous comment. 'Sorry. That was a stupid thing to say. I meant, we're always careful.'

'The night you came back off tour before Christmas. We had sex in your dressing room before you went on stage.'

That was down to him. He'd been so eager to see her, he hadn't even thought about using protection. He hadn't seen her for six weeks and had been horny as fuck. 'I'm sorry, Chloe. It's my fault.'

'I'm sure there were two of us in that dressing room. I know this is a surprise and you haven't had a chance to process it yet, but what's going on in your head?'

'I'm pissed at myself for not wearing a fucking condom that night. I wasn't thinking straight. Fuck! I'm so sorry, Chloe. I should have—'

'Hey, this isn't a blame thing. I should have said something, but I was so carried away in the moment I didn't. And here we are.'

Yeah. Here they are. What the fuck is he meant to say or do now? He'd be lying if he said kids had entered his mind once... well, ever. He knows it's what people think about as they get older, but he never did. He loves his brother's girls to death. But that's so different to having his own children.

'Are you okay?'

He blinks and looks up at her. 'What? Yeah. Sorry. Head's going a little crazy.'

She shuffles closer and takes his hand. 'I know it's a lot to absorb. I'm still trying to get my head around the idea myself.'

'Right.' He's being a dick. He knows he is, but he doesn't have the first clue what he's thinking. All he knows is that he needs to get some air. 'I might go for a drive.'

'But what about dessert and relaxing on the couch?'

He gets up, suddenly feeling like there's no air in the fucking room. 'I just need a few minutes. I'll be back in a bit.'

Chloe nods. 'Sure. Are you okay?'

'Yeah. Grand.' He smiles at her, but by the look on her face, it falls short. 'Back in a bit.'

She nods, then watches him as he makes a cowards escape.

Tate guides his truck down the pothole laden track leading to the beach and stops at the gate. The wind coming off the sea is freezing, so he grabs his jacket and woolly hat off the back seat, before he braves the beach.

He picks the nearest rock and sits down, watching the waves crashing against the stony beach.

Chloe is pregnant.

He's going to be a dad.

He kicks the stones at his feet and curses loudly. He can't be a dad. No way. After the events of the last year, he's more sure than ever he *shouldn't* be a father. He's a messed up recovering addict who can't keep his own life going the right way. How the fuck is he meant to be a father to anyone? It's impossible. And unfair on the poor kid.

And it's not like his own biological father would have won any awards himself. He's not exactly coming from a great gene pool. Kid is bound to be fucked up, just having him for a father in the first place. Which is why he doesn't want this. He doesn't want to be a father.

But Chloe wants kids. You'd have to be blind not to see that. Which leaves him with two options. He either comes clean, tells her he doesn't want kids, and loses her. Or he keeps his mouth shut, and plays the part of a dutiful dad, to keep her happy.

Neither option fills him with joy, but he doesn't want to lose her. He can't contemplate life without her. Not for one second.

He'd been a selfish dick most of his life. Relationships lasted until he got bored. He'd never given past girlfriends what they wanted - emotionally at least. Not until Chloe.

He's so deeply in love with her it scares him sometimes. Scares him how much of a hold she has on him. Hearing her voice when he is away. Holding her when he comes home. Lazy mornings in bed. She has made his life better in so many ways. He can't say goodbye to all that.

Tate curses when he realises he's scratching the inside of his left arm again. He's not going back to that again. He shoves his hands into his jacket pockets and curses himself.

He's more messed up than he thought. Since Dara opened the memories of his fucked up past, he can't seem to deal with things he'd usually shrug off. Not that Chloe's pregnancy is something that can, or should be, shrugged off.

No wonder people still walk on eggshells around him. No wonder Gregg and Bria couldn't tell him they liked each other. Everyone is terrified of pushing him over the edge and back to drugs. He's made his friends and family wary of him, and that hurts.

He was meant to be the strong one. The unflappable one. The one everyone else could lean on. Now he's a fucking basket case. A basket case who is going to be a father.

He can't tell her this isn't what he wants. He's not going to do that to her. For the first time in his life he's going to do the right thing. He wants a future with Chloe, no question. If accepting this baby means he can have a life with her, he'll do it.

Chloe

Chloe finishes straightening the living room again and sits down. Then gets up and walks into the kitchen. Nothing to tidy there either. She's already done that, twice.

He's been gone an hour. Sixty long minutes.

Is that a good sign? Does that mean he's really processing it? Or is he freaking out?

She pushes away from the counter and goes upstairs to the studio. His house is spectacular, but the studio is absolutely her favourite room. She could never get bored of the view over Blackrock and the sea beyond.

Chloe picks up one of Tate's many guitars and sits on the couch with it on her knee. He had given her a few lessons while they were away, and she wasn't actually too bad.

It helped that Tate is such a natural teacher. He should be, after studying music for years. Before he was signed, he'd made his living teaching piano and guitar. It's something she knows he misses, but with his schedule and rising fame, it became impossible to continue with. He still teaches her gran when he's free, even though she has to be the most stubborn, argumentative student he's ever had.

Chloe plays the intro to one of Broken's songs from memory. It's the song Tate sang to her in the kitchen, before they had sex on the counter top.

Her sexy musician had walked in on her listening to him on the radio, and took over the singing, while he touched her, undressed her, made love to her. He doesn't sing to her enough. And that's something she regrets.

She should ask him to sing for her more often. Or to play for her. There's something about Tate singing that moves her like nothing else. The husky edge to his voice sends shivers through her entire body.

She's seen him on stage with the guys, performing in front of thousands of screaming fans a few times now, but it still feels like the first time, every time.

It didn't matter how into the performance he is, he never forgets she's there, watching him. Every time he meets her eyes at the side of the stage, he winks or smiles. And every time he does, she has to stop herself from going out on stage and jumping on him.

No doubt the fans who have paid to see him, would be far from impressed if she did that.

Chloe watches the sea on the horizon. Would the baby look like him? Would their son or daughter have his deep blue eyes and his dark hair? She can't help but smile at the thought.

Or does, until she remembers why she's up in the studio in the first place. None of that will matter, if he's not on board with the pregnancy in the first place.

He's besotted with his nieces, but that's very different to having your own child.

She places the guitar back in the rack, then checks the security camera feed on the screen on the wall. Still no sign of Tate.

One hour and twenty minutes.

Where the hell is he?

Then she catches movement on the screen. About time. Chloe watches as he pulls his bike in to the driveway and the gates close behind him.

She had been desperate for him to come home, but now she's nervous about the upcoming conversation. The direction of her entire future hinges on what he says to her.

Tate

Tate drops his bike keys on the counter, then faces the stairs as Chloe walks down to him. He hates himself for it, but he didn't want to come home. He wasn't ready. Hell, he doesn't think he'll ever be ready. But he made his decision and he'll stick by it. For Chloe.

'Hey. Sorry I was gone so long.'

She pulls herself onto one of the bar stools and plays with the sleeve of her jumper. 'It's fine. You had a lot to think about. Are you okay?'

What a question. One he still doesn't know how to answer honestly. While he plays for time, he sits on the stool beside her and turns the ring on his thumb, as the awkward silence drags on. This should be a happy occasion. Chloe deserves for it to be a happy occasion. Instead she's getting him like this, and that's not fair.

The smile that makes an appearance feels weak at best, but her expression brightens a little, so it must be convincing.

'So I guess we're having a baby.'

If he could slap himself on the head without freaking her out, he would. What sort of a half-arsed statement is that to come out with?

'Is that what you want?'

He nods. 'I would have preferred a little more time with just you and me, but yeah.'

'I know. It's a lot sooner than I would have liked too, but...' she shrugs and smiles. 'Are you really sure you're okay about this, Tate? I mean, really sure?'

'Yeah.' God he couldn't be less sure about anything in his life, but she wants it. He can see it in her face. And if he can give her this, he will. No question.

Chloe runs her fingers through his hair as they kiss and, in that moment, he knows he's done the right thing.

Chloe rests her forehead against his and rubs her hand along his thigh. 'I put the ice cream back in the freezer. Do you want to continue from where we left off?'

'Yeah.' He needs to make this up to her somehow. He's failing miserably at the moment. 'You sit and I'll grab it.'

Chloe stretches out on the couch as he gets what they need, then joins her. Chloe snuggles up against him, taking a spoon from his hand. 'Where did you go?'

'The beach.'

She nods as she licks the ice cream off her spoon. 'I thought that's where you'd be.'

'It's my thinking spot.'

She holds up a spoon of ice cream which he accepts, not really tasting it. 'I have an appointment next week. Do you want to come with me?'

'Appointment for what?'

'The baby of course,' she responds, laughing at his confusion. And he can't blame her. He's on a roll with the stupid questions today.

'Yeah. Sorry. Of course I'll go with you. Just send the reminder to my phone.'

'You haven't asked the date.'

This time his brain catches on before his mouth fucks him over again. 'You know the due date?'

She takes another spoon of ice cream, waiting until she swallows it before she answers. 'Well, I can guess. If I got pregnant at your concert, I should be due in September.'

'Right.' He's not sure how to respond to that. 'So do you want to tell people or...'

Chloe pauses as she considers that. He's so far out of his depth on this one, he'll let her take the lead. 'Is it okay if we wait a little while? I mean you can tell family and the guys, but leave it at that for now. Is that okay?'

'Yeah. No problem.'

Chloe cuddles closer to him. 'I know this is a lot to take in. It is for me too. But we'll be fine Tate. We can do this.'

He nods. 'I know.' She thinks they can be parents to this baby so he has to believe her.

Chloe puts down the ice cream and climbs onto his lap, facing him. She's happy. He'd have to be blind not to see that.

'I was stressing about telling you. But now you know, I'm getting a little excited about it. I know it's very early and I'm trying to rein myself in, but I can't help it.'

He brushes his fingers through her hair, smiling when her face lights up. 'You're allowed to be excited.'

Her smile turns to a smirk, her eyes travelling down his body. 'You know, I'd really like you to take me upstairs. If you want to, of course.'

'Really? You're feeling okay?'

'At this moment, yes. I'm more than okay.' Her hand moves up his leg to his dick, brushing over it through his jeans. 'Please, Tate.'

He smirks down at her hand then peers up at her. 'You really think you have to beg me? You not feel what's under your hand?'

She squeezes him gently and he gasps. 'Oh, that?'

Chloe wraps her arms around his neck, holding on while he carries her up the stairs and lays her down on their bed.

'I love you, Chloe.' And he does. More than he's ever loved anyone before. She is his entire world.

Her soft hands pull at the bottom of his t-shirt, so he tears it off before leaning over her again, her incredible body fitting perfectly under his.

'How about you show me how much?'

She traces her fingers over his nipple piercing and the feeling goes straight to his dick.

'I love how you react like that.'

He kisses the side of her neck. 'I did warn you.'

Her hand moves down his chest and tugs at his belt. 'Get them off.'

She groans as he sucks her earlobe. 'How about we both strip and I'll meet you back here in two seconds?'

He pushes to his feet, making quick work of his boots, jeans, and underwear before covering Chloe's naked body with his own. Her hand slides down his chest again and finds what she wants.

She wraps her hand around his dick then circles her thumb over the head, brushing against the piercing, putting just the right amount of pressure on it to have him squirming. He's never had someone play with his piercings as much as she does, and he loves it.

Chloe wriggles down the bed and Tate watches as she flicks her tongue over the piercing, licking the precum off the black ring. Her thumb traces over the bar piercing the base of his dick, as she slips him into her mouth.

Tate braces one hand against the headboard and the other on the bed, fisting the sheet, as she sucks him. As she's playing with the piercing, she cups his balls, massaging them. Each time she moves up his dick, her tongue flicks against the ring, pushing him ever closer to the edge.

And she knows it.

His stunning woman slows down, and peers up at him. She winks and he groans aloud. 'Tease.'

'I'm not even a little bit sorry.'

He drops his head when she takes him deep into her mouth, then swallows, putting pressure on the head. 'Fuck Chloe... I'm going to come.'

He should have kept his mouth shut. She slows down, and he groans as his orgasm slips away.

'That's not playing fair.'

She laughs, the look she gives him, sexy as hell. He peers down at her, wedged between his legs. She takes his dick in her hand, holding it firmly as she runs her tongue over his balls, never breaking eye contact with him.

Her tongue moves up to the barbell, pulling against it.

'Jesus, Chloe!' It hurt, but in such a good way.

By the time she's led him to the edge countless times without letting him go over, he's worked up, sweating, and in desperate need to fuck her.

Chloe pushes back up the bed, then positions him where she wants him, groaning as the piercing drives her crazy when she grinds against him. 'I won't last long after what you just did to me.'

'I know. I want you worked up and desperate to come.'

He grips her by the legs and slowly pulls her towards him until he's completely filling her. She's right. He is worked up and more than a little desperate. But he doesn't want to be too rough with her. Not while she's... He glances down at her stomach and stops moving.

'Hey. Tate. Look at me.'

He convinces himself to look at her, rather than at her stomach. If he thinks about that too much, he'll pull out.

'I want my stunning boyfriend tofuck me, right now. Make me scream your name, Tate.'

Chloe moves her hips, reaching around to dig her fingers into his ass.

He sucks in a breath through clenched teeth. 'You're asking for trouble, you know that?'

'Oh I hope so.'

Chloe

Tate isn't with her - not fully. But she can hardly blame him. She's had a few days to try to process the news. He's had a few hours. Of course he's going to be a bit off. With a little encouragement from her, he's relaxing... well, not fully relaxing. That would defeat the purpose.

His massive body covers hers, the griffin tattooed on his chest right in front of her face, shifting as his body moves. He's worked up, her teasing pushing him to the brink so many times, he's ready to come. But he holds himself back. His movements are slow. Controlled. For now at least. He'll let go and she can't wait.

Tate looks down at her, his blue eyes filled with the promise of what's about to be unleashed.

'Put your hands over your head. Now.'

She doesn't hesitate, stretching her arms above her head. Tate wraps his hand around her wrists, pinning them together. His other hand grips her chin, holding her steady while he kisses her. Each swipe of his tongue against hers matches his hips, the slow steady pace frustratingly intense.

With each thrust of his hips, she moans and pushes back against him, desperate for him to stop teasing her and make her come. He smiles against her mouth, lifting his hips, moving his dick out of her, until just the tip is sliding in and out.

'You all worked up now, huh?'

'I'm taking it this is payback?'

His hand grips her wrists tighter when she tries to free herself. Or at least plays like she is. She has no intention of going anywhere.

'You didn't think I'd just let you come now, did you?' He lifts himself up and watches as his dick slowly slides into her pussy. God he's so handsome it hurts. She could watch him like this forever and never tire of looking at him. His tight stomach rolls as he thrusts into her, taking his time, making sure he buries himself deep, before withdrawing again.

'Please Tate. I need to come...' She's breathless now, her body tingling from her toes to her scalp. She arches her back, trying to get friction against her pussy, but every time she moves, he pulls back.

'Tate...'

'What?' he asks, knowing full well what she wants.

'Please. I need to come.'

'Beg me.'

'Please Tate. Please...'

He flips her onto her stomach, lifting her hips, before pushing into her hard and deep. She moans, pressing her face into the pillow as he fucks her like a man possessed. Whatever doubt he may have had initially, has clearly been shoved aside. He spreads her ass cheeks, driving himself deeper.

Chloe gasps when his fingers trace over her clit, swirling in slow circles, the pressure building in her with each swipe.

'You're going to come now, Chloe.'

Her *yes* is muffled by the pillow, but he hears it anyway, his fingers massaging her clit until she climaxes with an ear-piercing cry.

Tate grips her hip with his free hand, holding her in place as her orgasm brings on his own. He drops his head onto her back as he leans over her, his dick sliding slowly and steadily into her, as he comes.

He pulls her back against his chest, wrapping his arms around her, as he kisses along the side of her neck. 'That was fucking awesome.'

She manages to nod, but she's still a little spaced out. He laughs and slowly pulls out, before lowering her onto the bed.

'You okay?' he asks, as she flops back with her arm draped over her face.

'Fucked...'

'Glad to hear it.' He falls silent, so she peers out from under her arm. He's staring down at her stomach, a serious look on his face.

She takes his hand in hers, rubbing her thumb over the Celtic knot tattooed on the back. 'Are you really okay?'

He smiles and nods. 'Absolutely.'

But instead of cuddling up to her like he usually does, he climbs out of bed. 'I'm going to grab a shower.'

Before she can ask him to stay, he's already disappeared into the bathroom and has turned on the shower.

Well that's not a good sign. When they have sex, it's usually a battle to extract herself. He'd happily spend all day in bed with her. She can't remember him ever getting up so fast before.

But things are different now. They'll be different from now on.

And she's fine with that. She really is.

Chloe looks over at the bathroom door. In spite of what he said, she has a horrible feeling he may not be as thrilled about the news as he's letting on.

Gregg

The wind sends Gregg's hair into a frenzy as he steps out of the car. 'Jesus, it's freezing.' He pulls his woolly hat over his head, managing to contain most of his hair, then zips up his jacket. He climbs onto the bonnet of his Defender and looks along the beach.

Tate loves the beach. Anytime he needs to talk, he wants to go to the beach.

Like right now.

The text hadn't said much.

Need to talk. Beach at the farm.

Man of many words as usual.

But he knew Tate well enough to know that, if he needs to talk, something is seriously wrong. So, he'd left his house in Ashford and driven the ten minutes to Newcastle where Tate's parents live.

He finally spots Tate in the distance, and groans to himself. Well isn't this just perfect. Not only is he meant to meet him on the beach, but Tate is riding his demon horse.

God, Gregg hates that horse!

Jove feels the same about him. They have a mutual hate/hate relationship and that suits Gregg just fine. The horse is nuts about Tate, and vice versa. Unfortunately, all Jove fancies doing to Gregg is biting him. Horrible animal.

Maybe if he waits by the car, Tate will come to him, saving him from going anywhere near the sea. He sits on the roof of his car and can't help but smile as he watches Tate. He's a little envious of his friend.

Tate and Jove are in the water, the large black horse galloping through the waves. He can't see Tate's face, but he knows full well he's smiling. Getting out on Jove always cheered him up. It was his way of unwinding and letting go of all the stress of life.

Thankfully, Tate finally notices him and steers Jove towards him. Looks like he'll be spared a not so relaxing stroll on the terrifying beach.

Jove thunders towards him, sand spraying from under his hooves. Tate reins him in, and Jove slows as he moves towards Gregg. As he guessed, Tate is smiling. Jove is glaring and snarling at him. Well, probably not, but it feels that way.

The massive black horse snorts loudly as he comes to a stop beside Gregg's car. 'Good ride?'

Tate pats Jove on the side of the neck and nods, as he loosens his hold on the reins. 'Fucking brilliant! Think I needed that. Want a go?'

'Fuck off! And yes I cursed, but that called for a curse. Keep that thing away from me.'

Tate laughs and pulls Jove back a step. The smile fades, as he rubs the side of Jove's neck. There is something on his mind.

'You want to talk from up here, or do you fancy doing this on solid ground?'

He swings his leg over the saddle and drops to the ground as Gregg climbs off the roof of his car. 'Thanks for coming.'

'Of course.' Gregg lets Tate pull up Jove's stirrups in peace.

Tate suddenly curses and turns around. 'I am such a dick.'

'Oh I know that, but any reason in particular?'

'I shouldn't have called you to the beach. I'm sorry. We can walk in the field. There's a big hedge between it and the beach. Or we can go somewhere else.'

'I'll go for the field.'

'You sure?'

'I need to get over this, Tate. I'll walk in the field.'

He follows Tate through the gate, keeping to the other side of Jove who, as always, is attached to Tate like an giant dog.

'Chloe is pregnant.'

Tate's blunt statement comes with no build up. Gregg stops and grabs Tate's arm, pulling him to a stop. 'She is?'

Tate nods, but looks far from happy about that. 'She told me last night. I fucked up, Gregg. It was the day we got back from touring. I was so excited to see her... well, you can guess.'

'Wow. Okay, so this is a big thing for you both. How is she?'

Tate starts walking again, so Gregg follows him. 'She's a bit queasy, but seems fine other than that.'

'And how does she feel about the baby?'

Tate shrugs. 'Happy, I guess.'

'Hold on. You guess? Have you not spoken about it?'

'Of course we have. It's not planned, you know. We're both trying to get our heads around it.'

'I'll bet. Congratulations, buddy. Really.'

'Yeah. Thanks.' He massages the back of his neck, as he stays quiet for another few minutes. Gregg never thought about any of them having children. It was bound to happen at some stage. They're heading towards their forties. He knows it's been on his mind lately. Not that he's anywhere ready for something like that with Bria. Not yet anyway. But he would like a family with her, at some stage.

He'd never heard Tate mention children. Not once. Maybe that had something to do with his own childhood. Maybe he's just never thought about it. Until Chloe came on the scene, he was hardly the settling down kind of guy.

'And what about you? How do you feel about it?'

Tate smiles briefly at him. 'Happy.'

'Try again, buddy.'

'Terrified.'

'Better.'

Tate stops and looks at him. 'How the fuck is that better?'

'Because it's the truth. Of course you're terrified. That's natural. I'm sure Chloe is too. Can I ask you something?'

Tate nods.

'Please don't take this the wrong way, but do you want to be a father? It's just that I've never heard you mention it before.'

'I'm doing this with Chloe.'

'That's not what I'm asking.'

'I don't know how I feel, okay? But I've got time to figure it out and get used to the idea.'

'Right.' That wasn't exactly the answer Gregg was hoping for, but he's not really surprised. Tate is loyal. Always has been. Which is great... most of the time. But Chloe needs him to stay with her and the baby because he wants to. Not because he feels like he has to.

'Tate, maybe you should—'

'Gregg. I asked you to meet me so I could tell you. I don't need a discussion about it. I've made my decision.'

'Yeah, but this comes down to more than you feeling duty bound to—'

Tate squares up to him. 'What the fuck? You think that's what I'm doing?'

'Hey, don't get your knickers in a twist. I'm just looking out for you. Both of you. I kind of like you and Chloe, quite a bit.'

'Yeah, well it's all fine, okay. Trust me.' He backs away, but he's still tense and on edge. So much for the relaxing ride on Jove.

'Whatever you say. I'm here if you need to talk about anything though.'

He nods and continues down the track again. 'Oh, and I don't want you to say anything to anyone else. It's too soon. We want to wait another few weeks.'

'Of course. I won't even mention it to Bria.'

'Actually, my sister has known since the wedding. She got Chloe a pregnancy test. That's what was going on when they disappeared for a bit.'

'And there was me thinking they were comparing their boyfriends.'

'I hope they never do that. Your girlfriend is my sister.'

Gregg grimaces. 'Yeah. Good point.'

Tate nods towards the gap in the hedge. 'You feeling brave?'

Gregg instantly tenses. 'What?'

'Do you want to move onto the beach? Just walk along the sand at the top of the beach?'

'I don't know if I can...'

'I'm scared of the dark,' Tate says. 'Clowns too, but for a very different reason.' He smiles and Gregg can't help relaxing a little. 'I still have to sleep with the light on sometimes. Dara chaining me to a bed, in a pitch black room, didn't help. Asshole. But I'm trying to get past it. Chloe helps. We practice getting me used to the dark. We turn off the light and she holds me or talks to me.

'I figured that maybe if we try something similar with you, it could help.' He shrugs and smiles again. 'Fuck knows. It's just an idea.'

How the hell Gregg stops himself from crying he'll never know, but he hangs on to his composure. Tate gets it better than he thought he would. Tate always slept with the light on while they were away, but he just thought it was because they were in a strange place, or maybe he just preferred it that way.

'Sounds like a good idea.'

Tate steps down from the grass path onto the sand, followed by

Jove, who wanders off to sniff some seaweed. Gregg stays where he is, unable to get his feet to move from the grass.

Tate holds out his hand. 'I've got you, Gregg. I promise.'

He feels like a right wuss, but he takes Tate's hand, holding onto it like his life depends on it. When he's not dragged into hell in the first few minutes of having his feet on the sand, he loosens his grip on Tate's hand. 'Sorry.'

'For what? You're doing great. You want to walk down here for a bit? Not anywhere near the sea, I promise.'

'Okay. Think I can manage that.'

They walk in silence for a few minutes, Jove following behind, pausing every now and again when something catches his interest.

'Did you get a message from Dillon?'

Gregg takes a second to register the question. Just putting one foot in front of the other is taking all his concentration. 'Dillon? Yeah. He said he doesn't want us at the sentencing tomorrow.'

'Got that one too. No visits today either. You think he's pulling back?'

Gregg shrugs, then stops to look at the sea as a particularly large wave crashes against the sand. Tate positions himself between Gregg and the surf, blocking his view.

'You good?'

'Sorry. Yeah. Just the sound of the waves.'

'Let's keep walking.'

Gregg moves again, thankful that Tate is guarding him. Not that the sea will suddenly spring legs and run after him, but better safe than sorry. Gregg shoves his hands into the pockets of his jeans to stop fidgeting. He's fine until there's a lull in the conversation and his mind goes off on him.

'So you think he's pulling back? Dillon I mean.'

'Probably. You know him. He's not one for the touchy, feely emotional stuff. I'm sure he'd prefer to keep to himself and deal with it alone.'

'So we let him? He could go away for a month or two.'

'You want to force Dillon to do something he doesn't want to?'

'Yeah. You're probably right But we're ignoring him on this one. We're going to the sentencing.'

Gregg snorts. 'Too right we are. Stuff him and the *push everyone away* crap that he does. Hey, I spoke to Max. Pippa was the one to call the Garda at the wedding.'

Tate isn't surprised to hear that. 'Figures. Do you think he'll get a custodial sentence?'

'I think so, buddy. It's not his first slap on the wrist. I'd be shocked if he didn't.'

'Fuck.'

They walk in silence for a few minutes, before Tate points back the way they came. 'Probably should head back. I told Chloe I'd be back in a few hours. Don't want her to worry after my recent disappearing acts.'

Gregg nods eagerly. He's proud of himself for lasting as long as he has, but he's wound so tight he swears he's going to break.

'You okay though?'

'Yeah. Stressed out, but I'm not freaking out, so that's a plus, right?'

Tate drapes his arm across Gregg's shoulders, silently supporting him as they make their way back up the beach.

Dillon

It's been a hell of a long time since Dillon hasn't been in control. As he listened to his sentence being read out in court, he realised he'd lost the control he needs to survive. Lost the control he desperately clings to.

One month. Four weeks. Thirty days.

No control. No decisions. No freedom.

It could have been worse. He knows that. But four fucking weeks is pretty bad in his eyes.

He taps his fingers on the table in front of him and tries to stay strong. He needs to, or else this is going to be a fucking nightmare. He doesn't let his emotions get the better of him often. It's never a good thing, but when he stepped into the court room and saw Tate and Gregg with his sisters, he'd come fucking close to crying.

He told them not to come. Pretty much ordered them to keep away. The band had been dragged through the press enough the last few weeks with his fuck ups. He didn't want them anywhere near this.

But they'd ignored him and he couldn't be more grateful. As much as he tries to push people away, they refuse to let him. And that means more to him than they'll ever be able to understand.

He tried to persuade his sisters not to come, but had lost that battle too. The two of them are nearly as stubborn as he is. They'll tell Luke the verdict, if he picks up his phone. Which he probably won't. He's not due back from honeymoon for another few weeks. Knowing Pippa, she'll keep him out of the loop until then. It's probably fair enough, given what he did at their wedding.

He looks up as the door opens and Clara is shown into the room, followed by Eva. The Garda closes the door behind them and they both hurry over to hug him, barely giving him a chance to get to his feet.

Eva cries as she buries her face against his chest. 'Hey. I can't breathe!'

'Sorry.' She wipes her face and takes his hand instead, as he gives Clara a one-armed hug.

'How are you, Dill?'

He sits down, each sister refusing to let go of his hands. 'I'm fine.'

Clara nods and smiles at him. 'Of course you are. You're always fine. I can't believe this is happening, Dill. I didn't think—'

'It's okay, Clara,' he says, squeezing her hand. It's not. It's as far from okay as it can get, but he doesn't want his sisters worrying about him. He'd put them through enough over the years. More than enough.

'Is there anything...' Clara stops talking and shrugs. 'What am I saying? There isn't anything I can do, is there?'

'There is actually. Would you keep an eye on the houses for me? I had cleaners in yesterday to give the two houses a good going over.

The fridges are emptied - just in case I wasn't going home today. But it might be an idea to check in case I missed anything. I offered Gregg the cottage a while ago. He might move in. Might not. He's got a spare set of keys. I don't want him walking in to something stinking the place down.'

'Of course.'

Her eyes water but, as usual, she keeps a handle on it. Clara is strong. Always has been. When their parents disowned him, Clara stepped up to look out for him. She's always been there for him. His rock and support, even when he didn't deserve it.

Eva on the other hand, is a big softy and can't hold back the tears. 'This is so unfair. Is there nothing your lawyer can do?'

'She did what she could, Eva. Hey, it's only four weeks. I've been on tour longer than that. I'll be out before you know it.' He pauses, then asks the question he doesn't want the answer to. 'Have you told... do Mum and Dad know? About today and the sentence?'

Eva looks at Clara, then back at him.

'I'll take that as a yes.'

Clara squeezes his hand, then gives him the worst excuse for a smile he's seen for a while.

'And? Not surprised, huh? Or, do I deserve everything I'm getting? I can see Dad throwing that one out there.'

When his sisters look at each other again, he knows he hit the nail on the head. Why does he keep doing this to himself? Why can't he just accept that they hate him and move on? He should have got the message by now. It's been over twenty years. It's not like it happened yesterday. Instead he keeps picking at the scab, reopening the wound, over and over again.

'Forget it. It's fine.' He's probably just ensured his parents would never, ever, speak to him again. Not that he could see a reconciliation anywhere in their future. Kind of impossible to apologise or make things up to them when he has no fucking idea what he did wrong. It was obvious they never loved him. When he came out it just gave them the excuse they needed to disown him.

'I'm sorry, Dill.'

He smiles at Clara, even though he feels like throwing up. 'Seriously. It's—'

'Fine,' his sisters finish for him at the same time.

Dillon laughs and pulls them both into a hug. 'I'm going to miss you both.'

They hang on to him for a long time, before sitting back in their chairs. Eva blows her nose on a tissue, while Clara fixes him with one of her no-nonsense looks. 'You keep your head down and please, for the love of God, do not get into more trouble.'

'I promise. I'll be on my best behaviour.'

'I know *your* best behaviour. You'll need to do better than that. I mean it Dill. Don't do anything to make this worse for you. I know you can take care of yourself, but I know you can have a temper when pushed. You need to rein that in for the next four weeks. Promise me.'

'I promise.' The door opens and two officers step inside and look at him. 'Right. I guess that's me then. I better go before I get into more trouble.'

His sisters hug him tightly, but he refuses to let their emotions get to him. He can't. There's time enough for that later when he's alone.

Luke

Sitting on the balcony of their private villa in the stunning Maldives, the clear blue ocean in front of him, Luke is in paradise.

They're only a week into their honeymoon, but it feels like a lot longer. He turns the wedding ring on his finger. It feels like he's been married for months, not one week. But it hasn't been a normal week by any means.

He smiles as Pippa joins him, leaning over to give him a kiss. 'I'll be back in two hours. Are you going to be okay here alone?'

He nods. 'Of course. Enjoy your massage.'

'Oh I will. See you later.'

He keeps the smile on his face until she leaves the villa. Once he's sure she's gone, he takes out his phone and turns it on. They promised each other there would be no phones while they were away. It's their honeymoon. They deserve to be away from all the mundane everyday drama - or at least that's what she said. Luke isn't sure exactly which mundane drama she's talking about.

He plays with the wedding ring as he waits for the phone to power up. He thought he'd like the feel of it. But so far, his marriage hasn't been something he necessarily wants to remember.

Or at least the wedding part.

He understands why Pippa wanted to leave on honeymoon the night of the wedding as planned. She had put a lot of time and effort into planning every detail of the day and the honeymoon. Of course she didn't want any of that wasted.

But that didn't help him feel any better about walking away from Dillon after his arrest. Pippa had called the Garda. It's not something he's happy about, but he understands... mostly. It was her special day and Dillon was spoiling it. Luke didn't feel the same, but the damage is done. No going back.

Dillon didn't lose his temper often. When he did it was disastrous and usually ended up with him in legal bother.

The thing that Luke doesn't get is why he lost his temper. He can't think of any reason why Dillon went berserk like he did.

His phone finally turns on. After being off for a week, the battery is on ten percent, but it will do for now. As the notifications come in a knot forms in Luke's stomach. Dozens of messages from both Gregg and Tate. But it's the message from Dillon's sister Clara, that hits him hardest.

Dillon has been sentenced to four weeks for what he did at the hotel. Luke peers at the words, carefully reading them again and again just to be sure.

He loads a browser and types in Dillon's name. It's true. Not that he'd doubt Clara, but it's all over the internet. He's in prison. While Luke is relaxing in the Maldives, his best friend is in prison.

He opens a new message, but stops and closes the phone down again. It's too late. He can't contact Dillon, and there's no point replying to Tate and Gregg at this stage.

They needed him last week and he wasn't there for any of them.

Being on honeymoon is no excuse as far as he's concerned. They're his family. He should have at least spoken to them. Should have spoken to Dillon before he...

Luke closes his eyes and curses to himself. He can't think of Dillon in prison. It doesn't make sense.

And his wife put him there. He's not blaming her for what happened, but he wishes anyone else would have called the Garda except her. It just feels like another barrier between his new wife and his best friend.

Luke gets up and slides his phone back in the case where he found it. He wants to talk to Pippa about Dillon, but he's not about to begin married life by fighting with her. He promised he'd leave his phone off. Turning it on and then wanting to discuss the man who put their wedding in the papers for all the wrong reasons wouldn't go down well with her.

He'll just have to get through the next three weeks, then go home and figure out how to make it up with Dillon.

With nothing else to do, Luke grabs a beer from the fridge and sits back on the balcony, the guilt of abandoning his friend eating him up.

Tate

'Fuck, fuck, fuck!'

Tate lowers the guitar and scrunches the piece of paper, launching it at the wall. It lands in the bin on top of the others. He's been trying to write for two hours, but everything he puts down on paper is shite. Worse than shite. Broken Chords hits the top of the charts every time they release a single. What's in the bin wouldn't get anywhere near the charts.

He's lost it. Whatever talent he had for writing songs, had now up and left him.

Fucking perfect.

He gets up and leans against the floor to ceiling window, looking out over Blackrock and the sea. Maybe it's just a temporary glitch. He's still processing the fact he's going to be a father. Of course he can't concentrate. His head is all over the place.

Not that his fans would accept that as a reason. They need to release a new album. Which means having at least one fucking new song. Right now he doesn't even have one measly line.

Besides, it doesn't feel right doing stuff like this while Dillon is beginning his first day in prison.

Fucking Pippa.

Dillon was out of line, but he doesn't deserve to be locked up for a month. He was heartbroken. If Pippa had a heart, she'd get that, instead of calling the cops. Tate has had a few run in's with her over the years. Run in's he wouldn't tell Luke about, but this is a whole new low.

She was threatened by Dillon. Any idiot could see that. Luke and Dillon had a special relationship. They always had. Maybe that was partially down to Dillon's feelings for Luke, but Tate doesn't think so. They bonded years ago while they were still in school, and had been inseparable since then. Or were, until Pippa began pulling Luke away.

He looks over his shoulder at the guitar resting on the couch. They'll just have to find a way to deal with whatever shit is going on in their personal lives. Their careers are a whole different matter. The future of Broken depends on him and the songs he writes.

No songs. No band. End of their dream and all the hard work.

He sits back on the couch and takes out a fresh sheet of paper. He's old school when it comes to writing. No fancy programs or apps for him. Not until he's got something to work with at least.

Then someone knocks on the door, and he shouts out harsher than he intended. 'What?'

Tate lowers the guitar when Chloe peeks around the door. 'Hey. Sorry to interrupt. Your parents are here. They need to talk to us.'

He nods and she shows them into the studio. After hugging him briefly, Rick and Becca sit on the huge leather couch against the wall, and Tate gets a really bad feeling. They don't just drop in on him.

'What's happened? Are you both okay? Has something happened to Shane or Bria?'

'No love,' his mum replies. 'We're all fine. I promise.'

'Then what's with the tense family meeting thing going on here?'

Rick smiles at Chloe. 'Why don't you take a seat.'

Chloe sits next to Tate and Rick looks at Becca for a minute. He's getting seriously weird vibes from his parents. 'Okay, what the fuck is going on?'

'Tate...' his mum scolds when he curses.

He nods apologetically. 'Sorry.'

Rick clears his throat and looks up at Tate. 'We got a letter for you today in the post.'

'Right. What is it?'

His dad holds it out and Tate takes it from his hand. As soon as he sees his pre-adoption name on the envelope, he wants to throw up.

James Reilly only exists on court documents and official paperwork relating to those first horrific six years of his life. And in his nightmares. He can still hear his father calling him, using that name to draw him out from hiding.

The minute he was adopted, his name was changed to Tate Archer. It was the first step towards his new life.

'I can't do it.' He passes the letter to his dad. 'You open it.'

Rick takes the letter back from him and tears it open. He slides the page out of the envelope and quickly scans the contents. 'It's from Mountjoy Prison. Your father had a heart attack two days ago. They were unable to resuscitate him.' Rick looks up at him. 'He's dead, Tate.'

Chloe and his parents fix their attention on him as he replays the words over and over again. The bastard is dead. The man who haunts his dreams and made his life hell for years, is gone forever. He swallows as the bile rises in his throat. 'Back in a sec.'

He hurries down to his bedroom and just manages to get to the toilet, before he throws up. The next few minutes are spent with his head down the toilet, until he finally runs out of anything to throw up. He slumps back against the bath and concentrates on just breathing, until he hears a knock on the door.

'Can I come in?' Chloe asks from the doorway.

He nods, so she comes in and sits on the edge of the bath beside him. 'I'm so sorry, Tate. I honestly don't know what to say to you.'

'Nothing you can say. Fucker is dead.' He angrily scrubs his hands over his face and curses loudly. 'I wasn't expecting to hear anything about him again. Kind of knocked me for six.'

'I know. Your parents are downstairs. Are you feeling up to talking to them?'

He gets to his feet and washes his face. 'No thanks. I've wasted enough time thinking about that fucker. Spent hours in therapy talking about him. I'm done.'

'Tate, you can't just—'

'Can't just what? He's dead, Chloe. It's done. Over. I guess I can just put it all behind me and move on with my life. Forget what he did to me. Forget what he did to my mother.' Tate clenches his jaw to stop his pathetic outburst. 'I've got to get out of here.'

'No, Tate. I don't want you going off by yourself.'

He ignores her and storms down the stairs. She's just trying to help, but he feels like he's suffocating. He needs to get the hell out of here before he screams. He grabs his helmet from the cupboard and pulls open the patio door. His bike is still outside from earlier when he took it for a spin.

'Tate. Stop please. Where are you going?'

'I just need some air, okay. I'll be back in a bit.'

'Don't go like this. Stay for a bit, please. You've just had a shock.'

He knows it's a dick move but he swings his leg over the bike and starts the engine, cutting off anything else she says. He puts on his helmet and pushes the remote for the gate. As he's pulling into the Blackrock traffic, he glances in his side mirror at Chloe, standing in his driveway looking after him.

Chloe

Chloe opens the door and lets Gregg into the house. 'Thanks for coming over so fast. I'm worried about Tate and I don't know who else I can talk to.'

Gregg sits her down on one of the bar stools, and crouches down so he's at eye level. 'What happened?'

'He's going to kill me for telling you, but I'm worried sick.'

'About what?' Gregg asks.

'His parents came over with a letter from the prison. His father died of a heart attack. Tate... I don't know how to describe it. He just shut down. He threw up a few times, then took off. He wouldn't tell me where he was going and he's ignoring all my calls and texts. His parents have headed back to their house in case he shows up there to take Jove for a ride.'

'Damn it,' Gregg mutters as he sits down beside her.

'I've never seen him like that before. I'm scared for him, Gregg. Really scared.'

Gregg pulls her into a hug, then smiles at her. 'Don't go worrying yourself, okay. He's not going to do anything stupid. Tate's not good at dealing with things at the moment. He probably just needed to go for a spin, clear his head, and then he'll be back. He's got you and this little one to come back to. Believe me, he's not going to fuck that up.'

Chloe smiles at Gregg but isn't put at ease by his words. Tate's reaction to the baby had hardly been encouraging either. 'Do you have any idea where he would have gone?'

'I'm guessing as his truck is outside, he took his bike. That'll make tracking the fucker down a smidge trickier, but luckily Broken Chords' biker gang is on hand to help.' He grimaces as he looks around the room. 'Okay, well one member of the gang. I'm flying solo, but no fear. I'm on the case. You make yourself a cup of tea and I'll find your grumpy Prince Charming.'

She stands on the front doorstep and watches as he climbs on his bike. Gregg will always get top marks for trying to cheer up any situation, but she's not an idiot. She saw the look that passed across his face as he left the house. He's as worried about Tate as she is.

10

Tate roars and throws the stone into the sea. He picks up another and hurls it after the first. And another. And another. By the time he's finished, his arm is aching and a little of the anger has gone out to sea with the stones. He drops down onto the rocks and stares out at the crashing waves.

He really should head back. The sky is darkening, hinting at one hell of a downpour heading his way, but he can't face going home. He can't face Chloe again. Not until he gets himself together at least.

He laughs to himself on the deserted beach. Not the best plan. At this rate, he won't be seeing her for quite some time. He's been trying to get himself together for a year now, and is doing a shite job at it so far.

His father is dead.

So why isn't he happy? Or even relieved at the least. But he's just angry. Angry that his father has come back into his life and made him feel helpless and off-balance again.

Tate scratches his arm through his jacket and gets up to pace the shore. His phone vibrates in his pocket, but he ignores it. He needs more time. For what he doesn't know. Maybe to get himself together. Maybe to fall apart even more. He just knows he can't face anyone right now.

He's so sick of feeling like this. So sick of second guessing everything, and still being haunted by his past. A few years ago he was confident, sure of himself. This is verging on fucking pathetic and it's getting old.

Getting clean was supposed to be a good thing. His life was meant to improve. But apart from Chloe, he's struggling with every other aspect. She deserves so much better than him. Their kid deserves so much better than him.

He peers out to sea and admits the truth to himself. His mind isn't blank. The same niggling thought has been with him since he got back to Ireland and, no matter how much he tries to ignore it, it won't leave him.

If his old dealer showed up right now with some gear, he'd bite his fucking hand off, and he hates himself for that.

After taking off his jacket, he scrubs a hand over his face and walks into the sea. It was kind of *his thing* to swim in his clothes. He did it regularly when out with Jove. The urge would take him and he didn't fight back. Kind of like what he did with drink, and then drugs.

He stops when he's up to his waist, and just looks at the water swelling around him. A completely random thought hits him. He's an orphan now. Not that he considered Ken Reilly his father. Rick Archer is. Always has been, but now his biological father is gone, he's the last one left in his first family.

James Reilly is officially gone. He died along with his bastard of a father. No one else called him by that name. Well, no one he really remembers. Social workers and doctors probably did, but meeting the

Archers was his first solid memory. As soon as he met them, he felt safe again.

Or did, until Dara unlocked the nightmares and brought his fucked up childhood back.

'Bit cold for a swim isn't it, buddy?'

Gregg really would prefer not to go anywhere near the sea, but if Tate doesn't move his ass, he might have to drag him out. Not something he's overly keen on.

Gregg looks down at the pebbles by his feet. It's a few harmless pebbles. He knows that, but his feet won't move past the grass growing at the top of the beach. He shoves his hands into his pockets and takes a deep breath. He can do this.

But he can't.

No way his body and mind will connect and move him onto the beach. He licks his dry lips, and shouts over to Tate. 'C'mon Tate! I don't want to come in and get you.'

Empty threat, but Tate doesn't know that.

Thankfully, his mate isn't going to force him to take a dip. Tate turns and wades out of the water. He picks up his jacket and trudges up the beach, joining Gregg on the grass.

Chloe was right to call him. Tate's gone into his head again. He knows him well enough by now to see that.

'Chloe told you, didn't she.'

'Don't you go getting mad at her. She's worried about you, buddy. Taking off like that is understandable, but she wanted to make sure you were okay. Are you?'

Tate shrugs. 'I should be glad, shouldn't I?'

'There's no rule book on how you should feel when your abusive, murdering, father, dies in prison. What I do know is that you can't bottle it up. Not again.'

'You worried I'll use again, is that it?'

Gregg was expecting that. 'Yeah, I am. And that's not me having a go. Just looking out for you.'

'I know you are. I just wish everyone didn't automatically assume I'm going to use again.'

'I'm not assuming anything. You're my best friend, Tate. I don't want anything to happen to you.'

Tate smiles and nods. 'I'm sorry I worried you. You know, I had a bizarre thought before you arrived. Everyone who knew me as James is gone. I've always thought of the Archers as my family, but it just hit me that my old family... I don't know. I'm all over the fucking place. Ignore me.'

'Of course you're all over the place. And between you and me, I prefer you as Tate. You're not a James.'

That at least earns a laugh. 'Is that right?'

'Absolutely. You are so not a James. Besides, James didn't have a family he could depend on. He didn't have friends watching out for him.'

'Yeah, I get it. And Tate does.'

'Too right he does.' Gregg leaves Tate thinking about that for a minute, before he heads in to the next part. 'So, are you going to see him?'

Gregg winces at the look Tate gives him. 'What?'

'You're next of kin. You can see him if you want.'

'Why the fuck would I want to do that?'

'I don't know. It's an option though.'

Tate gets up and Gregg knows he should have kept his mouth shut. 'No fucking way!'

'Okay, buddy. I get that. It's just an option if you want.'

'I'm not going to give my nightmares a face.'

Gregg pauses, waiting until Tate looks over at him before he speaks again. 'But maybe giving him a face will help to quash the nightmares.'

'Is knowing what Angel looks like helping your nightmares?'

Gregg grimaces and looks out at the sea. Tate got him there, and he knows it. 'Fair point.'

'Why am I not happy, Gregg?'

'Like I said, there's no right—'

Tate shakes his head. 'No. About the baby.'

That shuts Gregg up for a second. 'You're not?'

'I don't think so. I should be though, shouldn't I?'

'I've never been in that position. Have you told Chloe how you feel?'

'Don't be ridiculous. Of course not.'

Gregg is getting an uneasy feeling about this. 'Right...'

'Don't look at me like that. How could I tell her that I'm worried I'll be just like my father? I'm an addict, Gregg. What sort of role model is that for any kid.'

Gregg thought Tate would be thinking something along those lines, but didn't want to suggest it in case he made things worse. Which is too easy sometimes with Tate.

'You're nothing like him. I've known you for all but six years of your life. Fair enough, you're a moody shite at the best of times, but I wouldn't be friends with you if you weren't a decent person. You know that. You need to tell her how you feel.'

Tate shakes his head. 'I can't do that to her. Not happening.'

'So what? You lie for the rest of your life? Jesus, Tate. You can't be serious about this.'

'What's the alternative? If I tell her the truth I'll lose her, Gregg. I won't let that happen.' He pushes to his feet and slips on his jacket. 'I'm heading home. Feel free to follow me to make sure I don't do another runner.'

Gregg looks over his shoulder at Tate as he walks back over to his bike. Well that's one hell of an awkward situation he's just stuck himself in the middle of. He gets why Tate doesn't want to lose Chloe, but this isn't going to end well for either of them.

11

Bria

Gregg pulls up outside the restaurant and it takes Bria a few seconds to realise where they are. 'We're going here for dinner?' She's always wanted to come to this restaurant, but felt it would be silly to spend so much on a meal.

'No. I just brought you to the car park. That's it. Back home.'

She slaps him on the chest. 'Hilarious. I mean, are you sure?'

'It's our two month anniversary. That's a big deal. Of course I'm sure. Why do you think I got all dressed up in this swanky suit?' His smile falters a little. 'This is your favourite restaurant, isn't it?'

She kisses him. 'It is. Thank you.'

'Phew! You had me worried for a bit. I had to pull some serious celebrity strings to get in here.'

'I'm not surprised. I guess dating you has its perks.'

He winks and pulls the small cooler from the back seat of his

Defender. 'Oh I have many useful perks, my dear Bria.' Gregg takes out an insulin pen and untucks his shirt. 'After dinner I'll make sure to show you some more of those incredible perks.' He winks at her as he gives himself his shot, then packs everything away. 'Right, that's me all set for an expensive meal. Shall we check out what their pizza is like?'

Bria laughs as he opens his door, walks around the front of the car and opens her door. She takes his hand, stepping down carefully from the Defender. 'I don't think they do pizza.'

'Ah nuts. That's the only food group I know.'

The door is opened for them, and they are shown to their table by an immaculately dressed woman, who is giving Gregg a little too much attention for Bria's liking. It's at times like this that she realises exactly who she's dating.

Having grown up with Gregg, she rarely thinks about him as the celebrity drummer that he is. It's only when random strangers mentally undress him in front of her, that it hits her. Not that she could really blame the woman. Gregg is flat out gorgeous. And the fact he doesn't have a clue how good looking he is, just adds to his appeal.

After the woman is finished fussing over them, she leaves them alone and Bria relaxes a little. As she sips her chilled water, she discretely looks around the room. More than one set of eyes are turned in their direction. 'You've been spotted.'

Gregg peers over the edge of his menu and grins. 'I'm an international superstar. Of course I've been spotted. Rock god, remember?'

'How could I forget? You remind me often enough.'

He wiggles his eyebrows and focuses on the menu again. 'Jesus. It's a good thing I am a rock god. Have you seen these prices?'

Bria can't help but laugh aloud at the look on his face. 'Bit more expensive than McDonald's right?'

'Too right. So, you get the new design you're working on wrapped up?'

Bria nods and takes another sip of water. 'Thankfully. Actually, I had a little good news today.'

Gregg leans over the table, his full attention on her. 'Don't leave me hanging here.'

'Well, after the success of the show you were a part of, it looks like we'll be running another one. And I'll be creating half of the outfits.'

Gregg smiles widely and grabs her hands across the table. 'Wehey! That's amazing, Bria.' Then his eyebrows drop. 'Hang on. You're not going to suggest I get this stunning ass of mine back on the catwalk, are you?'

'No, I'm not. Well, unless you want to of course?'

Gregg shakes his head emphatically. 'Hell no. I mean of course I would, if you desperately needed me to, but give me a packed out stadium any day over that. Downright terrifying.'

He may have been terrified, but Gregg had performed like a pro that night. Seeing her outfit on his incredible body, was the highlight of her career to date. Having Gregg Egan's name against her work, still makes her smile every single day.

They order their meal and, after a while, Bria ignores the attention her dinner date is attracting. It's impossible not to relax in his company. Once their meals arrive and Gregg has politely chatted to the waitress, they are left alone.

'Does it not get annoying?'

Gregg chews and frowns at her. 'What?' he asks around a mouthful of food.

'All the swooning.'

He wipes his mouth with his hand, ignoring the napkin on the table beside him. She swears he does it on purpose, because he knows it winds her up. 'You get used to it. When you're as studly as I am, it's part of life.' He winks and points his fork at her. 'But you know all about that. You fell for my irresistible charm.'

'How could I resist?' she replies sarcastically.

'Exactly! How could you? But seriously, it's part of the game. I don't even notice it anymore. And that's not me being big headed. If I focused on that, I probably wouldn't leave my house. Got to ignore it. First lesson your big brother taught me.'

'Speaking of Tate. Have you seen him recently?'

Gregg shakes his head, sending a lock of hair over his forehead. 'Think he's spending time with Chloe. You know, so they can get their head around the baby and the news about his father.'

'Yeah. He's gone quiet.'

Gregg clears the last piece of food from his plate, then sits back in the chair. 'You worried about him?'

'Of course I am.' Tate had been her rock for her entire life. Until he overdosed, she knew he would be there for her no matter what. It didn't matter what problem she threw at him, he'd deal with it and always make things better. But now he's having so much thrown at him, she doesn't feel like she can talk to him like she used to. Not only that, she's seriously worried he's not coping with his own problems in the first place. He was never a big talker. Now he's bordering on withdrawn at times.

Gregg frowns as he stares at his empty plate. 'He's got a lot to deal with.' He smiles weakly and shrugs. 'He just needs time to process everything.'

'And what about you?'

'Me what?' he asks, looking confused.

'How are you, Gregg? I mean really. No laughing off the question.'

He licks his lips and plays with the buckle on his cuff for a few seconds. 'Ah I'm grand.'

'Gregg...' Her tone does the trick.

'I don't know. I guess I just thought I'd be getting over it by now. Or even that it would be a smidge better. But I'm talking about it with my therapist. I swear.'

'I know you are.' No doubt her nightmares are very different to his, but the memory of watching the man she loves disappearing under the waves, wakes her most nights. 'It will take time, Gregg.'

He nods. 'Got any idea how long we're talking?'

He smiles as he asks, but Bria isn't fooled for a minute. 'I wish I could tell you that. I really do.'

'You and me both. Anyway, we're out for a romantic evening. Enough of that sort of talk. It'll seriously bum me out.' He smiles as he takes the dessert menu from the waitress, waiting until she leaves, before he rolls his eyes. 'I swear if I have to keep smiling I'm going to get a sore jaw.' He points to the cheesecake. 'Ooh. That's got my name written all over it. So,' he says putting his menu down. 'You fancy heading back to mine for the night?'

Bria takes a sip of her wine, as she decides what to say. She desperately wants to spend the night with Gregg. That's not the problem. It's more *where* he wants to spend the night, that's giving her issues.

'Okay,' Gregg says, putting his own glass down. He leans over the table and looks at her. 'What is it?'

'What's what?'

'Don't even go there. Lately, every time I mention going back to my place, you go all lukewarm on me. Now I know you're still totally in love with me. How could you not be, right?'

She laughs and takes his hand. 'You are irresistible.'

'Too right I am. So, I know it's not me. C'mon. We've been through a lot together. You know you can tell me anything.'

Bria licks her lips, unable to put into words what she's feeling. A few weeks ago, being with Gregg in his house had been so easy. It was homely and comfortable. Now it's different. Now it's the place where Angel had been spying on him - on them. Where he'd been taken by force and nearly killed.

Gregg reaches across and tilts her chin up. Bria looks into his brown eyes for a moment, before her attention is drawn to his uncovered wrist, and the scar left by the restraints Angel used on him. 'Look at me.'

'I'm fine, Gregg. Really. And there are people watching us.'

'Fuck them,' he says, surprising her. Gregg didn't tend to curse much. 'I couldn't give a damn if the whole restaurant is looking at us. I'm only concerned about you. What's wrong?'

'I know we said we wouldn't talk about her, but I can't help it. I want to be with you, but every time I'm in your house I...'

She can see her words hit him straight in the gut. He grimaces and scrubs his hand through his hair, messing the already haphazard style. 'Shit,' he mutters. 'I'm sorry, Bria. I thought it was just me.'

'Just you what?'

'I kind of feel like I'm still on camera there. But I didn't want to bring it up in case I upset you.'

'And I didn't want to, in case I upset you. I just can't get it out of my head. When I'm in your bed and I look up at the ceiling, I can still see the camera there, recording everything we're doing. And I know a lot of people made sure the house is safe, but my head keeps going off on a tangent.'

He rubs his thumb along her cheek. 'I know we're trying not to give Angel much air time, but you should have told me. And yes, I should have told you too. Bria, I want you to be comfortable around me. Thinking like that when we're together... it's yuck. Definitely not what I want happening.'

'I am so comfortable around you, you know that. It's just...'

'My house, right?'

'Yeah. I'm sorry.'

He takes her hand and grips it firmly. 'Hey. No apologising for that. To be honest, I've been off the last few weeks too. My house doesn't feel right anymore. I was trying to prove to myself and everyone else that I was grand, you know. That what Angel did isn't a big deal and I'm over it.' He leans closer and lowers his voice. 'Between you and me I'm kind of failing at that.'

'It's only been a few weeks. Of course you're not over it. But I honestly don't think you can move on while you're in that house, with her house next door.'

He slumps back in the chair and purses his lips. 'Well, that's that then.'

'What is?'

'It sounds to me like I need to start looking for a new house.'

Hearing Gregg say those words lifts a weight from her shoulders. She knows, without a doubt, she wants to spend the rest of her life with him. No question. She knew that, long before they finally admitted their feelings.

But that house is getting in between them and she hates it. They've only been a couple for a few weeks. A few short weeks, and he's already been kidnapped, given an insulin overdose, chained to a jetty, and nearly drowned by Angel. Is it too much to ask for a little normality? Just the two of them exploring their new relationship, like every other new couple on the planet. Even for a celebrity like Gregg, everything that's happened is far-fetched.

'You know, I feel a smidge better saying out loud that I need to move,' he admits.

'Me too. We could always use my place until we figure out what to do?'

Gregg frowns then smiles widely. 'Actually, I have another slightly more private option. Dillon offered me one of his houses after the whole Angel thing. How about I take him up on that?'

'Really?' Bria and Dillon had grown closer over the last few weeks, but staying overnight in his place with Gregg is a bit weird.

'I mean his cottage, not the place in town. He takes people there for... entertainment. Whatever, no way I'm going near that place! And it'll only be for a few weeks while I look for a new house. When he's released, he could very well kick me out. And you should see the cottage. It's right on the sea. Nothing around for miles. It's stunning.'

'Right on the sea? Are you sure you can handle that?'

He shrugs. 'Only one way to find out. I'm willing to give it a shot.'

'And you're sure he won't mind? I know he doesn't let anyone near the cottage.'

'I'm sure. Hey, he likes you. You've officially been added to Dillon's approved list.' Gregg shrugs and smiles at her. 'Finding a new house, selling mine, and buying a new house won't happen overnight. It could take months. I just don't want to put us on hold while I sort it all out.'

'Well, if you're sure Dillon is okay, I'll absolutely stay over the odd night in his house.'

'Oh the odd night? You putting me on rations?'

'Okay, more than the odd night then.'

His grin puts any doubts out of her mind. She'd heard from the guys that, apart from his sisters and the guys, Dillon never let anyone near his cottage. But if he made the offer, she's going to take him up on it.

'So that's sorted?'

Bria picks up her dessert menu. 'Yeah. I think it is. Now let's get dessert, then go back to mine for the night, to work it all off. When will you be able to get in touch with Dillon?'

'Tate is visiting him in a few days as it happens. I'll ask him to run it by Dillon again and we'll go from there.'

'But is it not a little insensitive asking him while he's in prison?'

'I'll make sure he asks tactfully, I promise. Now, let's get these desserts sorted. I plan on working it off at least twice.'

Chloe yawns and rolls over, patting the bed beside her. No Tate. She opens her eyes and feels the bed beside her again. It's cold, which means he's been up for a while, or didn't make it to bed in the first place.

He can't keep going like this. The stubborn man needs sleep. She completely understands his reaction yesterday. Everything to do with his father hit him hard, and there's nothing she can do to help. He refuses to talk to her about it, and she's tried. He's opened up about his heroin dependency, and the kidnapping. Over the last few weeks, she's heard every detail of what Dara did to him, while he held him captive.

But the six years with his father, is still firmly locked in his head.

She wants so desperately to help him, but she's lost. It's all completely alien to her, thankfully. Nothing in her life can begin to compare to what he went through. It's all well and good saying that he should talk about it. Without knowing what he's going through, she doesn't want to keep pushing him and risk doing more harm than good.

Until the letter arrived yesterday, she had no idea Tate was called James Reilly for the first six or seven years of his life. That detail is the part that's going around and around in her head. Shouldn't she have known that? His name was changed and she had no idea. What else doesn't she know about the man she's living with?

Chloe climbs out of bed and steps into the shower, letting the power jets work into her muscles. Of course he changed his name. It was all part of his fresh start when the Archers adopted him. Perhaps being called James brought back horrific memories for him.

She scrubs her hair, quietly cursing herself. What does it matter that he changed his name. He's been Tate for over three decades. The problem is, the fact she didn't know, highlights how little she actually does know Tate.

She glances down at her stomach. She's having a baby with someone she's known for less than a year. They haven't even celebrated his birthday together. His thirty-seventh birthday is in two weeks. She had planned to do something special for him. He was in rehab this time last year so she absolutely wants to make this one a memorable birthday for very different reasons. So far, between the baby and his father, it's going to be memorable all right.

After getting dressed, she goes downstairs to make breakfast.

Music is blaring from the gym, so she leaves Tate to his workout. Much better he takes out his frustration on the equipment, than on her.

She's clearing away her dishes when he eventually appears. Judging by the amount of sweat pouring off him, he's more than frustrated by the appearance of the letter.

'Did you get any sleep at all?'

He turns on the kettle and shrugs. 'Few hours.'

Chloe doesn't bother replying to that lie. There's no way he got a few hours judging by the size of the rings under his eyes.

'Do you want something to eat?'

'I'll grab some cereal in a few minutes. I'm just going to have a shower first.'

She makes him a bacon sandwich instead of letting him have his usual Coco-Pops, and pours a cup of strong coffee. Tate storms down the stairs just as she's finishing plating it up and grabs the food. 'Thanks. I've got some work to do. I'll see you later.'

'Tate! Hang on. Is that it?'

'What?'

'You've barely said two words to me since your parents brought the letter around. I'm worried about you.'

He turns to face her and his hard blue eyes lock on her. 'Don't mention that fucking letter again.'

Chloe takes a step back, momentarily surprised by the anger he's directing straight at her. 'I get you're upset, but don't take it out on me.'

'I'm not taking it out on you. I've got work to do and you'll be late. You'd better go.'

'Oh knock it off, Tate. You're angry. I get that, but this isn't my fault.'

'I know. I'll see you later.'

'You really think I'm going to head off to work and leave you here in this mood?'

He slams the plate on to the counter, sending the sandwich spilling on to the surface. 'I'm fine! The fucker is dead. End of subject. I don't want, or need to talk about it. Go to work.'

'No. I'm not leaving you while you're like this.'

'I promise you won't come home to find me unconscious on the couch, with a needle sticking out of my arm.'

Chloe stares at him, not quite believing he just said that. Clearly he's on the same page. He closes his eyes and curses under his breath.

'Fuck, Chloe. I'm sorry. I didn't mean that. I'm such a... I shouldn't have said that.'

'No, you shouldn't have. Have a great day, Tate.' She grabs her bag and keys and goes out to her car. Tate doesn't follow her, so she gets into the car, heads out the driveway, and towards the school. About five minutes down the road she pulls over, and phones Gregg.

'Chloe. What a nice way to start my day.'

'Are you free today?'

'I knew you'd come around to my way of thinking. I'm a much better prospect than Tate.'

'Not quite why I was calling. We had a massive row and... well he threw a comment at me, and now I'm terrified of leaving him alone all day to brood.'

'Oh great. What did my delightful buddy say?'

'He's been in a dire mood since he came home yesterday. I think he spent the night working out again. I told him I didn't want to leave him alone while he was like that, and he countered with... well he basically told me I didn't have to worry about finding him on the couch with a needle in his arm. I wasn't even thinking about him relapsing, Gregg. I just didn't want to leave him all worked up like that. But now, I am thinking that. I know he over thinks things sometimes. I just... God, he can be so infuriating. '

'Idiot! Him not you. Don't worry, I'll go check on the eejit. Might give him a kick or two for being an ass.'

'He apologised for what he said, but I'm just worried now. I'm not back until nearly four.'

'Don't fret. I'm on the case. I'll be with him in about twenty minutes. You go to work, okay.'

'Thanks, Gregg.'

'No need for thanks. I'll keep in touch with you.'

She ends the calls and pulls back into traffic. Until Tate mentioned relapsing, she hadn't thought about it. If she's being honest, she was more concerned he'd start drinking again before he went anywhere near drugs. After hearing what he just said, things have flipped.

Tate

Tate opens the door and glares at Gregg. 'Perfect. She called you?'

Gregg pushes past him and fills the kettle. 'Now, who would you be talking about?'

'Cut the crap, Gregg. I'm seriously not in the mood.'

'Oh I know that.' Gregg sits on the counter and clasps his hands together. 'From what I hear you're in one impressively foul mood. Now, please correct me if I'm wrong, but a little birdie mentioned you told her not to worry about finding you with a needle sticking out of your arm. Personally, I find that hard to believe. I mean, you wouldn't just throw a comment like that out there. Not after the hell you went through to get clean. Would you?'

'Are you done with the whole dramatic retelling?'

'Tate, this is serious. What the hell were you thinking?'

He drops onto one of the bar stools and runs his hand over his face.

'I get it, okay! It was a shitty thing to say. It kind of popped out before I could stop it.'

'But it did pop out and you sent your girlfriend to work worried sick about you. Good move, buddy.'

'Are you done?'

'Nope. Not even close. Your father is dead, Tate. It's something you need to deal with.'

Tate scratches his beard and looks out the window. He's got no interest in going there - ever. He's just starting to get his head right after the memories of his past came back to him.

'I don't want to talk about it, so please drop it.'

'So you're going to stick your head in the sand and forget about it? Brilliant plan.'

'What the fuck do you want from me?'

'I want you to talk. That's the only thing we all want.'

Tate slams his fist onto the counter. 'You want me to talk. Fine. I'm fucking terrified, okay! I'm terrified I'm losing my mind again. All this shit is swirling around in there and I don't know how to deal with it.'

He curses and gets up to pace his living room. 'My life is finally back on track, Gregg. My career - our career, is going better than I ever thought it could. I was getting on top of all the shit from my past. Getting on top of my addiction. And I've got an amazing, fucking gorgeous woman I'm completely in love with. Why did this have to happen now? Why, when things are finally going well, does he have to come back and fuck it all up again?'

'Okay, I get that, Tate. I really do, but like you said you're on top of it. You've got Chloe, your family, your band mates. We're all here to support you. But you need to deal with the fact he's dead. Talk to us. Talk to your therapist. Just talk.'

He resists the sudden urge to scratch the inside of his left arm. The old track marks had healed months ago, but the pull to keep scratching the site had been a habit he couldn't break - not until Chloe. He can't go back to all that.

He hates that he made that comment to her, but it came from his own fear more than anything. Using heroin hadn't been a conscious decision he made. He just sort of fell into the habit to deal with his nightmares. He knows he doesn't want to go down that path again, but it's always a possibility he can't fully shake.

The thought of her finding him like that, is enough to turn his stomach. His parents found him the first time, and that's something he'll never be able to get over. Neither will they. 'I will. I promise. I've got an appointment later today.'

Gregg stares at him for a long time then finally nods. 'Fair enough. So, we're heading out for a few hours.'

'No. I just want to stay here. I'm—'

'You are not staying here for the day brooding alone. We'll take the bikes to the track for a few hours. And don't even try to tell me you're not in the mood, cause I won't believe you. You're always in the mood to beat my ass on the track.'

Tate smiles at that. A few hours on a motorbike sounds like the perfect way to blow off some steam. 'Fine.'

'I promise I'll have you back in time for your meeting.' Gregg heads towards the door from the house to the garage, then stops. 'And I know I'm no expert by any means, but maybe you should think about apologising to Chloe. It's just a thought,' he adds quickly, holding his hands up in front of him. 'Maybe a quick text or something like that for starters.'

Tate nods and pulls out his mobile.

I'm so sorry for how I was this morning. I honestly didn't mean what I said. I love you x

It's pathetic and barely an apology, but it will do until he sees her later. Hopefully, she'll give him a chance to apologise properly.

Chloe

By the time school finishes for the day, Chloe is exhausted. She wants to go home and have a long soak in the bath. But that would mean seeing Tate. After what happened this morning, she's in no rush to go home and face him. Gregg had sent her a message saying he'd dragged Tate to the track for the day, then dropped him at his therapist for his appointment.

That gives her a little comfort. At least he's talking to someone about what's going on in his head. That is assuming he is actually talking. Knowing Tate, he could very well be doing a lot of staring, or skirting around what's really bothering him.

He's an expert at evading awkward questions thanks to years of being interviewed, and it's infuriating at times.

But she can't hide from him forever. He'd sent her a message apologising, so at least he knows how wrong his comment was. She doesn't want to think about him like that. It was bad enough when Dara gave him heroin just before Christmas. It was a few shots and he'd recovered quickly from it, but seeing even a small part of that aspect of his past terrified her. The last thing she needs is that image in her head again - especially when it's put there by Tate himself.

Gathering her bags, she walks outside and stops when she sees a large black truck parked beside her car. Tate is sitting on the bonnet, cap and sunglasses on, as if that will help to disguise who he is.

Seems he knew she'd be less than keen about going home, and decided to meet her half way. After taking a deep breath, she crosses the road and walks over to him.

'I wasn't expecting you.'

'Yeah. Sorry about ambushing you. I just wanted to apologise to you in person.' He shrugs and smiles a little. 'I thought you might not be rushing home to see me. Not that I blame you,' he adds quickly. He gestures back to his truck. 'I got dinner. I thought we could sit at the seafront and eat.'

She smiles and his face brightens. 'I'd like that. I presume it's fish and chips?'

He nods. 'Yeah, but posh fish and chips. I went to a restaurant and convinced them to whip me up something special for you.'

There's a first time for everything. He usually goes for a traditional take away over anything fancy. He's clearly making an effort.

She climbs into his truck and he drives around the seafront, parking in a relatively private spot facing the sea.

'Probably best we stay in the truck.'

He's right. It's a beautiful evening, drawing the crowds out for a walk around the seafront. He passes her a heavenly smelling box. She unwraps it and takes a deep breath. The food smells incredible. It is fish and chips, but it's very different to the usual fare. It's more like what you'd get in a proper restaurant. And not a cheap one at that. 'This smells incredible. Thank you.'

'I wanted to take you there for dinner, but wasn't sure it would be such a good idea until I did a bit of grovelling first.'

He passes her a knife and fork, but doesn't dig in. 'Chloe... about what I said this morning. I can't tell you how much I wish I could take it back.' He finally looks up at her, his blue eyes glistening. 'I was angry and tired. Which is no excuse. And I shouldn't have taken it out on you.'

She reaches across to take his hand. 'I need you to talk to me, Tate. I know you're trying to deal with your father's death, Dillon's arrest, and the baby. I know it's a lot at the same time, but you're not alone. I love you, you grumpy git.'

He laughs and squeezes her hand. 'Fuck knows why.'

'Well, you do have one or two endearing qualities. Gregg said you were going to talk to your therapist today.'

'Yeah. It helped a little I guess. I just wish my past didn't keep getting shoved in my face, Chloe. Just when I feel like I'm getting out from under it, it comes back to punch me in the gut. Why can't James Reilly just stay buried and leave me the hell alone?'

That's the most honest he's been with her about the situation. 'Maybe you need to get it all out in the open so you can finally move on from your time as James. It's just a thought.'

He stares out the window and shrugs. 'Maybe. Anyway, I'm getting off the point. Can you please forgive me for that fucking shite comment?'

'You scared me Tate. I wasn't even thinking about that, until you threw it at me.'

He grimaces at that. 'Fuck. I'm a right dick. I promise that's not on my mind. I don't know where the comment came from. I didn't even realise I was saying it until it was out.'

'I hope not. That's not an image I want in my head.'

His face drops as he nods. 'Yeah. I get that.'

'Tate?'

He looks up at her again. 'No, Chloe.'

'Sorry?'

'I don't want to use again. I swear.'

'Honestly?'

'Yes. But I'd be lying if I said I didn't think about it from time to time. But it's not in the sense that I consider getting in touch with my old dealer. It gets to me the most when I'm stressed out. Then it weasels its way back into my head, but I can cope with it. I promise. I know what to do. Know how to distract myself. You've got nothing to worry about.'

'Okay. But just make sure you keep talking, Tate. I'm always here for you.'

He reaches across and kisses her. 'I promise. Now eat up before it goes cold.'

Chloe tucks into her amazing dinner, relieved and glad that he came to sort this out with her. But that doesn't mean she's just going to stop worrying. She knows Tate well enough by now to know when he's pretending things aren't as bad as they actually are.

And something tells her this thing with his father has hit him harder than he's willing to admit.

13

Tate

Tate sits at the white plastic table and looks around the stark room. It's fucking miserable in here.

The door at the end opens, then a guard walks in, and brings Dillon over to the table. Tate waits until the guard has stepped to the back of the room, before he gives Dillon his full attention.

The extravagant bassist is a shadow of himself. He's only been here a week, but it's already clear this place is taking its toll on him. Dillon's green eyes are bloodshot, and the black rings under them are impressive. His hair is tousled and without his lip and nose piercings he doesn't look like himself. Tate clears his throat, and gives a pathetic attempt at a smile. 'Hey.'

Dillon nods and looks around him. 'Thanks for coming.'

'What the fuck are you thanking me for? We're not going to leave you here and not visit.'

Dillon nods again and chews the side of his lip where his piercing should be. 'I'd offer you a drink, but it tastes like piss.'

'I'm grand. How are you getting on? You look tired.'

'I am a bit. I'm fine though. Counting down the days. Looking forward to having my own space again.'

Tate thinks he looks anything but fine. 'You're detoxing, aren't you?'

Dillon nods and attempts a smile. 'Funnily enough, they're not keen on me using while I'm in here.'

'Are you doing okay?'

Dillon shrugs. 'Mostly,' he says, looking away from Tate, which is a sure sign he's lying. Either detoxing is hitting him hard. Or he's still managing to get his hands on drugs even in here. Which probably isn't impossible.

'So, how's Chloe?'

Tate nearly has second thoughts about telling him, but it's not fair to keep him out of the loop. 'She's pregnant.'

Dillon's smile is absolutely genuine. 'Congrats, Tate. That's amazing.'

'Yeah it is.'

Dillon leans on the table and looks in his eyes. 'You're not sure, are you?'

'What? I am.'

'No you're not. It's a big fucking deal, Tate. It's normal to not be sure. You talking to Chloe about it?'

'She's really excited about it.'

Dillon narrows his gaze, his green eyes serious as he glares over at him. 'I didn't ask that.'

'I don't know, okay. I mean I should be, shouldn't I?'

'Fuck knows. I've never had anyone tell me I'm going to be a father. But you love her, right?'

'Of course I do.'

'And she loves you.'

110

Tate sighs and slumps back in the chair. 'Yes. So what? That means we'll live happily ever after with our child?'

Dillon goes quiet for a minute. 'My folks love each other to death but they can't stand me. So, no. I don't think you'll all live happily ever after, just because you love each other.'

Tate instantly wishes he could take back his comment. He wasn't thinking - as usual. 'Sorry, Dillon.'

He shrugs. 'What I meant is that it's a good base for talking about all this. You are so fucking good together. Any idiot can see that. Yeah, having kids might not have been on your radar now, or even ever. But that doesn't mean it's a fucking disaster. It's something you need to talk about together. Honestly.'

'I don't want to hurt her.'

Dillon nods and smiles. 'I get that. You told her you're up for it, didn't you?'

'I am.'

'Like fuck you are! I know you, Tate. You're no more up for it than I'm up for spending even a second more in here. You lied to her?'

'Fucking rich coming from you. Have you told Luke how you feel about him?'

Dillon's face drops and Tate, yet again, regrets his words. He's on a fucking roll today. 'Dillon—'

'He's married, Tate. Do you really expect me to give him a call while he's on honeymoon? Hey Luke. What's the weather like? You enjoying your honeymoon? Oh, while I'm talking to you, fancy divorcing your new wife and being with me instead? Yeah, I know you're straight too, but fuck it. Give me a chance and I'll change your mind about the whole *fucking a guy* thing.'

'Dillon. I didn't—'

He shakes his head and looks at the coffee vending machine in the corner. 'Forget it.' After glaring at the vending machine for another minute, Dillon sighs and leans on the table again. 'I'm in love with my straight married friend. Fucking tragic, and that's before you even bring my current living arrangements into the equation. You're in a solid relationship with a woman who loves you, although fuck knows why. Grumpy fucker like you,' he adds with a small smile.

'Thanks.'

'I'm being serious, Tate. You're going to be a father. It's not a bad thing. Hell, we both know what it's like to have parents who aren't keen on us. I reckon out of everyone, we'd be pretty fucking great dads.' He shrugs and picks at the corner of the table. 'Can't see that in my future. But you have this chance, Tate. Don't write it off without really thinking about it.'

Tate and Dillon look over at the door as the guard steps inside and looks at his watch. 'Oh yay. Time to go back.' Dillon gets up and hugs Tate.

'Are you going to be okay in here?'

Dillon grins widely. 'Why? You offering to bust me out? I'm fine, Tate. Really. You go home and have a proper talk with Chloe. Thrash it out. Be honest with her. Tell her you're freaking out. Fuck, Tate, she probably is too. It's normal.'

'Yeah. Thanks. Will do. You look after yourself.'

Dillon nods and walks away. 'Have been for years.' He stops at the door and looks at Tate over his shoulder, before being led from the room.

Tate drops back into the seat and looks at the closed door. Dillon is broken. He's trying to hide it, trying to act normal. But like Dillon said, they know each other too well at this stage.

He doesn't want to leave his friend here. If he's like this after a week, what's he going to be like after four?

Bria

Bria gets out of Gregg's car and looks around the outside of Dillon's house. It's a mess. Weeds everywhere, chipped paint, seriously overgrown garden. 'Are you sure this is the place?'

Gregg grins as he walks around the front of his car. 'Ah you see, that's part of the deception.' He drapes his arm across her shoulders and gestures to the crumbling facade. 'Now, if I were to tell you a world famous rock star lived here, someone worth a fair few Euro, would you believe me?'

'Believe you? Nope. I'd think you're nuts.'

'Exactly. But nuts I am not, my dear Bria.' He takes her hand and leads her over to the door, complete with a chipped doorstep and a fair growth of moss. He unlocks the door and keys in the alarm code.

When Gregg opens the door from the small hallway to the living area, Bria's jaw nearly hits the ground. Exposed beams, a massive fireplace with a wood burner, huge windows overlooking the sea. It's immaculate and she loves it.

Gregg stands beside her with his hands on his hips. 'Good deception, huh?'

'Are you kidding me! This house is beautiful. Are you sure Dillon lives here. It's not very...'

'Dillon.'

She laughs. 'Yeah. It's understated and subtle.'

'Yeah, well the pad in town is the loud and obnoxious place. Just like the owner. He comes here to relax. Get away from all the stress and craziness.'

'I can see why. I thought the view from Tate's house was good, but I could stand here all day and just watch the sea.'

'As tempting as that sounds, how about I show you around first.' He takes her hand and leads her through the vast living room to a corridor at the side of the room. Gregg nods to the first door they pass at the back of the house. 'That's his room, so we'll leave that door shut. The next one is the gym.' He opens the door and she peers into the well equipped gym, again with a full floor to ceiling view of the sea.

'Does he not get people walking along the beach looking into his house? This whole side is one big window.'

'One way glass. All the view, with none of the nosy parkers.' She follows him back out of the room and along the corridor. 'Bathroom,' he says, gesturing to a door on the other side of the passageway. 'And this is our room.' He opens the door and Bria smiles widely when she steps inside.

Like the rest of the house, the white walls, wooden floors, and exposed beams give the room a warm, homely feel. The bed is enormous, the heavy wooden bed frame a perfect match with the beams. 'Oh Gregg.'

'Yeah. I know. Ensuite is in there. So that's it. You reckon it'll do for the next few weeks, until I figure something else out?'

She walks over to him and wraps her arms around his neck. 'Oh I reckon it'll more than do. It's so far from what I imagined. I thought I'd feel weird being in Dillon's house, but I don't.'

Gregg brushes her hair behind her ear, then kisses her on the forehead. 'I know it's not ours, or even mine, but I will find a new house. I promise. Even if I have to rent somewhere, I'll do it. I just want you to be happy, Bria.'

'We both need to be happy, Gregg. You may smile all the time, but I know you well enough to be able to tell the difference between your genuine smile, and your fake one. The latter has been making an appearance more lately. And I'm not criticising you. I'm really not. I just wish you had more to genuinely smile about.'

'I'll be grand. Just need my old noggin' to get with the program.' He taps the side of his head and attempts a grin, but it's a little forced. 'Seriously, I'm doing okay, Bria. And you never know, maybe taking a break from the scene of the crime, will be just what I need. And I'll be heading away in a few weeks with the band, so that'll help too. I think all this hanging around brooding, certainly isn't helping.'

She loves him for always being bubbly and cheery, no matter what. But if he's pretending, just to keep her happy, that's not fair on him. What Angel did to him, changed him. Took some of the spark from him.

Being in his house didn't help. She should have said something sooner, but didn't want to upset him, or draw attention to the problem. But even after being in Dillon's house for this short time, she can already see the difference in him. He's holding himself differently. More of the old confident Gregg is coming to the surface. And he's right. Getting back on stage will help him so much.

'You know, I miss seeing you on stage.'

Gregg grins and it's absolutely genuine. 'Is that right?'

'Oh yes. I've spent years watching you from the side of the stage playing the drums. Watching the sweat glisten on your arms as you play. Wanting to brush the damp hair from your forehead. Desperate to jump on you the second you stepped off stage.'

He licks his lips and swallows. 'Is that right?' he repeats.

'And you know the best part?'

'I'm really hoping you're going to tell me.'

'Next time you perform on stage, I'll be waiting backstage for you as your girlfriend, and I will absolutely jump on you the second we're alone.'

'Interesting.' He presses his tall, solid body against hers. Bria takes a long breath, breathing him in, the spiced orange and vanilla scent he wears as addictive now, as it was the first day she smelled it. 'And what exactly would you do to your sexy rock god boyfriend?'

'I didn't mention rock god.'

'I'm guessing he is.'

'That's a shock.'

He nuzzles against the side of her neck and she sighs. Everything about Gregg turns her on. Has for a long time, well before they admitted their feelings to each other. Being with him is easy, but lately life had come between them, tainting their very new relationship.

Part of that is her fault. She knows that, but Angel had come too close to taking him from her, too close to killing him in front of her.

It's ridiculous that she's letting his house get to her like she is, but she can't help it.

He grips her chin in his hand and tilts her head back. His messy hair is hiding his left eye as he leans closer. 'Be here with me.'

'I'm sorry—'

He presses his lips to hers, cutting her off. The kiss is slow and deep, instantly distracting her from her dark thoughts. He keeps his hand on her face as he pulls back and smiles at her. 'Now, I believe you were about to tell your sexy, drop-dead gorgeous drumming God of a boyfriend, exactly what you would like to do to his studly body.'

Bria smirks at him. 'I think you added quite a bit of poetic licence there, Gregg.'

He shrugs and gives her one of his wide grins. 'Not if it's the truth.' He pulls off his t-shirt and flexes his muscles. 'See. That there is one hell of a studly bod.'

The devil face tattooed on his chest shifts as his muscles roll. 'Dave is looking at me.'

He glances down at the face and smirks. 'Think he likes you.' Gregg pulls her against his chest, pressing his crotch against her. 'Don't stop now. I'm on the edge here babe.'

She reaches down and rubs his dick through his jeans. 'Feels like you are. So, are we still on the concert scenario?'

'Yep. I'm all pumped from an epic show and need you to help me work off all the excess energy.'

'Right, well, I probably would want to start by licking this the second we're alone.'

He hardens under her touch. 'I'd probably be on for that.'

Her hand slides lowers, brushing against his balls. 'Then I'd move my attention down here, licking and sucking them.'

A small groan escapes from Gregg.

'Then I'd slowly move back up and slide your dick into my mouth so I could suck it.'

His throat moves as he swallows deeply. 'Okay, still with you.'

She skims her fingers up his side, loving the way his muscles twitch under her touch. 'I'd run my hands all over your sweat slicked skin as I suck you, taking you deep into my throat—'

'You know,' Gregg says, clearing his throat. 'I'm not quite getting what you're hinting at.'

She grabs him by the belt and guides him back towards the bed. 'Does my sexy drumming God need a demonstration?'

He purses his lips as he considers that for less than a second. 'You know, what the hell! I think that would be best to avoid any confusion.'

Bria unbuckles his belt so she can open his jeans, then shoves him back onto the bed. She sits on the end of the bed and takes off his boots, jeans, and underwear. Without hesitating, she takes his hard dick in her hand and licks the tip, slowly working her way down his shaft to lick his balls.

She stops and peers up at him. 'Is that helping at all?'

He nods eagerly. 'Oh yeah. I'm a tad slow off the mark though. Better keep going, just in case.'

Gregg's hands rest on her head as she draws one of his balls into her mouth and runs her tongue along it, before moving to the other one. She wraps her lips around his cock, taking him deep into her mouth. His back arches off the bed as he groans aloud.

She swirls her tongue around his dick as she sucks, taking her time to tease him in as many was as she can. His body tenses and relaxes under her, the movements hypnotic and a serious turn on. His body is absolutely perfect, his huge chest tattoo only highlighting it in all the right ways.

Bria could listen to Gregg's sounds all day. She loves seeing him like this, all worked up and sexy as hell. It's such a contrast to the joker most people see. She's the only one who sees him like this. The only one who will ever see him like this if she has her way.

'Don't stop, Bria. So close...'

She traces her fingers along his balls, gripping the base of his shaft with her other hand. Gregg gasps, his hand gripping her hair tighter as she works him.

Bria groans along with Gregg when he comes down her throat, eagerly taking everything he gives her. She runs her tongue slowly along him, sending a spasm up his body.

'Did you get what I was trying to tell you?'

He lifts his hand, giving her a thumbs up. 'Yep. All good. I'm absolutely with you.'

She moves up his body, lying on top of him. 'What's the stupid grin for?'

'My beyond beautiful girlfriend just sucked my dick. I have a lot to smile about.'

She screeches as he suddenly grabs her, rolling them over.

14

Gregg

Gregg looks down at the beautiful woman laid out under him. His girlfriend. Bria smiles seductively at him, wiggling her hips to encourage him to move. But he doesn't. He just needs to look at her for a minute. To admire her.

Bria slides her hand around the back on his head and pulls him down. She kisses him, her tongue owning his mouth, claiming him as hers.

'I love you, Gregg.'

'I love you, Bria.'

She releases him and wiggles her hips again. 'Now stop admiring me and show me what that studly body of yours can do.'

'Are you ready? Cause it's going to be intense.'

Bria gestures to his jeans on the floor. 'Will you just get a condom and stop messing about. In me. Now!'

'Whatever you say.' He grabs a condom from his wallet and kneels over Bria as he slides it on. 'You ready?'

She slaps him on the stomach, then sits up and flips him onto his back. 'Wow! Getting feisty there, Bria.'

She grins, straddling him. Her pussy rubs against his dick as she grinds against him. Her soft moans increase as she uses him to rub against her clit. And he has no arguments.

Bria's strawberry blonde hair is draped over her shoulder, covering her breasts. Each time she moves, her nipples peek out through her hair, teasing him.

'Lick them.'

Never one to argue with her, he pushes up, capturing one nipple between his lips. Her groans get louder when he sucks it, pulling and nibbling on it. When he moves to the other side, her movements become less controlled.

She shoves him back against the bed and holds his dick upright as she lowers onto him. Gregg gasps when her tight pussy squeezes him in all the right places. He will never ever get tired of being with Bria. Never get tired of how she feels.

Bria slowly moves down his shaft, taking more of him each time her hips rise and fall.

'You good, babe?'

She sighs loudly and opens her eyes to look at him. 'Never better. Hands over your head Mr. Rock God.'

He does as he's told and she laces her fingers with his, pinning his hands down. This side of Bria is one he can't get enough of. She's demanding and likes to tell him what to do. And he's more than happy to oblige. Why wouldn't he?

She'd never restrain him. Not after what happened, but he loves when she holds him back like this. Having his beautiful woman sitting on top of him, with that look in her eyes is not something he would ever say no to.

He's not an idiot.

She leans over to kiss him, her tongue exploring every single inch of his mouth as her hips move in a slow steady circle on him.

'That's a little teasing.'

She nips his bottom lip, tugging on it before letting it go. 'So not sorry,' she mutters as she lets go of his hands and moves to his neck.

He gasps when she moves down to his nipple, scraping her teeth over it. 'And I so wasn't complaining. It was... damn it... that's... forget it. No idea what I was saying.'

She smiles as she lifts off him, then drops back, taking him deep.

'Good. That's the plan.' She sits back on him, resting her hands on his chest. 'Now you stay put and leave this to me.'

'No intention of going anywhere.'

Bria keeps her eyes locked on his as she moves on his dick, faster and faster until she's panting and her cheeks flushed. Her fingers dig into his chest, her nails scraping against his nipples as she holds on.

As she fucks him, her eyes travel over his body, taking him in. He gets attention wherever he goes. Part of the band thing, but the way she looks at him is different. This is someone who is in love with him.

She drops onto his chest, resting her damp skin against his. 'Your turn.'

Without missing a beat, Gregg takes over, his thrusts matching hers. Bria grabs his hair, pulling his head up so she can kiss him.

She's so close. He can feel the slight trembles, her breathing faster, her movements more urgent.

He slides his hand between them, his fingers easily slipping over their wet skin. As soon as he rubs his fingers over her clit, she shudders, her pussy gripping him firmly. 'Fuck, Gregg!' She doesn't hold back on the shout as she comes, and it doesn't take long for him to follow. Hearing her let go like that is enough to send him over the edge himself.

The two of them stay sprawled on the bed for a long time, and he's in no hurry to move. Bria is flopped across his chest, her arms to either side as she breathes heavily.

Pretty perfect.

God she feels so good on him like that.

He missed this. Missed just being with Bria, without any of the crap that's been getting between them, ruining the moment.

'Rocked your world, huh?'

She blindly swipes at him, whacking him on the arm as she laughs. 'So modest as always.' She lifts her head and peers at him, her eyes glossed over. 'But yes. Fucked.' She rolls off him and drapes her arm over her face. 'So fucked.'

'I too am so fucked.' He takes off the condom then rolls over and drapes his arm across her stomach. 'I love you.'

She opens her eyes. 'I love you too, Gregg.' She brushes his damp hair back from his forehead. 'It was like it was before.'

Gregg kisses her. 'Yeah. I know. So, it was definitely the house that was causing the problems.'

Bria traces her fingers along the lines of the tattoo on his chest. 'I'm sorry.'

'Hey, I'd prefer it was a house and not us. It's good to know we're still hot as hell together.'

She moves back from him. 'Are you kidding? Of course we're hot as hell together. We've got years of pent up attraction to work off. We'll be like this for decades at least.'

He grabs the throw from the end of the bed and pulls it over them. 'No arguments from me.'

She brushes her fingers over the lines of his tattoo, her silence instantly setting off alarm bells. 'What is it?'

'I was just... well, we're close to the sea here. Are you sure you'll be okay with that?'

'I can hear the sea when I'm outside the house, but not in here so I'll be fine. Right now, sorting out the housing issue is more important than my fear of the sound of water. Being with you like this is so important to me. I spent so long wanting you, now I actually have you, I won't let anything get in the way. I will get over this, I promise.'

She kisses him, pulling him close to her. 'We'll get through it together. I'm with you every step of the way.'

'Thanks, Bria.'

'No thanks needed. I presume you're hungry? Should I order a take away?'

'Pizza?'

She rolls her eyes as she climbs out of bed, waving her sumptuous ass in his direction as she walks away. 'Whatever my sexy Rock God wants.'

He makes a mental note to thank Dillon repeatedly for opening his doors to them. Kind of takes the fun out of it knowing Dillon's locked up, but his gesture means so much to Gregg.

For the first time in weeks, Gregg feels like he may possibly be able to get his old life back. Of course he'd had sex with Bria a lot over the last few weeks. There was no problem there. It just wasn't like it was before he was taken.

But this was. And it's such a relief. He knew they were okay, but he wants more than just okay - for both of them.

They'll have dinner, then go and grab their things. Time to put their relationship back on track.

The freezing water rises slowly, covering his legs, then up to his waist. He struggles to get free from the chain, pulls and tears at the restraints, desperate to get free, before the water engulfs him completely.

In the background she's laughing. Smiling down at him from the top of the jetty, taking pleasure from the fact he's going to die.

Gregg gasps through the thick gag when the water reaches his chest, soaking through his t-shirt, the icy waves making breathing difficult. He's getting weaker, finding it difficult to stay awake. She'd already given him a few shots of insulin. And he's freezing. Colder than he's ever been before.

He splutters as a large waves hits, submerging him for a terrifying few seconds. Water fills his mouth as wave after wave hits.

Gregg shouts out, frantically trying to push out of the water, but he's held firm.

'Gregg! It's okay.'

He opens his eyes and scrambles up the bed, still trying to get himself out of the water.

But he's not in the sea.

He's in bed with Bria, in Dillon's house.

Bria kneels beside him and rubs his leg, but he flinches, and pulls away. 'I'm sorry. Just still in my head.'

She sits beside him and gathers him in her arms, as he does his best to steady his breathing and his heart, which feels like it's about to burst out of his chest.

'Are you okay?'

He nods, even though he's far from okay. He knows he's safe, but he can still hear the damn sea swirling around him. 'I just need a minute.'

She runs her hand through his damp hair as he concentrates on breathing slowly. Then his watch goes nuts. His blood sugar levels are all over the place. He's not surprised. The nightmares are vividly realistic and he wakes up downright terrified.

'I'll get you a shot. Do you want anything else?'

'No. Thanks.'

As soon as she leaves the room, he flops back on the bed and stares up at the ceiling. It's only the first night in Dillon's house. He was stupid to think the nightmares would instantly disappear. Moving house isn't a magic cure for everything that's in his head. It's a start though.

Bria smiles at him as she rejoins him in the bedroom. She kneels on the bed again and passes him the pen. He twists it to the correct dose and injects it, passing the pen back to Bria.

'Thank you.'

'Don't be silly.' She passes him a slice of toast which he accepts, then she quickly checks the sensor taped to his stomach to make sure it's still secure.

His diabetes is part of his life now. Has been for a few years since he was diagnosed. But it's something he deals with in private as much as possible. It's not that he's embarrassed or ashamed of it. He just didn't want to draw attention to it.

Bria and the guys were always aware of it, but after Angel nearly killed him by giving him too much insulin, they had insisted on learning everything they could about his condition. Having Bria and the guys watching his back means the world to him.

She lies down and strokes along his arm, tracing his tattoo. 'Was it the same nightmare?'

He nods. 'Oh yeah. It's a classic at this stage.' He attempts a smile, but falls short. 'Sorry for waking you up.'

'Why are you apologising for that? You know, I have nightmares about what happened too. I get it… well to a certain extent. I'm not comparing mine to yours, but it's not something you can help or stop. Believe me, I wish it was.'

'You and me both. Damn it. I'm awake now. I might as well get myself a drink to go with my toast. Fancy one?'

'No, thanks.'

Gregg wanders into the kitchen and turns on the kettle. As he waits for it to boil, he looks out the window at the sea, beyond Dillon's overgrown garden and chews on his toast.

He's being ridiculous. Unless he decides to move into the midlands, he's going to be near the sea at some stage. He needs to get over it.

He opens the patio door, letting the cool sea air into the house. Instead of freaking out, he closes his eyes and takes a long, deep breath, just listening to the waves.

After spending hours in therapy, he should be at least able to stand here and not get a panic attack. Bria slips her hand into his, but doesn't say anything. Just stands in the doorway, listening to the sea.

'Do you... I know it's a bit weird, but can we maybe go for a walk?'

'You want to walk on the beach?' she asks.

He shrugs and looks over at her. 'I think so. Tate has babysat me on the beach a few times. It's getting easier. Well, a little easier. I'd like to try with you too, if that's ok?'

She hugs him tightly. 'I'd love to. Maybe not in our underwear though.'

Gregg grins at her. 'Yeah, I don't think the world is ready for that. We're too damn sexy.'

Ten minutes later, Gregg is at the edge of the beach holding Bria's hand like it's a lifeline.

'You okay?'

'Yep. No problem. Well, maybe a little problem.' She points the torch along the stony beach and waits for him to take the lead. Gregg puts one foot in front of the other. Then does it again. And again. All the while, Bria's thumb strokes his hand, the steady rhythm easing him.

'So, you know that new collection I'm working on?'

'What?'

'The new collection I was talking about at dinner.'

Gregg smiles. He knows what she's doing. 'Yeah. The one you promise I won't have to wear.'

'Well you didn't quite say you'd never wear any of it. From what I remember, you said you would step on the runway again, only if you really, really, had to.'

'I know the world went mad for model Gregg and I love you to bits, but no.'

She laughs and nudges his arm. 'Ah Gregg. Be a sport. You looked so good in leather.'

'Well obviously I did, but that's beside the point.'

'I'll twist your arm again. Just wait.'

He pulls her against his chest and hugs her close to his body. 'I'll do anything for you, you know that.'

Bria brushes his hair back from his face and smiles. 'I know. I'd do anything for you too.'

'You already have.' He rests his forehead against her and shuts his eyes. 'Thank you.'

'Want to keep walking?'

'Why not.'

She links arms with him and rests her head against his shoulder as they walk down the beach.

15

Gregg unlocks Dillon's front door and drags his bag inside, dumping it by the door. He rests his hands on his hips and smiles as he looks around the cottage. It's not his, but it'll more than do - for the moment at least.

'Can you get the fuck out of the way?'

'Sorry, buddy.' He shoves his bag out of the way with his foot, letting Tate squeeze by, with another two bags.

'Why did I get the heavy bags?' he asks, glaring at Gregg.

'Cause you've got the bigger muscles, buddy.'

Tate sneers at him and dumps the bags, dropping one on Gregg's foot.

'Ouch! You did that on purpose!'

'I know.' Tate smirks and goes into the kitchen, putting on the kettle as Gregg massages his bruised foot.

'You're a dick, Tate.'

'So you keep saying,' he replies, taking two mugs from the cupboard. 'How long are you camping out here for?'

Gregg shrugs and sits on the couch, smiling when Tate passes him a cup of coffee. 'Depends.'

'On what?'

'Dillon, mainly.'

Tate leans back, draping his arms along the back of the couch. 'So what made you decide to take him up on his offer? You'd been so dead against it.'

'It's Bria. I mean she's fine, but something came up at dinner a few nights ago and this was the solution. For the short term at least. I didn't know what else to do.'

'What happened?'

'Okay, so I asked if she wanted to come back to mine after dinner for se... some tea,' he adds quickly when Tate's eyes narrow. 'Yeah. Some tea.'

'Thanks for that shite attempt at not making things awkward.'

'Noticed that huh?'

'Yeah. Kind of. Move on. Please.'

'Right, okay, so anyway, she wasn't keen on coming back to mine. She'd been iffy about it for a while, but she only fessed up at dinner. She keeps thinking about Angel.'

'Ah. That would kill the tea drinking mood.'

'Exactly.'

'You haven't been relaxed there either though, have you?'

Gregg hates admitting it. Hates how much of a failure he feels, when he says someone had scared him like that. He plays with the buckle on his medic alert cuff.

'Gregg?'

'No, buddy. I guess I'm struggling.'

Tate nods. 'Why are you giving yourself such a hard time about this? You're allowed to not be okay. You know that, right?'

Gregg drops his head onto the back of the couch and sighs. 'I'm pissed off Tate.'

'About what?'

'Everything. No. Well, not everything. That's a little dramatic.' He rolls his head to the side and looks over at Tate. 'I miss not being happy.'

Tate nods. 'Yeah. I hear you. Is your house causing the major problems?'

'Yep. Just my house. And the fact her house is next door. I mean what the hell was I thinking? I'm living in the house I was taken from, and living next door to the house where I was chained up. Talk about self-sabotage.'

'You've done nothing wrong. You didn't want her to run you out of your house. I get that. But I think it's time to admit enough is enough. You need to sell up, Gregg.'

Gregg nods. He'd come to that conclusion himself, but it's not that simple. The guys had generously gifted him nearly half a million Euro a few weeks ago to help pay off both his and his parents' debts, but he didn't have enough left to just go and buy a new house. Not before taking the time to sell this one first.

'I know that'll take funds,' Tate says after a short silence. 'I could always—'

'Not a chance in hell, Tate. You've done more than enough for me. Thanks, really, but no.'

Tate nods. 'Fair enough.' He pauses for a moment and plays with the ring on his thumb. 'You really love her, don't you.'

Gregg grins widely. 'Yes. I really do, Tate. And I'm happy to sell up. Happy to live in a rental for however long it takes. I just don't want to stuff things up with Bria after I've finally convinced her to give me a chance. I just wish... I wish I could be with her, without all the other stuff interfering. I keep telling myself I'm over what Angel did to me, but I'm not.' He glances down at the scar around his wrist. He'd given that to himself trying to break out of the restraints. Permanent reminder of Angel.

'It was only a few weeks ago. It'll take time.'

'Yeah. I know. I'll use this place until Dillon gets out. See where I go from there.'

'Why not his flat? It's closer to Bria's work.'

Gregg grimaces, earning a glare from Tate.

'What?'

'I'm not poking around in that place thanks all the same. That's where he takes his dates back to. I already know too much about his private life. Don't think I could handle knowing more.'

'What the fuck are you talking about?'

'You know, his whole *tying people up* thing.'

'I think it's called bondage, Gregg.'

'Oh listen to the big expert. Excuse me. Bondage then.' Gregg stops talking and slowly looks up at Tate. 'Hang on! You knew?'

'Yeah.' Tate smirks at him. 'You honestly telling me you didn't?'

'No, I damn well didn't! He mentioned it out of the blue while you were away. Talk about deer in the headlights. You should have seen the look on his face, at the look on my face. He thought it was hilarious.'

'Would have loved to see your face when he told you. I can't believe you didn't know.'

'Yeah well clearly I'm all sweet and innocent, unlike the rest of you.'

'Well if it's any consolation, he only does that at his Dublin apartment. This place is sweet and innocent like you.'

'Oh ha ha, buddy.' He pushes off the couch and takes two packets of crisps from the cupboard. Gregg hands one to Tate and drops back on the couch. 'So, enough about me. How's Chloe? Is she sick at all?'

Tate shrugs, as he examines the label on the crisps. 'A bit. She's not too bad though.'

'That's good. How are you? Did you tell your therapist about what happened to your father?'

Tate takes a long time to answer. Longer than he needs to. He's stalling. 'I'm grand, and yes.'

'Bullshit.'

'Excuse me?'

'I know when you're keeping stuff from me. And that is exactly what you're doing right now.'

Tate slouches back on the couch and drops his head, mirroring Gregg's posture a few minutes ago. 'I don't know, Gregg. It's just this shit with Dillon getting locked up. Luke is still ignoring all of us, which is fucking weird. Then my asshole father dies.'

'You're not going to add your baby to that particular list, are you?'

Tate lifts his head and looks at him. 'Of course not. I know I should be happy or excited, or something, but I'm not. And I don't know why. I've got all this other stuff sapping my energy and that's so wrong. I know it is.' He pauses and scrubs his hand over his face. 'Fuck. I'm a dick. I've got a beautiful girlfriend who is crazy about me, even with all my problems. Why can't I be there for her when she needs me?'

'Yeah, but if you're not so sure about the baby—'

'I've made my decision,' Tate says, pulling his ringing phone from his pocket. 'Drop it, Gregg.' He glances at the screen. 'It's Bria. What's up?' he asks when he answers the call

Gregg watches as the smile drops from Tate's face. 'Yeah. I'm with Gregg at Dillon's place. What? When? Fuck, I'll be right there.'

He lowers the phone onto his lap and stares into space.

'What is it?'

'It's Chloe. She's in hospital. She's lost the baby.'

16

Chloe

Chloe lies in bed and listens as the front door shuts. A few minutes later, she hears Tate's truck pull out of the driveway, the heavy roar of the engine fading as he drives away.

He had to do some promo shoots, so will be gone for most of the day. He wanted to stay with her, but she told him to go to work. Physically she's fine so doesn't need him to babysit her. But, hearing him driving away, she realises she did want him to stay with her. It's too late now. She's not going to call him back and mess things up with Ellen and the guys, by forcing them to reschedule the shoot.

They'd spent the last week alone together, trying to come to terms with the loss of their baby. Tate was over it though. He's upset for her and is doing everything he should to comfort her, but it's for her benefit. Ever since she told him the news in the hospital, she's been unable to shake the thought that he might be relieved. Not that he's happy about it. She doesn't believe that, but he's definitely not as upset as she is.

And that's bothering her.

Of course she was scared when she found out she was pregnant. She may deeply love Tate, but they were still getting to know each other. She was still trying to find her feet in his crazy world. Having a baby so soon, was far from ideal.

But she wanted it.

Chloe rolls onto her side and rubs her hand over Tate's pillow. Being with Tate is incredible. He's a stunning man and is completely devoted to her. She knows that. It took her a long time to accept that he doesn't look at anyone but her. Took a long time to accept he politely ignored every single adoring fan who threw themselves at him.

Her future is with Tate. Or at least she thought it was. After seeing his reaction to the miscarriage, she's not so sure they're on the same page. He shut down on her in the hospital. He held her. Comforted her. But, as much as she's tried, he hasn't once even given a hint as to how he feels about it.

She'd tried so hard over the last week to get him to open up, to talk to her about the miscarriage, but he did his usual *bottling it up* thing. He kept changing the subject, or lavishing attention on her. Anything to avoid actually telling her how he feels.

She's losing him. Little by little, Tate is pulling away from her. It started after she told him she was pregnant. Then his father died, and he literally withdrew in front of her eyes. He hadn't recovered from that, and now losing the baby was too much for him to face.

The problem is, it's something she needs to face. She can't continue going on with life, as if nothing happened.

He bottles things up. She can't. It's not how she's built.

Chloe pulls his pillow up to her face and breathes in the incredible scent of leather and sandalwood. His scent. The tears start to flow as she hugs it to her.

She needs to get her head around what happened, but can't do that while she's hiding her true feelings from Tate. They're both dealing with different things, and she can't help him and herself, at the same time.

After crawling out of bed, she wanders downstairs and looks around the living room. The tears continue to stream down her face as the realisation sinks in.

She needs space to think. To talk. To cry.

As much as she wants to believe otherwise, she can't do that with Tate. Not while his head is on other things.

Tate

That photo shoot is going to go down as the most painfully long, desperately boring shoots of his life.

He should have called it off, but had left it too late. At least the photographer wasn't interested in getting him to smile. It was rare for photographers to go down the happy, smiling theme when it came to the band. He was all about the grumpy fucker theme today. It was his thing at the moment and he's getting bored with it.

He looks up at his house and sighs. He has to leave his grumpy fucker self in the car. Chloe doesn't need that. She's struggling with the miscarriage. He's trying to be supportive and sympathetic. He really is, but he knows he's failing miserably, and he hates himself for that.

There's no fucking rule book or manual, for this sort of thing. It's not helping that his fucking father is still at the back of his mind. The prison contacted him again, asking if he wanted to arrange the funeral. He'd sent it to his lawyer to deal with. Any response he would have personally sent back, would have been less than professional.

He couldn't give a fuck if they threw his father's body in the sea, in the dump, or whatever. As long as he doesn't have to deal with it, he couldn't give a flying fuck where he ended up.

Chloe knows nothing about the second letter. It arrived the same morning he collected her from the hospital. She didn't need to worry about that, on top of everything else.

He sighs again and looks at the side of the house, noticing the back end of the battered pick up peeking around the corner.

Chloe's gran Dorothy is here. He loves her to bits, but all he wants to do is curl up on the couch with Chloe. Talking to anyone is far from appealing.

He pushes open the door of the truck and climbs out, less enthusiastic about going inside than he was when he first pulled into the driveway.

Tate steps into his kitchen and nearly walks straight into Dorothy, as she heads towards the front door. 'Shit. Sorry. Hi, Dorothy.'

'Tate.' She smiles at him, but something is off. 'I'll be in the car Chloe, whenever you're ready.'

Tate goes into the sitting room, the unsettled feeling jumping a level when he sees Chloe sitting on the arm of the couch with her coat on. 'Hey. You heading out with your gran?'

She shakes her head. 'No. I'm going to stay with Gran for a while.'

He drops his keys on the coffee table. 'What? Why?'

'Come on, Tate. You know why. I can't keep going around in circles with you like this.'

'What the fuck are you talking about?'

'We lost our baby, Tate. I need to talk about that. I can't just move on and forget it happened.'

'Jesus, I know that. I'm here for you. You can talk to me.'

She slowly shakes her head as she plays with the strap of her handbag. 'I've tried, Tate. I really have, but I don't think we're coming at this from the same place.'

'What do you mean by that?'

'I'm going to ask you something, and I need you to be entirely honest with me.'

He forces himself to uncross his arms in an attempt to appear even a little less defensive than he's feeling. 'What?'

'How do you feel about us losing the baby?'

He pauses and turns the ring on his thumb. 'I'm gutted you had to go through all this.'

'That's classic Tate avoidance. Why aren't you answering the question?'

'I did answer.'

'This is really serious. I need you to answer the question. Please. Do you want to have children?'

'Well, yeah, I guess. What about you? Do you want kids?'

'Yes. Until I got pregnant I wasn't so sure, but coming so close... yes Tate. I really do want children. But I want them with you. I'm not saying right now necessarily, but at some stage. The thing is, I don't want you to just agree to keep me happy. Or to keep me, full stop. Please Tate. Just be honest with me.'

The ring on his thumb gets a serious amount of attention before he finally meets her eyes. 'To be honest, I don't know, Chloe. But if you do, then I'm fine with that. But not yet. I'd like more time just for us. It's not even been a year since we met and it's been an emotional roller coaster of a shitshow. I think we desperately need some time just for us.'

Chloe nods slowly and smiles at him. 'Were you just going to go along with this? Raise a child you didn't want, just to keep me happy?'

'No. Of course not. I wanted it.'

'*If you do, then I'm fine with that?* I wish I could explain to you how much I love you for saying that. The fact you'd do that for me...' She smiles at him, but he's not feeling overly thrilled about whatever she's about to say. Then his attention falls on the bags at her feet.

'So instead of staying and talking about this, you're going to leave me. Is that it?'

'It's not that simple, Tate. I'm grieving, okay. I am, but you're somewhere else. And I understand that. I really do. I know your father dying has completely thrown you. But I need to spend time on myself right now.'

'So this is my fault?'

She takes his hands in hers and smiles sadly at him. 'Absolutely not. You've done nothing wrong. It's the situation that's fucked up.' She laughs and wipes her eyes. 'I want children, Tate. I want them with you, but if you're just going along with it to keep me happy, it won't work. As much as I want it to, it's not fair on anyone.'

'Chloe—'

'No. Let me finish, please. I don't want you to humour me. You'd end up hating me, Tate, and I don't want that. I just think it's best we have some time—'

'Don't finish that sentence. I'm begging you.'

She sits on the arm of the couch again and takes a minute before she speaks. 'We each need time to think about what we want. I love you, Tate. I love you so much, but I need to figure out if that's enough.'

'Fuck, Chloe. Don't leave me. Please.'

'I'm not leaving you. But surely you can see this isn't working, for either of us. I know you have so much to deal with right now, and I know you're struggling. But you won't let me help you. You keep pushing me away, Tate. And I understand why, I really do. But I'm struggling too. I'm trying to get my head around what happened. I need to talk about it, to deal with it, but I feel like I'm doing it alone.'

'Chloe, you're not alone.'

'I am, Tate. When it comes to how I feel about the miscarriage, I'm alone. You've refused to discuss it with me at all, and I can't keep going like that. It's not fair on either of us. So I'm going back to Gran's for a bit.'

'But I'm going away on Friday. Will you be back by then?'

'I don't know, Tate. I don't know if we can fix this, as much as I'd like to.' She wipes tears from her face and smiles at him. 'I love you so much, Tate.'

He pulls her into a tight hug, burying his face in her hair. 'I love you too. I'm sorry. Please don't leave. I'm begging you, Chloe. Stay.'

She pushes back from him and sniffs. 'I need some time to think and so do you. There's plenty of food in the fridge, so please don't live off chips while I'm gone.'

'Can I call you?'

'Give me a few days and I'll call you, okay.' She picks up her bags and Tate watches as she walks away from him.

Chloe

Chloe somehow keeps it together until her gran's battered pick-up pulls out of Tate's driveway. As they drive back towards Newcastle, the tears refuse to let up. The switch is on and she can't stop the flood.

'He was devastated, Gran. You should have seen his face. I broke him.'

'Of course he was devastated. He loves you. Any fool can see that. But sometimes love isn't enough, Chloe. You're doing the right thing - for both of you. You need this time to figure out what you both want. A bit of space will do you both the world of good.'

'What if we still want different things, Gran? What if this is it for us? What if I've left his house for the last time?'

Her gran pauses as she manoeuvres through the traffic. 'I don't know, dear. I hope it's not the end for you and Tate. I really do, but if it is, better now, than five or ten years down the road after marriage and a little one. That would be horribly unfair on both of you. And any children you might have had. They'd deserve more than a father who was playing the part, because he wanted to keep you happy.'

Chloe nods as she wipes her face. Her gran is right. She knows that, but it doesn't make walking away from Tate any easier. She's never been so in love with someone before. But love alone isn't going to fix this for them. She wants a family. Tate doesn't.

How exactly is time apart going to solve that problem?

'I'd better call Gregg or Bria. Let them know to keep an eye on him. I don't want him to do something stupid because of this.'

'Hey, you don't go thinking about things like that. If Tate decides to drink or use because of this, that's one-hundred percent on him.'

She takes out her phone and opens a text to Bria. 'I have enough going on in my head without adding that to the pot.'

She sends the message and leans against the window, as they make their way back to Newcastle. Chloe desperately hopes this is a short term relocation, she really does. She honestly can't imagine a life without Tate in it.

Luke

Luke stares at the pristine cream paint on the wall. They arrived home from honeymoon last night. The month away with Pippa had been great, but the time had crawled. Dillon should be released in a week and he can't wait to see him. That's if he can convince himself to visit him. Dillon may not want to talk to him after he disappeared for the month.

Deep down he knows Dillon would understand. He was on honeymoon. It wasn't that he was intentionally ignoring him. Even though that's exactly how he feels.

But if it meant keeping Pippa happy, taking a break from his phone was something he had to do. And it had made her happy. They'd done everything a newly married couple should do on honeymoon. It was different to how it is here. Maybe it was the change of location, or the married couple buzz. He doesn't know what it was, but he wishes he could get it back.

In the vast ensuite at the far side of the room, Pippa is in the shower scrubbing her perfectly flawless skin clean. He doesn't blame her. Sex hadn't been great. It never is. Even while on honeymoon he struggled to keep her happy. But she hadn't minded while they were in the Maldives.

He knows she needs more from him.

But he doesn't know what. Or how. And he tries. He really does. He desperately wants to make Pippa happy, but there's something wrong with him. Something he can't fix. Everything he does disappoints her.

Including sex.

He glances down at his dick. She seems happier now they don't have to worry about using protection. Pippa had booked him in for a vasectomy a few weeks before they got married. She didn't want to have children. She worked hard to look the way she does. He tried to convince her he would love her no matter what, but there was no way she would let any *brats* ruin her perfect figure.

He didn't like when she used that word - especially when she was speaking about his brother's children. But she always laughed off his comments when he mentioned it.

Besides, Pippa didn't have time for children, even if she wanted them. She has such an active social life. Every day she seems to have a brunch, or lunch, or shopping, or a spa trip planned. There was always something to occupy her time. There's no way she could give that up to raise a family. It would be impossible. Or so she told him.

Not that he hadn't tried to convince her otherwise. He really did. He could organise his schedule around hers, or even take a step back from touring if he had to.

But she stood firm and booked the appointment for him.

He always thought he'd be a father one day. He wanted to be a father, so badly. He genuinely believes he'd be a good father, but she had hinted otherwise.

But there's no point thinking about what might have been. It just won't be happening for him, and he has to accept that. At least he has his nephews. But it's not the same. Not at all. But he can spoil them rotten. Make sure he's the best uncle they have.

A shiver works through his body. He's sore and cold, and desperately wants a shower. Luke wriggles his fingers, trying to get some feeling back. The pins and needles are irritating. The cuffs securing his wrists and ankles to the ornate four poster bed are too tight, cutting into his skin.

He knows he's bleeding. He can feel the warm blood around his wrists.

He's only ever been with Pippa, so he's got nothing to compare it to, but he's heard Dillon talk about sex enough times to know it should be enjoyable. Shouldn't it?

So why isn't it for him? Pippa enjoys herself, so that's the main thing. He just wishes it didn't hurt so much.

She thought his struggling was part of whatever game she was playing. She always did. If she knew he was genuinely in pain, she would have stopped. He's sure of it. If she really thought he was being serious, when he begged her to let him go, and that he didn't want this, she absolutely would have stopped.

There's no way she'd have had sex with him if she really believed he didn't want to. That would be...

She wouldn't do that to him. He closes his eyes and turns away from the wall. He's her husband. She loves him. It was all part of the game. Okay, so he didn't enjoy it as much as she did. Or at all. But he wants to make her happy. He loves her.

So why does his stomach drop when the water turns off, and she joins him on the bed?

Her blonde hair is wrapped in a towel, but she's left her body uncovered. He's lucky. He knows that. Pippa is so beautiful. Why she picked someone like him, he'll never know.

She leans over and kisses him, her tongue pushing into his mouth. He resists for a moment, but she convinces him to let her in. He's tired. He just wants her to unlock him, so he can shower and get some sleep.

'Can I just grab a shower first?'

She smiles sweetly at him as she runs her finger down his chest to his dick, rubbing her hand along his length. 'What's the rush. You're so sexy like this. Lying there waiting for me.' But her smile dies when his body doesn't respond the way she wants it to. It's happening more and more lately, and he has no idea why.

'Seriously? I thought you'd be ready to go again.'

'I'm sorry. I'm just a little tired.' He hopes it's just tiredness, but he's worried there's something else wrong with him. He's only thirty-seven. Surely he shouldn't be facing problems like this yet.

'Tired? How can you possibly be tired? You didn't do anything.'

He swallows thickly and smiles, even though he's getting increasingly nervous. She straddles him, leaning on his chest as her blue eyes meet his, one long nail flicking against the piercing in his nipple.

'Tell you what. How about I leave you here like this for a bit. You can get some rest. Besides, I like the idea of you being up here, spread out like this, naked, and waiting for me.'

His heart speeds up, until he's convinced he's going to have a heart attack. 'No, please. My arms are getting sore. Can you just let me out for a few minutes? I promise I'll come right back. Please.'

'Oh come on, Luke,' she pouts, her perfect lips pressing together. 'Where's your sense of adventure? We've got nothing else planned today. I want to spend it with my sexy rock star husband.'

'I know, but—'

She swings her leg over his, standing back on the beige carpet. Her phone rings on the dressing table so she holds up a hand to silence him as she answers. 'Astrid, hi. What? No nothing at all. Go ahead.'

She grabs her robe from the back of the door and hurries from the room, leaving Luke staring after her.

'Pippa! Please...'

But she's gone. He can hear her voice fading as she goes

downstairs. He closes his eyes and does his best not to freak out.

She's done this before. She's left him for hours while she went about her day, coming back every now and again to *play* with him, when she got bored.

He pulls himself up the bed to ease the pressure on his arms but there isn't much give in the chains locking his ankles to the bed. The headboard presses against the top of his head, the carvings uncomfortable against his scalp, but his arms can move a little. The thick raw line circling both wrists has stopped bleeding. The cuts weren't deep, but sting like crazy.

His fault for pulling as hard as he had. He should have just lain there and let her... She says they were making love, but it didn't feel like that. Dillon enjoys using restraints and being dominant. He gets that. But something about what Pippa does is different. Dillon's partners come back to him again and again. They enjoy what he does to them, with them.

Luke can't stop looking at the marks on his wrists. He must be doing something wrong. Pippa enjoyed herself. So it must be him.

He's cold but until she unlocks him he's going to stay cold.

He looks over at the wall again, mulling over what just happened. There's definitely something wrong with him. Sex should be enjoyable. Not something he dreads.

She's going to finish her call and want to have sex again.

He'll just have to try harder next time. It's like she keeps telling him - it's his job to make her happy.

17

Tate

Tate doesn't look away from the sea as a car pulls in beside his truck. He's still not sure why he made the call. Still not convinced it was his best idea. Fuck that. He's positive it's the worst idea he's had since he made the same call over a year ago.

Eddie climbs out of his BMW and gets in beside him, the smell of his cologne turning Tate's stomach the second he gets a whiff of it. 'Baltic out there.'

Tate doesn't bother responding. Eddie has a habit of talking whether he gets a response or not. He's one of those people who you instantly dislike. Tate can't put his finger on what exactly he has the issue with. Something about his cocky self-confidence grates on Tate's nerves. That and the fact he's a drug dealer.

'I must say Tate, I thought I was hallucinating when I saw your number pop up on my screen. I didn't think I'd be hearing from you again.'

Tate peers across at him, but doesn't say anything.

'Glad to see you haven't lost your talkative streak. How the hell do you manage when you're interviewed? Must be a dream for the sad fucker asking the questions.'

'Are you done?'

Eddie smirks, but there's nothing friendly about the gesture. 'As you wish. What's going on here, Tate?'

'I told you on the phone.'

'And I heard you.' He pats the pocket of his coat. 'I have what you asked for.'

'So why are you asking me what's going on?'

Eddie settles back in the passenger seat and looks out the window at the sea. 'I sell drugs Tate, so morally I don't have a leg to stand on. But you, my friend, cut it close last time. And I mean really fucking close. Heard you technically died on the way to hospital. Are you really sure you want to go there again?'

Tate holds out some Euro and looks over at Eddie. 'Do I owe you extra for the lecture?'

Eddie pulls the package from his pocket and throws it on Tate's lap. 'You're a real piece of work, you know that. Just looking out for you. I'd prefer my product didn't kill Tate Archer. It's not good for business.'

'I'll do my best not to fuck up your business.'

Eddie takes the money from Tate and nods. 'Appreciate that. I'll leave you to it. You know where I am when you need more.'

'I won't.'

Eddie laughs loudly as he climbs down from the truck. 'Oh Tate. If I had a Euro for every time I heard that, I wouldn't need to supply rich bored celebrities like you.' He blows Tate a kiss, then slams the door, whistling to himself as he walks back to his car and drives away.

Tate slips the packet into his pocket and looks back at the sea. Technically, he hasn't done anything wrong... yet. Just because he bought it, doesn't mean he'll use it. He just wants it in case things get bad.

Eddie doesn't know what he's talking about.

Dillon

Dillon climbs out of Ellen's car and leans down to look in at her. 'Cheers for the lift.'

'I know you would have preferred Tate and Gregg to collect you, but I didn't want that publicity. Under the radar is best. Give you time to settle in before you face the cameras again.' She reaches out, grabbing onto his hand. 'Are you sure you want to be alone right now? I could stay for a bit if you want.'

'I'm grand, thanks.' After being confined with so many other people for the last month, he desperately needs time alone.

'Okay, well you know where I am if you need anything.'

'Thanks, Ellen.' He closes the door and waits until she's left the parking garage. Once her car has disappeared around the corner, he turns and walks into the elevator. He'd have preferred to go back to his Wicklow cottage, but he had told Gregg and Bria they could stay there until they're sorted.

After the fucked up situation with Angel, the couple deserved a break. It took Gregg long enough to admit staying in that house was a mistake, but he needed to figure it out for himself. Dillon would have been sorely tempted to raze the fucking house to the ground, if he'd been in Gregg's shoes.

The elevator arrives at the top floor and he drags his sorry ass over to his door. It's been four weeks since he was last here, but it feels longer. A hell of a lot longer.

He unlocks the door and turns off the alarm. Dillon looks around his penthouse, the lavish surroundings very different to where he spent the last month. He wanders into his kitchen, randomly opening cupboards, finding them full of food. His sisters were clearly here stocking up for his return.

No alcohol. None in the fridge either. They removed everything. 'Fucking perfect.'

He grabs a bottle of water and stands in front of the floor to ceiling window overlooking the Liffey. His phone rings again. It's been ringing non stop since he was released. Without looking at the name on the screen, he dismisses the call. The last thing he wants is to talk to anyone. Well, except for Luke. He won't be ringing Dillon though. Not now he's married to that bitch. He should be back from honeymoon now. No doubt he's probably enjoying spending time with his new wife - as he should.

Time to accept that fact and move on with his life.

Dillon screws the lid back on the bottle and throws it on the couch then walks into his bedroom. He desperately needs a very long, hot shower, along with a haircut and a shave. He can smell that place on him. It's everywhere, coating his skin and his hair.

He shrugs off his suit jacket, throwing it in the corner. The suit will be dumped. No way he's wearing it again. It takes a few attempts to take off his shirt, but he eventually works it down his arms, wincing as the material pulls against his skin.

The reflection facing him in the mirror on the wall, is a far cry from the one he's used to seeing. No piercings. Messy hair. Unkempt beard. He's a fucking state. His body has taken a hit too. He's lost weight and muscle definition, which seriously pisses him off. It'll take ages to build that up again. And then there's the other painful issue.

A few of the inmates had seen him as a soft target. Out in this world he's anything but. His reputation as the bad boy of the band is well founded. He'll fight - verbally or physically. He doesn't care. He'll hit and punch and kick when he needs to. But in that place, he was in a whole new world. In there, if he fought back, he'd only make things so much worse for himself.

So he'd taken what was thrown at him by the other inmates. It went against every part of his being, but he'd taken the jeerings. He'd taken the punches. He'd taken the kicks. Taken everything thrown at him without fighting back.

More wounds to add to the knife scar Angel left him with a few weeks ago. He'd brushed the injury off at the time, but in truth, she had freaked him out. If the knife had gone a little deeper, he might not be here.

He gingerly touches his ribs and winces. Nothing was broken but they'd cracked one and bruised everything else. His chest is like a fucking rainbow from yellow to green to purple and black. Both arms too. Breathing is still painful, but getting easier. No one knew anything was happening, until that last particularly bad attack, which landed him in the prison hospital. He was good at hiding things. Years of experience at that.

He'd asked the prison to keep the injuries quiet, and they'd been more than happy to comply. It's not like he was about to point fingers at the culprits. The only thing they could do was keep him in a cell by himself for that last week of his stay, which was even more depressing.

He doesn't do well left alone with his thoughts. There's so much going on in his head, and most of it terrifies him. That's where drugs, drink, and sex come in. They help distract him, help numb him. Without his usual distractions, he'd brooded about shit that, under normal circumstances, he left locked away.

Normal circumstances.

He laughs harshly, aggravating his ribs. What the fuck is normal for him?

Stuff the shower. His body needs a good soak to get rid of the stench. He turns on the bath taps, and faces his reflection in the mirror again. He looks beyond shite. After taking a ridiculous amount of time to trim his beard he lowers into the hot water, wincing as his sore muscles protest.

Dillon lies back and closes his eyes, letting the water soak into his abused body. He honestly doesn't have a clue what to do now. His life plans at this moment consist of the bath.

Then what?

When he gets out of the bath, what next? Luke isn't around to talk to. Tate and Gregg would come over in a heartbeat, but he doesn't actually want to talk about the last month.

He'd give anything to forget about the last two fucked up months of his life. Hell, why stop there? Why not wipe out the last year? Ten years? Wipe it all. All thirty-nine years. Start from scratch and... and what?

He'd still have the same parents who hate him, for no reason that he can think of. Coming out hadn't helped, but they'd hated him long before that. They love Eva and Clara, but not him. They call his sisters, meet with them regularly, have dinner together.

But he's never invited. He hasn't been in his parents' house since he was seventeen. He knows his sisters have tried to talk his parents around, with no luck. In their eyes he doesn't exist any more.

He's nearly driven himself insane trying to figure it out over the years, with no answers coming to him.

'Stop!' He thumps his fist against his forehead. 'Don't go there.'

Fuck, he needs a drink. Or something stronger. Anything to shut off his brain. He's so fucking tired, but his head isn't giving him a break. He shuffles around in the bath and looks through the open door into his bedroom. One of his favourite guitars is in the stand beside his bed.

He hasn't picked up an instrument since well before Luke's wedding. He loves music. Loves how he can get completely lost whenever he's playing and singing. And he's really fucking good at what he does. When he was a kid, playing guitar and singing to himself, was one of the few things that made him truly happy. Knowing that his stunt may have cost him a career he adores, is more than he can bear.

Broken Chords is his life. The guys are his family. Without either, he's back to being alone. And he can't handle that. Not again. He needs to be on stage. It's part of who he is. Standing in front of a crowd, doesn't matter the size, brings him to life. He thrives on the attention. Fuck, he needs it.

Negative attention or positive, he doesn't care. Somehow, he always managed to come out on top. Even when he did something stupid, his popularity never took a hit.

Until now.

Ruining his best mate's wedding is unforgivable. No way he's going to come out of this without taking an impressive hit to his popularity. He'll be lucky if he's not booed off the stage next time. If he ever gets on a stage again.

He must drift off, only waking when he inhales a mouthful of bath water. The next few minutes are spent clearing his lungs, in between wincing in pain as the coughing fit jars his ribs.

He tries, and fails, numerous times to haul his aching body from the water. Maybe a shower would have been a better idea. When he finally drags himself out of the water, he wraps a towel around his waist and walks back into his bedroom.

He's hungry, but can't be arsed going near the kitchen. Instead he climbs into bed, still wet, and wrapped in a towel, staring over at his guitar, until he eventually falls asleep.

Tate

Tate looks at the bag on the table in front of him, as he paces his personal studio. To his left, the floor to ceiling blinds are pulled back, filling the vast room with light.

He loves this space. It's where he comes alive as an artist. Ninety percent of their recent songs were written up here.

Now he's ruined that. Instead of a piece of paper and a guitar holding his attention, it's a syringe of heroin.

He shouldn't have prepared the drug. But he'd done it without thinking. Now his brain has finally kicked in. Better late than never, but a little too late for him to be able to walk away. He glares at the bag and paces back and forth in front of the window. Like hiding the fucking thing in a sandwich bag will make it less threatening.

'Idiot,' he mutters as he scrubs a hand over his face. 'Stupid, fucking idiot!'

He kicks the couch, sending it banging against the wall.

So if he's such an idiot, why is he still in the same room as it? Why hasn't he disposed of it, and picked up the phone to his sponsor?

Because he wants the fucking thing, and he can't bring himself to get rid of it.

'Jesus, Tate. What the fuck are you doing?'

He slumps on the couch and rests his chin in his hands, as he glares over at the package. Ever since he got back from Canada, his mind has been a mess. It's not getting better either. He'd done most of what he was told to do when he was struggling, but it's not working.

There isn't a chance in hell he'd consider going back to rehab. It's not like he'd actually done anything to warrant that. Not yet anyway.

He just needs a fucking break. Just wants to feel like he's actually in control of his life for the first time in well over a year. Dara. The baby. His father. Dillon. Chloe.

It's one thing after another. Each blow sending him back to square one, while he's still trying to recover from the one before. He can't keep doing this. Can't keep fighting.

Why can't he just wake up in the morning, and not have to worry about something? There's always something waiting to kick him in the gut, and he's so done with it all.

He's not a saint by any means, but he's certainly not a bad person. He must have been a right arsehole in his past life, to deserve this shit now. The thing that's really pissing him off, is the knock on effect it's having on Chloe. She is the single most amazing thing in his life, and now all this shit has driven her away. Forced her to leave him and their home.

Okay, so maybe some of that was his fault. His reaction to the pregnancy and miscarriage was beyond terrible. He knows that, but if everything else hadn't been going on, maybe he would have dealt with that part better.

Maybe.

Or maybe he's just a fuck up who would have messed things up for them eventually anyway. It's not like he has a solid track record for long term, healthy relationships.

Astrid was the longest one before Chloe. Fucking tragic.

And now he's getting angry thinking about Astrid.

God he hates that woman. He'll never forgive her for well and truly shoving that knife in his back. He's not a junkie.

He looks over at the bag.

He's not. While they were together, he used from time to time but nothing serious.

She's as bad as Pippa. The two of them are leeches. Clinging on to their celebrity partners, desperate to make a name for themselves. And it worked. Probably more so for Pippa, thanks to marrying Luke, but Astrid hadn't done too badly.

Good luck to her. As long as she keeps far away from him he'll die happy.

All he wants is Chloe.

That's it.

He'd happily walk away from the fame. From the music. From the money. He'd give it all up, if he could just have her back in his arms again. God, he misses her so much.

He pulls out his phone and considers calling her, but decides against it when he looks at the bag again. How fucked up would that be. He needs to get rid of that first, then call her.

Ten minutes later, he's still staring at it.

He just needs a few hours of peace. Just a few hours without stressing about the nightmares and the long and painful list of mistakes he's made. Maybe if he slept, things wouldn't seem so desperate.

One hit wouldn't send him over the edge again. It had taken days of constant using to hook him the last time. And it's not like he'd need more, if he managed a few hours of decent sleep.

Tate reaches out and takes the bag from the table, turning it over in his hand.

He doesn't have anything planned for the rest of the day. He could take this and get some sleep. Wake up fresh tomorrow.

He's still trying to justify what he's thinking about doing, as he takes off his hoodie. The list of reasons why this isn't such a bad idea are still going through his mind, as he ties the rubber tube around his arm, holding one end with his teeth as he takes the syringe out of the bag.

He looks down at the vein, clearly visible in the crook of his elbow.

What the fuck is he doing?

He stops, the needle inches from his vein. Is he really going to do this?

Tate closes his eyes, but instead of helping clear his head, his father's face appears, sneering down at him. The smell of stale beer consuming him. The sickening sensation of his father's body pressing down on him. The helplessness and paralysing terror growing, when he realises what's about to happen.

Before he fully knows what he's doing, Tate opens his eyes and slides the needle into his vein.

18

Gregg shoves the pizza box in Tate's face as soon as he opens the door. 'What took you so long? I nearly had to eat it all myself.'

'What are you doing here?'

He drops the box on the counter in the kitchen and takes a couple of bottles of juice from the fridge. As he opens them, he gets his first look at his friend. 'Thought you could do with some company. Damn buddy. You look like shit.'

'My girlfriend just left me. You expect me to be doing a fucking dance or something?'

Walked into that one. Gregg passes him a bottle and gestures to the living room. 'Let's eat in there.'

Tate frowns at the bottle, then slowly nods and drops heavily onto the couch. Gregg passes him a slice of pizza, but Tate shakes his head and glares at the bottle in his hand instead.

'Ah come on. You need to eat something.'

'I'm not hungry.'

Gregg chews on his pizza. He knows full well everything he says to Tate is either going to rub him up the wrong way, or push him further into the slump he's in.

Not that Gregg can blame him.

Chloe is absolutely the best thing that's ever happened to Tate. He's as gutted as his friend is about this hopefully, temporary split. Fingers crossed it is just temporary and they'll get over it. Chloe is so good for Tate.

'Okay so I'm going to ask. Have you talked to anyone about the baby?'

It takes Tate a good minute or so to look away from the bottle to Gregg. 'What?'

'The baby, Tate. Have you spoken to anyone about it?'

'No. It's done. Nothing to talk about.'

Gregg isn't surprised by that answer. 'Ah come on now. Of course there is. Chloe is talking about it. You need to do the same.'

Tate furrows his brow as he glares over at him. 'How do you know that?'

'I think she told Bria…' his voice trails away as Tate's jaw clenches. He's firmly stuck both feet into this big mouth. 'They're friends, Tate. They're going to talk.'

'So you know more about my fucking girlfriend than I do?'

Gregg puts the pizza back in the box and wipes his hands on his jeans. 'It's not like that, Tate. She was just getting it off her chest.'

'And Bria blabbed to you?'

'No. Bria wouldn't do that. I was in the room too.'

'Fucking perfect. So was I the only one not invited to this big heart to heart? Does the whole band know what's going on?'

'It wasn't like that, Tate, and you know it. She was just talking to her friend and I happened to be there. That's it. It wasn't a conscious decision to include me. I mean it.'

Tate snorts, then flops back on the couch, his anger under control again. Gregg takes a drink of juice as he examines Tate. That was intense, even for Tate. His mate is off, in a weird way, but Gregg can't put his finger on it.

He groans as his mobile buzzes in his pocket. Then Tate's one vibrates on the counter. 'It's Ellen,' Gregg says checking the screen. 'She wants to meet tomorrow to discuss this weekend.'

'What's happening this weekend?'

'We're meant to be in the UK. We're performing, remember?' Although by the look of their front man, Gregg very much doubts the performance is on his radar at all. The guy is in bits. There's not a cat in hell's chance he'll be up for singing anything. But that's his decision.

There's no way Gregg is going to interfere. It never goes well. All that did was put up a rather thick, immovable wall in front of him. Tate is the sort of person who needs to reach a decision without anyone badgering him. Stubborn git. 'We're leaving on Friday.'

'Right.'

And that's it. Nothing else on the subject, so Gregg fires a message back to Ellen agreeing to meet. If Tate isn't up for it, they'll just have to cancel. It's not the first time. Tate in rehab. Dillon in prison. They've been a bunch of unreliable disasters the last year or so. It's a downright miracle Vox are still playing ball with them. Then again, disasters or not, they're high earners, so that probably gives them a little leeway.

'So are you still on for tomorrow? Tate? Hey! You with me or what?'

Tate turns and nods. 'Sorry. What?'

'Are you okay? You're acting a bit weird.'

'Thanks for that.' Tate glares at him and takes a drink.

'I didn't mean it like that. Oh forget it.' Clearly he's in one of his moods. 'Okay, so I asked if you're still on for the party tomorrow?'

'What party?'

'Luke and Pippa's party to celebrate the fact they survived honeymoon.' He chuckles to himself, but Tate just looks at him. Gregg clears his throat. 'Right, so Ellen kind of wants us there for a bit. Show a united front, or something like that.'

'Is Dillon going?'

Gregg shrugs. 'I'd presume so. It's not like I want to go, but Ellen said we only have to go for an hour.'

'Spending five fucking minutes with Pippa is too long. I'm not going.'

'Ah now, buddy. Ellen said—'

Tate pushes to his feet and slams the bottle down on the table. 'Fine! Whatever. I'll go to the fucking party.'

Gregg doesn't say anything as Tate goes into the kitchen and searches the cupboards. Gregg silently watches him as he rummages in his kitchen. An unpleasant thought hits him, but he doesn't want to allow it to settle.

He wouldn't... would he?

Gregg shakes his head. No way. Tate had been through hell, while he was coming off drugs last year. Gregg had seen some of it first hand. It was horrible seeing how painful and miserable his detox had been. Okay, so Tate isn't in a happy place, but he wouldn't do that.

'Hey, do you mind if I spend the night. I don't fancy heading back to my place.' He had planned on staying with Bria, but he's not so sure Tate should be left alone.

'Whatever.' Tate drops back on the couch and passes him a packet of crisps. 'What time is this party tomorrow?'

'Eight I think.'

'Bria going too?'

Gregg shakes his head. He had considered bringing her, but decided against it when Chloe left. Tate would need a wing man, and he fully intended to support him.

Besides, Bria wasn't exactly chomping at the bit to go to the party. Strangely enough, Pippa didn't have a huge fan group among the band, or their partners. 'Think she's got work to do. Some fancy design that needs to be finished.'

'More outfits for you to prance around in.' Tate actually smiles which is nice to see.

'She's promised me that won't be happening again.'

'It suited you.'

'I was a natural, I get that. Doesn't mean I fancy strutting my stuff again, thank you very much.'

Tate stretches out on the couch and turns on the TV. After a few minutes silence he sighs. 'I miss her, Gregg.'

'I know, buddy. It's not over though. You know that, right? She just needs to get her head straight.'

Tate nods as he stares at the TV, but doesn't respond. Gregg leaves him to his thoughts. He seems a little calmer now than he was when he first arrived.

Maybe Gregg was seeing things earlier. His girlfriend had a miscarriage, then left him. That's bound to throw him off course. No wonder he's not quite himself.

Doesn't mean he's going to leave him to his thoughts though. He'll stick around until it's time to go to the party tomorrow. Make sure he doesn't do anything he's going to regret.

Dillon

Dillon wakes with a start and takes a second to look around the room. No concrete walls. No bars. No noise. He takes a shuddering breath and wipes his face as he looks over at his phone. Eight pm. He's been asleep for a few hours but still feels like shite. So much for sleeping until the morning.

The intercom on his door sounds. That must have been what woke him. 'Go the fuck aw—'

He frowns at the image on the security camera. It's Luke.

Dillon's heart races as he stares at his friend. He looks good, but he always does.

The buzzer goes again. 'Dillon. I need to talk to you. Please.'

Dillon's hand moves without any consideration for the argument he's having with himself. He presses the button to respond. 'Come in. I'll be out in a sec.' He buzzes Luke into his flat, then slumps back on the bed. Now what?

For the past few weeks he's been desperate to speak to Luke. Desperate to clear the air as much as he can. But now he's fucking terrified about seeing him again.

He hears the door close behind Luke. Too late to run. He might as well get it over with. After throwing on a pair of jeans and a long sleeved t-shirt, he takes a calming breath, straightens his shoulders, and heads into the living room.

The second he gets a proper look at Luke, he knows something is wrong. His friend looks terrible. 'Hey.'

'Hey. Can I sit?'

Dillon nods and gestures to the couch. 'You want something to drink?'

'No, I'm good thanks.'

Dillon sits beside him on the couch, and the two men keep the awkward silence going for a few minutes. It's a silence Dillon isn't keen on breaking.

He's so relieved Luke called round to see him, but there's only one reason he'd do that after so long. He wants to have it out with him. Luke doesn't scream and shout. Never did, but that doesn't mean he isn't able to get pissed off. Dillon has been on the receiving end of it from time to time - usually when he pushes his friend too far.

Screwing with his wedding would fall into that category.

He stifles a yawn, hoping Luke didn't notice. Leading up to the epic disaster at Luke's wedding, he was taking drugs to go to sleep, and more to wake himself up in the morning. Spending a month inside, hadn't helped him sort out his sleep patterns.

He's wound up and his fucking brain is refusing to give him a break. He's always been like that. People don't think he gets stressed out or bothered by anything, but it's the exact opposite. He works fucking hard to keep his mask on in public - sometimes with his friends too, but it's exhausting, and lately, required drugs to help him keep it in place.

'How was your honeymoon?' Not that he wants to think about what Luke and Pippa got up to on honeymoon, but it's what friends ask.

'Yeah, it was good. Are you okay? I wanted to get in touch with you when you were in prison, but...' he shrugs and looks away.

Dillon knows full well Pippa probably didn't want him to talk to his embarrassing, criminal friend. If she's to save face in front of her social media followers, she'll want to distance herself from him. Which is more than okay by Dillon. It's the threat of losing Luke that's scaring him.

'It's fine, Luke. I just kept my head down and counted the days. It's done.'

Luke nods and looks him up and down. 'You lost weight?'

'Yeah. I'll have to kick my ass to get the bulk back.'

'You look different without your piercings. Are you going to leave them out?'

Dillon meant to put them back in before the bath put completely forgot. 'I'll put them back in. Really looking forward to dealing with the ones in my dick. That'll be fun.'

Luke laughs. 'Ouch. Good luck with that.'

'I'll need it. I'll let you know how I get on.'

'Please don't. I'd prefer not to think about your dick.'

They both laugh at that and, for a moment, it feels like it used to. But then Luke turns to look at him. He so sad and that kills Dillon.

'Dillon, I'm so sorry I went away without seeing you.'

'Fuck that, Luke. To be honest, I thought you wouldn't want to set eyes on me again. I am so, so, sorry for what I did. I wish to fuck I could go back and slap some sense into myself... but I can't. I never wanted to ruin your wedding like I did.'

'You didn't ruin it, Dillon. And I'm so sorry Pippa called the Garda on you. I had no idea until we went away, that she did that. I thought it was the hotel.'

Dillon shrugs. He wasn't in the slightest bit surprised Pippa did that. Bitch hates him. 'It's grand. I deserved it. Do you hate me?' Dillon flinches at his pathetic question. He hadn't planned on asking like that, but his mouth just screwed him.

Luke shakes his head. 'No. Never. You're my best mate, Dillon. You're a nightmare, but I'd never hate you,' he adds with a smile. 'So I don't know if you heard, but Pippa is having a party. Sort of like a back from honeymoon gathering.'

Dillon nods. He had heard, and he has an idea where this is going.

'Okay, Pippa... she thinks... It's just that after what happened—'

'It's okay, Luke. I get it. You'd prefer I wasn't there.'

Luke briskly shakes his head. 'No! I want you there, Dillon. I do. It's just...'

Dillon smiles, trying to take the load from Luke's shoulders. 'Hey. I wouldn't want me there either. You two deserve a decent party - especially after what I did to your reception.'

'I'm sorry.'

'Stop. Really. I don't have a problem with it. I mean that. I'm sure I can figure out something to do.' He winks and Luke smiles. This isn't Luke's fault so he's absolutely not going to hold it against him.

'Thanks. I'd better go.'

Dillon nods. Yep - he'd better go and report back to the bitch. Tell her he did her dirty work. 'No problem.' He walks Luke to the door and keeps the painfully fake smile on his face. 'Have a great time tomorrow.'

'Yeah, thanks. You too.'

Dillon leans on the open door and grins. 'Oh you know me. I always do.' Luke disappears into the elevator and Dillon drops the smile. Fucking perfect.

And so it begins.

He knew there would be repercussions for his actions, but wasn't prepared to hear his best mate actually telling him he wasn't invited.

He gets the feeling his life is about to get a hell of a lot more lonely.

19

Tate

Tate grabs his coke from the bar and glares into the glass. He wants to go home. This whole evening has dragged on too long already. He checks the time. Fuck. Ten minutes. He's been here for a lousy ten minutes.

But he can't leave. The painfully boring drinks party is being held at Luke's house, by his equally boring wife. If it wasn't for Luke, Tate would have blown this fiasco off, but he wasn't going to bail on his friend.

He scrubs his hand over his face, but he can't wake up. He didn't sleep last night. The night before either. Chloe helped to keep the nightmares away... most of the time. The drugs hadn't helped much either.

There's no magic fucking cure to make his life better. There's no wand he can wave to bring Chloe back home, where she belongs.

Beside him. The thought that this might be his life from now on, terrifies him.

He glances around the room, but can't see anyone he can be bothered talking to. Gregg and Luke are at the back of the room, talking to people he doesn't recognise. He needs Dillon at times like this. He could always be counted on to make these events less painful.

If Ellen hadn't insisted he be here, he would have ditched it the second he heard Pippa had banned Dillon from the evening. They go to events as a foursome. End of story. The fact that bitch actually made poor Luke tell Dillon personally, is pissing him off just as much as Dillon being banned in the first place.

'Are you going to get me a drink?'

The second he hears her voice, Tate's skin begins to crawl. 'What the fuck are you doing here?'

Astrid smiles as she slips onto the stool beside him. 'Pippa and I are friends, remember. That's thanks to you.'

Too fucking right it is. She crawled up the social ladder hanging on to him as tight as she could.

'Stop glaring at me like that. Why are you so hostile with me?'

He leans over, getting right in her face. Her perfume is familiar and he doesn't like it. 'I told you at the wedding. You know full well why I don't want you anywhere near me. I'm done talking to you, so please, fuck off, and leave me alone.'

'You can't even just talk to me?'

He turns on her, the anger building in his gut. 'We never talked, Astrid. We fucked. That's it. Then you fucked me over, so no, we can't talk.'

She grabs his arm, as he tries to turn away from her. How he doesn't physically shove her off him, he has no idea. Something stops him, and he's so grateful.

'Hand. Off. Now.' His tone is low and deadly serious, but she doesn't take notice.

'There are a lot of cameras here, Tate. Best to sit down for a few

165

minutes instead of making a scene. That won't help your career. Probably not your relationship either.'

She smiles sweetly and pushes out the stool he was sitting on. He slowly sits down, but doesn't put his drink back on the bar. He's not staying. 'Talk. Fast.'

'I'm sorry about you and Chloe.'

The look he gives her does the trick.

'Sorry. That's none of my business. I know you're slightly irritated about what the press *thought* I said.' She pauses, as he rolls his eyes and looks away. 'Whatever, I still care about you.'

'I don't need you to care about me, Astrid. What I need is for you to leave me alone.' He sighs and slams his palm down on the bar. 'What is this, huh? Why are you bugging me? I told you at the wedding that I'm not interested. Leave. Me. Alone!'

She combs her blonde hair back from her face and pouts. 'Wow. Still have a grasp on sweet talking I see.'

'If I was planning on sweet talking anyone, it certainly wouldn't be you. What do you want?'

'I just want to make things right between us. I hate all this tension. I know you didn't think we had anything deep and meaningful, but I did. Does that make me a terrible person, Tate?'

He wants to keep glaring at her, but doesn't have the energy right now. 'Whatever. It's done.'

'But it's not if you still hate me. Do you hate me?'

Yes, but right now he just wants her to leave him alone. 'I don't hate you. I'm fucked off with what you did, but it's not important anymore. Forget it and move on. Please.'

She reaches out and takes his hand. 'Friend?'

Tate pulls his hand back. 'No. We're not friends because, as I said, you fucked me over. But I'll talk to you civilly if I bump into you. That's the best I can do.'

That pout of hers comes back, but he's not falling for it. When they were together he might have given her a hug. Maybe. But after she told the press he'd been a heavy drug user for years, he'd lost anything that may have resembled feelings for her.

He stands up and takes his glass off the bar. 'See you around.'

Astrid jumps to her feet and reaches up to wrap her arms around his neck, pulling him down for a hug. It lasts the grand total of a second, before he grabs her by the arms and unlocks her. 'Goodbye Astrid.'

Ignoring her ridiculous pout of disappointment, he makes a beeline for Gregg.

'Oh no buddy. Not again!'

'Not again what?'

'You have that same look you had at the wedding.' Gregg nods towards Astrid, staring over at them. 'She got you again, didn't she?'

'I don't know what her fucking deal is, but it's gone beyond pissing me off. I told her I don't hate her, and to move on from what happened. I'm hoping it'll shut her up.'

Gregg raises his eyebrows, but doesn't say anything.

'What?'

'You do remember what she was like, right? She was a teeny bit obsessed with you. It was the end of the world when you used your brain, instead of your dick for thinking, and dumped her.'

'I told you not to mention my dick and her in the same sentence. And it's done. I've got more important things going on, without wasting any time on her. Let her leech off someone else. I'm sure Pippa has a friend or two she can cling on to.' He takes a drink of the coke and grimaces. It's gone warm. 'Fuck, when can we leave this thing?'

Gregg shrugs, looking as pissed off as he does. 'Soon I hope. It's not even like we can talk to Luke. Pippa should just handcuff him to her and be done with it. You'd swear she's afraid someone else is going to jump on him or something.'

'She's always been like that with him.' Tate places his glass on a tray, as a waiter whizzes by him. 'Have you spoken to Dillon today?'

Gregg shakes his head. 'I sent him a message. To be honest, I didn't know what to say to him, so kept it to a text. I can't believe she told him not to come. How low is that?'

'Are you really surprised?'

'I know. It's still shite though. He's having a hard enough time as it is without singling him out of things like this.'

'We should go and see him tomorrow. If we survive this hell of course. Have you seen Chloe lately?'

Gregg does that awkward face he always does when he's in a situation he wants out of.

'Sorry. Forget it. I don't want to land you in the middle of this.'

'You're not. And yes I have. She's been talking to Bria a lot.'

'Do you think I should try to … I don't know…'

'Yes. You need to talk to her. You can't sort this out unless you two are actually in the same room as each other.'

'But what if we can't agree? I mean, what if she wants one thing and I don't know if I do? I love her to bits, Gregg, but…' He doesn't know what he wants, so how can he even consider talking to her. Knowing his luck, he'd end up making things so much worse.

'I guess that's what you need to figure out for yourself. If you honestly don't want kids, you need to tell her.'

'But then I'll lose her.'

'You don't know that for sure either way. What is guaranteed is that, unless you're both honest about what you want, it will come to an end sooner or later.'

'Am I a terrible person? If I don't want kids, I mean.'

Gregg pulls him over to the side of the room, where there's a bit more privacy. 'Ah no, don't be silly. Not wanting kids is your choice, buddy. No one is going to judge you either way. Pippa doesn't want kids, which is probably a good thing.'

'She doesn't?'

Gregg shakes his head. 'I remember Luke mentioning it a while ago.'

'But Luke loves kids.'

Gregg shrugs and sips his juice. 'Maybe he changed his mind. What I'm getting at is that it's normal. Nothing to feel shitty about. But you need to be honest with her and with yourself. You both deserve that.'

Gregg is right, but that doesn't help him figure out what's going on in his head. Being surrounded by all these people isn't helping either. He can't think straight with all the noise, and drink, and loved up couples, all around him.

'I think I'm going to head.'

Gregg pops his glass on the window sill next to him. 'No problem. I'll drive you home.'

'I don't need you to.'

'I drove you here. You plan on walking back to Blackrock or do you fancy that lift?'

'Fair point. I might take that lift after all.'

He makes his way through the room, his attention being drawn to Astrid as she waves at him, a huge smile on her face.

Dillon

Dillon sips his whiskey, still nowhere near tipsy, let alone drunk. He's been at the bar for about an hour, alone, feeling pissed off and sorry for himself at the same time. Fucking pathetic.

Luke, Tate, and Gregg are probably digging into expensive nibbles and even more expensive champagne, while he's holding up the bar considering if he should go completely mad and treat himself to a packet of Scampi Fries.

Glamorous lifestyles of the rich and famous.

He can feel Jason staring at him from across the room. He's forbidden his security to sit with him. No point feeling sorry for yourself, if you're not doing it alone. Makes it so much more miserable.

Uninvited.

Story of his fucking life. Although, since finding fame and fucking fortune, he'd been invited to more events then he can remember. How tragic is it to be specifically asked not to come to his best mate's wedding party or whatever the hell the party is for.

Everyone is going to be there. Everyone except him.

'Stop feeling fucking sorry for yourself.'

He doesn't do this. He never does the *woe is me* shit. He gets hit, packs it away with everything else he can't be bothered dealing with, and moves on. He doesn't wallow.

Prison has done this to him. Getting knocked around and being able to do nothing about it, fucked with his head. There wasn't a lot else to do when he was in his cell, except feel sorry for himself.

He curses himself again, then downs the rest of his drink.

What he needs is sex. It's been weeks since he's been with anyone. No wonder he's stressed out.

He'd even take a woman at this stage. He's veered away from women for years, but beggars can't be choosers. And with the lack of decent men here tonight, he might just have to break his rule for one night.

The blonde bartender smiles as she places another drink in front of him. She doesn't recognise him. He wears glasses when he's using a computer or watching TV, but lately he'd taken to wearing clear lenses when he's out. It's amazing how the addition of pair of glasses can completely transform him.

He still gets attention, but it's got nothing to do with his fame and that's just fine by him. He's not in the mood to be all polite. He just wants a fuck without the celebrity oohing and aahing.

She continues serving other customers, but her eyes dart back to him every minute or two. He sips his whiskey, peering at her over the rim of his glass.

Looks like he's on to a winner. She's doing a fairly decent job of undressing him with her eyes.

Time to go to work.

It takes less than ten minutes. Not exactly a record, but not his worst effort.

She unlocks the store room and closes the door behind them, locking it again. 'So,' she says, giving him what he presumes is a seductive smile that needs a little work. 'I'm Rachel.' She holds out her hand and he shakes it.

'Ryan.' He always used his surname in situations like this. Easier to disappear afterwards.

She opens her mouth to talk again, so he kisses her, shutting her up. Rachel hesitates for a second, startled by the suddenness of his kiss, but quickly gets with the program. She groans as her tongue finds his.

'Oh God,' she exclaims as she pulls away from him. 'It's pierced. I've never been with someone with a pierced tongue.'

'It's not the only place I have piercings.'

He grins when she instantly looks down at his dick. Before she can comment, he kisses her again. He needs to move this along before his head processes he's with a woman.

He's attracted to women as much as men, but swore off women when *she* broke his heart. Easier than trying to fake it when his head threw her face in place of whoever he was fucking at the time.

Better safe than sorry though. He spins Rebecca or whatever the fuck her name is, around to face the wall instead of him. Less personal, but they'll both get what they want from this.

'Bend over.'

She must be as on for this as he is, quickly bending over, resting her arms on the boxes in front of her. He pushes her tight black mini skirt up and over her ass. The black thong gets slipped to the side, then he rubs his fingers over her pussy. She's soaking. That's good. Less time to get her ready.

Fuck, he's being a selfish ass, but he can't help it. In his playroom, he'd take his time with her, slowly work her, slowly tease her, edging her again and again until she was begging and pleading with him to let her come.

In a grotty stock room of a pub, she's going to get a quick fuck and that's it.

He takes out a condom, slipping it on. He catches her staring at his dick over her shoulder. The three barbells crisscrossing the crown tend to get attention. They're a little severe, but he fucking loves them. Loves how they look, mainly. And it's not as if he's ever had one complaint from anyone he's stuck his dick in. The piercings hit all the right spots inside, intensifying the feelings. Who's he to argue with that?

He rests his hand on the back of her neck, pushing her head down as he slides the tip of his dick to her wet pussy.

She's tighter than he was expecting, her walls squeezing him as he slowly slides in. He may want a quick fuck, but he's not about to hurt her by shoving into her.

'You good?'

She nods quickly, a moan escaping her lips when he slides out a little before pushing back in again, slower than he would have liked.

'That feels... God it's incredible.'

He has to agree with her. It does feel pretty fucking amazing. He'd forgotten what it's like to fuck a woman. Dillon grips her hips, holding her steady as he moves, keeping a hold on himself for the first few thrusts.

She moans loudly.

'Shut the fuck up,' he hisses.

He has no problem with an audience, but getting her fired isn't part of the plan. No doubt her boss wouldn't be too happy with her fucking the customers. Or letting them fuck her.

She has no intention of keeping the noise down, her groans increasing in volume when he slams into her, driving his dick deep.

Dillon pulls her back against his chest, and wraps a hand around her waist to hold her in place. 'Open your mouth.'

In all fairness to her, she does exactly what he says, which is a serious turn on for him. He slides two fingers into her mouth. 'Suck on them like it's my dick.'

She hesitates for the briefest of moments then closes her mouth around his fingers. 'Good girl. Use your tongue too.'

He's not far off now. Neither is she. Her whole body is trembling, her tongue soaking his fingers, sucking on them as he picks up the pace again.

Usually, he'd try to hold himself back, but this is purely about getting that release. Needing that release.

He's pounding into her now, their damp bodies slapping against each other. Then she comes, her body trembling, her walls squeezing him tight. Her teeth dig into his fingers as she screams, the sound stifled somewhat.

The pain of her biting him is exactly what he needs. With two last thrusts, he buries himself deep. Dillon drops his head onto her shoulder as he rides it out.

Once his dick is done, he slowly pulls out of her and takes off the condom, tying a knot in the end. While she's still splayed out on the boxes, he pulls up his boxers and jeans, fastening his belt as he examines her dripping pussy laid out in front of him.

He's tempted to fuck her again, but decides against it. Might just call it a night and go home and get wasted.

She pushes upright and turns to face him. Her face is flushed. 'Wow. I mean... that was... wow.' Her smile fades when she realises he's dressed and ready to leave. 'Are you going?'

'Your break will be over in a bit.'

'Oh. Well are you going to hang around? We could continue this after my shift.'

Dillon slides his hand around the back of her head, pulling her in for a kiss. He keeps it slow, using his tongue to fuck her mouth, exploring every inch of it before he pulls away. 'Thanks but no.'

He leaves her to sort herself out, ignoring her muttering something about exchanging numbers, or something like that. He doesn't hear her. He's already out the door and heading back to the bar. He makes his way out the front door and down to the SUV parked to the side of the car park.

Jason joins him at the car and unlocks it. 'Get your itch scratched?'

Dillon glares at his bodyguard, then climbs into the car. 'Just drive me home.'

Jason does an exaggerated bow, then slides in behind the steering wheel and starts the car. 'You do realise the whole point is that I have eyes on you all the fucking time, right?'

'You really want to watch me fuck? All you have to do is ask. I might even let you join in.' He gets a kick out of the look on Jason's face.

'You really are a dream to work for, Dillon, you know that?'

'Oh yeah. Anyway, I was fine. She didn't even know who I was. It's all good.' He lies back and closes his eyes, putting an end to the conversation. The sex had killed the whiskey buzz and, as much as he wants to be alone, he also can't bear the thought of going home and drinking himself to sleep... again.

'Stop at the next bar we get to.'

'Ah now I reckon you've had enough. You should—'

'Stop at the next fucking bar, Jace.' He fixes the man with his best *don't fuck with me look*, only turning away when Jason curses under his breath.

A few more drinks then he'll head back to his monstrously expensive penthouse and wallow in misery until the morning. Not a perfect plan but fuck it, it's what he does.

Luke

Luke grabs his phone from the bedside table, quickly silencing the vibrating as he climbs out of bed and closes the door behind him. He grimaces when he sees Jason's name on the screen. Dillon's security only calls him for one reason, and it's never good.

He answers the call, keeping an eye on the door as he speaks quietly. 'It's three am, Jason.'

'Sorry Luke. I need your help though.'

'What's he done now?'

'Take a guess.'

'Drunk and loud.'

Jason snorts. 'Got it in one. I tried to convince him that going out wasn't the best idea, but you know him. I seriously got the short straw when I was assigned to this stubborn asshole. I managed to get him out of the pub before too many photos were taken, but it wasn't easy.

Think he's making up for the last month without drink.'

'Where is he now?'

'In my car, in the parking lot at his place. The problem is, he won't get out of the car. Keeps asking for you. I'm sorry Luke, I know you've got your party thing tonight, but it's like trying to move a tank. He won't budge.'

'It's fine, Jace. Everyone's gone. I'll be there as fast as I can. Just try not to deck him before I get there.'

Jason laughs. 'Sorely tempted, but it would go against the fact I'm employed to keep him in one piece. See you in a bit.'

Luke ends the call, and looks back at the bedroom door. She won't be happy about him sneaking off like this, but he has to go. When Dillon gets like this, his stubborn streak increases tenfold.

Luke has no idea why, but he's the only person Dillon isn't obnoxious with when he's drunk. Poor Jason could quite possibly be stuck with Dillon in his car for a few hours, unless Luke convinces him to move.

He opens the bedroom door a crack, and peers inside. Pippa is still asleep, her petite form buried under the enormous duvet. Luke creeps inside, grabs some clothes, then closes the door behind him. He gets dressed in one of the spare rooms, then hurries downstairs. After scribbling a quick note to Pippa, he puts on a pair of boots, takes his jacket off the hanger and unlocks the door into the garage.

It feels good to be outside in the fresh air. The party wasn't too bad, but the house had been filled with her friends. He had nothing in common with most of them. He'd breathed a sigh of relief once the last of the boring guests left, looking forward to crawling into bed and getting some sleep.

But Pippa had other ideas.

He hadn't been able to give her what she wanted... yet again. He'd tried, but his body was dead against it and no amount of encouragement from Pippa had helped. Everything she did just hurt him so she gave up, disappointed in him once again. Now he's tired, his dick and wrists are sore, and he has to think of some way to make it up to her.

She'll hear if he takes his Range Rover, so he bypasses it and takes his helmet from the shelf. Luke pushes his bike outside, making sure to lock the garage door behind him. Once he's a little way down the road, he climbs onto his bike, wincing when the saddle presses uncomfortably against his groin, and fastens his helmet.

It takes him only twenty minutes to get to Dillon's place, thanks to the late hour. He drives into the underground garage, and spots Jason's SUV parked in his spot next to Dillon's one. Luke pulls into the second visitor's parking space, and shuts off the engine, as Jason climbs out of his car. Dillon appears to be asleep, his eyes closed and his head resting against the window.

Before he gets off his bike, he makes sure the leather cuffs are securely fastened around his wrists. The leather bands are part of his everyday wardrobe, hiding the scars from the cuffs she uses on him. Better to wear them, than face the questions. Questions he's not sure how he'd answer, without making it sound like he was complaining about sex with Pippa.

'You okay, Luke?'

'What? Sorry. Yeah. How bad is he?' Luke asks as he climbs off his bike and peers through the window at Dillon.

'Oh he's bad. Drunk, and he downed some pills too. No idea what, but they hit on the way home. He's zoning out.'

Luke glares through the window at Dillon, who takes no notice. 'Perfect. Okay, let's get him upstairs.'

Jason opens the door, reaching out to prop Dillon up as he slumps to the side. 'I rang ahead while I was waiting. Pete is on the door tonight. He's unlocked the service elevator for us.'

That's something at least. Dillon's well-to-do neighbours haven't taken kindly to the drunken, and usually loud, rock star coming home at all hours.

Dillon shoves Jason away. 'Get off me.'

'Dillon. It's Luke. Time to get you inside.'

Dillon frowns and tries to focus on Luke, but he doesn't seem to be able to. Then he grins sleepily, and falls out of the car. Luke and Jason catch him before he lands on his face or ass, and help him upright. 'Hey!'

'Hey yourself,' Luke mutters as he positions himself under one of Dillon's arms. He pauses to let Jason support Dillon from the other side. 'Ready?'

Dillon nods at him. 'All set. For what?'

'I was talking to Jason, but it would help if you could walk too.'

'Will do. Lead the way.'

Jason shakes his head and nods towards the door. 'Let's go then.'

They half drag, half carry him into the elevator, and prop him up against the wall, as Luke hits the button to the penthouse apartment. Dillon frowns over at him, then turns his attention to Jason. 'Hey.'

'Hey. Again.'

'You've got that same old disapproving look on your face.' He laughs and hits his head back against the wall.

'Dillon—'

Dillon holds up a hand, then jabs his finger into Luke's chest. 'You too.' He gestures haphazardly between the two men in front of him. 'Same fucking look on both your faces. Always judging me.'

'Dillon, we're not judging anyone.'

He tries to poke Luke again, but misses, tipping forward until Jason catches him and holds him back against the wall.

'Let me go!' He shoves Jason away, and glares at him. 'I didn't ask you to babysit me, Jace. You could have gone home and let me fuck in peace.'

The elevator door pings and opens, not a moment too soon. Dillon can get nasty when he's like this. The sooner they can get him to bed, so he can sleep it off, the better.

'Believe me, Dillon. I'm seriously wishing I had.' Jason props him up against the wall, as Luke opens the door and helps Dillon inside his apartment. They bring him into the bedroom and sit him on the edge of the bed, both breathing heavily as they look down at him. 'You're one heavy fucker, you know that,' Jason mutters, as he wipes his face.

'You know what, Jace? You're not half bad looking,' Dillon mumbles as they turn on the light. 'I'd do you.'

Jason snorts. 'Wow. That's one hell of a compliment, but I'll have to pass, thanks anyway.'

'You have no fucking idea what you're passing on. I'm really good. I mean really fucking good.' Luke pushes Dillon in the shoulder and he flops back on the bed, laughing to himself. 'I've got them lining up to spend time with me.'

Jason pulls off Dillon's boots. 'I don't doubt that, but again, I'll pass. You're not my type.'

'What the fuck is wrong with me?' Dillon asks, lifting his head to glare at Jason.

'You're a bloke.'

Dillon waves his hand and drops his head back on to the covers. 'Minor detail. Give me half an hour and you'll change your mind.'

'Oh would you just lay off!' Luke snaps, as he manhandles Dillon up the bed. 'Leave Jason alone, and get some sleep.'

Dillon rolls onto his side, turning his back to Jason. 'Whatever. I'm tired.'

Luke searches the pockets of Dillon's jacket. Apart from a pack of sour apple sweets, there's a small, empty plastic bag. No indication of what had been in the bag. 'What did you take?'

Dillon shakes his head. He's not going to tell him. Awkward git never does.

'Should I ask what he got up to?' Luke isn't so sure he wants to know. Dillon's sex life is eye-opening at the best of times.

'He had some personal time with one of the bartenders. Disappeared with her for about twenty minutes or so.'

That surprises Luke. 'Her? Really?'

'Surprised me too. I've given up trying to figure out what's going on in his head though.'

'Yeah. I know what you mean. Can you grab some water?' Luke asks, covering Dillon with the duvet.

Jason nods and heads into the kitchen and Dillon rolls back over to peer hazily at him. 'Stay.'

'Yeah. Sure.' Luke takes the water from Jason and rests it on the bedside table. 'I'll stick around for a bit. You can go, Jace.'

'You sure you're okay with him?'

'Oh fuck off Jason!' Dillon snaps, sitting up suddenly. 'If I can't fuck you, you're no use to me. Don't need a fucking babysitter.'

'Gladly,' he counters, glaring down at him. 'They don't pay me enough to deal with you when you're like this.'

'Well get used to it. This is what I do.' He collapses back on the bed. 'Over and over and over again. One long fucked up party.'

Luke nods to Jason. 'It's okay. He just needs to sleep it off.'

'I'll give Andy the heads up. Let him know you're here.'

'Thanks.'

As Jason locks the front door behind him, Luke lies down beside Dillon. He's settled again, his eyes closed and his breathing steady.

He's always been confrontational when he drinks. The drugs he took tonight seem to have taken off some of the aggressive edge, but he seems to gravitate towards picking a fight when he's like this.

Luke has lost count of the number of nights he's babysat his friend. He doesn't have an issue staying to make sure he doesn't do something stupid. It's more that he deeply wishes Dillon wouldn't get into this state in the first place.

He plays the hard man. Pretends to be fine, but he's far from it. Luke doubts he's truly been happy for the last twenty years. Well, except for those few months when he was seeing a woman about a decade ago, who seemed to be able to find the real Dillon, under all the crap and bravado. But then she left, and he took a steady fall. One he still hasn't recovered from.

Luke's phone vibrates in his pocket. It's Pippa. He braces himself for the inevitable fight, and answers the call.

'Where are you?'

'I'm sorry. I'm with Dillon. He's—'

'Drunk.' Pippa finishes. 'Come home. He's big enough to look after himself.'

'He's in a really bad way, Pippa. I can't leave him like this.'

'But you can leave me? We're just back from honeymoon and you're leaving me for him.'

'I'm not leaving you. It's one night.'

'Can't Jason watch that he doesn't choke on his own vomit? That's what he's paid to do after all. Come home.'

Luke closes his eyes, the headache already building as Pippa's tone drops. But he can't leave Dillon like this. There's no way he'd do that to him. 'I'm sorry...'

Silence.

Then she ends the call.

He stares at the screen, the dread weighing heavily in his gut.

'You okay?'

Luke jumps, dropping the phone onto the bed. 'I thought you were asleep. You scared the hell out of me.'

Dillon's green eyes are unfocused, but serious. 'You can go. Don't want you getting into trouble because of me.'

'I said I'll stay. Get some sleep. You look shit.'

Dillon grins then closes his eyes. 'Asshole.'

'I know you are.'

'Why are you still hanging around?' Dillon asks after a few minutes of silence. His speech is a little slurred, either thanks to what he took, or exhaustion.

'You asked me to stay.'

Dillon angrily shakes his head. 'I mean with me, full stop. Not here now.'

'I've asked myself that quite a few times,' Luke says, smiling to take the sting out of his comment.

'She hates me.'

'Who?' Luke is struggling to keep track of Dillon's drunken thoughts.

'Your *wife*.' He near on spits out the last word, like it's poison.

'She doesn't hate you,' he lies. Pippa absolutely hates Dillon.

Dillon snorts, scrubbing his hand over his face, as he rolls onto his back again. 'She had me arrested.'

'I know. I'm sorry.'

Dillon shakes his head, sending one of the pillows tumbling off the edge of the bed. 'My fault. Always my fault.' He laughs harshly and closes his eyes. 'Tired. It was too loud in there. Couldn't sleep.'

'In where?'

Dillon buries his head under his arm. 'Prison. I hated it, Luke.'

He hasn't said a lot about that month, and Luke hasn't pushed him, worried about forcing his friend to relive that time.

'They thought I was an easy target. Some soft celebrity. Your *wife* would like that. It would make her fucking day.'

Luke sits up when he hears that. 'Were you a soft target? Did something happen to you while you were in prison?'

He nods but doesn't look at him. 'Didn't fight back. Didn't want to get in more trouble. Bruises are gone now.'

Dillon was beaten up in prison and didn't say anything. 'Dillon—'

'I keep fucking up, Luke.'

'No, you—'

'She left me, Luke. I loved her so much, but she couldn't stand me either.'

He's not talking to Luke anymore. His voice is barely audible. He's in his head again and that's never a good thing.

'Everyone leaves me in the end. Fucking jinxed.'

'I'm not going anywhere, Dillon. I promise.'

After a minute or two, Dillon rolls back to face him, but can't seem to focus on him. 'We'll see.' Then he closes his eyes and takes a shaky breath. 'I love you.'

'I love you too, Dillon.'

He scrunches his brows. 'No,' he mutters angrily. 'Doesn't matter. Forget it.' He rolls onto his back and sighs loudly, but doesn't say anything else, so Luke assumes he's passed out. He kicks off his own boots, and settles back on Dillon's bed.

He's not tired. Far from it. The fight with Pippa is still at the front of his mind. He understands why she's not happy with Dillon. When his friend thrashed one of the rooms at their wedding, it had put the day in the papers, for all the wrong reasons. Pippa will probably never forgive Dillon for that.

Which puts Luke in such an awkward position. He's stuck between two of the most important people in his life. Stuck playing referee when they clash. Which they do too often for his liking.

'I'm in love with you. It killed me watching you marry her.'

Luke holds his breath for a second then turns to look at Dillon. He's facing him again, but his eyes are closed. 'What did you say?'

Dillon licks his lips and buries his head under his arm.

'Dillon?'

He gets nothing but a low snore. He's gone.

What the hell was that? Did Dillon just say that he loves him? As more than a friend?

They're close. No doubt about that, but is there a possibility Dillon's feelings run deeper than just friendship? He never hinted that he might have feelings. But this is Dillon after all. He rarely talks about anything apart from music or sex.

As Dillon snores softly beside him, Luke's thoughts go off on a tangent, second guessing so many times they've been together. Trying to see if there was more to each moment than just friendship.

Luke knows Dillon has never got on with Pippa. They've always clashed, but it never sat right with Luke, that Dillon would react as he had at their wedding. They're so close. Dillon would never do anything to cause him upset or embarrassment.

But if he did actually have feelings for him, could that have tipped Dillon over the edge?

I'm in love with you. It killed me watching you marry her.

Luke feels sicks. No wonder Dillon flipped. He was watching someone he loves marrying someone else.

Luke curses himself and turns his back to Dillon. Now he's being big-headed. Dillon doesn't fall in love... well, hasn't for years. He has sex. No strings attached, sex. There's no reason he would change his M.O. - especially for someone like Luke.

It was nothing. Just an off-the-cuff drunken comment. Nothing more. It can't be.

He closes his eyes and plans what he's going to say to Pippa when he goes home tomorrow. The fact she hung up on him as she did, tells him he's in for a *fun* time when he goes home. If given the choice, he'd prefer to stay here with Dillon.

21

Tate

Tate opens the door and steps aside as Ellen pushes her way into his house. He frowns at his watch. It's barely eight. He'd finally dropped off around four. There's a lot of strong coffee in his immediate future. 'Morning, Ellen. Please come in.'

She doesn't comment on his sarcasm, as she drops her bag and a file on the counter and looks around at him. 'Can you get dressed. I don't want to do this with you half naked in front of me.'

He glances down at his boxers and shrugs as he sits on one of the bar stools. 'Do what?'

She sighs. 'Fine. When were you going to tell me about Astrid?'

Tate scrubs a hand over his face as he tries to wake up. He's wrecked and desperate for a fix, which isn't helping his mood. 'You've lost me, Ellen.'

'You and Astrid are apparently back together again.'

Tate stares at Ellen for a long few minutes as the words register. 'I'm sorry. I'm what now?'

Ellen pulls a page out of her file and Tate pushes upright on the stool. He hates when she produces pages from that file of hers. It's almost always bad news.

'This is a copy of an article that's running... sorry, has run in today's papers.' She holds up the page and Tate gapes at the photo.

'Fuck!'

'Yes, Tate. Fuck indeed. Now correct me if I'm wrong, but that appears to be you, and that woman you're hugging is Astrid. Naturally, you're getting back together and the world has gone mad about it, with mixed feelings. I would imagine ending your relationship with your girlfriend, to get back with the true love of your life, might have something to do with that. Chloe is extremely popular with your fans. Astrid... well, not so much.'

'This is all bull, Ellen!'

'Yes, Tate. I know that, but I'm not the one in control of these articles. I also can't control what your fans read, or what they believe. So, back to my first question. When were you going to tell me?'

Tate grabs the page out of Ellen's hands and glares at the photo. It was taken at Luke's house last night. 'There's nothing to explain. I can't stand this fucking woman. You know that. She ambushed me at Luke's wedding and again at Pippa's party last night. Tried to convince me to give us another shot. I said no, Ellen, I swear. I love Chloe. I'm not going to do anything to fuck that up.'

'Yes, but you have to see how it looks to the rest of the judgemental world. Chloe moved out, and a short time later you're seen with Astrid. It's not painting you in a fantastic light.'

'You think I care about that? Chloe's going to see this. It's the last fucking thing we need right now.' He gets up and leans on the sink as he stares into the garden. 'Someone took that picture on purpose. I was walking away from her when she launched herself at me. The hug barely lasted more than a second. That's it. And I left a few minutes later with Gregg.'

Ellen sighs and places the paper on the counter. 'I know you, Tate. I know how you feel about Chloe, but this is giving out mixed signals to the rest of the world. And Astrid wasn't someone Vox was entirely on board with you dating anyway. I didn't tell you this at the time, but she approached quite a few papers after your overdose, offering to sell them your story.'

Tate shouldn't be surprised to hear that, but it still hurts like a kick to the gut.

'We're trying to protect you. I mean that. She made quite a bit on you. A truly disgusting human, taking advantage of your situation like that.'

He nods. Too fucking right. 'So what happens now?'

'I need you to get dressed. Anthony and his team want to see you.'

He groans as he looks up at her. 'Oh that's not good.' The owner of Vox only ever calls people in when he's seriously unhappy. 'You think he's going to drop us?'

'He just wants to talk to you, face to face. I seriously doubt they'd drop the band from the label. You're earning them a pretty penny at the moment. We just need to figure out how to deal with this.'

'Yeah, but it's been nonstop bad publicity. I cost them a fortune when I overdosed. This won't help.'

'Don't stress about it, Tate. Get dressed and we'll see what he has to say.'

'But I need to talk to Chloe.'

'Anthony first, then by all means, talk to Chloe.' Her face softens as she smiles at him. 'Forgive my bluntness but you look terrible. Are you okay?'

'No, I'm not fucking okay,' he snaps. 'Sorry. I'm just... I need to sort things out with Chloe and this fucking Astrid thing isn't going to help that.'

'Chloe knows you would never go back to Astrid. Anyone who knows you, won't doubt that.'

He grabs the page and holds it up to her. 'There's a picture of her dumb-ass boyfriend hugging his ex, all over the press and social. Whether she believes me or not, she's going to have to look at this. It's online forever. Fucking bitch!' He slams his fist onto the counter top. 'I knew she was up to something. I've heard nothing for months and *accidentally* bump into her twice in the space of a few weeks.'

'Is there anything I can do to help?'

'Turn back time a few weeks, so I don't fuck up in the first place?'

She packs her files away and stands up. 'If only I had that ability. With what you four go through, it's sorely needed. Get dressed. Let's get this over with, so you can talk to Chloe.'

Dillon

Dillon comes back to consciousness thanks to a heavy hammer knocking repeatedly against the side of his head. He groans and licks his lips. God he feels shite. He doesn't usually suffer from hangovers. The mix of pills he took are probably to blame. He's going to kill himself one day if he's not careful.

He opens his eyes and smiles when he sees Luke asleep beside him. Suddenly the headache doesn't seem too bad. Waking up beside Luke is the perfect hangover cure.

Luke's dark brown hair is tousled and standing up in dishevelled spikes. Dillon's eyes move down to admire the irritatingly addictive piercing under Luke's bottom lip. Lips he's thought about kissing more than once.

Then there's Luke's body. It may be hidden under a grey tight fitting t-shirt, but Dillon knows it. He's committed it to memory. That perfectly sculpted rock hard body covered in tattoos which highlights every ridge and dip.

Luke takes a deep breath and the t-shirt presses against his pecs, the piercings in his nipples straining against the thin material for a moment. Like Tate, he has both pierced with a bar, and Dillon has dreamt of licking those piercings too many fucking times. All said and done, the guitarist is fucking gorgeous.

He curses himself and slowly turns away from Luke. He's one sick fuck. Luke is his friend. He's been there for him through so much shit. The guy doesn't deserve for Dillon to be thinking about him like this.

And there's the small issue of him being married.

And straight.

And his best friend.

He has to stop doing this to himself. Luke is with Pippa. End of story. It's never, ever, going to happen. All he's doing is driving himself crazy.

Feeling utterly disgusted with himself, he slides out of bed and decides to shower in the spare room, so he doesn't wake Luke. Using the wall to support himself, he drags his sorry ass down the corridor to the spare room.

He had slept in the same bed as Luke, after he'd fucked a random woman in a store room.

God he's disgusting. Seriously fucked up. He got himself into a state, then dragged Luke into his sordid night. He doesn't remember a lot of what happened after he left Rebecca or Rachel or whatever. He does know that Jace wouldn't have called Luke, unless Dillon had insisted.

He strips out of his clothes and steps into the shower, turning the water on full. He scrubs his skin, trying to cleanse the previous night from his body, as well as his memory.

Luke doesn't deserve to be his crutch every time he takes things too far. The problem is, his brain fucks him over every time. He's got this inbuilt need to call on his friend - no matter how embarrassing the situation.

Dillon groans and looks down at his dick. The damn thing wants Luke as much as he does. All he has to do is think about Luke and his body gears up for something that will never happen. The circle of piercings around the tip are digging into him, doing nothing to calm him, or it, down. He needs to deal with it. No choice.

He fists his cock and runs his thumb over the piercings in the head. Not for the first time, his brain takes him on a fucked up ride. Instead of his thumb rubbing precum over the black piercings, it's a tongue. Luke's tongue.

He shouldn't be thinking like this. It's not right, but his mind, his body, they both need Luke. It's so fucked up, but lately, thinking of Luke is the only way he can come. Thinking about Luke's lips around his dick, sucking him until he comes in his mouth. Then Dillon would return the favour.

Fuck, he wants Luke's dick in his mouth so badly. Wants to run his tongue over Luke's balls, to feel the soft flesh under his tongue as he licks his way up Luke's dick, before sliding him deep into his throat.

Dillon's fist pumps faster, his hips joining in, as his mind assaults him with the image of him on his knees in front of Luke. Of locking eyes with Luke as he uses his tongue and mouth to drive Luke insane. Of watching Luke's body clench and release, his eight pack rolling, as he pumps into Dillon's mouth, rubbing his dick against the piercing in Dillon's tongue.

As the fantasy plays out in his mind, Dillon wraps his other hand around his balls, squeezing them firmly. He needs to come, but not yet. He doesn't want this to end. Doesn't want to come back to his painfully lonely reality.

The pressure builds in his balls but he refuses to let up, pumping his fist, swiping his thumb over his piercings with every draw of his hand.

In his mind, Luke is still fucking his mouth, his firm body covered in a fine sheen of sweat, highlighting the stunning tattoos as his hips thrust, driving his dick deep into Dillon's throat.

Dillon drops his head back against the shower wall. His body is vibrating with the tension, his own hips thrusting in time with his hand.

Not yet. It can't end yet.

His balls throb in his hand. His dick like stone, the piercings tugging against the most sensitive part of his body, as he runs his thumb over them.

In the fucked up fantasy playing out in his mind, Luke takes control. Dillon prefers to be in charge, but he'll submit to Luke any day. He fists Dillon's hair, holding his head steady as he thrusts harder into Dillon's mouth. Dillon chokes on Luke's thick cock, but Luke is relentless, his hips driving his dick further down Dillon's throat. He digs his fingers into Luke's ass cheeks, steadying himself as Luke fucks his mouth.

'Look at me,' Luke commands. Dillon peers up at the impressive body towering over him. Luke's brown eyes lock on to him as he moves faster, making Dillon gag with each powerful thrust. 'You're going to swallow it all.'

Dillon whimpers as Luke's body bucks against him. Luke comes down the back of his throat. His hips continue to pump as his dick pulses in Dillon's mouth.

Back in the real world, unable to hold back any longer, Dillon releases his balls and bites his bottom lip, as he comes hard against the shower wall. He tips forward, bracing himself with one hand, while his other continues to pump his dick.

The orgasm keeps on coming, powered by the seriously hot fantasy playing in his head. He presses his face against the side of his outstretched arm, desperate to muffle the shout.

If he was alone he'd be loud. Fuck, he'd roar the place down. But with Luke still asleep down the corridor, he stays quiet. Which just makes the orgasm so much more intense.

His dick finally decides it's done, so he releases it and clenches his fist, thumping it against his leg, as his body shudders.

That was one of the most intense orgasms he's had for a hell of a long time. That's one hell of an imagination he has. One hell of a self-sabotaging, fucked up imagination. He's not doing himself any favours letting his mind run away like that. But he can't help it.

He slams his fist against his thigh again. What the hell is wrong with him? This can't be normal. The all-consuming guilt that hits when he jerks off, or has sex, can't be normal. But that's what sex is like for him. It's something he needs. A basic function he craves.

Until after.

Once he comes, all that's left is disgust, shame, or sometimes no feelings at all. Just emptiness. He's not sure which is worse.

He watches his cum slowly slide down the glass wall of the shower and his stomach hardens. Right now he's disgusted at himself. He used his friend to get himself off. It doesn't matter that it was all in his head. That nearly makes it worse. The Luke in his head isn't the real one. Luke will never be with him. Not like that.

After rinsing off his now quiet dick, and the shower, he dries quickly and curses himself. In his rush to leave Luke he'd not taken any clothes with him.

He wraps a towel around his waist and walks down the corridor back to his room, glancing at the door to his playroom as he passes. He might have to start calling in subs again to take his mind off Luke. Before the whole prison fiasco, sex was a daily thing for him. And that was on a slow day. But since he was released, he's lost the taste for it.

He wasn't being big headed when he told Gregg he's good at it. He's seriously good. He has a list of partners desperate to spend time with him again and again.

Or at least he did.

He hadn't turned on *that* phone since he got out. A part of him didn't want to know if his voicemail was full... or empty.

He comes to a stop at the door to the kitchen. Luke is standing at the counter making coffee, looking fucking incredible as always. 'Morning. How's the head?'

Dillon immediately thinks back to the shower and his throat tightens. He nods as he gets his head back on track. 'Yeah, not too

192

bad,' he lies. It's killing him. 'I'll just grab some clothes.'

'Coffee?'

'Yeah. Thanks.'

He hurries into his bedroom and throws on a pair of black jeans and a black tank top before joining Luke at the counter. They spend a few minutes drinking their coffee in silence. He should offer Luke breakfast at least, but he doesn't think he can stomach even looking at food let alone cooking anything.

'Thanks for staying last night.'

Luke smiles as he sips his coffee. 'No problem. I would prefer you didn't keep getting into that state though. You're going to kill yourself someday.'

Dillon nods, not liking the guilt that hits him. 'Yeah. Sorry. Just had a bad day.' To add to the bad day before that, and the day before that, and every fucking day.

'Can you promise me something?'

Dillon peers at him over the rim of his coffee mug. 'What?'

'We're heading off in three days. Can you lay off until we get back? The performances this weekend are important.'

'I'm not going to screw it up for the band.'

Luke places his cup on the counter and turns fully on the bar stool to face him. 'This has nothing to do with Gregg, Tate, and me. It's about you. This is about you getting back on stage where you belong. I don't want you to screw it up, for you.'

'I know. I'm sorry. My head's just been all over the place lately. I'm thinking of calling it off. The shows I mean. I'm all over the fucking place. No one wants to see a car crash on stage.'

'You're being dramatic. You need to get back on stage. Besides,' he adds with a seriously sexy smile. 'You've always been a car crash. It's never stopped you from being popular.'

'Thanks,' he replies sarcastically, trying not to focus on Luke's mouth. 'Why am I still friends with you?'

'Because you're unbelievably difficult to be friends with and no one else will have you.'

'Again, thanks.'

Luke winks at him, then sips his coffee again. 'Do you remember anything from last night?'

Something in his face worries Dillon. He knows he can talk shite when he's off his head, but the way Luke is looking at him makes him wonder if he said a little too much. 'Bits. Why?'

'You mentioned something that happened in prison. You said the bruises are gone.'

Fuck, fuck, fuck. Dillon takes a mouthful of coffee while he gets his thoughts in order. 'Just my usual drunken shite.'

'You were beaten up.'

'No.' Luke raises his eyebrows but doesn't say anything. 'Fuck! Okay, I was roughed up a little. I was able to handle it. I'm fine.'

'Why didn't you say anything?'

He gets up and puts his empty cup in the dishwasher. He could do with something stronger to wake him up, but he's not about to take anything with Luke still here. 'Say what exactly?'

'Did you tell any of the guards?'

Dillon leans against the counter and laughs. 'Yeah right! Like that would have helped. It was a few bruised ribs. It's done. Move on. Please.'

Luke takes a laboured breath as he stares at him.

He needs Luke to go now. Images of what he did in the shower come back, turning his stomach. There's one sure fire way of getting Luke to leave.

'I've got someone coming around in a bit. I better make myself look half decent.'

That does the trick. Luke nods and puts his cup in the dishwasher. 'Good luck with that. You look terrible.'

Dillon sneers at him. 'Fuck off!' Luke grins and grabs his coat from the couch.

'You want to meet up later?'

Dillon shakes his head. 'I'll be tied up for a bit. No pun intended,' he adds with a wink. 'Besides, you should probably spend some time with Pippa.' He desperately wants to see him later, but he can't keep doing this. He needs to take a step back. Let Luke spend time with his stuck up wife.

'Yeah. You're probably right.' Luke wanders over to the door and opens it. 'Call you later. And you're not bailing on the performances. Just lay off the drink and definitely the drugs. Please.'

'What about you?'

'What do you mean?'

'Are you laying off?'

Luke turns his attention to the floor, then slowly nods. 'Yeah.'

'Fuck off! No you're not. Bit rich you throwing out the advice when you're using yourself.'

'A bit of hash every now and again. Far cry from what you do, so don't even go there with me. Do you even know what you took last night?'

He doesn't, and that's not on. He should know.

'I don't want to have a fight with you, but I'm worried. Lately you don't seem to be able to get through the day without drinking, or downing some pills.'

'Go back to your wife, Luke. I'm grand. I'll give you a shout later, okay?'

Luke looks as if he's about to argue, but has second thoughts. Dillon watches Luke walk over to the elevator and disappear inside. Dillon slowly closes his front door and locks it. He turns and leans against the door, not sure what to do with himself. He desperately wants a drink but there's nothing in the flat.

Which means he has to go out.

Or he could do something useful for a change. Luke is right. He's going from one drunken stupor to the next. That's how things went downhill for Tate. It began with a few drinks, then some drugs, and escalated to heroin and an overdose.

He's not as far gone as Tate was. He knows that, but buying and taking random shit, from random dealers, will end badly if he's not careful.

His attention falls on the photo of his sisters and him, at one of his concerts. He won't do that to them. He won't let them find him minutes from death. Not again.

Clara and Eva made him promise never to do that to them again, and he intends to keep his word. It was twenty odd years ago, but they haven't got over it. And he hates himself for putting them through that.

Dillon grabs his phone from his bedroom and calls Clara. He's been dodging her since he got out of prison, but that ends now. He needs some normal, or he's going to go off the rails pretty fucking spectacularly.

'Dill?'

'Hey.'

His sister pauses for a second. 'Hey? You've been avoiding me and Eva since you were sentenced, and all you can give me is a hey?'

'Sorry. I...' He what? What excuse can he give for ignoring the only family he has left? He was ashamed. Embarrassed. Terrified he'd let them down yet again.

He adores his sisters. After his parents kicked him out, Clara took him in. She's fifteen years older than him and Eva ten years, so he's very much the baby of the family. But neither of his sisters ever treated him like he was a nuisance, or a bother. Not once. Not even when he deserved it.

The girls had been a rock to him, always at the end of a phone, always ready to listen, or just to let him come around and eat their food.

He didn't see Eva as often any more. Probably his fault. She's living in Cork, with her husband and three sons. She's got her hands full. He should make more of an effort to visit her.

'I guess I didn't know what to say to you,' he admits, truthfully.

'I get it Dill. But come on. Do you really think I'd be shocked by anything you do, at this stage? The part that upset me most, was you locking me out. I know you don't like sharing what's going on in your head, but you should know by now I'll never judge you. And believe me, you've thrown your fair share of interesting moments at us over the years. Don't shut me out. Or Eva. We both still love you, even though you are a stubborn, moody, eejit most of the time.'

'I don't mean to be.'

'I know. You're so good at it though.'

He laughs and it sounds strange. He can't remember the last time he laughed. 'And you're good at kicking my ass when I need it.'

'Oh absolutely! I'm an expert at this stage.' She goes quiet for a moment. 'Dill, are you okay?'

He closes his eyes and shakes his head. 'No, not really.'

'I've made too much food as usual. I'll expect you in about half an hour. Don't be late. Do you have any rock star plans for tomorrow?'

'No. Don't think so.'

'Great. Bring an overnight bag. You won't be fit to go anywhere after all this food.'

'Thanks, Clara.'

'I'm your big sister. It's my job to look out for you, no matter how much it irritates you. Now get a move on or I'll start without you.'

'See you in a bit.'

'Perfect. Oh and park that flashy Mustang of yours in the garage. I don't want the neighbourhood curtain twitchers staring at the house for the next day while you're here.'

'Will do. Thanks, Clara.'

'Dill, we're family. Stop thanking me. Now get moving, or I'll have to sample the chocolate cake, and you know I have no self control!'

'Put the spoon down! I'm on my way. Love you.'

'Love you too, Dill.'

He ends the call, feeling a little better about life in general. Maybe he can get through the day after all, without touching alcohol.

22

Tate

Tate pulls up at the traffic light and unclenches his fingers from around the steering wheel. The meeting with Anthony, and another six less than cheery people, had gone on for over an hour. They were going to keep working with the band, that was never really an issue.

Broken brought them in a hell of a lot of money. If they survived Dillon going to prison, Tate being photographed with Astrid isn't a big deal really. It was more the image of the band they were worried about. Being seen with Astrid so soon after *allegedly* dumping Chloe, was going to hit his relatively clean reputation.

They wanted the Astrid thing quashed, and for Tate to make a public statement about what really went on. Yeah, he's looking forward to that one.

He only wishes it were that easy to fix things with Chloe. Trying to figure out where his head is at, is difficult enough, without having half the fucking country watching him.

They're arranging for the band to do a few TV appearances over the next few weeks which will mean him having to go away. Timing couldn't be worse, but he doesn't want to fuck things up for Gregg, Luke, and Dillon by refusing.

He curses when he catches himself scratching the inside of his left elbow. It's getting worse.

When the fuck did he get so messed up? His job was hardly easy. They worked so hard to get where they are. It was stressful, tiring, and emotional at times. Since Dara sent him that fucking letter and opened the floodgates on his fucked up memories, he can't handle confrontations. A year ago he'd have laughed off the whole Astrid mess and moved on. Now he's over thinking it, and back to scratching his arm again.

He slams his hand against the steering wheel. 'Fuck!' He can't see Chloe when he's like this. Tate pulls over to the side of the road and searches through his contacts for his sponsor's number.

But it's not his sponsor's number he finds first.

It's Eddie's.

He stares at the number, as the traffic speeds past him on the motorway. What began as just one hit, had turned to three over the last two days. It's not like the last time. Last time he'd gone from hit to hit, no break in between, with no time for his body to recover.

He's still in control of this. Still has a firm hold on it. It's just for another few days. Just until the Astrid thing it put to bed and he can sort things out with Chloe. Then he'll be able to sleep again. Maybe another few hits and he can delete Eddie's number forever.

After seeing Chloe, he has nothing else planned for the rest of the day. He can meet with Eddie, go home, and get some peace. Get some sleep. Get it out of his system before he heads off to the UK.

No one will know. No one has to know. It's not like they'd understand. They'd assume he's relapsed. But he hasn't - not really.

There's just so much going around in his head. So much noise he needs quietened. He hits the call button and closes his eyes, as he silently begs for the call to be answered.

'Well, well, well. If it's not my favourite rock star.'

'Hey, I need you to sort me out again.'

Eddie is quiet for a long time before he speaks again. 'Again? Are you sure?'

'Is this a new part of your sales technique, cause it's not great?'

'Like I said to you before, I don't need a sales technique. You rang me, remember? Don't have a go at me for checking.'

'I'm sure.'

'Very well. You home?'

'Not there.'

'Where are you?'

Tate looks out the window, trying to get his bearings. 'Near Sandymount.'

'Okay. I'll meet you at the car park by the beach. I'm five minutes away.'

'Thanks.'

He ends the call and pulls back into the traffic. Once he gets what he needs from Eddie, he'll delete his number. One more hit to get him through the rest of the day. Tomorrow is bound to be better.

Chloe

Chloe takes her cup of tea outside to the garden, and leans on the fence overlooking the beach. No sign of Tate down there. Every time she comes out here, she half expects to see him thundering along the beach on Jove.

It seems like only yesterday she first saw him on this very beach, on his stunning horse. He had captivated her from that first moment. Watching him strip down to his boxers and go for a swim, hadn't turned her off in any way.

She can't remember ever wanting anyone as much as she wanted Tate that first day — and every day since then. She hates being without him. Hates waking up without his arms around her, hugging her close to him. Misses listening to him singing in the shower every morning. Misses coming home to him and telling him about her day and hearing about his. In the short time they were together, they had become such a large part of each other's lives.

This wasn't supposed to happen.

Even when he was at his lowest, she never contemplated being without him.

She smiles when her gran joins her at the fence. 'Are you okay?'

'I don't know. I miss him.'

Her gran squeezes her arm. 'Of course you do. And I'm positive he's missing you too. Chloe, I saw the photo.'

Chloe sips her tea as she checks the beach again, just in case he suddenly appears. The photo of Tate and Astrid was the first thing she saw when she checked her social accounts this morning. She knows Tate. Knows without a doubt he would never get back with Astrid, but seeing the photo had hurt.

'You know it's not true, don't you?'

'Of course I do, Gran. It's no secret how much he dislikes Astrid. Luke and Pippa were having a party at their house. Astrid is a friend of Pippa. She was bound to be there. She appeared at the wedding too. I just wish... it wasn't a nice thing to see. You know, Tate hugging someone else.' She sighs and looks back at the beach. 'But if we can't find a way through this, I'll have to get used to seeing him with other women.'

'One step at a time. There's nothing to say you won't get through this. It's only been a few days.'

'He's going away with the band. He'll be going out and...' Chloe hates the jealousy she's feeling. She has no right to keep him to herself when she's the one who left him.

'He loves you. There's no way he's going to do anything until you two decide what's happening. Don't let thoughts like that influence your decision.'

'Easier said than done. Oh ignore me. I'm all over the place.'

'I'll go and get lunch started.'

'Thanks.'

They both turn around when they hear a car pull into the driveway. Her gran smirks and nods to Tate's truck. 'Speak of the devil. I'll leave you to it.'

Tate climbs out of his truck and walks over to her. He looks incredible. Tired, but incredible.

'Hey.'

He smiles, but it's one of his fake smiles. 'Hi. You saw it, didn't you.' Tate leans on the fence beside her and twists the ring on his thumb.

The breeze sends his scent of sandalwood and leather in her direction, and it's like a comforting blanket wrapping around her.

'Yeah. I saw it this morning.'

'Fuck!'

'I know it's not true.'

He turns around to face her. 'What? You do?'

Chloe laughs. 'Of course! Tate, I've been with you long enough to know the difference between your *I want you* face and your *I'm trying not to deck you* face. Anyone with half a brain can see you were less than happy with her in that photo. I'm just glad you didn't actually hit her.'

This time the smile is genuine. 'You have no idea what a relief it is to hear you say that.'

She reaches over and takes his hand. 'Don't get me wrong. I'm less than impressed that she tried to pull a stunt like that, and brought our private life into her fantasy. Whatever is going on between you and me, is our business. And yes, I know there's no such thing as private when it comes to dating you, but I just would have preferred it wasn't something either Pippa or Astrid were talking about.'

He rubs the back of her hand as he nods. 'I know. I'm completely with you on that. A part of me is thinking Pippa pulled Astrid in to fuck with me, but I'm probably being paranoid.'

'Why would Pippa do that? I know you two don't see eye-to-eye, but deliberately messing with you like that?'

He shrugs as he looks out over the horizon. 'Okay, so I may have played down what went on between myself and Pippa a few years ago.'

Chloe waits, a little worried about what he's talking about. She thought the verbal fight Tate and Pippa had, was bad enough. She dreads to think how much worse it might have been.

Tate glances at her, before looking back at the beach. 'She came on to me earlier that night.'

'She what!'

'She'd been drinking a fair bit and followed me upstairs when I went to the toilet. I had to forcefully remove her hands. She didn't take it well. When we went back downstairs she started laying into the band. Having a bitch that we had to go away again. We argued, and I called her a money grabbing leech.'

'God, she's unbelievable. Does Luke know?'

'Fuck no! I thought about it, but I put the whole night down to too much drink. So anyway, she really doesn't like me. Feeling is mutual too. Getting all buddy with Astrid is a good blow.'

'I'm sorry, Tate. It's a mess.'

He snorts. 'Too fucking right.' He peers over his shoulder at her. 'I'll fix it though. I promise.'

'I know you will. How are you, apart from all that, I mean.'

'Missing you.' He looks at her and smiles. 'A lot. How are you?'

'Missing you too, but being here is helping.'

'I'm glad. Do you think you're ready to come home?'

She knew it would come up at some stage, but still doesn't have an answer that he's going to like. Being here is helping, but the problem is still there. She still wants to have children and, unless he says otherwise, he doesn't.

'I'll take that silence as a no.'

'It's not a definite no, Tate. I didn't leave the house so I could just think about losing the baby. I'm trying to figure out what I want out of life. This is a big deal.'

'You don't think I know that!'

His sudden flash of anger surprises her. It usually takes a lot to get him wound up. 'This is difficult for both of us. I'm not enjoying—'

'Then put an end to it,' he interrupts. 'Come home. Go upstairs and pack your bags and I'll bring you home.'

'Not yet. Nothing has changed Tate. We both want different things.'

'I told you I'd have kids with you if that's what you want. What else do you want from me, huh? What else can I say to you? You want me to sign a fucking contract or something?'

She takes a step back from him. This isn't Tate. Not her Tate. He rarely raises his voice at her or at anyone. He's more of a silent brooder than a hot head. 'I think it's best if we take a few minutes. We're both emotional.'

'What the fuck do you expect, Chloe? I love you. I'd do anything for you. Do anything to make this right, but you're pulling the strings here.'

'You're being unfair. That's not what I'm doing.'

'That's what it feels like. What do you want me to do?'

'There's nothing you can do. I want children. You don't. Please tell me you see that's a big problem?'

'I told you I'd have kids with you!'

'Oh great. Thanks! Let's start a family and raise kids whose father only had them, because he felt *obliged*. I honestly thought you'd be the last person to say that. I thought you'd understand how important it is, to be wanted by your parents.'

He clenches his jaw as he faces her, the anger barely contained. 'You saying I'd be like him?'

'Of course that's not what I'm saying! But surely you can see that it won't work? We either both want children, or we both don't. I'm not going to force you to do this, if it's not what you want.'

When he scratches his arm, alarm bells ring. He hasn't done that for months. But he's bound to be stressed. She is. And upset. And now, worrying about him.

He catches her looking at him scratching, so stops. 'So I have to sign up to this, to agree right now? If I don't, you'll what? Walk away. Leave me. End our relationship?'

'That's not what I want to do.'

'Then don't!'

She shakes her head, unable to form any words that will make this better for either of them. Without a word, he turns and walks back to his truck.

'Tate...'

He stops and look sideways at her. 'What, Chloe?'

'I'm worried about you.'

He laughs and shakes his head. 'You don't have to be. Let me know when you make up your mind about me.'

She watches in stunned silence as he climbs into his truck, and pulls out of the driveway, wheels spinning, as he tears down the road.

Bria comes back to their table with a tray of coffees and a couple of pastries, placing one of each in front of Chloe. They'd managed to find an empty corner table in the coffee shop.

Since she began dating Tate, she found people were beginning to recognise her more often. Bria too, thanks to being Tate's sister and dating Gregg. The attention is still hit and miss, but leaning more towards the hit as the months go by.

Bria takes a sip of her latte before sitting back in the chair and crossing her legs. 'You look terrible.'

'Oh wow! Thanks,' Chloe says, laughing.

'That was a bit harsh, sorry.'

'No, it's fine. I feel terrible. I had a massive row with Tate yesterday.' She rubs her face, as his harsh words come back to her. 'He was so angry.'

Bria leans on the table, frowning at Chloe's statement. 'He was angry? About what?'

'About what I'm doing to him.'

'Excuse me?'

'That's reading between the lines. We were talking fine, then he just flipped on me. I've never seen him like that, Bria.'

And she never wants to see him like that again. He has a temper. She knows that. She'd heard enough stories from the guys about their tousles over the years. Never in her wildest dreams did she imagine being on the receiving end of that.

He scared her. Not that she was scared *of* him - not for a moment. But, she's scared he's not dealing with everything that's being thrown at him. And she's to blame for some of that. She knows that, but allowing this issue between them to continue, would do them more harm than good long term.

'He can be a grumpy git at the best of times but not that bad,' Bria says. 'Then again, I'm not surprised he's out of sorts. And, that's not me having a go at you,' she adds quickly. 'It's just bad timing. I don't suppose you were able to figure things out with him, before he flew off the handle?'

Chloe shakes her head. 'I wish. He wasn't listening to what I was saying. He thinks I'm controlling this entire situation and leaving him hanging.'

Bria winces. 'Ouch. That's a bit harsh.'

'Is it?' She picks at a piece of her chocolate muffin. 'It was my decision to leave.'

'Whoa there. From what you told me, you had to go. The whole children conversation is a big one. And it's kind of important.'

'Have you had it with Gregg?'

'Not until this happened between you and Tate,' she admits. 'Seeing what you two are going through, sort of spurred on the conversation.'

'And I presume you're both on the same page?'

Bria nods. 'We are. We'd like that in our future, but we've only been a couple for a few weeks. Though, I guess knowing him all my life makes it seems a lot longer.'

'I probably should have had the talk with Tate long before now, but it didn't enter my mind.'

'Yeah, but the year with Tate was a bit crazy. I'm not surprised you didn't get to that topic.' She reaches across and rests her hand on Chloe's. 'Don't let his moods throw you off track. You've been through a lot. You need to figure out what you want. And in spite of what he thinks, so does he. I know you love him, and I know he loves you. You're right though. This is a big deal and he needs to face it.'

'Tate face something?' She tears a chunk from the muffin and pops it in her mouth. 'Maybe in the past he could, but recently, he clams up and hits the gym. Every single time.'

'Good point. If it helps, Gregg said he's been off with him too. I think his father dying has hit him hard.'

'Of course it has. He's not talking about it though. Every time I tried, he shut me down.'

'Same. Mum and Dad gave it a shot a few days ago but he changed the conversation.'

'Is he going to his meetings?'

Bria shrugs as she finishes her drink. 'He says yes.'

Hardly a definite confirmation.

'Listen, I'll give you a little insight into my stubborn brother. When he gets all defensive, you've already lost the fight. It's like he stops listening and is operating on auto-pilot. The only way you'll be able to have a civilised, productive conversation is when he's calm.'

'Any idea when that will be? He hasn't been calm since he heard that Gregg was kidnapped.'

'Don't remind me of that fun time,' Bria mutters, drily. 'That woman has a hell of a lot to answer for.'

Chloe sees something in her face that gives her reason to pause. 'Bria? Are you okay?'

She nods, then shakes her head. 'Not really.'

'Are you and Gregg okay?'

'Since moving into Dillon's house we're so much better. We're comfortable there. Not looking over our shoulder or wondering if someone is watching us. But... I don't know. I guess I shouldn't have been expecting a quick fix. Chloe, can I ask you something? It might seem totally insensitive, but how do you deal with Tate's nightmares?'

Chloe puts the pieces together. Of course Gregg would be having nightmares. How could he not? If a psycho stalker kidnaps, drugs, and tries to kill you, you'd get nightmares too. 'How bad are they?'

'It's not every night, but more often than not. It's strange. We both have the same nightmare. Gregg in the water, slowly disappearing under the sea. I hate it Chloe. Hate that he's living through it again and again. Hate that we both are.

'He's talking about the dreams, thankfully. And about his fear of water, which we're working on. He also let me give him his insulin shot this morning which is massive. He hasn't let anyone touch his insulin since she tried to kill him with it.'

'I don't blame him.'

Bria nods. 'I just hate seeing him like that. Gregg is so upbeat. Always is. When he screams in his sleep I just fall to pieces, Chloe. I need to be strong for him, but it's so difficult.'

'I know. I think when they dream about what happened, it gives us a peak into their memories that we never get to see at any other stage. It's unfiltered. Painful.'

Bria slumps back in the chair, and gazes out the window at the pedestrians pushing their way along Grafton Street. 'So I'm guessing no tips?'

'Sorry. All we can do is make sure they keep talking, and be there for them however they need us.'

At least Bria is with Gregg to help him. By leaving Tate alone, is she giving them time to decide what they want, or has she just abandoned him when he needs her the most?

23

Luke

Luke washes his face and peers up at the mirror over the sink. He feels rough. He's exhausted and in desperate need of a few hours in bed. He's spent most of the night watching over Dillon, making sure he was still breathing.

He's seriously worried about him, but there's not a lot he can do about it. Dillon has been using drugs in some form or other for years. Not as bad as Tate has been, but it was constant. And he's got a feeling it's getting worse.

He jumps, as Pippa pounds on the bathroom door. 'I ordered in your favourite breakfast. It's getting cold.'

'Coming.'

Just for once he'd be happy with a bowl of cereal, but Pippa preferred to either order in, or go out for breakfast. Waste of money and time, but it's what she wants, so he'll go along with it.

He takes a clean t-shirt from his drawer and puts it on, pausing for a second to examine his reflection in the full length mirror in the bedroom.

He's losing weight. His clothes are a little looser on his body. No surprise with all the vomiting. He thought it was a stomach bug, but he's been throwing up on and off for weeks. He probably should go to the doctor about it, if it keeps going any longer.

Luke trudges downstairs and joins Pippa at the ridiculously monstrous kitchen table. She pushes the plate of pancakes towards him. 'Eat.'

The pancakes on the plate are probably the most expensive pancakes in Dublin, but he hates them. Pancakes are her favourite. Not his. If he's being really honest, he doesn't know what his favourite breakfast is.

'What's wrong?'

He smiles at Pippa across the table. Her long golden hair is out and curled today. Her make up is perfect and her outfit new, as far as he can tell. She's beautiful. So far out of his league, that he still has no idea how he ever attracted her attention.

'Luke? Are you listening?'

'What?'

She rolls her eyes and drops her fork to her plate with a clatter. 'I'm talking to myself as usual. Am I boring you?'

He shakes his head quickly. 'No. I'm sorry.'

'You look tired.'

'I'm fine.'

'Maybe you should cancel this weekend.'

Luke's heart instantly beats a little faster. It's a common occurrence whenever work comes up. He can't help getting nervous about how the conversation will go. 'I'm fine. Really.'

She picks up her fork and continues eating her breakfast. 'I don't know why Ellen is bothering with this weekend. Dillon's career is over. No one is going to want to see him on stage after what he did at our wedding. And then there's the whole Tate situation.'

'What Tate situation?'

'Chloe of course. He dumps her, then gets photographed with Astrid. He's hardly a good role model.'

'He didn't leave Chloe. She just needs some time alone.'

'Exactly,' she says, 'Time alone, away from Tate. That's not a good basis for a relationship.'

Luke swallows deeply, then takes a piece of pancake, chewing slowly. He knows it's just going to come up again, so he's not keen on eating too much.

'Are you ever going to see them for what they are?'

He swallows the food. 'Please, Pippa. I don't want to do this again. They're my friends and I have to go this weekend. I want to go. I miss performing.'

'I know you do, but I don't want you being overshadowed by the others. With a little effort on your part, you could be so good.'

'Could be?'

'Tate is the lead singer, so he'll always have the majority of the spotlight. Gregg's personality alone ensures he's instantly liked by everyone. Dillon... well, he goes overboard to get attention. You don't stand out from the others.'

'Right.' The pancake is desperate to come back up, so he swallows to keep it in place. He thought he was okay on stage. Thought he could hold his own.

Pippa clears away her empty plate, glaring at his barely touched breakfast, before clearing it away too. 'I've spoken to you about this before. Look at you, Luke. There's nothing wow about you.'

He breathes in through his nose and out his mouth, but the churning in his stomach is building. His wife thinks he looks boring. Is that what she's saying?

He looks down at his jeans and t-shirt. He always dressed like this. He feels comfortable dressed like this. Did she want him in designer shirts and slacks? That's not him.

She sits on the chair beside him and rubs her hand along his leg. 'Don't do that sad face. I hate that sad face. You know I'm just telling you the truth. I've accepted the tattoos and the piercings. You know how much I hate them, but I agreed to let you keep them, didn't I? Can you not just let me help you? With my help you could look so handsome.'

She straddles his lap and lifts his chin, so he's looking at her.

'You could be so much better than you are. Don't you want that?' She leans forward and kisses the side of his neck. 'Don't you want to make me happy?' Her fingers rake through his hair, her nails scraping against his scalp, as she sucks his earlobe. 'That's what you want, isn't it?'

'Of course it—'

Pippa kisses him, cutting off anything else he was going to say. Her tongue pushes into his mouth, her hand gripping the back of his head, drawing him closer.

When her other hand slides between them, moving closer to his crotch, he panics. He doesn't know why, but his body decides it's had enough. He pushes her off his knees and stands up, barely making it to the sink, before he throws up the pathetic piece of pancake.

Luke rinses his mouth and the sink, before turning to look at his wife. She's sitting on the chair he had occupied, until he needed to bolt. Her face is blank, which usually means he's upset her. Of course he has. She wanted to have sex with him and he threw up.

Luke sits on the chair next to her and tries to take her hands in his, but she pulls them away and rubs her arm. It's then he notices the scratch on the underside of her arm.

'I scratched my arm on the table when you threw me off your knees.'

'I'm sorry—'

The slap she gives him, knocks his head to the side, jarring his teeth. He says nothing. He knows better than to react to what she just did. It makes things so much worse.

'You're sorry? What for? For hurting me, or for throwing up when I touched you?'

'Both. But I didn't throw up because—'

'Because the thought of being with me turned your stomach? No. Of course not. Why would I think that?'

'It wasn't. I swear. I don't feel well today. That's all.'

'But you were well enough to spend the night with Dillon? You left me alone last night so you could mop up his vomit. Then when I try to do something nice for you, by getting breakfast and then wanting to be intimate with you, you shove me away and throw up. That's one way to make me feel wanted.'

Pippa pushes his hands away, when he reaches for her again.

'Don't Luke. To be honest I don't even want to see you right now. Go upstairs and do your packing for the trip with your beloved band.'

There's no point trying to explain himself any longer. She's too angry with him and he can't blame her. He nods and gets up.

'I am sorry.'

'You always are, Luke.'

He waits until he's in their ensuite before he touches his cheek. It stings like crazy. That was one hell of a slap. The whole side of his face is red. She doesn't usually hit his face. Then again, he hasn't needed to throw up after she touched him before.

Luke sits on the side of the bath and concentrates on his breathing. His stomach is in knots and his head is killing him.

What is he doing wrong? He loves Pippa. She loves him. So why does he continuously let her down? The thing is, it's not even the slap that's bothering him the most. It's what she said about him.

He's far from vain. Never ever sang his own praises, or thought he was anything special. But hearing that she felt the same had hurt. Maybe compared to Tate, Gregg, and Dillon he is forgettable.

He's a good musician though. He knows he is. And a good singer. He wouldn't be singing with Tate, unless he could enhance Tate's already incredible voice.

He gets up and goes into the walk in wardrobe. He pulls a heavy storage box from the bottom shelf and opens the lid. Inside are dozens of awards and plaques he has won as part of Broken. Number one songs. Number one albums. Best rock band. Best rock song. You name it, the band has won it.

He digs down to the bottom of the pile and carefully slides one award out. This one is just for him. Luke Daly. Not Broken Chords. He won rock guitarist of the year two years ago. He even beat Tate, which was still hard to believe. Tate is one hell of a guitarist.

But he'd done it.

He frowns as a drop of blood hits the golden guitar. He wipes his nose and stares at the blood on his fingers. He hasn't had a nose bleed for years. It's probably down to the slap. Using his t-shirt to catch the blood, he quickly packs the awards away, and goes back in to the bathroom, before he drips blood on the beige carpet.

'What happened?' Pippa asks when she comes upstairs.

He shakes his head, as he presses the tissue to his nose. 'Just a nose bleed. It's okay.'

Pippa takes the tissue from his hand and examines his nose. 'You didn't get blood on the carpet did you?'

'No. Caught it in time.'

'That's something.' She gets a fresh tissue and holds it under his nose. 'I did this when I slapped you.'

'It's fine.'

'I was just so upset at your reaction. Do you have any idea how much you hurt me? And I don't just mean the scratch. My husband threw up when I touched him! God, could you imagine what people would say if they found out.'

'That's not why—'

'I know, but it still hurts.'

'I'm so sorry. I love you, Pippa. I love being with you. You know that.'

She purses her lips and looks at his nose again, dabbing a fresh tissue against it. 'Words Luke. It's actions that speak louder.'

He reaches up to take her hand in his. 'I will make it up to you, Pippa. I'll show you, I promise. Just give me a chance, please.'

She leans over and kisses his cheek. 'Tell you what. You get cleaned up and meet me in the bedroom. I might let you apologise properly.' She winks, then throws the bloody tissue in the toilet, before walking out to the bedroom.

He wipes the blood from his face, then stands up straight. He'll give Pippa what she wants. It's the least he can do. Luke unbuckles the cuff from around each wrist, leaving them on the sink, then goes into the bedroom to apologise to his wife.

Tate

Tate stares out the window of the minibus as it travels along the motorway. The two shows Ellen arranged in the UK are the last thing he wants to do, but this is for Dillon. The bassist needs to get back on stage. He knows that feeling all too well himself. The sooner the four of them perform again, the better.

He just wishes he hadn't left Ireland while things are so uncertain between himself and Chloe. He checks his phone again. Still no messages. He sent her a text last night, saying that he was heading away for the weekend, and she'd replied, telling him to have a good time. That was it. No kisses. No emoji. Just a few words. Nothing to help him figure out where he stands with her.

Beside him, Gregg mutters in his sleep. The guy can sleep anywhere, which comes in handy in their line of business. Dillon and Luke are in the row behind him, both staring out the window, lost in their own thoughts.

They're struggling. Each of them are dealing with shit, and dealing badly as usual. No doubt Dillon is worried about appearing in public again. Luke looks about as shite as Tate feels. He's pale, tired, and quieter than he usually is. But Tate has enough going on in his own head, without bringing Luke's marital issues into the mix.

Not only has he not deleted Eddie's number from his phone, he called him twice more. He subconsciously rubs the inside of his arm.

He'd taken his last hit just before he got on the flight. He should be okay until he gets to the hotel. Eddie has arranged for one of his UK contacts to sort him out if he needs it. The way he's feeling right now, he'll need it.

Being stuck in this fucking bus isn't helping him relax. He feels cooped up and twitchy as hell. To distract himself, he puts on his headphones and plays some music. He lasts less than one song before he gives up on that idea.

'Stop with the damn squirming,' Gregg mutters beside him. 'Some of us are trying to sleep.'

'Sorry.'

Gregg opens one eye and squints at him. 'What's got you all agitated?'

'Nothing. I'm just bored.'

Gregg frowns at his watch and grimaces. 'Well we've got about an hour left, so why don't you try to get some sleep. It'll be a late one.'

Gregg closes his eyes again, and is snoring within a few minutes. Tate puts on his headphones again and closes his eyes. There's nothing he can do except wait out the next hour.

Tate finishes his fifth, maybe sixth, cup of black coffee still feeling as knackered as he did after his first. Crawling into bed, and not reappearing for a year is the only thing he wants to do.

Performing is a bad idea. He knows Dillon needs to get back on stage but it just feels wrong and he has no idea why. It's not helping that he's wound like a fucking spring.

He'd left a few messages for Chloe, but she hadn't got back to him yet. He'll be lucky if she even listens to them. He scratches his arm, as he paces the dressing room.

What the hell is he doing here? Why did he leave Ireland without at least trying to apologise to her? Why did he even lose it with her in the first place? He was the one with the problem - not her.

His attention falls on his bag. One of Eddie's contacts sorted him out before he left the hotel. It's fucking pathetic. He can't even make it through one day.

It's just because he's stressed. That's the only reason. If his life wasn't falling apart again, he wouldn't need it.

And he desperately needs it.

He glares over at the door when someone knocks, stopping him from opening his bag. With a quick look at the bag to make sure it's closed, Tate opens the door and smiles at Sam. It's entirely forced, but she seems to be convinced by it. 'Can I come in?'

He steps aside, closing the door behind her.

'Are you not getting dressed?'

Tate glances down at his bare chest, forgetting that he was meant to be getting dressed. 'Yeah. Sorry.' He quickly crosses his arms, terrified she'll see the marks on the inside of his elbow.

'You've got an hour before you're on, but they want you guys ready in about ten minutes, if that's okay.'

She passes him the black shirt from the chair, then checks her notes as he slips it on, rolling up his sleeves to just below his elbows. 'The guys ready?'

'Yep. We're just waiting on the main man.' He takes the offered belt and slides it into the loops on his black jeans. Sam is helping to get him dressed, and he couldn't care less. He's seriously off his game.

She knows it too, if she's babysitting him like she is.

As he buckles his belt, he catches her staring at him in the mirror over his shoulder. 'What?'

'Are you sure you're up for this?'

'I'm fine. We need to get Dillon back on the horse.'

'I know that, but you're going through—'

'Sam!' he interrupts a little harsher than he intended. 'Listen, I appreciate you looking out for me, but I can do this.'

She nods, but you'd have to be an idiot to think he's convinced her for a second. She just knows better than to argue with him. 'Ready for hair and make-up?'

'Yeah.' He grabs his mobile from the chair and glances at the screen. No new calls. No message. Nothing.

She said she needs time. What's the standard *need a break* time? Is he heading into a month of this shite? Two months? Longer?

He can't handle being in this limbo for much longer. Sam grunts as he barrels into her back. Lost in his head he hadn't noticed she'd stopped at a door down the corridor. 'Shit. I'm sorry. I was miles away.'

'It's fine, Tate.' She opens the door and ushers him inside.

'About fucking time,' Dillon mutters from the far side of the room.

'Yeah, sorry. I'm on a bit of a go slow today.'

Gregg keeps glancing over at him, as his hair is dealt with.

'What?'

'You look tired.'

'Yeah. Thanks for pointing that out. I'm about to go on TV, so it's great to know I look shite.'

The woman doing his hair, grins to herself, which doesn't improve his mood. Her fingers rake through his hair as she styles it, grating on his already well grated nerves. She's just doing her job, but he wishes she'd get the fuck away from him.

'I didn't say you look like shite. Stop being dramatic.'

'I'm not being dramatic. Whatever, just sit still so she can fix that mop of hair. Good luck to her.'

Gregg holds up his middle finger, but keeps quiet until the team have made them camera ready. Tate frowns at his reflection. He has to give it to the hair and make-up artists. He's not nearly as rough looking as he was when he stepped into the room.

Sam opens the door as she checks her clipboard. 'Okay, time to get you guys down to the set.'

Tate follows Gregg, Luke, and Dillon into a room equipped with couches, drinks, and snacks. Dillon flops back on one of the couches and stretches out his legs. He's quieter than usual. Usually, he'd be buzzing by now, desperate to get on stage and soak up the attention.

Luke nudges Dillon in the side. 'Are you okay?'

Dillon doesn't immediately answer. 'Just want to get this over and done with, you know. If I survive this I'll be grand.'

'Survive?' Gregg says. 'They're not going to lynch you when you go out.'

'Fingers crossed,' Dillon responds, closing his eyes and resting his head against the back of the couch. Luke shakes his head and gets up to grab a bottle of water.

He shrugs at Tate. 'He'll be fine once he's on stage again.'

Luke sits down beside Dillon, and scrolls through his phone as Gregg joins Tate at the coffee machine. 'The vibe is off, isn't it?'

'Yeah. Big time. We've just got to put on a show and get the fuck out of here.'

Gregg slaps him on the shoulder. 'That's the spirit, buddy.'

'You know what I mean.'

Gregg nods. 'Yeah. I do. Sam's good though, isn't she?'

Tate tips two spoons of sugar in his coffee. Stuff the drugs, he's got a serious caffeine problem at this stage. 'Seems to know what she's doing. You happy with her?'

'Hell yes,' Gregg says. 'I don't think she's harbouring any secret infatuations for any of us either, which is a bonus.' Gregg may be joking about it, but his eyes betray what he's really thinking.

'You know, maybe we should all get away for a bit.'

'What? You've just got back from holiday.'

'No, I mean the four of us,' Tate says. 'Even for a weekend. Just... I don't know, get away from everything.'

'That might not be a bad idea. I can't remember the last time the four of us just hung out together, without any band stuff or whatever, in the way.'

Tate sips his coffee. They used to go away every year, just the four of them on a lads weekend. Their problems would still be there when they got back, but even having a few days away sounds fucking amazing.

Now if he can just get through this performance without making a fool of himself, it'll be a good start. That last coffee isn't sitting well in his stomach. He's seriously nauseous.

'I'm off to take a piss. Too many coffees.'

Sam grabs him as soon as he steps out the door. 'Are you okay?'

'Toilet. I'll be back in a sec.'

Tate bypasses the main toilet and goes back to the ensuite in his dressing room, smiling at the security guard blocking the door. He escapes inside and shuts the door behind him.

Then he bolts for the toilet and throws up. He slumps onto the floor and breathes heavily, as he waits for his gut to stop cramping. Fuck, he feels rough. He tears off his shirt, dumping it on the floor. He's too hot. He's burning up.

He's a fucking idiot to think he could do this without help. A little less than an hour before he has to go on. It's probably enough time. If he stays in here for a while afterwards, the guys won't know.

He pushes himself up the wall, bracing his legs to keep his ass from hitting the ground again. When he gets to the chair he collapses onto it and reaches for his bag.

He needs to sing. There's no choice. He's never called off a performance. Not once, and he's not about to start now.

Gregg

Gregg checks his watch and curses. Tate is going to be late if he doesn't get a wriggle on. 'How long does it take to have a piss?'

Dillon glances up, chewing on his lip ring. He's been doing that nonstop since they were brought down. Poor guy is nervous, not that he'd ever admit it. It would go against his hard man reputation.

'You probably should go and rouse him. We're going to have a riot if we're late.'

Gregg wanders down the corridor to the toilet and knocks on the door. No answer. He knocks again then opens the door. 'Tate, you in here buddy?'

Gregg wanders into the bathroom but all the stalls are empty. Maybe he went back to use the loo in his dressing room. The burly guard at the door takes a second to recognise him, his stern frown easing a little, but not by much. 'Hey. I don't suppose he's in there?'

'About ten minutes.'

'Can I go in?'

The guard shrugs, so Gregg knocks on the door. No answer. He opens the door and slips inside the room, closing the door behind him, leaving the scary guard outside.

Bingo. One lead singer sitting in the chair. 'No time for a chill out, buddy. We're on in a...'

His voice trails away when he sees the syringe in his friend's hand. Tate looks over at him, his expression blank and his eyes glassed over.

'Oh fuck! You stupid selfish dickhead!'

Tate's only response is to lie back in the chair and close his eyes.

He can't believe this is happening. Not again. Not after everything they went through the last time. The only thing he wants to do is grab Tate by the neck and give him a good shake. But he stops himself.

Getting angry isn't going to help. It's too late for that.

After glaring at Tate who continues to ignore him, Gregg pulls out his phone and calls Dillon. 'Hey. We got a problem. Don't say anything, but can you and Luke come to Tate's dressing room.'

While he waits for the guys to arrive, Gregg leans against the wall and looks over at Tate. He wants to shout and scream at his friend, but it's not going to get through to him right now. He's too far gone, and no amount of shouting will do anything to help them out of this pickle. Gregg pushes off the wall when the door opens and Dillon comes inside with Luke.

'What's the—' Dillon only has to look at Tate and he knows what the problem is. Gregg just manages to get himself in front of Tate, as Dillon launches at him. 'I'm going to kill the fucker!'

With Luke's help, they hold Dillon back, shoving him against the wall. 'Calm down. Losing it with him won't help,' Gregg says, getting right in Dillon's face.

Dillon nods, so they back away from him and turn to face Tate.

'We need to tell Sam,' Luke says. 'We're on soon. There's no way he'll be going on stage.'

Luke's right. He doesn't want to involve Vox, but they can't exactly perform without Tate. It would be kind of obvious if the singer was missing. He nods at Luke, then crouches down in front of Tate while Luke calls Sam.

'Hey buddy. How are you doing?'

Tate opens his eyes and frowns at Gregg. 'What are you doing here?'

'Came to find you. What have you done, Tate?'

He shrugs and closes his eyes again. 'I'll be okay in a minute. Just leave me alone.'

'Gladly,' he mutters, as Sam joins them in this nightmare.

She groans when she notices Tate, slumped in the chair. 'What's wrong with him? Is he sick? Oh please don't tell me he's sick! You're on soon.'

'I caught him shooting up.'

The penny drops and her mouth falls opens. 'Oh no! Please tell me you're joking? Not that you would be. That would be a terrible joke.'

'It's the fucking truth,' Dillon says turning away from Tate, to pace in front of the door.

'What are we going to do? I should probably call Ellen.'

'No! Just wait a few minutes.'

'Why, Gregg? He's high. There's no way I'd let him go on stage, even if he was able to. I can't handle something like this without her help.'

Dillon scrubs his hand over his face as he storms back and forth in front of the door. 'She's right, Gregg. He's a complete write-off. Unless someone else is going to take vocals, we're not going on.'

Gregg turns his attention back to Tate. 'Hey buddy. This is getting serious. Can you look at me. Come on. Lift your head and look at me.'

Tate slowly lifts his head and Gregg smiles, even though that's not what he feels like doing. Throttling Tate is incredibly tempting right now.

'Stop looking at me like that.' He scratches his arm, tearing at the skin like he did last year. It's like Gregg's gone back in time.

Gregg shakes his head and moves away from Tate, as he sends a message to Liam. He gets the feeling they'll need help to get Tate out of here.

Gregg brings Luke and Dillon to the far side of the room and lowers his voice. 'Anyone have any ideas?'

Dillon laughs harshly. 'Ideas? There are no fucking ideas. We're what? Ten minutes away from going on that stage, and he's fucked,' he says, pointing to Tate. 'No choice. We have to pull out.'

Luke scratches the back of his neck as he looks at Tate. 'Or you could take the lead, Gregg.'

Gregg frowns as he turns towards Luke. 'Me? Hang on. Why me. Why not you?'

'The fans are used to our songs with Tate in the lead with me. He wrote that new song for you a few weeks ago. If you sing that, we'll be home free. It's a new song with a new singer. It'll work Gregg.'

'Eh, no, Luke. There's no way I'm taking the lead.' He points to Tate. 'He does that.'

Dillon pulls an apple lace from the bag in his pocket. 'Today is fucking stressful enough, without all this shit being added to it. Tate is fucked. We have to get on stage or the band is fucked. Luke is right. Sing that song, Gregg. It'll save our necks. Buy us a reprieve, so we can sort him out. The last thing we need is more bad press.'

Gregg's mouth opens and closes for a few seconds, like he's a damn fish. 'But I can't sing.'

'Yes you can,' Luke replies. 'You're an amazing singer, Gregg. And that song is perfect.'

'Yeah, but you're the one who sings with Tate. You. Not me. No, you have to take the lead.'

'He wrote that song for you, not me. It's a few minutes. No interview. Just the song, and then we can sort Tate out. I know you can do it, Gregg. We've all heard you sing. And there's no way Tate would have written a song for you, unless he thought you could blow everyone away, singing it.'

Gregg is being backed up against an incredibly uncomfortable wall. Yeah he can sing and he's not bad, but he's also not Tate. People want to see Tate. Or Luke when he takes the lead on a few songs. They all sing as a group, but he's never taken the centre stage spot all on his lonesome.

Dillon looks past Gregg to Sam, who is frowning at her clipboard. 'Hey, Sam. Gregg wants to take the lead.'

'Hang on. I didn't say that!'

Her eyes widen and she smiles. 'The song Tate wrote for you?'

'What the hell? Does everyone know about that damn song?'

'It's my job to know,' she replies. 'So, are you up for it. It'll be perfect. No one has heard it before. It'll be a new experience. Oh, I think this will work.'

'Yeah, but what about Tate?' The wall is pressing firmly into his back. He gets the feeling he's about to go on stage, taking the lead for the first time. 'What excuse are you going to give?'

'Dodgy stomach or something like that. It happens. They'll be disappointed, but it's perfectly legitimate as an excuse.'

Gregg groans and looks over at Tate. 'Fuck! Fuck! Fuck!'

Sam squeezes his arm and smiles widely. 'I'll let them know,' she says, as Liam, Jason, Andy, and Ciaran pile into the room, instantly filling the space. 'Liam, short story. Tate is high. He won't be going on tonight. I'll need you, and maybe Jason, to get him out of here under the radar, and then sit on him in the hotel, until we finish here.'

The four bodyguards are clearly as impressed with Tate as Gregg and the guys are, but they stay quiet. They're employed to keep them safe, not have a go at them. Although, Tate deserves to hear whatever is going through Liam's mind at that moment. He's furious.

Tate comes to his senses a little, sitting up when he notices the heavies glaring over at him. 'I said I'm fine. I can go on.'

'Sam pulled you,' Gregg says, bracing when Tate turns to him.

'She what?'

'Oh come on,' Dillon says. 'What the fuck do you expect? We don't go on high or drunk. What the fuck are you playing at?'

Tate pushes to his feet, slightly unsteady. 'I'm fine to go out.'

Gregg stands in front of him, hating that Tate can't seem to focus properly on him. 'Sorry, buddy. If you were thinking straight, you'd get why we're doing this. Go back to the hotel with Liam. We'll talk later.'

Tate pushes forward, being blocked by Liam. 'You're not going on without me. You can't!'

Dillon opens the door and, even though the three of them want to stay and help Tate, they walk away from him and close the door, shutting out his shouts of anger.

Dillon leans against the wall and crosses his arms as he glares at the door. 'He's going to be fucked with us for doing this.'

'We don't have a choice, Dillon,' Luke says. 'He's going to be angry with us if we cancel, or if we go on without him. We can't win when he's like this.'

'Fair point.' He pushes off the wall and gestures down the corridor. 'Let's get this shit over and done with.'

Gregg follows after Luke and Dillon. This isn't the way today was supposed to go. Tate is using again and he has to go on stage in his place. If he survives the next few hours, he'll be amazed.

25

Tate

Tate has never been more humiliated, disappointed, and disgusted with himself than he is right now.

The guys had to go on stage without him.

First time that's ever happened. He knows Gregg took his place, and he couldn't be more proud of his friend. It was absolutely the right call. If they'd sung one of their known songs with someone else in the lead, it would have been weird. He just regrets missing Gregg singing that fucking song. His friend had refused to sing it, even though Tate knew it would suit his voice. The one time he actually sings it, and Tate misses it.

He'd been escorted back to his hotel room in secret, so no one saw him. Lead singer in a band, and he can't even get on stage because he fucked himself over, yet again.

It's a joke. He's a joke.

He should care more, but he can't think about anything except heroin. That's it. Just the fucking drug. He is desperate for another hit, craving it so badly he can barely think straight.

He's not tired. Not hungry. Not thirsty.

He wants a fix. Or Chloe.

How fucked up is that?

Does that mean he's putting drugs before Chloe?

That's even more fucked up.

'You want anything?' Liam asks.

Yes. Desperately. Tate shakes his head. 'Just go away, Liam. Please.'

Liam sighs loudly, but leaves him to wallow in misery alone. As much as he wants to stay in bed, his bladder has other ideas. He crawls out of bed, wincing when his head throbs angrily. He puts out a hand to steady himself against the wall, as his brain and skull get back in sync.

He lunges for the bathroom, just making it to the toilet before he vomits.

'Jesus, Tate. Are you okay?'

'Leave me the fuck alone, Liam.' He throws up again, with Liam hovering nearby, which just makes the whole experience so much worse. Once his stomach uncurls, he glares over his shoulder at Liam. 'Get out!'

Liam holds up his hands and backs out of the bathroom. Tate wipes his mouth, and slumps back against the massive bathtub. He scratches his arm, unable to stop himself from doing it, even though it just pisses him off even more.

He pulls up his shirt sleeve and glares at the raw marks on his skin. The cat is well and truly out of the bag now. No point trying to hide it. The guys know. Sam knows. Their security know. It's only a matter of time before Chloe finds out.

Then she won't need any more time to think about their future. It's done. Finished. He killed it the second he stuck a needle in his arm again.

He uses the bath to pull himself to his feet, then washes his face, disgusted at the pale, pasty face looking back at him. God he looks shite. The nausea isn't letting up and he's twitchy as hell. Pity he didn't remember anything except the high he got from the drug. The pain, the nausea, the infernal scratching. None of it entered his mind, until it was too late.

He shuffles back into the bedroom and collapses in the bed, wrapping the duvet around himself to keep out the chills.

They'll be back in a minute. Luke, Gregg, and Dillon will burst through the door and lay into him. Maybe Sam too. And he can't really blame them. It would be bad enough if they were in Ireland, but being away has just added another level of awkward to what he did.

There's no way he'll last another day without more. Not a chance in hell. Hours on the road, followed by hours on the ferry while he feels like this, is a hard no. He closes his eyes, burying deep under the duvet and tries to get some sleep before he heads into a massive fight with his friends.

Gregg is buzzing. No other word for it. The thought of getting up on stage and singing, nearly had him running for the toilet more than once, but he got through it. Not only that, he doesn't think he did too badly. They'd got a standing ovation, so that's a good sign.

Dillon had even cracked a smile and hugged him after. Another good sign. He's not one for hugging people for no good reason.

The only downer on the evening is Tate. And that's a whopping massive downer. One they're on the way to face right now.

Gregg stares out the window of the car and tries to get his thoughts in order. Not that preparation of any kind will make a difference. Tate isn't going to be thinking straight. The second he fell back to drugs, Gregg had begun to lose his friend again.

'How long do you think he's been using for?'

Dillon shrugs, as he glares out the window. 'Wasn't his first time.'

'It was probably around the time his father died and Chloe left,' Luke says. 'You know he can't deal with things since Dara took him.' He pulls out his ringing phone, glances at the screen, then silences the call.

'Pippa?' Dillon asks.

Luke nods. 'I'll call her later. Tate first.'

Gregg takes out a bag of gummy bears and offers them around, before taking one himself. All this stress isn't doing his levels any good. 'So, I'm guessing he'll be a dick when we confront him.'

'We confronting him?' Dillon asks.

'Yeah. Is that not the plan?'

Dillon takes another sweet from the bag. 'He's either going to be high, or wanting to get high. Not sure what talking is going to do. He's more stubborn than I am. It'll just force him to push back. We might just have to get him back to Ireland and try to figure it out then.'

'Oh, right. That easy, huh? How exactly do you expect us to get a six-foot-three, two hundred plus pound pissed-off man onto a ferry home? Or even get him out of the hotel. He's not going to go quietly.'

Dillon shrugs. 'Fuck knows. I guess it depends on how hard he's using. We could get back to the hotel and he's grand.'

Gregg raises his eyebrows as he stares at Dillon.

'I'm trying to be positive, okay.'

'Yeah well don't bother. Nothing to be positive about right now.'

'Don't have a fucking go at me, Gregg. I'm pissed off too, okay. Really seriously pissed off, but getting ourselves in a knot won't help. Worst case, I'll fucking deck him. Knock him out and shove him in the minibus.'

Gregg doesn't bother pointing out how unhelpful that comment is. Even though he suspects Dillon would absolutely do what he said.

The rest of the ride takes place in uncomfortable silence, which just gets so much worse when they're met outside Tate's room by a stony faced Jason.

'What's wrong?' Dillon asks his bodyguard.

He opens the door, and waits until they're in the hallway of the suite, before he answers. 'He's been throwing up, but it seems to be settling down. Hasn't puked for about an hour,' Jason tells them, keeping his voice low. 'I've called the transport in. We've made the decision to head back now. Get the overnight ferry home. He's settled, so best to get the fuck out of here while he's cooperative.'

Dillon kicks the wall and curses to himself. 'Better go get our stuff packed then. Cheers Tate.'

He leaves with Luke, but Gregg hangs behind to check on Tate. He's as angry as the others about what Tate did, but he's still worried about him. Again. He thought all this was behind them.

Gregg quietly creeps into Tate's room and over to the bed. Tate is flaked out on the covers, fully dressed. He barely flinches, as Gregg lifts his left arm to expose the inside of his elbow.

Even in the dim light of the bedroom, Gregg can see the track marks. This wasn't the first time. There must be at least half a dozen marks. Tate's probably been using again for a week or two.

Gregg sits on the edge of the bed and looks down at Tate. 'You stupid eejit.'

For the first time since Gregg entered his room, Tate stirs, looking up at him with slightly unfocused eyes. 'Hey.'

'Hey? Seriously?' He pokes Tate's arm right over the scars. 'You've been holding out of us.'

'Not now, Gregg,' he says, before turning his back on him.

Gregg shoves him onto his back, holding him down on the bed. It's the wrong thing to do, he knows that, but he's irritated. Singing on stage had been the best time he's had for ages. Now he's pissed off, and any small glimmer of happiness he had while he performed, has been well and truly dampened.

'Don't you dare do that, Tate. Not after the last time. Not after you nearly fucking died, you prick.'

Tate tries to dislodge him, but Gregg is seriously pissed, and not in the mood for playing nice.

'We went on stage without you, Tate. For the first time in the history of the band, you weren't on stage with us! Do you understand that? Do you even comprehend how messed up that is? We went on without our lead singer and main guitarist. What band does that?'

Tate swipes at Gregg, but he's too groggy to make any real impact. 'Gregg, get the fuck off me!'

'How long?'

'I've got a handle on it this time.'

'Oh you have, have you? Well that's just grand then, isn't it. What the fuck am I worried about?'

Tate glares at him, his eyes not quite right. 'Sarcasm doesn't suit you.'

'Yeah and heroin doesn't suit you, buddy.' Tate isn't getting it. There's nothing in his face to even give the slightest hint that he understands, or admits, how fucked up today was. 'Wasting my breath.'

He gets off Tate and sits on the bed beside him. Tate pulls down the sleeve of his shirt, trying to hide the marks.

'Oh I wouldn't bother with that now. That particular horse has well and truly bolted, buddy.'

Tate sighs and closes his eyes. 'Lay off. I'm fucked.'

'Too right you are.' Gregg shuffles up the bed and sits beside Tate. 'What happened, Tate? Was it your father? The baby? Chloe?'

Tate leaves the silence hanging for a long time, before he slowly turns around and hits Gregg with one hell of a cold glare. 'What I do, or don't do, with my body, is my fucking business.'

Gregg is immediately transported back to over a year ago, when he confronted Tate on his drug use outside his house. He was met with the same reaction he's getting now. Narky, confrontational, pissed off

Tate. On a good day, Tate is notoriously stubborn. Tate on heroin is unmovable. Gregg can talk to him until he's blue in the face, but he's not going to budge.

Which means he's going to have to do something he desperately doesn't want to.

He loves Tate like a brother, but watching him do this to himself the first time was unbelievably painful. He can't do it again. Not with everything else he's trying to deal with. He doesn't have enough left to give. Not if he wants to get his own head straight again at some stage.

'Okay.'

Tate frowns at him. 'Okay what?'

'You're right. It's your body. There's nothing I can do to stop you. But I'll be damned if I'm going to sit by and watch you try to kill yourself again. I won't do it. I can't. I love you too much, Tate.'

Tate nods towards the door. 'No one is forcing you to stay. I'm fine, so you either get off my case, or fuck off.'

Gregg gets to his feet, keeping composed, even though he wants to scream. He has no choice. He has to do this, or he risks doing himself more harm than good.

'Fair enough. I'll talk to Ellen when we get back to Ireland tomorrow.'

'About what?'

'I'm done Tate. I can't do this anymore. I'm leaving the band.'

Chloe

Chloe never thought she had a sixth sense. Sometimes she would get a feeling that something was wrong, but didn't put much stock in it. But when she woke up this morning, there was a heaviness in her gut she couldn't shake off.

She wanted to call Tate. Needed to hear his voice, but decided against it. After their argument, she doesn't feel like she can do that. Not without hurting him, or confusing the issue.

As the morning progressed, the feeling strengthened. Then when a deep red Mustang pulls into her gran's driveway, she knows her gut was right.

She watches Dillon climb out of his car, looking tired and pissed off.

Dillon has never called around. He glances up at the window and looks at her, his chest visibly rising and falling, as he takes a long breath.

She doesn't want to open the door to him. Something is wrong with Tate. She knows it. There's no other reason he'd be here. And he knows she knows. Dillon leans on the bonnet of his car, his arms crossed, patiently waiting for her to get herself together enough to go downstairs and open the door.

Which she does about five minutes later.

She gestures for him to come inside, leading him into the kitchen and taking a seat at the wooden table. Dillon casually glances around the room before sitting opposite her, chewing on his lip ring as he looks over at her.

Of all the band members, she has probably spent the least amount of time alone with Dillon. She barely knows him. Had barely spoken to him, other than casual chats when they were together as a group.

If she's being honest, she was always a little intimidated by him. He's roughly the same build as Tate, maybe not as tall, but still well over six foot. But it was the added air about him that made her a little uneasy. She's worked with enough people over her career, to know when someone isn't being themselves.

And Dillon isn't.

He's acting. This persona he allows the world to see isn't the real him. Which begs the question, what is he hiding from the world?

'Do you want a drink?'

He shakes his head. 'Better I just get to the point.'

'What happened?' Deep down she knows exactly what's wrong, but still needs to hear it from him, before she can allow herself to deal with it.

'Tate's using again. Gregg walked in on him shooting up in his dressing room, before we went on. Sam benched him, so Gregg took the lead instead. Jace and the guys brought him back to the hotel with a little resistance. We confronted him about it when we got back. Well, Gregg did mainly. Some of us were too pissed off to deal with it.'

He's clearly talking about himself.

'Gregg and Tate got into it and short story, Tate wouldn't admit he has a problem. Told Gregg to mind his own. So Gregg left the band.'

Chloe doesn't move. Just stares at Dillon, as his words echo in her head. None of it is sinking in. Not one bit of it.

'I'm sorry to land all this on you,' he continues. 'Gregg isn't up for talking about it. He's gutted. Really fucking gutted. Luke can't deal with what's going on. He ran back to Pippa as soon as we got back.' Dillon sits back in the chair looking utterly defeated. He's all alone dealing with this.

'Are you sure he's using? I mean, it might have just been a one off.' Not that it makes the slightest difference if it's once, or a dozen times.

'Positive. It's been going on for a few weeks. I really am sorry Chloe.'

'It's not your fault, Dillon. I appreciate you coming to tell me.'

She doesn't even realise she's crying, until he's kneeling in front of her, his arms wrapped around her. Chloe buries her face against his chest as she cries. She doesn't even care who's holding her, she just needs to let this out.

He releases his hold when she's cried out. Chloe sniffs and looks up at him. 'Sorry about that.'

He smiles and winks at her. 'No problem. It's a fucking shite situation. You're entitled to be upset. I know I am.'

'So is this it? Have we lost him to drugs again?' She meets his eyes, but drops her gaze to the black ring in the centre of his nose. His eyes are seriously unnerving.

'I have a plan of sorts, but I might need your help.'

'My help? What can I do?'

He gets up and perches on the edge of the table. 'Just be you. Be honest with him. Fuck knows, I'm making this shit up as I go. What I do know is that my family is falling apart, and I'll be damned if I'm going to sit on my arse and do fuck all about it. It's too important.'

'Do you think he'll listen? You know what Tate is like.'

Dillon gives her a smile that makes her nervous. 'Oh he'll listen. I'll make damn sure of that.'

Tate

Ellen closes her office door and smiles at Tate, as she walks around to the far side of her desk. He's tired, irritable, and needs something he doesn't want to admit he needs. Since they got back from the UK, he'd stayed in his house. He needed to get away from the disapproving looks he was getting from everyone around him.

The drive back to the ferry had taken place in seriously uncomfortable silence. Even Luke seems to be pissed off with him which was a new one. Luke didn't get pissed off with anyone.

Gregg's decision to leave the band was the main reason for the mood. Well, it possibly had something to do with him using again, but if they'd just lay off the judgemental looks, he'd be able to talk to them about it. But when Gregg made his announcement, Tate got the brunt of the bad feelings.

Fucking perfect.

It's not his fault Gregg is over-reacting. This isn't like the last time. Nothing like it. He's tired and stressed, so there's a chance it may have a stronger hold on him than he would like, but he'll get on top of it again. As soon as...

He stops that thought before it goes any further. Chloe is gone. He just has to accept that. She hasn't reached out to him since their row. Not that it's necessarily all up to her, but a little give and take would be nice.

'How are you feeling?'

Why is he the one doing all the running? How long is he supposed to just sit around and wait for her to make up her mind about him?

'Tate? Hello! Are you listening to me?'

'What?'

Ellen blows out a breath and clasps her hands together on her desk. 'I asked how you're feeling.'

'I'm fine. I just had a wobble.'

She peers over at him, not saying anything for a few minutes. 'A wobble? Sam pulled you from a performance. You. The lead singer. That's more than a wobble. What's going on, Tate? And I want the truth, not some *wobble* nonsense.'

He takes a second to rein himself in, before he responds. Being questioned like this isn't helping his mood. 'It was a one off. I get that it was a fuck up. I do, but Gregg did an amazing job.'

'I'm not questioning that for a moment. No one has any complaints about the performance. Gregg was incredible.' She leans on her desk and levels her gaze on him. 'You're the lead singer, Tate. You need to be on stage. You need to be singing. If you can't for whatever reason, I need to know why.'

'What the fuck do you want me to say, Ellen? It won't happen again, okay.' Her eyes harden as she looks at him. He hadn't planned to shout at her. It just came out that way, and now he's well and truly screwed himself.

'Why don't you take a second to calm down.'

'Jesus, Ellen. If one more person tells me to calm down, I swear I'm going to hit something.'

'Well, that's good to know. Do I need to get Liam in here?'

'No. I'm sorry.'

She grunts but doesn't look impressed. 'Gregg had a long talk with me. Do you have anything to say about that?'

'He wants to leave. It's his choice.'

She sits back and stares across at him. 'Did you seriously just say that? Your best friend wants to leave Broken, and all you have to say is that it's his choice? Now I know there's something wrong. You do realise what this means for Broken, don't you? Gregg is incredibly popular. We're going to take an impressive hit when he leaves.'

'We did okay without him before. We'll manage again.'

Ellen gives him a strange look, one that has him squirming in his seat. She's pissed off. Not that he can blame her. Losing Gregg is shite, but there's nothing he can do about it. Gregg over reacted and threw his dummy out of the pram. Now they have to deal with the consequences.

'I think it would be a good idea to take a break.'

Tate's mouth drops opens. 'Fuck's sake Ellen. What the hell are you talking about?'

'Tate, I sent four incredibly close friends away for the weekend, to perform as they've done countless times before. I got back four angry, upset men, who can't seem to talk to each other. Gregg is leaving. Dillon went on one of his all night drinking sessions, which Jace is getting on my back about. Like I have any control over him. Luke... well, I can't remember the last time I saw him smile. And you...' she pauses and slowly shakes her head, as she looks out the window.

'Take the time. Can you not see how wound up you are? You know you guys are friends, as much as clients. I'm speaking to you now as your friend. I'm worried about you. You're clearly stressed and agitated. Not to mention you look terrible, no offence.'

'Yeah. Thanks for that.'

'I'm being serious, Tate. I wouldn't be doing you, or the band, any favours by not stepping in. I'm giving you all a break. No performances. No interviews. No photos. Nothing. Just time off to get yourselves together.'

'I don't need time.'

She leans back in her chair and nods at his arm. 'You haven't stopped scratching your arm since you sat down. Now, I'm not going to officially ask if you're using again, because I'd have to make a note of the answer. You know that. What I will say is that, off the record, you need to get on top of it. Now. Go back to rehab. I'll sort it out for you. Please.'

'I don't need rehab.'

She sighs and shakes her head as she glares at him. 'Take the time off, Tate. It's not a request.'

'So that's it. Broken Chords are what? Done?'

'No. You're taking a well needed break. All of you. This isn't just a personal attack on you, in spite of what you may think. Dillon is just out of prison. Luke is on the verge of leaving. Or will, if what I heard on the grapevine is anything to go by. And Gregg isn't the same since Angel took him.

'You all need to concentrate on yourselves, Tate. For the last six years, the four of you have been working non stop. Take a few weeks - maybe a month or two. That's all I'm talking about. I'm hoping Gregg will come around and change his mind in that time.'

'Who decides when we're fixed?'

'Tate, stop trying to pick a fight with me. It won't work.'

'When?'

'I don't know, okay! When the four of you are ready to perform again. Or the three of you. To be honest, right now, I have no idea what the future holds for the band. Get some help, Tate. I'm begging you.'

She's backing him into a corner and he's far from impressed about that. He doesn't want time off. Working is one of the few things he has left, that helps distract him from everything else in his head. Without it, it's just him alone rattling around an empty house.

'So I presume that means a negative drug test from me, right?'

'You said that - not me.'

Before he actually does pick a fight, that would end whatever semblance of a career he has left, he stands up. She's not going to change her mind. If he keeps pushing, he's going to find himself out on his arse. 'Great. Fine. Thanks Ellen. Pleasure as always.'

He leaves her room, slamming the door behind him like a prize dick. Liam silently follows after him, his eyes burning a hole in the back of his neck, but he doesn't care. He just needs to get out of here and back to his house. Tate scratches his arm again, then curses, and drops his hand to his side as he enters the elevator.

'Can I say something?' Liam asks as the door closes and they travel down to the garage.

'What?'

'How long are you going to keep this up for?'

'Fuck, Liam! I've just had it all from Ellen. You're here to keep me safe. That's it. Mind your own fucking business.'

Liam nods, keeping his attention ahead of him. 'Watching you kill yourself, and saying nothing, isn't keeping you safe.'

Tate suppresses the groan. Liam got him there, smart git.

'Seriously Liam, give it a fucking break. I'm having a shite day as it is.'

'Understood,' he responds. Tate eyes the back of Liam's neck, waiting for some other comment or sermon. But there's nothing.

He leads Tate through the underground garage to the SUV, and opens the door for him. Liam pulls out of the car park, joining the late afternoon Dublin city centre traffic. Liam pulls up at a red light and passes Tate a bottle of water and protein bar. 'Eat that.'

Tate's first instinct is to throw it back at him, but he has second thoughts. He's starving.

'Where to?'

'Home.'

'Fair enough.'

'Is that it? No more lectures?'

Liam glances at him in the rear view mirror, before pulling away with the rest of the traffic. 'Can't see there's much point. I've said my piece. If you're not going to see sense for Gregg, you're sure as hell not going to for Ellen, or me. Waste of breath.'

'What is it with everyone? I don't have a problem.'

'Of course not.'

'What the fuck is that supposed to mean?'

'Exactly what I said. You don't think you have a problem. Fair enough.'

Tate bites his tongue, choosing to glare out the window instead of getting into it with Liam.

Gregg

Gregg watches the waves crashing on the beach about half a mile ahead of him. He's seriously stressed. Has been since he had the fight with Tate a few days ago.

Dillon and Luke had tried to talk him around, Sam too, but he's held firm. His head is struggling as it is, without having to worry about Tate.

The problem is, leaving the band didn't solve the Tate issue. He's still going to have to watch his best mate lose himself to drugs again. The only difference is, he won't have to watch him disappearing on a day-to-day basis.

Ellen was talking to their lawyers, to see if they can release him from his contract. Their manager had been amazing about his decision. She gets it. They all do in fairness, but that doesn't help the guilt that's gnawing away at him.

He's walking away from his friends, from a career he loves, to save himself.

Since Angel kidnapped him, he's been off balance. He's scared of things he didn't give a second thought to before. If he's going to put the ordeal and the nightmares behind him, he needs to concentrate on himself.

He smells Bria's perfume before she sits down beside him. 'I thought you might be here. Your mum has lunch ready.'

'Thanks. I'm not really hungry though.'

She lifts his arm and checks the screen on his watch. 'This says otherwise. You need your shot and some food. I don't want you keeling over on me.'

He pulls out a packet of gummy bears from his pocket. 'Got these bad boys to keep me going.' His smiles dies when she raises her eyebrows and hits him with a stern look. 'Yes. I know. Insulin and real food. I hear you.'

'Good.' She kisses his cheek, then rests her forehead against the side of his face. 'I love you.'

He smiles and squeezes her leg. 'Love you too. I'm sorry I'm being a miserable git.'

'I think you're entitled. I'm so sorry this is happening, Gregg. I wish I could make it better. I wish I could make Tate see sense, but I can't.'

He switches places with her when he realises she's crying. Gregg gathers Bria in his arms and kisses the top of her head. 'I'm sorry too. I should be able to do something for him. But he's not interested.'

'I keep toying with the idea of telling Mum and Dad about Tate. They need to know, but I'm also hoping he'll come to his senses any day now and everything will go back to the way it was.'

He peers over at her.

'Yeah. I know. It's not going to happen, right?'

Gregg shrugs. 'There's always a chance...' There's no chance. Tate has form. Sooner or later he'll fall, and this time he might not get up again.

'I did do something though, and please don't be angry.'

'What did you do?'

'I called Shane a few hours ago.'

Tate and Bria's older brother is one of the most decent men Gregg has ever met. He's cool-headed, but with a serious *don't mess with me* vibe. He's also massively protective of his younger siblings, especially Tate. Calling him would piss Tate off, but it was a good decision. 'You know what, I should have thought of that.'

'You don't think Tate will be angry? That it will just make everything worse?'

'Your brother is using heroin. How can you make things worse? So, what did he say?'

'He's going to try to come over.'

'From Canada?'

She nods. 'He's got a lot on with work but he's doing what he can. He'll keep me up to date.'

'Having Shane here won't hurt. Tate usually listens to him.'

His watch beeps at him, so Bria stands up and holds out her hand. 'Come on. Let's get you sorted.

They walk hand in hand back to Gregg's parents' house. After lunch he'll... Gregg frowns to himself. He'll what? Without the band or music he's not sure what he'll do.

They walk down the driveway to his parents' house, surprised to see a stunning dark red classic Mustang parked beside his car. He can count on one hand the number of times Dillon has been to his parents' place.

Dillon climbs out of his car and sits on the bonnet. 'You okay?'

'Yeah, just getting some fresh air. What are you doing here?'

'I just got a call from Liam. Tate lost it with Ellen. We've been benched for the foreseeable. All of us.'

'Shit. I'm sorry.'

Dillon pushes upright and walks over to them. He chews on his lip ring for a second, then sighs. 'I know you're trying to protect yourself after what happened, and I get that. Luke and I don't want to put any extra pressure on you, but we need you. The band needs you. Tate needs you.'

'Tate needs his next fix.'

'Tate needs his mates to kick some sense into him. He needs help, Gregg.' He pauses and scrubs a hand over his face. Gregg can't remember ever seeing Dillon so exhausted before. He can usually go on all night benders and still manage to look like he's just woken up.

'I'm seriously pissed off with him too, Gregg. But I'm not waiting for him to land himself back in hospital again. I know you don't want that either.'

'Of course I don't. But you know what he's like. He's not going to budge. If he had a go at Ellen, he's not going to listen to us.'

'Then we make him listen.'

Gregg narrows his gaze. 'How?'

'The way I see it, there's you, me, Luke, Andy, Jason, Ciaran, and Liam. That's a lot of muscle against Tate. I reckon we could make him see sense.'

Bria lets go of Gregg's hand and stands in front of Dillon. 'Hang on one second. You're not going to hurt him, are you?'

'Give me a bit of credit, Bria. He's my friend. I'm going to make sure he listens. Even if it means I have to pull out some of my restraints, to make him listen.'

'Your restraints?' she asks, confused.

'Please don't ask.' Gregg still hasn't quite recovered from the conversation when Dillon gave away a little too much about his sex life. 'You think it will work? Cornering Tate I mean, not the restraints part. It's a dead cert he'll get physical with us. You know that, right?'

Dillon shrugs. 'We can handle him.' Dillon kisses Bria on the cheek then walks back over to his car.

'Where are you going?'

'Tate's. You're coming too, Gregg. Get in the car.'

'Dillon...'

'Get in the fucking car, Gregg.'

'Fine. I just need a minute.'

'What for?'

'Shot and food. I'll be out in a sec.'

He unlocks the front door and hurries in to the kitchen with Bria following after him. 'Are you really going to do this?'

He opens the fridge and takes out his insulin, checking the dose on the pen a few times before he injects it into this stomach. 'Dillon's right, awkward git. We can't just do nothing.'

Bria wraps the sandwich Gregg's mum made for him. 'And if he still doesn't listen?'

'At least we've tried.' He takes the sandwich and kisses her. 'See you later.'

'Good luck,' she calls after him as he goes back out to Dillon. If this goes anything like he thinks it will, they'll need more than luck to get through it.

27

Tate

Liam pulls the SUV into the driveway of Tate's house. Thankfully the rest of the drive took place in silence, but he's still pissed off. Mainly at himself. Losing it with Ellen was a career destroying move. Of course she was going to be on his case about what happened in the UK. It's her job, and he's screwed her, Gregg, Luke, Dillon, and Sam, by not doing his.

'You need anything else?' Liam asks, turning in his seat to face him.

'No.'

'Suit yourself. You know where I am if you need me.'

He climbs out of the car, again being a dick by slamming the door. The sooner this day is over with, the better. Another fucking night alone with a pizza and some crappy show on TV. He won't call Eddie. At least he'll try not to.

He slides his key into the lock and steps into his hallway, shutting the door behind him, in case Liam fancies having another go at him. It takes a few seconds to realise his alarm is off. He's sure he put it on when he left. He probably forgot.

Then he opens the door into the living room and curses. Gregg, Luke, Dillon, Andy, Jason, and Ciaran are right at home in his living room. He turns to head right back out the front door, but comes to a stop when Liam steps into the hallway and closes the door behind him, blocking his escape. Probably not what he's doing, but that's what it feels like.

'Fucking rude to invite yourself into someone's house.'

'We need to talk to you, buddy,' Gregg says as he gets to his feet.

Tate groans and massages his forehead. Fucking headache is getting worse by the second. 'Listen, I've had it in spades today from too many people. I'm tired. Please get the fuck out of my house so I can get some sleep.'

'Or more gear,' Dillon says.

'No!'

'Fuck off, Tate!' Dillon rises to his feet and walks over to him. 'You said you've got a handle on this. So I'm guessing there should be no new track marks on your arm, right? Nothing but old scars.'

'Am I seriously getting a drug lecture from you of all people?'

Dillon's eyes harden. 'Yeah, so I'm no angel, but that's how I know you've got a problem. Do you not think I can see it?'

'How about you work on yourself first before having a go at me?'

'I am.'

'In prison you mean. How did that go for you?'

Dillon laughs and takes a step back. 'You really are a dick, aren't you? I lost a month of my life, because I took drugs and made a fucking idiot of myself. You've already spent three months in rehab after nearly killing yourself. How far are you going to push it this time?'

'What the fuck is it with everyone? I. Am. Fine!'

'Show me your arm.'

'Seriously, Dillon. Can you just go.'

'Show us your arm, Tate,' Gregg says, walking over to stand beside Dillon.

Tate looks around them to Luke and the bodyguards. 'Your turn now is it?'

Luke nods. 'We're worried about you Tate, so please stop being an ass about this. Prove us wrong. Roll up your sleeve.'

The overpowering urge to bolt from the room takes charge. He backs away, forgetting that Liam is behind him. Tate is a big guy, but Liam is bigger. His bodyguard uses his skills and training to quickly pin him back against the wall. 'We're trying to help you, Tate.'

'Yeah, it fucking feels like it. Get off me Liam!'

'Show us your arm.' Liam adjusts his grip, releasing pressure from Tate's left arm.

'Get off me!'

Gregg appears in front of him and looks at him over Liam's shoulder. 'Let us help you, buddy. You're hooked again. We can all see it. We'll do everything we possibly can to get you clean. We promise.'

He wants to scream at Liam to let him go. Curse and shout and fight to be released. But he's tired. And not just physically. He's tired of feeling like he's in a free-fall. He just wants everything to go back to how it was at Christmas. Just Chloe and him. Happy and in love. None of this shit, messing with his head.

But he's not ready to say he's addicted. He's not addicted, well not really. He just needs a few nights without the nightmares, and he'll be able to get on top of it again. He knows he can. He's sure of it.

He's not an addict. He's not. But if they see his arm, they'll think he is. He'd had a hit this morning. Just one, and he didn't plan on having another.

Gregg grabs his arm before Tate can stop him. He shoves the sleeve up, airing Tate's dirty laundry to everyone in the room. 'Jesus, Tate!'

He bucks against Liam, but the bodyguard is well able to hold him back. 'Get the fuck off me!'

Liam ignores him which does nothing to improve the situation.

'It's my fucking house. Let me go!'

Gregg taps Liam on the shoulder. 'Let him go.'

Liam steps back, but Tate stays where he is. He doesn't know what to do now. What to say. How to react. It's seven against one.

What he wants to do is grab his keys and leave them to it, but Liam is blocking one exit and Andy the other. He's trapped in his own fucking house.

'So what now, huh? Is this where you all take turns to tell me how I'm messing up my life, or that I'm better than this, or something else inspirational?'

'Stop being a dick,' Dillon says, lowering onto one of the bar stools.

'Me being a dick? You ambushed me in my house!'

'You know what I don't get?'

Tate glowers at Gregg. 'What don't you get?'

'We visited you in rehab last year. We got a bit of a look-see into what withdrawal was like for you.'

'I'm not—'

'Do you remember the vomiting?' Gregg says, ignoring his interruption. 'The fevers, the chills, the cramps?' He pauses, but Tate doesn't bother saying anything. 'Do you remember shouting at all of us, picking fights or crying, depending on how bad the day was. Do you remember all of that?'

'Yes!' he shouts, cutting Gregg off. 'I remember,' he continues quietly. 'Do you think I'll get myself to that stage again? It's not going to happen! I've got this.'

'Fuck you, Tate!' Gregg says, surprising him. Gregg rarely cursed. 'Fine. Well, as I'm unemployed at the moment, I'm at a loose end. Dillon and Luke are too, thanks to Broken being put on leave, because of you. We're going to stay here with you and see exactly how you've got this.'

'No you're not!'

'Yes we are. All of us. Take a seat on the couch and get comfy. We'll be here for a while.'

Chloe

Chloe peers up at the stunning white house, and her heart aches. She only lived with Tate for two months, but every minute of her time here had been memorable. Now she's nervous about going inside.

She considered herself one of the lucky ones. She hadn't seen Tate while he was using drugs. She had met him just out of rehab, so had never experienced the darkness that took over him, as it now has again.

Bria takes her hand and squeezes it. 'You don't have to do this.'

'I love him, Bria. Whatever is going on between us doesn't matter right now. He needs to listen to someone.'

'Just don't get your hopes up. According to Gregg's text, Tate isn't budging. He's convinced he's got the situation under control.'

'And the guys don't agree?'

Bria shakes her head.

'Okay. Wish me luck.'

She takes her keys from her bag and unlocks the front door, closing it quietly behind her. Even through the closed door to the living room, she can hear raised voices. Mainly Dillon and Gregg.

Chloe places her hand on the door handle, but stops before she opens it. She doesn't want to see him like this. He's a giant of a man, but he's gentle and sweet. He's rarely lost his temper around her, but she knows he has a fierce one when he's pushed or cornered. If he feels that way about what they're doing, he could lash out and that won't help anyone.

Chloe takes a breath, then opens the door. The guys are spread through the vast open plan room, taking up positions on the chairs and bar stools surrounding the marble counter. In the middle of it all, Tate is sitting on the couch, hands clenched firmly in front of him.

His head turns towards her, and he frowns. Chloe bites the inside of her cheek to stop herself from crying. It could be exhaustion or perhaps the drugs, but he doesn't look like her Tate anymore.

His deep blue eyes are bloodshot and sunken, the heavy black rings under each eye so much more noticeable, thanks to his nearly grey complexion. His strong jaw is sharper, his broad body a little smaller. He looks like he hasn't been eating properly, if at all, since she left.

He keeps his attention trained on her, refusing to say anything or to drop his gaze.

'Can you give us a minute. I'd like to speak to Tate alone.'

She is fully expecting an argument, but she doesn't get one. The room empties, Gregg, Luke, and Liam out the front door with Dillon, Andy, Jason, and Ciaran heading out the patio door into the garden. They're blocking him in. Making sure he doesn't run.

'Can I sit?'

'Why not? You can join the party.'

She takes a seat on the armchair opposite him. He's eyeing her suspiciously, like she's been pulled in as the emotional card to make him see sense. 'I saw the band on TV. Gregg was incredible.'

'Yeah. He was.'

'When you first brought me back here for dinner, you took me to the studio upstairs and opened up to me. About the drugs and your father. Do you remember?'

'I haven't lost my memory.'

His reply is harsher than she was expecting. He's got his guard up.

'You were open with me about why you got tangled up with drugs. You also spoke about how upset you were with Astrid's lies.'

'Why the fuck are you bringing her up?'

'You were so upset, because she told the press you weren't able to go on stage unless you'd had a hit or a fix... whatever.' She looks up at his face. He's not frowning at her anymore. He knows what she's

254

getting at.

'You were so upset, because the fans are the most important part of what you do. Each and every one of them pay to watch you, Luke, Dillon, and Gregg. They deserve to get the best out of you, every single time. You looked me in the eye, and said you have never, and would never, use, or drink before you perform.

'I want you to look me in the eye right now, and tell me you weren't going to perform after taking heroin. That you weren't going to go on stage and give a substandard performance, because you were on drugs.

'If you were, then I may not know you as well as I thought I did. You might not be the man I thought you were, because I thought your fans were the most important thing to you.'

Tate stares at her in silence for a long time, a muscle in his jaw twitching. She got to him. She knows she did.

There's no way Chloe would forget that conversation with him. Listening to him opening up about his addiction, and what his father did to him, was a turning point in their relationship. He had told her, expecting her to turn away from him. Instead, it gave her incredible insight into what makes Tate tick. Helped her understand his reactions to certain situations.

Bullying Tate won't work. Telling him to get help won't work. Nothing is going to change, unless he decides himself that he needs help.

The silence is killing her, but she lets it continue. His frown is gone, but he's not looking at her. His attention is on the coffee table in front of him.

Then it happens. The briefest of glances at the inside of his arm. If she'd blinked she would have missed it.

Time to up the ante. She takes her bag off the ground and gets to her feet. 'I guess I was wrong about you.' She makes it as far as the kitchen, before he stops her.

'Wait!'

She turns and looks at him.

'I was.'

Chloe walks back to the armchair and sits down. 'You were what?'

He swallows and scratches his arm, but he doesn't seem to notice he's doing it. 'I was going to perform while I was high.' He curses, and stops scratching, clenching his fists together instead. 'I was going to perform while I was high,' he repeats, almost like he's allowing the truth to sink in.

'Is that what you want? Is that the performer you want to be?'

'You know it's not, Chloe.' He drops his head into his hands. 'Fuck!'

She moves over to sit beside him. 'We're all here to help you, Tate. Everyone here today, is here because they care about you. But we can't help you unless you want it. You're big and bold enough to make your own decisions. It's up to you. No one is going to force you.'

He drops one hand from his face and looks over at her. 'What about us?'

'I don't know. I still love you. I want us to work this out, but we can't while you're using. That's not me giving you an ultimatum. I'm just being honest. There's no way we can even begin to talk seriously about our future, while you're on heroin. I won't watch you fade away in front of me. I can't do that.'

'Right.'

When he scrubs his hand over his hair, she can see the trembling. He's fidgeting, his hands moving from his hair to his face, then to scratch his arm, before beginning the cycle again.

Chloe looks away, holding the tears at bay. She hates seeing him like this.

Tate suddenly gets to his feet and paces the rug in front of the fireplace. All the while he runs his hand over his hair, back and forth in time with his footsteps. His agitation is growing by the minute. She doesn't know a lot about heroin or what he's going through, but she assumes it has something to do with that. She's never seen him like this before.

She makes eye contact with Dillon through the patio door, trying to tell him that she might need help in a minute. She hopes not, but having the guys outside might come in useful. Dillon moves over to the handle on the door, keeping his attention locked on Tate, but not coming in yet.

'So you want me to go back?'

'Back where, Tate?'

He stops for a second, then changes direction. 'Rehab.'

'I think that's the best thing for you, don't you?'

He shakes his head over and over as he pulls on his hair. 'I hated it. Hated the way they looked at me like I was this fuck up. I'm not, Chloe. I'm not like that.'

'I know—'

But he's not listening to her. He's in his head somewhere. 'Everyone there was so... messed up. I'm not like them. I'm not!'

She makes eye contact with Dillon again. Tate is acting very strangely and it's making her nervous.

'They kept talking to me like I have something in common with them.' He scrubs his hands over his hair as he picks up the pace. 'I don't.'

He scratches his arm as he paces, tearing at the inside of his elbow, leaving red gouges on his skin.

'I'm not...' he doesn't finish the sentence, just mutters to himself. 'I could do it here. I could stay home and stop using.'

'I don't think that's such a good idea.'

He changes direction again, frantically tearing at his arm. 'I know I can stop. I'm not addicted, Chloe. I'm not! I'm not like them. I'm not an addict!'

Chloe is about to reply, but he stops and slams his fist into the mirror over the fireplace, shattering the glass. Before she can react, Dillon and Andy are on him, blocking Tate from Chloe, while Ciaran drags her off the couch and over to the staircase.

As the others come in the front door, Ciaran forcefully directs her up the stairs. 'I need to stay with him! Please Ciaran!'

'No, you need to go upstairs until they calm him down. If he hurts you it'll kill him, you know that.' Chloe wants to argue back, but one look at Ciaran and she knows it would be a waste of time.

He ushers her up the stairs into the master bedroom, standing at the door to make sure she stays put. Defeated, she sits on the edge of their bed and listens to the noise coming from downstairs.

'What's wrong with him? Why is he acting like this?'

Ciaran leans against the doorframe and crosses his arms. 'I'm guessing he's worked up because he needs another hit. He's addicted, Chloe. As much as he says otherwise, he's hooked again. I'm sorry, love.' He goes out into the landing, coming back less than a minute later with Dillon.

'How is he?' she asks.

Dillon curses and shakes his head. That's all she gets from him, as he storms past her into the bathroom.

'Dillon? Is he okay?'

'Does he sound like he's fucking okay?' he shouts from the bathroom. 'He's going nuts.'

'Can you calm him down?'

'He'll run out of steam in a bit,' he says, banging cupboards. 'Where's your first aid kit?'

Chloe joins him in the bathroom and takes the kit from the cupboard under the sink, handing it to him. 'Oh God. What happened to your face?' His nose is bleeding, there's blood on the corner of his mouth, and his eye is red.

'Tate hit me.'

'What? How many times?'

'More than once.'

Chloe can't believe Tate injured Dillon so badly. 'Sit down and I'll clean that up.'

'It's fine—'

'Sit!' she shouts, startling him into silence. 'I've had more than enough hassle from uncooperative rock stars today. Just sit down and stop arguing with me. Please.'

He shuts his mouth and sits on the edge of the bath. Chloe fills the sink with warm water and starts with the cut on his forehead. 'Sorry about that. And sorry he did this to you.'

'You're allowed to be pissed off. We all are. And you don't apologise for him. Ever.'

'I know, but this whole thing is a mess.'

'Ouch!'

'Sorry, it's nasty.'

'Fucker got me with his ring.'

She puts a plaster on the cut then focuses on his split lip. 'He got you right on your piercing. It's covered in blood. Would it be easier to take the lip ring out?'

'No. I might not get it in again. Just clean the blood. I've busted my lip before. It'll be fine.'

She concentrates on his lip, trying to get as much of the blood from around the black piercing as she can. 'I shouldn't have left him. After we lost the baby I mean. I should have stayed and tried to work it out.'

Dillon takes her hand and lowers it from his face. 'This is down to Tate, not you. He made the choice to use again. It would have happened whether you left or not, so don't blame yourself. I mean that.'

His green eyes meet hers and she gets a little reassurance from his no nonsense look.

'You were getting through to him, Chloe. I could see it in his face, even from outside the house.'

'But that's all gone now if he's having a tantrum.'

Dillon laughs, then winces and touches his split lip. 'Tantrum? Yeah, that sounds about right. Don't reckon I'll use that word around him right now though. I'd get more than a split lip. Don't worry. Gregg will talk him down. We'll try again once he's calmed down.'

She nods and sits back, examining his face again. 'All the blood is gone, but you're going to be left with some impressive bruises.'

He stands up and stretches. 'I can handle a few bruises. Thanks Chloe. You stay put for now, okay. I'll give you a shout when Gregg has worked his magic on our boy.'

She follows him back out to the bedroom and stops at the door. Tate is shouting, begging them not to send him back. Something crashes to the floor and Chloe peers over the banisters into the living room below.

Liam and Andy have Tate pinned to the wall beside the fireplace. Tate is frantic, thrashing to get free, shouting obscenities at them, in between pleading with them to let him go.

Ciaran takes her by the arm and gently guides her back to the bedroom, closing the door behind them, silencing Tate's shouts.

Tate

He's had some impressively embarrassing moments in his life. Moments he wished he could go back and redo if given the chance.

Withdrawal last time topped that list. He doesn't remember a lot of it, thankfully, but what he does remember will stick with him forever. Going through that while surrounded by sympathetic strangers was so humiliating.

They cleaned up his vomit. Took his verbal abuse. Held him back when he turned physical. Comforted him when he broke down. Watched him fall apart time and time again.

Until this moment, he didn't think it could get worse.

He'd lost it in front of everyone. In front of Chloe.

Gregg somehow managed to talk him down, again. The whole thing is a blur and he's kind of grateful for that. One minute he was pacing the room talking to Chloe, and the next he was sitting on the ground beside the fireplace with a bloody fist.

He knows he hit the mirror. He's not bothered about that. It's the bruises and bandaged cuts on Dillon's face that make him sick to his stomach. No one had said anything about how he got the injuries, but Tate knows it was him.

Gregg crouches down in front of him, looking at him like he expects him to flip again at any second.

Which he could. He'd scared himself.

He buries his head under his arms, trying to block everyone out.

He didn't realise how far he'd fallen. He honestly hadn't seen it until Chloe said what she did.

Of course he didn't.

He's an addict. Always will be. It doesn't matter what he does, he'll carry that label for the rest of his life. Maybe it's time he accepted that. He didn't admit he had a problem the last time, until he nearly killed himself. What made him think this time would be any different?

Pure pig-headed stupidity probably.

That, and the fact he's weak.

And a fuck up.

Why else would he be back here again after all the pain and utter hell he went through the last time?

He looks up from under his arm when he hears someone coming down the stairs. He knows it's Chloe. That's the worst part of the whole fucking mess. Now he can add her to the list of people who have seen him at his worst.

He can't look at any of them. Can't bring himself to face the disappointment. She sits beside him and wraps her arm around him.

'Are you okay?'

He shakes his head. No point pretending any longer. It's not like he could convince anyone after that fucking disaster of a show he just put on.

'So what's the plan?'

Even without looking, he can feel all eyes in the room on him, waiting for him to decide what he wants to do.

The problem is, he doesn't know what he wants to do. He hated rehab. Hated every second of his three months there. But what's the alternative?

Does he just continue using like he is and hope for the best? Hope that he doesn't land himself in hospital again. Hope that he doesn't die.

Then he makes the mistake of looking at Chloe. She's crying because of him. He loves her and, instead of planning a future with her, he's lost her and let her see him like this.

'We're not going to force you to do anything you don't want to.' She smiles at him, but as she's still crying, it doesn't improve how crappy he feels. 'It's got to be your decision.'

'I'm sorry.'

'We're not looking for an apology, buddy,' Gregg says. 'You can apologise till the cows come home. That's not what we're here for. We're here for you. Here to support you, if that's what you want.'

Tate looks down at his arm, disgusted at the marks on his skin. 'I don't want this.' He curses and scrubs his hands over his face. 'Fuck! I don't want to be like this.'

Chloe rubs his arm, the movement soothing, in spite of the shitty situation. 'You know what you have to do then, don't you?'

Yeah he does. 'I need to go to rehab.' He can almost feel the collective sigh of relief go through the room.

'You sure?' Gregg asks.

He nods. 'Yeah. I'm sure.'

Gregg pats him on the shoulder and smiles. 'We've got you, buddy. I'll sort it out, okay.'

He nods and rests his head on Chloe's shoulder when she pulls him close. 'It's the right decision, Tate.'

'I know. Fuck! My parents.'

'You should tell them in person,' Luke says. 'I can drive you there and wait while you talk to them if you want.'

He'd rather do pretty much anything else than face his parents as he tells them he's using again, but he needs to do it. He needs to look them in the eye when he tells them he's done this to himself again.

'Yeah. Okay. Thanks.'

Gregg stands up and rubs his hands together. 'Great. So we have a plan. Why don't you get cleaned up then Luke can take you to your folks?'

He nods and goes upstairs, not complaining in the slightest when Chloe follows after him. Without a word, she helps him take off his clothes and leads him into the shower, making sure the water is at the right temperature before manoeuvring him into the stall.

He half-heartedly washes himself, then takes the towel she hands him. Any energy he may have had, disappeared as soon as he mentioned the word rehab. His mind is already back there, reliving everything he went through the last time.

Chloe hands him a fresh t-shirt, underwear, and jeans and he gets dressed without paying much attention to what he's doing.

'You've made the right decision,' Chloe says as he sits on the edge of the bed to put on his boots.

'I know. Doesn't make any of this any easier to deal with.' He scratches the back of his head, suddenly embarrassed. 'I let it get me again. I'm so sorry Chloe. You don't deserve this. Any of it. I... fuck...I don't know.'

When she takes his hand, he could shout for joy. 'It's okay, Tate.'

'No, it's not okay. I've been the worst fucking boyfriend to you the last few weeks. I wasn't there for you when I should have been. I messed up again and again, and nothing I say or do, can ever make up for that. I should have supported you. Instead I fell apart and did this to myself. You deserve so much better.' He pauses and drops his gaze from her face. 'Our child deserved better.'

She sniffs and he looks at her face.

'Shit. I didn't mean to make you cry.'

'You didn't. I think I just needed to hear you say that.'

'I should have said it sooner.'

'None of that matters now, Tate. The important thing is you, okay?' He closes his eyes when she runs her hand through his hair. It feels familiar, comforting, and exactly what he needs right now. 'Do you... should I come with you when you go to rehab?'

'No. It's bad enough you've seen me like this. I don't want you there. Please.'

'Okay.' She smiles at him, straightening the pendant around his neck.

'Not much of a good luck charm is it,' he says, looking down at the griffin on the chain around his neck.

'I wouldn't say that.' She kisses it before slipping it under his t-shirt. 'I think it's working just fine.' Chloe rubs her hands over his chest and nods. 'I better let you go so you can talk to your parents.'

'Yeah. I suppose so.' She stands up and holds out her hand. Tate takes it, hanging on to her as he goes back downstairs.

Luke passes him a jacket then grabs his car keys from the counter. 'You set?'

'No. But it's not going to get better by putting it off.' Chloe pulls him into a hug, holding on to him for a long time before she lets him go. 'Bye Tate.'

He kisses her on the cheek. 'Bye Chloe,' then he follows Luke out the door.

Tate climbs out of Luke's car and faces his parents' farmhouse, the dread weighing heavily on him. He can think of at least a dozen things he'd rather do than go inside, but he needs to do this. They deserve to know.

He looks behind him as Liam pulls in, blocking the driveway. Is he here for Tate's protection or Luke's? After what happened in the house it could be either one.

'I'll wait here for you.'

'I'm not going to do a runner Luke.'

'I know. I'll be here.'

Tate gives up trying to fight Luke. He's not going to leave. Tate closes the car door and walks up to the steps leading to the front door.

As usual, his mum's sixth sense is scarily reliable. Before he even gets to the steps, she's opened the door to greet him.

'This is a nice surprise. Can you stay for...' Her voice trails away as she examines his appearance. He must look shite if her reaction is anything to go by. Then she looks over her shoulder to Luke and her confusion grows. 'What's wrong?'

'I need to talk to you. Is Dad here?'

'Yes. Come in.'

She keeps up the scrutiny, as he steps into the hallway and follows her into the living room.

'Rick! Sit down, Tate. Do you want a drink?'

'No. I'm good.'

He sits on the two-seater couch, as his mum disappears into the kitchen. When she comes back a few minutes later, his dad is with her.

Without his usual greeting, Rick sits on the three-seater with Becca and looks over at him. 'What's on your mind?'

'Right.' He catches Rick frowning at him, and Tate realises he's scratching his fucking arm again. Great start. 'Okay, Chloe is back living with her gran.'

The silence hangs for a moment before Becca nods. 'We know, love.'

'How the fuck... sorry,' he adds quickly when she frowns at him. 'How do you know?'

'Come on, Tate,' Rick answers. 'She lives just up the lane. Did you not think we'd find out?'

'Fair point.' And one he should have thought about. 'So she's taking a break. From me.'

He waits for them to say something, but they just look at him.

'A few days after Luke's wedding, she told me she was pregnant.'

That gets a reaction. Becca covers her mouth with her hands, while Rick grins widely. Both reactions wither away, when they pick up on the fact he's not sharing in their joy. 'You're not happy about that, are you?' his dad asks.

'It's not that. I mean yeah, I probably could have handled her telling me, better than I did. Screw that. I know I could have handled it better. She told me, and I just shut down. I did the exact opposite a supportive boyfriend should have done.'

'Hey, sweetie, it's a shock. I'm sure she understands that. You've got time to get your head around it. Both of you.'

'She lost the baby two weeks ago.'

'Christ,' Rick mutters under his breath. 'I'm sorry, Tate. For both of you.'

Tate shrugs. 'Again I fucked that up.' His mother doesn't scold him for cursing. Her mind is on other things. 'I let her think it might have been the best thing to happen. We've only been together ten months or so. I didn't mean it to come across like that, but the letter had come about my father, and my head was messed up. It doesn't excuse how I reacted.'

'Oh Tate. Why didn't you tell us sooner? You've been dealing with all this on your own. We could have been there for you.'

'There's actually a bit more I need to tell you, Mum.' He rolls up his left sleeve and holds out his arm. He can't look at their faces. Doesn't want to see the disappointment and shame.

'Jesus Christ, Tate! Are you fucking stupid or something?' Tate has heard his father pissed off before. This is more than just pissed off. 'Look at me, Tate. Now!'

He does as he's told and hates what he sees. His mother is crying, her attention on the marks on his arm. Rick, however, is beyond furious.

'I asked you a question.'

'Yes. I guess I am stupid.'

'Too right you are.' Rick pushes to his feet and paces, scrubbing his hand over his hair again. 'How long have you been sticking that shit in your body?'

'A few weeks.'

'Perfect. I presume Chloe knows.'

'She does now.'

'I knew I shouldn't have given you the letter from the prison. I knew it. But I thought you could deal with it. Guess I was wrong.'

'I can't do this again.' Becca slowly stands and shakes her head. 'I can't, Tate. I can't sit by your bed again, wondering if you're going to wake up. Wondering what damage you've done to yourself if you do wake up. Not again.'

'I know, Mum. I—'

She shakes her head sharply. 'No, Tate. You don't know. You honestly don't have the first clue.' Then without another word she leaves the room, slamming the door behind her.

The silence stretches on for what feels like hours. He's never seen his mother like that. He wasn't the best behaved child, but she never, ever, turned her back on him like she just did. Never turned away from him. Not once. Watching her walk away has left him feeling physically sick.

'Tate.'

He lifts his head and faces his father, now back on the couch opposite him.

'What's the plan? I mean, please tell me you have a plan?'

'I'm going back to rehab. Gregg is driving me there in the morning.'

'Okay, that's something I guess. I presume the guys know everything?'

'They cornered me a few hours ago. Gave me some home truths.'

'Glad to hear it. You're staying here tonight and I will drive you there myself tomorrow.'

'I need to pack—'

Rick points his finger at Tate. 'You're not going home. I don't want you leaving my sight until I personally check you in to rehab. Do you understand me, Tate?'

He nods once.

'What happened to your hand?' Rick asks, nodding at Tate's torn knuckles.

'I hit a mirror. Dillon too,' he adds quietly.

'Jesus Christ. I'm not sure I even know you anymore. I thought you had more sense, Tate. I really did. I thought, after what you did to yourself the last time, you'd steer clear.'

Rick shakes his head, barely controlling his temper. Tate can't blame him. He's just thrown a lot at his father, and none of it is good.

'I'm sorry. I know I've let you down.'

'No. You've let yourself down, Tate.' He sighs and shakes his head. 'It's done now. No point beating you up about it. I'll tell Luke he can go, and then I'll call Gregg. He can pack some things for you. You can stay in your old room, not the annex.'

'I'm not going to do a runner.'

'And I'm not taking any shit from you, Tate. I will not let you throw your life away, because of your arsehole of a father. I wouldn't be doing my job if I did. I don't give a damn if you're thirty-seven years old. You're going to do what I say without argument. So help me Tate, I will lock you in your room if you give me any trouble.'

'I won't. I want to get clean.'

'Yeah. So you say.'

'You don't believe me?'

'I don't know what to believe any more, Tate. I really don't. I thought you had a handle on this but...' he shakes his head then stands up again. 'Empty your pockets.'

'Dad, I don't have any—'

Rick raises his eyebrow and Tate stops talking. He stands, then drops his keys, mobile, wallet, and a handful of change on the coffee table.

'Do you have any on you at the moment?'

'No.'

'Forgive me if I don't quite believe you. Take off your boots and sweatshirt. When did you use last?'

'A few hours ago.'

'How are you feeling?'

'Okay.'

Rick crosses his arms and glares at him. 'Why don't you try the truth this time.'

'Not good. I feel sick.'

'Yeah well you've got a lot more of that heading your way.'

When Tate's stripped to his jeans and t-shirt, Rick gestures to the stairs. 'Go on. I'll bring you up something bland to settle your stomach.'

Utterly ashamed and disgusted with himself, Tate climbs the stairs and drops onto the bed in his old room.

He did this.

He killed the trust he'd taken the last few months to rebuild, and he hates himself for it.

Luke

'About time.'

'Sorry. I had to drop Tate to his parents' house.'

Pippa sits on the chair in front of the dressing table and crosses her legs. 'Why? Was he drunk? Oh please tell me he's not drinking again?' Her eyes narrow. 'Were you drinking with your friends?'

He quickly shakes his head. 'No! I promise I wasn't. He just needed a lift—'

She holds up her hand, stopping him in his tracks. 'Forget it! It's done now. Just don't do it again, Luke. I've been waiting for you.'

'I'm sorry.' She nods, so he decides to make his escape before she thinks of something else he's done to annoy her. 'I might work out for a bit.'

Pippa places her makeup case on the dressing table and shakes her head. 'You don't have time. I said we'd meet Astrid in an hour.'

'Astrid?'

'She wants all the gossip from the wedding and honeymoon. We're meeting her in town for dinner.'

Luke deserves an award for restraining the groan. He really doesn't like Astrid. In truth, he's not too fond of any of Pippa's friends. Compared to the guys, her friends are from a different planet. It's all about which designer they're wearing, what restaurants they're eating at, and who they're eating with. He'd much prefer pizza on the couch any day.

And Tate's ex isn't on any list of people he wants to spend ten minutes with, let alone an hour or so over dinner. It was bad enough she was at their wedding and the party the other night. He's had enough Astrid to last him a lifetime.

'I have an idea,' she says glancing over her shoulder at him. 'Why don't you call Tate? See if he's free.'

'I really don't think that's a good idea.'

'Why not? He's broken up with Chloe, so it's the perfect idea. Tate and Astrid belong together.'

Tate and Astrid were a car crash waiting to happen. The only thing Tate was interested in, was sex with Astrid. Nothing deep and meaningful. Much to her annoyance and disappointment.

'He's really not a fan of hers, Pippa.'

'You could convince him otherwise. I mean it won't be too difficult - especially now that Chloe is out of the way.'

'Tate is still in love with Chloe. There's no way I'm getting in between them. Maybe you should go and meet her alone. I'll stay here. I'll just be in the way anyway.'

She leans against the edge of the dressing table and crosses her arms. 'What's the problem, Luke? Why don't you want to come to dinner with me? Oh, I know. You're going to see *him* again, aren't you?'

'Who?'

She snorts loudly as she glares over at him. 'Don't give me that!

You know full well who I'm talking about. Dillon.'

'What? No.'

'I'm such an idiot. You weren't with Tate at all, were you. You were with Dillon.'

'No. I swear. Tate is going back into rehab, okay. He's using heroin again.' He instantly feels like he's betrayed Tate, but she'll find out sooner or later.

Pippa stares at him for a long few minutes, then sighs dramatically. 'Well, that's put an end to that, hasn't it. Astrid will be devastated.'

He keeps his mouth shut. Astrid's feelings are not on his radar in the slightest. He's seriously worried about Tate.

'So Tate is gone, and so is Dillon. That's just perfect for your career isn't it?'

'Tate will be out soon, and Dillon isn't gone. He's still part of the band.'

Pippa turns on the stool and fixes him with an impressive glare. 'Do you really think that? Dillon was in prison, Luke. Prison. Do you really think Vox will take him back after that? He's hardly the picture perfect role model for your adoring fans. And you do realise he got drunk at our wedding, and destroyed the place? Do you have any idea how embarrassing it is to have the best man arrested during the dancing? I'm surprised I can show my face in public. It's humiliating.'

'He's had a rough time—'

'Rough time? Dillon is selfish. That's what it boils down to. He does what he wants, when he wants, and to hell with everyone else. He proved that at our wedding. I don't want you seeing him anymore.'

Luke takes a second to process what she just said. 'Not see him? We're in the band together. I have to see him.'

Pippa rests her arms on her crossed legs. 'Well, I've been thinking about that.'

'Thinking about what?'

'You and the band. I think you should go solo.'

Luke stares over at her for a long time, before he can form any words. 'Solo? No! I'm not going solo!'

'Why not? There are at least three labels who would jump at the chance to sign you.'

'You've approached other labels?'

'Of course. You need to know your options, before you decide who would be the best fit.'

'Pippa, you can't talk to other labels about me. I have a contract with Vox. I'll get into trouble.'

She waves his concerns away. 'It's fine. Everyone is sworn to secrecy.'

Luke stares over at his wife, not quite believing what he's hearing. He has no intention of leaving Broken. Ever.

'The others are holding you back, Luke. You're in Tate's shadow. In the shadow of a lead singer, who has a heroin problem he won't be able to shake. You know that as well as I do. If he's going back into rehab for the second time in twelve months, that's really not a good sign.'

'But he's not holding me back. I'm on vocals with Tate.'

'Exactly! *With* him. It should be you at the front, not him. So that's why leaving the band is the perfect solution. Think what you could do, where you could go, without them keeping you back.'

He shakes his head over and over. He can't leave the band. He can't. Broken is his only escape. Being with the guys on stage is the only time he genuinely feels happy.

And safe.

'No...'

'Excuse me?'

'No, Pippa. I'm not leaving. I can't. I've made a commitment to them.'

She clenches her jaw, her foot bobbing up and down, as she throws her best disapproving look in his direction. 'You've also made a commitment to me, Luke.'

'I'm sorry, and I know you're trying to help, but I'm in a contract with Vox. Even if I wasn't, I don't want to leave the band. I love being in Broken with my friends. Really love it.'

'More than me?'

'What?'

'Do you love Broken more than me?'

'Well, no. Of course not.'

'Yet you're happy to ignore my feelings, for the sake of the band.'

'No, that's not what I'm doing. I just enjoy what I do. You know that. I love you Pippa, but I really don't want to leave Broken.'

Luke swallows thickly, as she silently glares over at him. She's furious. He listens to the tap of her painted nails on the dressing table, as she throws daggers at him.

Then things take a turn. Instead of imaginary daggers, she picks up her heavy jewellery box and throws it at him.

The corner of the ornate and expensive box hits him in the side, tearing his skin. He yelps and stares down at the blood oozing from the wound. 'Pippa—'

But she's not listening to him. 'We're married now, Luke. You can't be selfish anymore. You need to think about both of us, and what's best for us as a couple. That means taking my feelings into consideration for once. You've put the band before me for years. It's always the guys before me. You can't do that anymore. I come first, and the band second.'

He presses his hand to the wound, still in shock at what she'd just done. She'd hit him before, but never drawn blood like this. 'I'm sorry. I'll think about it, okay?'

'Think about it?' She shakes her head and rises to her feet, slowly stalking towards him. 'Think?'

He cowers as she nears. 'Pippa, please.'

'Please! What about me Luke?' She attacks him, striking his head, face, and chest. He buries his head under his arms, but it doesn't do much good. She's in a blind rage and won't stop until she's finished.

'What about me, Luke?'

He switches off, as she strikes him. Gets lost in his head, as she hits and slaps him again and again. She eventually runs out of steam, and lowers onto the bed beside him, breathing heavily.

He owes her an apology, but is terrified he's just going to make things worse. She's never lost her temper with him quite like that before. After a long silence he lowers his arms and looks over at her.

She's crying. That's his fault. He tries to take her hand, but she pulls it away, so he slowly slides to his knees in front of her, wincing when the movement pulls on his torn side.

'Pippa. Please look at me.'

She sniffs and wipes her face. He hates that he seems to keep upsetting her no matter how much he tries not to.

'I'm sorry, Pippa. I didn't mean to upset you.'

'The band is clearly more important to you than I am. I just wish I knew before we got married. I could have saved myself a lot of heartache.'

'The band isn't more important than you are.'

She wipes tears from her eyes and looks down at him. 'You've got a funny way of showing it. You keep pushing me, Luke. Keep disappointing me, then I lose my temper, and something like this happens. And now I feel guilty. I shouldn't have to fight three other men for my husband's attention. Surely you can see that? Why do I even have to point it out to you?'

'I'm sorry. You're right. It should be you first. It's my fault, not yours. I'll leave the band.'

'You will?'

He nods, ignoring the hollowness in his gut. 'Of course.'

'And Dillon?'

'I'll walk away. Can I see him one last time? Tell him I'm done.'

'I suppose so. Knowing him, he'll keep coming back, until he hears it from you in person. You can see him tomorrow. You're spending today with me.'

She cups the side of his face and runs her thumb along his cheek.

'I love you. I don't want to get angry with you, Luke. I hate it, but I can't keep going like this. I can't keep fighting for your attention. You can't keep pushing me aside when the guys or Ellen calls. It's unfair and makes me feel worthless. Why would you do that to me?'

Luke is now buried under a mound of shite he can't dig himself out of. He's made his wife feel like she's coming second to his work, and that's not right or fair on her. But he doesn't know how to make it right. He never knows how to make it right.

'Nothing to say to me?'

He smiles, even though he wants to throw up. He always wants to throw up. His gut has been all over the place the last few weeks. He swallows a few times, in an effort to stop himself from making this so much worse by being sick. 'I'm sorry. I don't want to keep letting you down.'

He relaxes a little when she smiles at him. 'I forgive you. Why don't you get cleaned up and we'll go out.'

Luke nods and pushes to his feet, then goes into the ensuite. He stares at the bloody gash on his side, but can't be bothered doing anything about it. It's going to be one hell of a bruise. Just like the one on his other side, from the night before their wedding. She'd shoved him against the corner of the granite work surface in their kitchen. But, that was his fault too, like always.

He doesn't know why he keeps disappointing her, keeps letting her down, keeps making her angry. He tries so hard to make her proud, but keeps falling short. The fact she married him at all is still a surprise.

He looks at his reflection in the mirror and doesn't recognise himself anymore. His skin is grey, his hair limp, black rings surround his eyes, and he's losing weight. His appetite has been non-existent lately. When he does eat, he usually throws up after. No wonder he looks like hell.

Maybe she's right. Maybe leaving Broken will make things better for them.

But he doesn't want to leave the band.

Really doesn't want to. Being on stage is the only time he feels fully at peace. He loves every second of it. Loves singing and playing the guitar.

But he has no choice. He can't put the band before his wife. What sort of a person would that make him?

Tate

'What the fuck are you doing here?'

Shane pushes past his brother and walks into the bedroom. 'Nice to see you too.'

'But... you're in Canada.'

Shane looks around him and shrugs. 'Clearly, I'm in Ireland.'

Tate stares stupidly at his brother for another minute, before he finally moves. He sits on the edge of his bed and stares at his brother. 'Okay, so you going o answer me now? What are you doing here?'

Shane sits on the armchair and scrubs his hand over his short strawberry-blond hair. 'Well, baby brother, I'm here because you're in a bit of a pickle, from what I can make out. Bria gave me a shout yesterday. Thought it would be a good idea if I made an appearance.''

'I'm not in a pickle.'

Shane laughs, as he rests his boots on the table in front of the armchair. 'Is that right? You see, I heard that Chloe had a miscarriage and that she's moved out. And that Gregg left the band, and the rest of you have been told to take some time off. That your father died and that you are sticking fucking poison in your veins again, and are heading to rehab in a few hours. Did I hear any of that wrong?'

Hearing Shane relay the last few weeks in such a straight, to the point way, is like a punch to the gut. 'So you came all the way here to have a go at me?'

Shane leans forward, shaking his head. 'Don't get all defensive with me. You push, and I guarantee I'll push back harder. I'm here to talk - not have a go.'

Tate sighs, admitting defeat, as he slides up the bed and sits back against the headboard. Shane is the one person Tate would never get into a fight with. He'd done it enough over the years and never came out of it well. Shane wins every argument – verbal or physical. That's why he made such a damn impressive lawyer.

'Sorry. I'm just... I don't know.'

'Can I join you?'

He nods, so Shane sits beside him on the bed.

'I hear you're grounded.'

He laughs at that. 'Yeah. Fucking tragic, right? You better watch it yourself. Thought the groundings finished when we left school.'

'It's certainly a new one, Tate. How are you holding up?'

He angrily shakes his head. 'Not good. Did you see Mum?'

Shane nods slowly. 'I did.'

'Is she still angry?'

'I'd say she's more upset than anything. She'll come around.'

'I don't think so. I've let them both down. Dad pretty much strip searched me, before he sent me up here. I've never seen them like that.'

'They're worried about you, Tate. We all are.'

'I know.' He curses and scrubs his hands over his face. 'You didn't have to come all the way here though.'

'Why wouldn't I? I'm your brother, Tate. I've done everything I possibly can to look out for you since Mum and Dad first brought you home. I wish... I don't know. I'm annoyed with myself, I guess.'

'For what?'

'Leaving,' Shane says, turning to look sideways at him. 'I moved away and I feel like we lost that closeness we had. I regret that.'

'Jesus, Shane! This isn't on you. You helped me so much when I was growing up. You got me out from under the bed, remember?'

Shane smiles at that. 'You spent two fucking days hiding under there. Didn't think you'd ever come out.'

'I trusted you though. I remember that like it happened yesterday. You were the first person I trusted.'

'Yeah, and I abandoned you.'

'You fell in love and found an amazing career. Me too... until I fucked it up.' He turns his head to look at Shane. 'I'm sorry.'

'I know you are.'

'I never wanted you to see me like this. Or Chloe. Fuck, I never wanted to be like this again.' He closes his eyes and drops his head back against the headboard. 'I've done nothing but hurt her. I love her and I treated her like I didn't care about her. I drove her away, Shane.

'I love her so fucking much. All I wanted was a life with her. Instead I was a dick to her, then stuck a fucking needle in my arm again. I can't blame her for leaving me.'

'You were both struggling with what was going on. You had a lot thrown at you over a short period of time.'

'That's a reason, but not a fucking excuse, Shane.' He twists the ring on his thumb as he glares at the wall in front of him. 'She told me she was pregnant, and I froze, Shane. I gave her nothing. I just couldn't get any words out.'

'It was a shock no doubt.'

Tate nods. Shock is right. 'We've been together for less than a year, and it's been a shite fucking year at times. I... I guess I was just hoping for a bit of time for us, you know. Just to be together, without any drama. I mean we hadn't even talked about kids. Hell, we've only been living together for a few months. I couldn't get my head around having a baby. I felt like I was suffocating, Shane. Like there was this weight on my chest, and I couldn't fucking breathe.

'And it's not like I'd be up there with all the best role models. A junkie and alcoholic, who can't sleep, because he's having dreams about his abusive father who killed my mother. How the fuck does all that make me a good dad? What if—' he stops himself before he voices his worry. Shane's already looking at him like he's pathetic.

'That doesn't mean you'll be a bad father, Tate.'

'Maybe not, if it was in my past. But I'm using again.'

'You're facing that head on. You will beat it again.'

'I hope so. He raped me, Shane. A lot. My father, I mean.'

Shane automatically tenses beside him. Tate may not have ever mentioned it to either Shane or Bria before now, but he knows, deep down, they suspected what his father had actually done to him.

'That's the first time I've ever said that out loud. It kind of feels good to say it. I've been trying to ignore it. Hoping it would go away. Think I've just been making things so much worse for myself.'

'Thank you for telling me. If you've never said it out loud, I presume your therapist doesn't know?'

Tate shakes his head. 'I've been hiding it behind my drug problem and the other abuse.'

'But not anymore?'

He turns to look at his brother. 'I have to start facing all this head on. I've spent the last year hiding from everything. Using my past, and my father, as an excuse for using drugs, and fucking things up with Chloe and you guys. It's all a lie though.'

Tate has no idea where all this is coming from, but he's not going to stop himself now it's finally coming out. For the first time since he overdosed, he's being honest, truly honest with himself.

'Loads of people have shitty childhoods, Shane. Far worse than mine. And Dara was only able to fuck with me, because I was already using drugs. That was on me. I've been using for years - long before he unlocked all the memories I'd buried. If I wasn't already being a dick, I wouldn't have reacted the way I did.

'And Chloe...' he takes a long breath and closes his eyes. He's exhausted and really wants a fix fucking badly. 'She deserves so much better than me. I should have held her, when she told me she was pregnant. I should have moved my fucking arse and hugged her. God,' he says, hitting his head against the headboard. 'That entire scene is on replay in my head. I was horrible. In the hospital too. She'd just lost the baby and I made her think it was a good thing.'

He turns to look at Shane again.

'No wonder she ran.'

'You know you *both* lost that baby. Not just her.'

He takes a few seconds to process that. He never thought about it like that. 'Yeah. I guess so. Do you think I'd be a good father?'

Shane smiles widely. 'Oh my God, yes! Absolutely. Have you not seen how your two nieces worship you?'

'That's different though.'

'Tate, you are ridiculously protective. Always have been. The way you are with them and with Bria, Chloe too. You'd do everything in your power to keep them all safe. Isn't that what every child deserves? Isn't that what you wanted as a child, when you were being hurt?'

He nods and swallows thickly.

'I know without a doubt, you'd be insanely protective of your child, and that you'd love him or her, more than anything else in the world. That's who you are, Tate.'

Tate wipes his face. He doesn't cry. But maybe he needs to let it out. He hadn't thought about it like that. Why hadn't he?

He'd been so focused on his father and his past, he hadn't allowed himself to think beyond that. Shane is right. He always is. Growing up Shane had looked out for him and, in turn, he looked after Bria. Just because his father was a sadistic bastard didn't mean he would be. He's not like him. Nothing like him.

He was raised by Rick and Becca. They're his parents - not Ken Reilly

He closes his eyes, not bothering to wipe the tears from his face. Bit fucking late to have this epiphany. 'It's gone, Shane. It's too fucking late.'

'I know, but that doesn't mean it won't happen for you again. One thing at a time, Tate. Get clean then talk to Chloe.'

He nods. 'So fucking tired, Shane.'

'Lie down. You need to sleep.'

'I can't sleep. Haven't been able to sleep for ages. Fucking head won't shut off.'

'Remember when you couldn't sleep after Mum and Dad brought you home?'

'Story of my fucking life.'

Shane picks up the remote from the bedside table and turns on the TV. He shuffles down the bed and flicks through the channels until he finds something that interests him. 'Lie down, close your eyes, and just listen to the TV. You'll drop off in no time.'

Tate gets under the duvet and slides down beside his brother. 'Will you stay?'

'Of course. Now shut up and go to sleep.'

Tate closes his eyes, taking comfort from Shane's reassuring presence, just like he did when he was a child, as he finally drops off to sleep.

30

Tate

Tate gets out of the shower, then tightens his grip on the towel when he sees Gregg sitting on the end of his bed. 'You scared the shit out of me!'

'Sorry buddy. I just brought some stuff over for you.'

Tate glances at the bag on the floor. 'Thanks. Dad called you?'

Gregg nods. 'Oh yeah. Wow. He can be intense, can't he?'

Tate grabs a pair of boxers and put them on in the bathroom, before rejoining Gregg in the bedroom. 'You think? He grounded me last night. Or near enough to it.'

Gregg grimaces, as he passes Tate the t-shirt from the bed. 'Oh dear. Not a good look for someone hitting forty.'

'I'm not hitting forty you fucker.'

'You're closer than I am,' Gregg adds with a grin.

Tate holds up his middle finger, before pulling on his t-shirt and the jeans that Gregg throws at him. 'So, I see Shane made an appearance last night.'

'I know. He's going to take me to rehab, instead of Dad. I think I've put my parents through enough as it is.'

'Might be less traumatic for you too. So, you okay about this?'

Tate fastens his belt before he answers. 'No.' He's far from okay. He's dreading it.

'It's the right thing, buddy.'

He laces his boots, then lies back in the armchair, staring out the window at the sea in the distance. 'How the fuck did I end up here again, Gregg?'

'I wish I knew, Tate. But you're here, and you're dealing with it.'

Tate laughs harshly, then rests his chin on his hand as he watches the waves. 'I have to do it differently this time. I'm going to keep ending up back here, unless I do it differently.'

'That's the first step. At least you know where you went wrong. You'll be home in no time, Tate. You'll see.'

Tate fists his hand, squeezing tightly as a cramp works through his arm. He gets up and paces beside his bed, tapping his hand against his leg as he walks. 'I hope you're right.' He adds scratching his arm, to his pacing, but he's beyond caring. He stumbles, as Gregg suddenly appears in his face. 'What are you doing?'

'I think we should go for a walk.'

'What?'

'You're about to peel your damn skin off. We'll go for a quick walk on the beach to clear your head. Then Shane can get you checked in. That sound good?'

'Dad's not going to let me leave the house.'

'Leave that to me. Grab a sweatshirt and I'll meet you downstairs in five.'

Tate doesn't think Gregg will be able to convince his dad for one second, but it's worth a shot. He needs to get out of here. Needs to do anything other than crave the very thing that's got him into this fucking miserable situation again.

He grabs a hoodie from the drawer, then slowly makes his way downstairs, like he's a teenager sneaking out of the house.

He gets as far as the bottom step, before Rick comes out of his study with Gregg in tow. 'Ten minutes Tate, then you'll need to head. Any longer and I will send out the search parties. I promise you.'

Tate nods and follows Gregg through the kitchen and out the back door. 'How the fuck did you manage that?'

Gregg grins widely and pats himself on the back of the shoulder. 'Clearly the sun shines out of my arse. Parents love me, buddy.'

'Yeah, well, whatever the reason, thank you.' Tate smiles as he approaches Jove's stable. The huge horse lifts his head over the door and nuzzles the side of Tate's face. 'Hey buddy. I fucked up again, so I have to go away for a bit.' He stops talking, as his throat closes up.

Going on the road is a regular thing. He's had to say goodbye to Jove, to his family, to Chloe, countless times. But this is so different. He's not going away with his four best friends. He's going away alone, to spend the next who knows how long, picking his brain apart.

Bit dramatic but that's how it feels.

Tate gets himself together then grabs the lead rope from outside the stable, attaching it to Jove's headcollar.

Gregg is convinced Jove has it in for him. Always has, but this is the first time he doesn't complain, as Tate leads his horse out of the stable and follows Gregg through the gate onto the beach.

As Shane turns off the main road, Tate resists the urge to shout at him to stop and take him home. But then he thinks about Chloe, and the life he wants with her. Desperately wants. More than all the fame and fortune, he wants Chloe. And that means sorting himself out.

He's hurt too many people by relapsing. He's got too many people to make this up to. Himself top of that list.

And his Mum.

He'd tried to talk to her before he left, but she just hugged him then walked away. She'd been here with him before. Watched him do the exact same thing to himself a little over a year ago. He can't blame her for not being able to deal with his actions.

He stuffs his hands under his armpits, but he can't stop the trembling. God he needs another hit. It's not even been a day and already his body is missing it.

'You okay?'

He stops himself from lying. That's what has landed him back here again. Pretending he's okay, when he's far from it. 'No. I feel fucking rotten.'

Shane nods, then seems to push the car a little faster. As they come out of the trees, the facility comes into view. Back here again. He lost three months of his life in there last year. Three miserable, painful, fucking depressing months. Coming off drugs the first time had been beyond humiliating. But instead of learning his lesson he'd run back to the easy fix, without remembering all the shite that came with it.

Shane pulls up in the visitors car park and turns to look at him. 'You need a minute?'

'I'd prefer to get in there and start the clock. I don't feel so good.'

Shane squeezes his shoulder then climbs out, and grabs Tate's bag from the back seat.

Tate pulls himself out of the car, turning when he feels someone looking at him. When he sees who it is, he knows he must be hallucinating. Chloe waves at him from beside her car parked a little further down the car park.

'I'll wait by the door,' Shane says, waving at Chloe before walking over to the door.

'Chloe. What are you doing here?'

She smiles again and he swears it's the most amazing thing he's ever seen.

'I know you told me not to come, but I had to.'

He wants to hug her, but he's not so sure it's his place anymore. He stuffs his hands into the back pockets of his jeans, partially to stop himself from touching her, but also to stop the infernal trembling that's working through him. 'How are you?'

'I'm good, thanks.' She looks critically at him. 'You're in a bad way, aren't you?'

He nods. 'No one to blame but myself. Listen, I'm glad you're here. I should have said this yesterday, but I wasn't thinking straight. Thank you for what you did... you know, for making me see sense.'

'You did that yourself. You just needed us to maybe give you a nudge in the right direction.'

'Nudge? It was a fucking kick. But I needed it, so thank you.'

She pulls his hand from his pocket and squeezes it. 'I'm so proud of you, Tate.'

Tate squeezes her hand, then lets it go. 'There's nothing to be proud of, believe me.' He winces as a cramp twists his gut.

'Are you all right?'

'No. Not really. Shit,' he mutters as he doubles over.

Chloe takes his arm and supports him as the cramp works through his gut. 'We better get you inside.'

'No! Wait. Can we talk? Please.'

'Tate, you're in pain. You need help.'

'Not now. When I get out.' He pauses, then vomits in the perfectly manicured flowerbed beside him.

Chloe runs her hand through his damp hair as he retches again, mortification adding to all the other shit he's feeling. He never wanted her to see him like this.

'Of course we'll talk. I love you, Tate. Now please let me get you inside.'

He manages to pull himself together enough to look up at her. 'Hold on. You love me?'

'Yes. That was never the problem, Tate. Now please let me get you inside before you well and truly destroy this flowerbed.'

Dillon

Dillon opens his front door and frowns when he sees Luke standing outside his apartment. 'Hey.'

'Can I come in?'

Dillon steps aside. 'Sure.'

He puts on the kettle, instead of grabbing something stronger. Luke doesn't look in the mood for alcohol. In fact he doesn't look in the mood for anything. For someone who just got back from a month on a tropical island, he's pale and pasty. Fucking knackered too, if the black rings under his eyes are anything to go by.

Dillon absently scratches his chest and considers putting on a t-shirt. He's just out of the shower and had been lounging around the house in his boxers. Luke slumps onto the couch and stares at the wall opposite him. There's something on his mind. It's fucking obvious.

'I might just throw on some clothes.'

'Are you okay?' Luke finally asks.

Dillon sits beside him, surprised by the question. 'Me? Yeah. Why?'

'Just after what Tate did to you yesterday. Your face looks sore.'

The kettle boils so he pours two cups of coffee and passes one to Luke. 'It fucking hurt at the time. Tate packs one hell of a punch.'

'Did Gregg contact you about him?'

Dillon nods. 'Yeah. Glad Shane managed to get back to see him. It'll be weird not having him around for a bit, but better than losing him.'

Luke looks back to the far wall, as he wraps his hands around his mug of coffee. 'You remember in school when that asshole from woodwork kept having a go at me before class?'

Dillon nods, not sure where this is coming from, but hey, if Luke is talking to him he's not going to stop him. 'Yeah. Simon something.'

'That's the one. Remember what you did to him?'

'Too right I do! I ended up in detention for a week because of that fucker. It worked though.'

'Are you surprised? You had his hand in a vice and were threatening to hammer a nail through it.'

'Fucker deserved it.'

Luke shuffles closer, and leans across him to put his cup of coffee on the table. Dillon holds his breath for some reason. He's not usually nervous around people, but something about Luke tonight is throwing him off course.

It different, and he can't figure out why. It's like Luke is quieter than usual, but not his voice. It's more the air around him. There's something off with his friend.

Luke's arm brushes against his bare leg, as he sits back in the couch again, sending a shiver through Dillon's body. Yeah, cause that's what he should be thinking about right now.

Why the fuck didn't you get dressed you self sabotaging prick?

'You've always looked out for me, Dillon. I don't mind it though. It's nice to know you've got my back.'

'Sure thing.' He eyes his bedroom door. Maybe he should make a dive for it. Add a few protective layers. Not that it's going to make a difference. He's the one with the problem - not Luke.

Being half naked around the guys was part of life. Between photo shoots and living on top of each other on tour, they'd lost any shyness ages ago.

That's what he gets for letting his fucking mouth run away with him at the wedding. Saying the words out loud, telling Gregg and Tate that he's in love with Luke, makes being around the guy awkward as anything.

It's like the truth is out there and everyone knows. Well, everyone in the band except Luke, thank fuck. But it's like there's a spotlight shining on him, highlighting every move.

'I'm getting cold. Better throw on some clothes.'

Fucking lame excuse but he's grabbing it and running. Dillon pushes to his feet but Luke stops him.

'What happened?'

His escape comes to a premature end. 'What happened when?'

'At the wedding.'

Out of the statement, the one thing that hits Dillon is the fact Luke called it *the* wedding instead of *his*.

He shrugs. 'I told you. Too much drink mixed with some shit I shouldn't have taken.'

Luke meets his eyes and Dillon squirms. Never done that before. Ever. He's a damn good Dom. Has been for years. He's never found anyone he couldn't look at straight on without flinching. Other people squirmed. Not him.

'I know you Dillon. I'm asking you to tell me the truth.'

'Truth. What truth? I got wasted and took some shit I shouldn't have. End of story.'

'You're lying to me. It's like the Simon thing again. You completely lose it when you think someone is hurting me. Always have. You have an inbuilt need to look out for me.' Luke pauses and for the briefest moment, Dillon swears the guy is going to cry. 'Do you think someone is hurting me?'

Well that's one hell of a question, and he has no idea how to answer it.

During his time in prison, he'd thought about Luke a lot. Constantly in fact. There wasn't a lot else to do, other than regret what he did, and beat himself up for messing up their friendship, and the most important day in Luke's life.

But as for someone hurting him? Is being married to a controlling bitch technically hurting Luke? He seems happy enough, sometimes. Doesn't he?

Who the fuck is he to judge? He's had one relationship worth anything, and that ended as badly as it could. When it comes to anything long term, he's clueless.

Luke is waiting for him to answer. Instead, Dillon flips the question around, firing it back at Luke. 'Is someone hurting you?'

His hazel eyes drop, focusing on the table instead of Dillon. Is that a yes? But then Luke lifts his head again and shakes his head. 'You still haven't answered my question. Why did you do what you did, at the wedding?'

Dillon doesn't miss that Luke wasn't entirely convincing in his own reply. He's still looking for the truth about the wedding though, and Dillon gets the impression Luke isn't going to drop it.

But is he really being a friend to him by lying?

Dillon has tried to keep his feelings for Luke bottled up. Tried to tell himself he's being stupid and to move on. Luke is straight. End of story. But Dillon's feelings didn't care about minor details like that.

It didn't help one bit that Luke is downright fucking gorgeous. His hair, his face, his sculpted body, his genuinely decent soul. Everything about the guy is perfect.

But as much as Dillon wants to be with him, he values their friendship much more. Luke was there for him when his parents threw him out for being bi. Luke had made him see that life was worth living, even though, for a long time, he didn't agree.

The least he owes him is honesty. He's already put a strain on their friendship. He's got nothing else to lose at this stage.

He sits back down and, ignoring the growing desire to empty his stomach, grows a set and faces his friend.

'Because I'm in love with you. I've been in love with you for years. You got married and I lost my head. Doesn't excuse how I reacted. Nothing will ever excuse that. And I know you don't feel the same. I mean you're straight, so it's fucking ridiculous, but... yeah. That's it.'

Dillon holds his breath as he waits to see how Luke reacts to hearing the truth.

Luke turns his head and looks at Dillon. He's not shocked or surprised to hear that. Did he know all along?

They just stay looking at each other in silence. Dillon glances at the stud in Luke's chin instead of his face. He can't look at his face. This is getting a little intense for his liking, but he doesn't want to turn away. Which makes no sense at all.

Luke has him firmly locked in his sights and, for the first time in his life, Dillon hasn't got a clue what to do. The tables have turned, and he's powerless to do anything about it. No control. No dominance. No clue how to react. Luke's eyes have full control of him.

Then the world shifts on its axis.

Luke leans over and kisses him. Dillon freezes when Luke's lips touch his. The kiss is soft and barely more than a brush of his lips, but it's the best thing Dillon has experienced. Luke is actually kissing him. Straight, married Luke. The realisation hits and Dillon pulls back.

'Hold up. What's going on here?'

'What's wrong? Don't you want to?' Luke asks, as his dark brown eyes hold Dillon in their spell. Something that's equal parts fucking awesome, and downright terrifying.

'No! I didn't say that. I'm just confused, that's all. I mean you're straight.' It's probably the most ridiculous thing he could have said in the moment, but the entire situation is confusing him. He's in his boxers on the couch, his mouth inches from Luke's.

'Please, Dillon. I just need to... I want to...'

He shouldn't. He knows he absolutely should get up and put a hell of a lot of distance, and clothes, between them ASAP. But he stays where he is, staring stupidly at the man he's loved for years.

'Are you sure you want this, Luke? I mean really fucking sure?'

Luke nods and moves towards him again. This time Dillon doesn't hold back. He doesn't want to hold back. He slides his hand around the back of Luke's head and pulls him closer, crushing their lips together. He teases Luke's mouth open and slides his tongue in, groaning when his tongue finds Luke's.

Then Luke's hand is on his chest and Dillon's cock goes from hard to downright throbbing. Dillon traces his palm down Luke's hard chest, loving the way the muscles moving under his skin.

Dillon pushes Luke back against the couch and covers his body with his own. Luke's arousal presses against his stomach and Dillon has to fight to calm down. He moves against him, the sensation of their dicks rubbing against each other through their clothes, is mind blowing.

Dillon has been with his fair share of guys over the years, but something about even being with Luke like this, is so much better than anything he's had before.

He slides his hand under Luke's t-shirt, running his fingers over his pierced nipple which feels so good, and then back down towards his jeans. Afraid to move too fast, Dillon stays outside and rubs him through the material. Luke groans against his mouth and Dillon loves how it sounds.

Then he's thrown back into the painful reality of his life. Luke turns to stone under him, and not in a good way. He fights to get out from under Dillon, scrabbling up the couch, nearly falling over the arm, in his attempt to break free. Dillon stands up, holding his hands out in front of him. 'Sorry, Luke I didn't mean—'

Luke shakes his head, as he looks anywhere but at Dillon. 'It's my fault. I shouldn't have done that. It was absolutely a mistake and I should never have let it happen. It was wrong on so many levels. Sorry.'

'No, that was down to me. I—' But Luke is already making a beeline for the door. 'Wait, Luke! Don't go like this! Please! Just sit for a sec.'

'I'm sorry, Dillon. I really am.'

Then he's gone, slamming the door behind him with a heart wrenching thud.

Dillon has no idea how long he stares at the door. Maybe Luke will come back, big grin on his face and tell him the whole thing was a joke. But as he stares at the door, fighting back the growing tightness in his throat, he realises he'll probably never come back.

Wrong on so many levels.

He drops onto the couch and plays the whole scene out in his head again. He'd asked Luke twice if he was sure. Didn't he? He can be a dick at times, but he'd never force himself on anyone. Luke said he wanted it.

Wrong on so many levels.

What does he mean by wrong? Dillon's head instantly goes back to his parents' kitchen when he was seventeen. He'd worked up to telling them he was bisexual for weeks. Weeks of convincing himself they'd be fine about it. That he's their son and they'd love him unconditionally.

But they were far from fine. And as for loving him unconditionally, he learned the hard way from too many people, there's no such thing.

His parents had used that same word. *Wrong.* He's wrong. Flawed. A disgrace. Disgusting. Disowned.

He paces his living room, keeping his eyes on the door, as if Luke is going to magically reappear. Luke can't have meant *wrong* the same way Dillon's parents had. He wouldn't say that. Not knowing how much it broke Dillon apart, when he heard it from his own mum and dad.

The anger builds, squeezing his chest, as he continues to pace.

'I'm not *wrong!*' He slams the heel of his hand against his forehead. How can one fucking word bring him back two decades? One measly fucking word. He can still see his mother, clear as fucking day, pointing at him across the kitchen table, spitting that word at him. Using it as a weapon, which tore him apart.

Dillon sits and clasps his hands together, as he continues to glare at the door. No one else is going to make him feel that way again. Not even Luke.

Dillon picks up Luke's half empty coffee cup and hurls it against the wall. The cup explodes, showering the floor and wall with coffee. There's no fucking way he's just going to let Luke throw that comment at him, then leave like that!

Whatever about him regretting it or whatever, that's something Dillon will have to deal with. But they've been friends for nearly thirty years. You don't get to kiss someone, then leave like that. It's not on.

Dillon throws on some clothes, then grabs his jacket and helmet from the hallway. He nearly lost his friend once because of his stupidity. He's not about to go for round two.

31

Luke

Before he's even slipped his key in the lock, the door is yanked open and Pippa stands aside to let him in. 'Well? Is it done?'

He kissed Dillon.

He went there to talk to his friend and he made a move on him instead. What the hell is wrong with him? He suspected Dillon liked him as more than a friend. Why did he push him? Why did he make Dillon say the words? Dillon has done nothing except support him, and he thanks him by being downright cruel.

Pippa gets in his face, her stilettos helping her get a little closer to eye level with him. 'Are you even listening to me?'

Dillon will probably never speak to him again. He deserves to lose him as a friend after doing that to him.

She pushes him in the shoulder. 'Luke? Stop doing that spacing out thing. Look at me.'

He looks at her, but all he can see is Dillon. See the hurt on his face, as Luke ran like a coward.

'Did you tell him to leave you alone?'

'No. I was going to but... I didn't.'

'I can't depend on you to do anything. One job, Luke. You asked if you could see him so you could tell him.' She narrows her eyes and takes a step back. 'Did you lie to me?'

'No.'

But he did. He had no intention of telling Dillon he couldn't see him anymore. Not for a second. He knows Pippa will get her way. She always does. His time with the band is done, but he didn't want to be the one to tell his friends he was leaving. He can't do it. He doesn't want to.

She turns and storms up the stairs. Luke waits for a second, then follows, before she can shout at him. Pippa glares over at him when he steps into their bedroom, then holds out her hands. 'Keys.'

'What?'

'I want your house, car, and bike keys.'

'Why?'

'Because clearly I can't trust you. You asked to see him and I agreed, on the condition you told him you were leaving the band, calling an end to your toxic relationship. Instead, you what? Had a beer with him?'

'No, I swear.'

'So what did you do?'

Nausea has him doubling over. He's going to throw up.

'What did you do Luke?'

He shakes his head, unable to get any words out. Not that he'd tell her. He'd never tell her.

'Luke! Did you take drugs with him?'

He pushes himself upright, but is still no more in control of his stomach than he was a few seconds ago. 'We just talked. I don't feel great. I need to sit down.'

Pippa pushes him back against the wall. 'You're going to stay right there until I believe what you're saying.' She digs into his pocket and pulls out his keys. 'No more heading off alone. You're not capable of following basic instructions, so how can I trust you?'

'You can trust me. I promise. I love you, Pippa. Only you.'

She tears his phone and wallet from his jeans. 'You keep saying that Luke, but then you go and do the exact opposite of what you say. We've only been married a few weeks and already I can't trust you.'

She turns on his phone and checks the messages. 'Dillon. Dillon. Dillon. Dillon. All Dillon. What a surprise.' The phone is thrown onto the bed, then she searches through his wallet.

'Pippa, please...' He says the words at the same time she finds the hash.

Pippa looks at the small bag in her hand then back at him. 'You just lied to me again.'

'It helps with the stomach cramps. I just...' He shuts his mouth. She's right. 'I'm—'

'Don't you dare say you're sorry!' She grabs her hairbrush off the dressing table beside him and hits him straight in the side, reopening the wound from the jewellery box. Pippa adjusts her grip, and strikes him again and again, the heavy wooden hairbrush adding a punch to each blow.

'You lied to me!' She hits him in the gut, and when he doubles over, she strikes him on the side of his head. Luke falls back against the wall, and slides to the ground, as his head spins.

But he should have stayed on his feet. The savage points on her stilettos hurt more than the hairbrush, sending waves of pain through both his legs as she kicks him.

Luke has no idea how long she punishes him for, but when she eventually stops, he's numb. He knows he's in pain, but none of it is registering with him. Not yet anyway.

Somewhere near him he can hear Pippa breathing heavily. But he doesn't look up. He stays in his cocoon on the floor, leaning against the wall with his arms over his head.

After a while he hears the shower running, and the stall door sliding closed. Only then does he lower his arms and look up. Then the pain hits. His arms, legs, chest, and head hurt like hell. Moving slowly, he reaches up to touch the side of his head, wincing when he touches something wet. His head must be cut.

He flinches as Pippa steps out of the bathroom, a towel wrapped around her body. She completely ignores him as she gets dressed, then sits at the dressing table to do her hair and make up.

'I'm meeting Astrid at the spa in town. I'll be gone for the rest of the day. I need time to think about how I can forgive my lying husband. Or even if I can.'

She peers down at him as she puts on her earrings.

'You know I was hurt by my lying ex. I told you that, Luke. I thought you of all people would never treat me like that.'

He swallows, trying to moisten his mouth but decides against speaking.

'I thought you were a better person. I thought I could trust you.'

She turns back to the mirror, then gets up and walks over to the bed. She slips his keys, wallet, and phone into her bag. 'Have a long hard think when I'm gone. There's water in the cooler beside the bed. I'll see you tonight.'

Pippa closes the bedroom door behind her, and Luke hears the key turning in the lock. He stays on the floor for a long time, just staring over at the door as the events of the last few hours play on repeat in his head.

He hurt his best friend.

He hurt his wife.

He's lost his best friend.

Maybe lost his wife.

Dillon doesn't forgive easily. There's no way he'll be able to forgive Luke for playing with his feelings like he had.

Luke loves Dillon to death. But not like that. So why the hell had he kissed him? He's not attracted to Dillon. He knows that. He was just... he doesn't know what. Confused. Upset. Lonely.

And lying straight to Pippa's face is unforgivable. Her last boyfriend had lied to her. She'd told him that enough times. He knew how much it had hurt her. He's a cruel man. No two ways about it. He's managed to hurt two of the most important people in his life, because he is selfish.

He slowly stretches his legs out, trying to ease the cramps that are progressively getting worse. As soon as he moves his left leg, something in his knee clicks and the pain shoots up his leg. He leans over and vomits on their expensive beige carpet.

After a ridiculous amount of time and effort, he manoeuvres his bruised, battered body over to the bed and, after taking a bottle of water from the cooler next to her side of the bed, pulls himself onto it. Unable to touch his leg without screaming in pain, he resorts to dragging himself across the vast bed, pulling his leg along for the painful ride.

How can he make this right with Dillon and Pippa?

What can he do to make it better?

Why does he keep hurting them?

Why does he keep messing up?

He lies back on the bed, soaked in sweat from the effort, and desperately trying not to throw up again, as he looks out the window.

It's him. He's the problem. He hurts them. He's the liar. He messes up continuously.

They'd probably both be better off if he wasn't in their lives.

That single thought replaces all the others, as his eyes move from the window to the bottle of sleeping pills on Pippa's bedside table. She was prescribed them to treat her insomnia. Which she said, was down to worrying about what he was getting up to, while he was on the road.

He reaches out and picks up the bottle. She filled the prescription a few days ago. It's a new bottle.

Luke lies back on the pillow and stares at the bottle.

Maybe they would all be better off, if he wasn't around to screw things up for them.

Maybe.

Dillon

Dillon climbs off his bike, and keys in the code for Luke's gate. It opens, which surprises him a little. He'd half expected Pippa or Luke to have changed the code to keep him out.

He rides his bike down the ridiculously long sweeping driveway, to the equally ridiculously imposing mansion at the end. This house was Pippa's dream, not Luke's. But just like everything else in his life, Pippa held the reins.

He brings his bike to a stop at the bottom of the steps leading to the front door. He may have stopped a little suddenly, leaving a deep groove in the perfectly raked gravel. Fuck it.

Dillon rings the doorbell, hearing it echoing inside the massive house. Three rings later, there's still no answer. Luke isn't picking up his phone either. Just the answering machine.

'Luke! It's Dillon. Stop ignoring me, or I swear I'll beat the crap out of you when I see you. Luke?'

He ends the call and curses. There's a strong chance he's ignoring him, but it's not really Luke's style. He wouldn't leave him standing out here like this.

Dillon peers in through the window into the hallway. Luke's jacket is on the chair at the bottom of the stairs. He wanders around the back of the house to the garage. Luke's car and bike are there.

Fucker is in the house ignoring him. Wow, he must really be pissed off.

Dillon wouldn't usually use the keys the guys have given him. They all have spare keys for each other's house, but he'd be less than

302

impressed if one of them let themselves in to either of his houses, while he was there. Could walk in on something they'd prefer not to see.

Dillon shakes his head as he looks down at the key in his hand. Fuck it. He needs to sort this out. He slides the key into the lock and steps into the entrance hallway. The stairs in front of him splits in two before it gets to the first floor. After trying the rooms downstairs he climbs the staircase. 'Luke? Luke!'

Still nothing. Dillon picks up the pace. Something is off about this whole thing. He runs down the hallway to the master bedroom and tries to open the door. But it's locked. Pippa's car isn't here, so he's not in there with her.

More convinced than ever he needs to get inside the room, he kicks the door until the lock finally caves. Dillon pushes the door open but can't convince himself to step inside the room.

Luke is lying on the vast bed, fully dressed.

But he's not moving.

If he was asleep, Dillon crashing through the door like a bull would have woken him.

Dillon knows it's only a second or two he's frozen for, but it seems like a lifetime.

His feet unlock from the floor and he rushes across the room to his friend. Luke's arms are covered in fresh wounds and bruises, there's blood on the pillow beside his head, and one of his legs is twisted at an unnatural angle. It looks like someone beat the shit out of him, then locked him in and left him to die.

But that's not the bit that scares him the most.

Luke is too still. Dillon focuses on Luke's chest, but it doesn't move. He's not breathing. Ignoring the deathly grey colour to Luke's skin, he places two fingers on the side of Luke's neck and holds his breath. No pulse.

He drags Luke down the bed onto the floor, and straddles him. When he moves Luke, he spots an empty pill bottle, along with a piece of paper on the bed beside him.

I'm sorry. You deserve better than me.

'Fuck, Luke!' While he begins one handed CPR, Dillon digs his phone out of his pocket and calls for help. 'Yeah, I need an ambulance. I think my friend has overdosed. He's not breathing and there's no pulse. I'm doing CPR but you need to get here now!' He gives the operator the address and the code for the gate, then throws the phone onto the floor.

'No you don't, you fucker! Don't you dare die on me!'

Hot tears pour down his face, as he fights to keep Luke alive. He can't die. He won't let him.

'Damn it, Luke! Wake up. Please!'

Dillon keeps his focus on Luke's face, hoping to see some sign of life. A twitch or a blink or anything to let him know his friend is still alive.

But there's nothing.

32

Dillon

'Here. Hey, Dillon?'

He looks up at Gregg and frowns at the cup in his hand. 'What?'

'Coffee.'

'Sorry. Thanks.' He takes the cup and Gregg sits on the couch beside him. The room falls silent again as the two men stare ahead of them, each lost in their own thoughts.

At least they have the room to themselves. The family room they've been given is just down the corridor from where Luke is fighting for his life.

He has no idea how long had passed since he found Luke on his bed. He kept up CPR until the paramedics arrived and took over, dragging him away from Luke so they could work on him. There was nothing he could do but watch from the side of the room, as they fought to save his life.

He'd never felt more helpless in his entire life. Still feels utterly helpless.

Luke's parents and brother, Alex, are with Luke. Pippa too, but that's only right. He may hate her, but she is his wife. Dillon was allowed to see him for a few minutes, but it was far from long enough.

When he closes his eyes, all he can see is Luke's still body lying on the bed. He needs to make sure he's still breathing. Needs to make sure Luke's chest is rising and falling. That it doesn't stop moving.

He puts the coffee cup on the table beside him when his hand shakes. He's a fucking mess. He thought seeing Tate hooked up to all those machines was bad enough. It had torn him apart seeing his friend like that.

But this is so much worse.

Tate wasn't bruised and beaten. Tate hadn't overdosed intentionally. *He* hadn't been the one to find Tate. What if he hadn't gone after Luke? What if he had stayed home and brooded about the fight? What if Luke had died?

He can't believe something was getting to Luke so badly, that he felt there was no other option. He has an incredible career, is fucking gorgeous, and is genuinely the nicest person you could ever meet. There's no reason he can think of for doing something so drastic.

But he had, and now he's fighting for his life.

Luke appeared so small and broken lying in the hospital bed. There were too many machines keeping him alive. Too many tubes and wires attached to him. Too many bruises and cuts covering his body, his crushed leg being supported until he was strong enough for surgery.

The doctors don't know if he's going to get through this. It's down to Luke and time now. But Tate got through it and Luke will too. He has to. He needs to.

Gregg has been sitting with Dillon since they arrived, but he's not talking. There's nothing to say. He knows Tate would want to know about Luke, but Gregg hadn't been allowed to speak to him. Not about this. And Dillon gets that. Tate needs to concentrate on himself right now. Hearing about Luke might jeopardise his recovery.

'Max? What are you doing here?'

Dillon stirs himself out of his thoughts when Gregg speaks. He looks up at Max, as he closes the door behind him, and takes a seat next to Gregg.

'Has something happened to Luke?' Something must have happened. There's no other reason for him to be here.

Max shakes his head. 'No, Dillon. He's holding his own at the moment. I actually need to speak to you and Gregg.'

'About what?' Gregg asks, pushing himself up in the seat.

'The hospital called us in. It seems that Luke has a lot of old injuries on his body, as well as the ones he sustained today.' He opens his notebook and frowns at the page. 'Cracked ribs, a broken finger, and old bruising on his arms, chest, and legs.

'Add that to the concussion, broken leg, and many more cuts and bruises, well, you can see why they were a tad suspicious. He's also got some weird puncture wounds on his leg, but they have no idea what caused those.

'Now you guys are fairly tight. I don't suppose you have any idea what might have happened to him?'

'He does track days on his bike every now and again, but I don't remember him ever saying he fell off,' Gregg answers, looking over at Dillon.

'He doesn't fall off,' Dillon says. 'He's a good rider. He's had a few bumps, we all have, but nothing that serious.'

'And the door was definitely locked when you got to the house?'

He nods, the image of Luke lying on the bed coming back to the front of his mind.

'From the outside or inside?'

'I don't know. I didn't see a key, but I wasn't paying that much attention. I was focused on Luke.'

'Right.' Max taps his pen on the notebook and chews the inside of his mouth, as he thinks.

'What's up? I know that face.'

Max shrugs at Gregg. 'Don't know. His wife mentioned the track days as the reason. His parents are clueless. Brother too. Seems like it might be clumsiness.'

'But you're not buying that, are you?'

Max looks over at Dillon. 'You're his best friend. What do you think happened? Why would he attempt suicide?'

'Do you not think I've been wondering that same fucking thing since I found him? I don't know. He has no reason to. I mean... he's... there's nothing.'

'And what about his temper?'

'Temper? What the fuck are you talking about? He doesn't have a temper!'

'It's been mentioned that he can fly off the handle from time to time. Hits walls and other inanimate objects.'

Dillon and Gregg look at each other at the same time, shaking their heads. 'No way,' Gregg says before Dillon can get the words out.

'Luke doesn't have a temper. He's never even raised his fucking voice!'

'Right.'

'What the fuck does that mean? You're not suggesting he had a tantrum and beat himself up, are you?'

'I'm just getting the facts, Dillon. That's it.'

He gets up and walks over to Max. 'Luke is gentle. He's kind. He's decent. There's no way he hurt himself or anyone else. Ever.'

'Okay. That's all I need for now. His family will stay with him for the moment. You should probably go home and get some sleep.'

Gregg shakes Max's hand. 'We're good. Thanks.'

The door closes behind Max, and Dillon gets lost in the silence again. He hates silence.

'I'm going to grab something to eat,' Gregg says, moving towards the door. 'You fancy anything?'

'No.'

Dillon sinks into the armchair, and tries to get his mind off the dark thoughts that are taking over.

Luke isn't violent. Never has been. Where the hell did that come from? His parents wouldn't have said that. Neither would Alex.

Which only leaves one person.

But why would she say that Luke is violent?

It doesn't matter how many times he says it to himself, there is no fucking way he'll ever believe Luke would raise a hand to anyone. It's impossible.

So why would she say that?

And why would Max ask if the door was locked from the inside or the outside?

Dillon stares at the floor, forcing himself to relive that scene.

Nothing makes sense though.

He does know that Luke hasn't fallen off his motorbike for years. He knows that Luke wouldn't hurt a fly. But, he knows that Luke has changed over the last few years. He's quieter. He's pulled away from both him and the rest of the band. He's smiling less, unless he's on stage, when he really comes into his own.

It's really the only time he seems even remotely happy. And it's also the only time he doesn't have Pippa hanging off him.

He doesn't know how long he stares at the wall going over every single detail, every conversation, every interaction, between Luke and Pippa.

She wouldn't... would she?

His whirlwind of thoughts are interrupted, when Jason opens the door and steps aside to let his sister, Clara, into the room. Without a word she takes him in her arms and holds him as he breaks down.

'It's okay, Dill. Luke is strong. He'll get through this.'

Dillon buries his face in her shoulder. He wishes he could believe Clara. He really does, but he's known Luke for decades. Luke was never reckless. Never acted irrationally or without thinking things through. If he made the decision to kill himself, it was just that. His decision. It wasn't a spur of the moment reaction to something. It was a choice.

And that's the part that terrifies Dillon.

Dillon scrubs a hand over his face trying to get himself to wake up. He's on his fourth cup of coffee and that's his limit. He stretches out on the chair beside Luke's bed, but his muscles are locked, so gets up instead.

He needs to work out, to get rid of some of the tension that's clamping down on his body. But he's not leaving. They'd tried to get him to leave. Short of calling in security to drag him out, he's not fucking moving until his friend wakes up.

If he wakes up.

Dillon curses himself and paces. He's not even going there. No way. Luke will wake up. There's no other option. Tate woke up. He had to be resuscitated like Luke and he made it. Luke would too. He has to.

As he walks back and forth, his eyes lock on the cuts and bruises on Luke's bare chest and arms. Barely controlled anger burns deep inside him.

He's spent every minute of the last fifteen hours going over all the options again and again, until he was driving himself crazy. But no matter what way he comes at this, he ends up in the same place every single time.

Pippa.

Luke's wife is hitting him. He's positive about it, and it has nothing to do with the fact he fucking hates the bitch. He knew there was something wrong. He could see his friend disappearing in front of him over the last few years. That night when they'd kissed, Luke had tried to tell him.

Do you think someone is hurting me?

He was trying to tell Dillon what was going on, and he had missed it, because he was too busy drooling over him, and trying to make himself feel better.

It's his fault Luke is here. All he had to do was listen to what his friend was telling him. Read between the lines. See all the warning signs.

Be the friend Luke desperately deserves.

Why hadn't he done something? Said something. He should have dragged Luke away from that cow, kicking and screaming, if he had to. Maybe if he'd trusted his gut, his best friend wouldn't be in a hospital bed.

Pippa had done her duty visits to Luke, showing her face every few hours, crying and gushing over her husband in front of the staff.

Dillon had made sure he steered clear of her while she was here. He didn't trust himself not to have it out with her. It's the last thing Luke needs. Besides, it's probably best he gets the truth from him, before he does anything stupid. Again.

He stops when he hears a strange sound coming from behind him. He stares at Luke but there's no movement. Then his eyes open briefly.

'Luke?' He rushes over to the bed and peers down at him. 'Luke?'

Maybe he was imagining it. Some sort of fucked up hallucination or something like that. He's been staring at Luke for so long he wouldn't be surprised.

When Luke groans and tries to pull the tube out of his mouth Dillon nearly shouts out loud. He pushes the button at the head of the bed.

'Hey, Luke. It's Dillon.' He gently moves Luke's hand back down. 'You need to leave that there for a sec, okay.'

Dillon steps aside as the nurse comes to check on him. 'He opened his eyes. Groaned too.'

She gestures over to the door and he obediently leaves and stands beside Andy outside.

When he's finally allowed back into the room, he barely manages to not cry like some fucking idiot. Luke turns his head and smiles at him. It's nothing like his usual smile, but he'll take it.

Dillon sits down in the chair he's spent countless hours in. 'Hey. About fucking time.'

Luke nods, but doesn't say anything. Dillon wipes his eyes, trying to stay strong for his friend.

'You scared the hell out of us.'

'I didn't mean to. I'm sorry.' His voice is weak and barely more than a whisper, but it's the best sound Dillon has heard for a long time.

'Nothing to apologise for, Luke. What happened?'

Luke turns away and looks at the foot of the bed. His expression changes, and Dillon realises he's seen that look so many times before. Until Luke overdosed, he didn't realise what that look meant. It's his friend shutting down. He wasn't going to talk, just like every other time Dillon asked if he was okay.

Dillon leans back in the chair and decides to take a risk. He knows Pippa and Luke's family are on the way. As soon as they arrive, he'll be kicked out and Luke will be with *her* again.

'How about I give you my take on it? Then you can just nod, or shake your head, at the end. That sound okay?'

Luke turns to look at him again, so Dillon takes that as a yes. 'Okay, so you meet Pippa and fall in love. I mean I get that. She's stunning. At first, things are great, but something changed. Maybe you can't figure out when, or maybe you can remember the exact moment. But things took a turn.

'I don't think it was too bad at first. It might have been comments, something meant to bring you down. You weren't giving her enough attention, or a fan got too close, or you had to go away too much. I'm hoping it wasn't going on for years, but thinking back I reckon it was.'

Luke frowns, and drops his gaze briefly. Dillon instantly knows he's on the right track. Luke is trying to hold them back, but he can see the tears. He feels like a bastard, but if Luke won't tell him what's going on, he'll have to help him out.

'Then it turned physical and she hurt you. Maybe even blamed you for forcing her to do that. Pippa probably apologised, and did all the *it'll never happen again* shit.

'But it did. By the look of the bruises and cuts, it happened a lot more. I'm guessing when you called off photo shoots it was because of the bruises. You were trying to hide them.'

And there are the tears. Luke is silently crying, and Dillon's heart is breaking. He rubs his hand over his face, willing his own tears to stay back, until he's finished.

'But you couldn't tell us. Couldn't tell me. Maybe you felt weak or embarrassed because a woman was hitting you, controlling you that way.' He pauses to clear his throat. 'Maybe you didn't think anyone would listen to you, or believe you. You felt alone and miserable and were hurting so bad, but couldn't see how to help yourself.

'I know you tried to tell me what was going on, but I didn't hear you.' And now he's crying too. 'So you took the only course of action you thought was left. You tried to end it all, just to make it stop. Am I right?'

Luke nods once. 'I'm sorry, Dillon.'

Dillon gets up and gathers Luke in his arms as he sobs. 'Hey. It's going to be okay. You're safe, Luke. I promise I'll never let anyone hurt you again. I swear.'

Pippa

Pippa clutches the strap of her Chanel handbag and watches as *that man* cries all over her husband. Since she began dating Luke,

Dillon Ryan has been a constant thorn in her side.

Every. Single. Day.

And now she knows why.

Dillon is in love with Luke. She can see it now. Gregg is worried about him, but he's not acting the way Dillon is. He's devastated, gushing all over Luke in a display that is, quite frankly, sickening.

The beige leather strap twists around her fingers as she walks away, locking herself in the bathroom, while she gets her thoughts straight.

She'd listened to every word Dillon had put in her weak husband's mouth, the anger building as Luke just played along. Not once did he stop Dillon, or correct him. Not once. He lay there, blubbering to himself as his *boyfriend* filled his head with all those thoughts. All those lies.

She'd done nothing wrong. She's positive of that.

Luke needed to be controlled. It's the kind of person he is. Weak and impressionable. That's why Dillon was able to get his claws into him as he had. Luke is so naive he will believe anything he's told. Clearly he thought more of Dillon than he did of his own wife.

She wouldn't be surprised if Dillon had made a move on Luke. She shudders and paces the bathroom, her heels clicking on the tiled floor. No. She has no doubts she'd know if Dillon tried anything with Luke. There's no way he would have been able to keep something like that from her. Luke's not that clever.

No, what she just witnessed between Dillon and Luke was all down to Luke's junkie, alcoholic friend.

Years of her life have been invested in Luke. Years of moulding him into a man she could be with. Years of building her own social standing, by allowing him to drag her to event, after boring event. Years of mixing with loud, badly dressed people she had to smile and talk to, just because they were in a similar field to Luke. God it was tedious, but she'd hung off his arm, smiling graciously at every single dull, self-obsessed performer.

She's not saying that being with Luke is a chore. Far from it. In spite of his complete lack of style, the piercings, and horrendous tattoos, he is an attractive man. The four band members are good looking in their own way - even pain-in-the-ass Dillon, but Luke is different. He didn't shout or draw attention to himself.

Sometimes she wished he would, but he wouldn't be so willing to please her if he had the confidence of the others. Under all the tattoos and piercings, he's genuinely sweet, caring, loving, and equipped with a stunning body. She had married quite a catch.

Initially Dillon wasn't too much of a worry. He was always there, but didn't get in the way. But, as time went on he seemed to be there more and more. Always judging her. She could see it in his face. That *cretin* whose own family can't stand him, had the audacity to judge her. How dare he!

She wrings the Chanel strap in her hands, wishing it was Dillon's interfering neck instead.

He's ruining everything for them. For her. She's invested too much time in her relationship with Luke. She has too much to lose by walking away at this point. Luke is worth millions of Euro. She's tried numerous times to figure out his exact worth, but has no idea. No one in their right mind would walk away from that. And she doesn't plan to.

Unfortunately, if Dillon has his way, Luke may say, or do something which could change all that for her. If even one person believes the story Dillon put in Luke's head, her happily ever after is as good as finished. The life she's built for herself will end. The expensive cars, the designer clothes, bags, and shoes, the stunning mansion she picked for them to live in. All at risk because of that sex crazed disaster.

Pippa takes Luke's phone from her bag, and glares at the list of missed calls and messages from Dillon. It's clear the drunken lout is obsessed with her husband. Unnaturally so. How desperate must he be to go after a straight, married man? Pathetic.

But that's what Dillon is. A pathetic drunk who will most certainly drink himself into the grave, or overdose in the next few years. When that happens she won't be shedding any tears over him. He deserves everything he gets, and so much more.

Pippa frowns when she notices a voice message from him to Luke. She plays the message, her smile growing when she hears Dillon very clearly threatening to beat up Luke if he didn't answer the door. She plays the message again, the smile firmly in place.

Well, isn't that interesting. She taps a long painted nail against the phone as she paces again, slower this time.

What would the authorities think if they heard Dillon threatening Luke, moments before he was found injured? She doubts they'd dismiss it as a coincidence. Dillon has a well documented habit of losing his temper. It wouldn't be a stretch to think he lost it with Luke.

She faces the mirror and stares at her reflection for a few minutes. Then she sniffs and takes a shuddering breath.

'You have to help me. I think Dillon Ryan hurt my husband.' Her eyes water and she forces a few tears out. 'I just found a message on his phone. Dillon was threatening Luke.'

Pippa nods and smiles, dabbing her face with a tissue. Not a bad performance. She takes out her mobile and searches through the contacts, stopping at Max's name. She could call the nearest station, but she likes the idea of Max being the one to speak to Dillon. He's more than familiar with Dillon's record, so might be more open to believing what she says.

After fixing her hair and reapplying her lipstick, she dials his number and tries not to smile too much. This day might end up being one for the memory books. She can't believe she's about to get rid of Dillon once and for all.

33

Dillon

Dillon puts on his cap and sunglasses, as he leaves Luke's room and makes his way to the car park, followed by Jason. His best mate had eventually cried himself to sleep. It was the most heart-breaking thing he's witnessed. And he's seen some crap in his life.

Luke is sensitive. Always has been, but not in a bad way. Anything but. He's sweet and caring. Genuinely decent too, which is rare nowadays. But he never cried. Never. Seeing him fall apart like that, tore Dillon to pieces.

He'd give anything to be able to put him back together. Give anything to gather him in his arms and not let him go. But he can't make this better for him. No one can.

Luke needs to find his own way through this shit, and it won't be easy. That bitch did a real number on him. She took that beautiful man, and pulled him apart a piece at a time, until he had nothing left in his life, except pain and misery.

He reaches the car park and sees Gregg sitting in his car beside the entrance. 'Give us a minute, Jason.'

His bodyguard nods, and waits by his own car, while Dillon climbs into the passenger seat of Gregg's car. Unable to hold back the anger any longer, he shouts and thumps the door.

'Hey!' Gregg grumbles as he turns around to glare at him. 'Watch the new car. What the hell is up with you?'

'Pippa's been beating Luke.'

Gregg's eyebrows shoot up. 'Pippa's been what?'

'That bitch has been abusing him, Gregg. He admitted it, before crying himself to sleep. I told him what I thought went on and he broke down. After a bit, he gave me what I'm damn fucking sure was only an edited version of events.

'It started with verbal put-downs and escalated to throwing things at him then slapping and punching him a few months ago. Then she...' he curses and shakes his head. 'I think she raped him, Gregg. More than once. Luke didn't say as much, but reading between the lines I'm sure she did. He's got restraint marks on his wrists.'

The atmosphere in the car takes a serious nosedive. 'Fucking bitch!' Gregg peers out the window for a long few minutes. Dillon has never seen Gregg so angry before. He tended to stay level-headed, helping to control both Dillon and Tate when they lost it. But this is a whole new scenario.

He suddenly curses out loud, and slams his hand against the steering wheel. Gregg closes his eyes and takes a few breaths to calm himself. 'Why the hell didn't he tell us?'

'Too embarrassed? Too scared? Didn't think anyone would believe him? Didn't know what she was doing to him was fucked up? I don't know.' He rubs his forehead. He needs a drink. Badly.

Gregg nods then turns in his seat to look at Dillon, his controlled ex-Garda face on. 'First thing we need to do is try to keep that bitch away from him.'

'I know.'

'If she's been manipulating him, he could cave and head back. If she has that level of control on him, he won't be able to stop himself. We need to protect him.'

Dillon nods as he stares out the window. 'Too right. I called his brother, Alex. Filled him in. He's going to talk to Luke himself when he sees him.'

He felt shite calling Alex, but Luke's brother is decent. Luke's whole family are. They're the kind of irritatingly perfect family you see on TV. Supportive. Loving. Protective. A far cry from his own situation, but it's exactly what Luke needs right now. There's no way Dillon was going to broach the subject with Luke's folks. He'll leave that to Alex.

'That's good. He's got his head screwed on. Is Luke going to report it?'

Dillon shrugs. 'He's not ready to even go there yet. Knowing him, I seriously doubt it. I know,' he adds when Gregg turns to look at him. 'He's been abused for years and kept quiet. It's his MO now. Can you really see him making a fuss about this?'

Gregg slowly shakes his head. 'She can't get away with this. There's a chance this assault could be put on her, but it'll be his word against hers, for the rest of the abuse.'

'But if she did it once, surely it's not a stretch to believe she would have done it before?'

'She could say it was a one off. Lost her temper, or he drove her to it. This is Pippa we're talking about. She's a devious cow at the best of times.'

'Is the ex-Garda wanting a bit of old fashioned revenge?'

'The ex-Garda wants to give Pippa a taste of her own medicine, yes.' He shrugs, then smiles sadly. 'But, that's not going to help anyone. We have to do this Luke's way, but that doesn't mean we can't protect him.'

'Too fucking right!' Dillon would much rather a bit of the revenge he mentioned, but Gregg is right. That's not going to help Luke. 'We'll talk to Alex first and see what he wants to do. It's so fucked up, Gregg. Luke thinks it's his fault she hit him. Bitch has him thinking he's not worth anything. I didn't see what she was doing to him, Gregg. How did I not see it?'

'None of us did.'

'We should have.' He isn't usually one for physical contact unless it's on his terms, but when Gregg wraps his arm around his shoulder, Dillon doesn't pull away.

He rests his head against Gregg's chest, as his friend holds him close. It's what he needs, but would never have asked for.

This is on him. Luke had told him that he was being hurt... well, in a roundabout way. But the more he thinks about it, the more his cry for help burns in Dillon's memory. He'll never be able to forgive himself for not hearing him. Never.

Dillon rubs his eyes. He's beyond knackered and desperately needs a good night sleep in his own bed. But, there isn't a chance in hell he's leaving Luke. No way. Not while that cow is wandering around like she owns the fucking place.

Luke's family should be here in a few minutes and, as soon as Alex speaks to Luke, the truth will come out. It has to. Luke and Alex are close. Really fucking close. There's no way Luke would hide the truth from his brother if Alex asked him directly.

But instead of Alex walking into the family room, Dillon is immediately on edge when Max arrives accompanied by two Garda, and looks directly at him.

'What are you doing here?' Gregg asks.

Max clasps his hands in front of him and nods to Dillon. 'Actually, it's you I'd like to have a word with. Can I borrow you for a minute.'

'Me? Why?'

'I'd prefer to do it in private. How about you and me take a spin down to the station.'

'Max, what's going on?' Gregg asks. 'What's Dillon *supposedly* done that warrants pulling him away like this?'

'It's in relation to Luke.'

Dillon rises to his feet. 'Luke?'

Max sighs and crosses his arms. 'Listen, I don't want to make this official. Please Dillon. Don't make this harder than it has to be.'

'Make what harder? What the fuck is going on? I haven't done anything. Hang on. Do you think I did something to Luke?'

Then the shit really hits the fan. Pippa bursts into the room, mascara running down her face. She points an accusing finger at Dillon. 'I want him away from my husband.'

'Mrs. Anderson-Daly, please leave this to us.' Max tries to step in between them, but Pippa pushes past him.

'Get him out of here!'

'Mrs. Anderson-Daly. Please.'

'It's her you should be talking to. Not me.'

'Dillon—' Gregg warns, but he's beyond caring at this stage. He doesn't like what's going on here. Doesn't like the way that bitch is looking at him.

Max approaches him, his hands out in front of him. 'Dillon. Take a breath and think about this. I just want a chat. That's it.'

'A chat? Are you serious? He beat up my husband!'

'Oh don't you even go there. I didn't lay a fucking finger on him! Why don't you stop this fucking show and tell us what really happened to him, Pippa? Go on!'

'All I'm doing is protecting my husband.'

'Fuck off!'

Max steps right up to him, forcing him back against the wall. 'Dillon. Last warning.'

He's fucking seething, but Max gets through to him. Or does, until

Pippa winks at him, before dramatically wiping the tears from her face.

In that moment, any remnants of self control evaporate. Pure uncontrolled anger takes over. All he can see is the man he loves, broken and dying on that bed, after she beat him up.

Before Gregg or Max can react, he launches himself at the bitch, knocking her to the ground. Gregg and Max haul him back, before he lands on her, but that doesn't mean he stops trying to get his hands on her. All he wants to do is wring her fucking scrawny neck.

One of the Garda helps her to her feet, while the second moves in to hold him back. Gregg gets right in his face and says something to him, but all he can focus on is Pippa, being supported by a Garda as she trembles. It's all an act. Everything is with her.

He fights to get free, but four against one isn't fair odds. 'Get the fuck off me!'

Somewhere through the rage, he hears Gregg talking to him, but all he can focus on is the smug fucking grin on Pippa's face.

Max's voice joins with Gregg's and he's forcefully spun around, his face pressed firmly against the wall. His arms are held behind his back, as handcuffs are fitted.

Dillon keeps fighting to get free. He can't stop himself. Max holds him against the wall, using his body weight to keep him in place.

'Jesus, Dillon! Take a breath.'

He wants to, but all he can see is her smile. The bitch is going to pin this on him. He's going to be blamed for hurting Luke. 'I'm calm, okay. Let go.'

'No can do,' Max says. 'You feel those cuffs? I just arrested you... again.'

'What? Why? I didn't do anything.'

'You assaulted Pippa in front of us, and then resisted arrest. We just wanted to talk to you, Dillon. I wasn't planning on doing this, but you left me no choice.'

Dillon hits his forehead against the wall. 'Fuck! I didn't hurt him,

Max. I swear. It was her. Not me.'

'Get him out of here,' she shrieks from somewhere behind him.

'You fucking bitch!'

Max pulls him away from the wall and two Garda grab him by the arms. Dillon glares over at Pippa, ignoring whatever Max is saying to him. The smile she keeps giving him when no one is watching, isn't helping to calm him down.

He wasn't against using his fists when the situation called for it, but hitting a woman has never entered his mind.

Not until now.

If he wasn't cuffed, he'd quite happily wipe that fucking smile off her face.

Max gets in his face again. 'Hey. You listening?'

Dillon nods, keeping his attention on Pippa.

'Time to go. I'm asking you not to cause a scene, okay. Just walk quietly.'

'No! I can't leave.'

Max grabs him by the arm and moves him towards the door. 'You're a serious pain in my butt, Dillon. Walk.'

Gregg gets between Max and the door. 'Please Max. Don't do this. He's emotional right now. He's worried about Luke. We all are.'

'You want to join your mate here?'

'Not exactly.'

'Then move, Gregg.'

Dillon knows he should walk out peacefully, but something won't let him. He doesn't want to leave Luke alone with her. 'Max, please no! Don't do this.'

Max ignores him and gestures to his colleagues. Dillon is dragged out of the room and along the corridor away from Luke. He looks back towards Luke's room but the door is closed. Does Luke even know what's happening?

Then Alex and Luke's parents arrive, walking along the corridor towards Luke's room. They stare over at the scene in front of them, and Dillon feels sick as Pippa speaks quietly to them.

When they focus on him again, he knows they believe her. He can see it in their eyes. Dillon opens his mouth, but no words come out. His throat has closed up.

The Garda haul his ass into the service elevator, as Luke's family watch. Before the doors close, the last thing he sees is Pippa standing at Luke's door. She waves at him, then blows him a kiss.

Luke

The pain isn't as bad when he wakes up again. His leg is still sore but it feels weird more than seriously painful. The surgery to put his leg back together must have gone okay. He'd been taken away after his parents and Alex saw him, to have it repaired.

He can't really remember what happened to his leg. Had she kicked him and he fell or kicked him after he fell? Everything is a blur, but he doesn't want to think about it at all.

He takes a longer breath, hoping he picks up on Dillon's familiar cologne.

He's not that lucky.

Instead it's her. His wife is beside him. The scent she wears is expensive and recognisable. It's all she's worn for the last few years.

He lies perfectly still, terrified she'll notice he's awake.

He's messed everything up so badly and Pippa will be furious. He'd tried to make things better for everyone by getting rid of the problem. Him.

But he messed that up too. His parents told him Dillon saved his life. That wasn't supposed to happen. Knowing that Dillon was the one to break into their bedroom and find him, will only drive Pippa's anger to new levels.

He should have taken more pills. Or bolted the main door to the house. Changed the code on the gate. There are a dozen things he could have done to stop Dillon finding him, if he hadn't been locked in.

But being locked in the room hadn't left him many options. It was a badly thought out, rushed plan that backfired, hurting everyone he cares about, again.

His attempt to appear asleep fails, when a tickle catches the back of his throat. It's been irritated since he woke up with the tube down it.

The scent of her perfume comes closer, as she runs her fingers through his hair, brushing over the wound on his scalp again and again. 'Morning sleepy head.'

With no choice, Luke opens his eyes and forces himself to smile at her. Pippa's make-up and hair is perfect as usual. For some reason he thought she'd appear a little dishevelled. But she always looks perfect. Him being in hospital wouldn't change that.

'How are you feeling?'

'A bit sore.'

'I'm not surprised,' she says as she strokes his hair. 'That was quite a tumble you took. You really need to be more careful.'

She's smiling, but her eyes are hard. She's upset with him.

Pippa shuffles a little closer. 'So, do you have anything to say to me?'

'I'm sorry.'

'Is that it? You tried to kill yourself, Luke! On our bed. In our bedroom. And you let Dillon find you! I mean what the hell were you thinking?' she hisses, glaring down at him. 'What reason do *you* have to even consider killing yourself?'

'I don't know. I didn't think. I'm sorry.'

'It's a little too late for that now. I was trying to protect you, Luke. You're clumsy. You fall and hurt yourself.'

'Pippa—'

'I also had to tell them you sometimes lose your temper and damaged the house.'

'What?'

'I told you Luke, I was trying to protect you. How can I do that now after you've betrayed me so badly?'

'I didn't mean to.'

She reaches over and kisses him. 'Never mind that now. It's done. And I've taken care of the situation you were, for reasons I still don't understand, unwilling to deal with.'

'What situation?'

'Dillon. He won't be bothering you again. Now, I think you and I need to have a little talk about what you *believe* took place in our house, the night you hurt yourself.'

He hears her words but can't seem to get himself past what she said about Dillon. What did she do? His first thoughts are that she hurt him. But that's not possible. Dillon is tough. He can stand up for himself.

'Hey, you're awake!'

He doesn't notice Alex come in until he's right by the bed. Luke glances at Pippa, who is clearly less than pleased about his brother's arrival.

'Hi, Alex. I don't mean to be rude, but I'd like to spend some time alone with my husband.'

'Oh my baby brother doesn't mind if I stay. Do you Luke?'

His first thought is to tell Alex to go, but stops himself. Alex is giving him one impressively intense look. It was the look they gave to each other when they needed to talk, without their parents overhearing.

Alex needs to talk to him and, even though she'll be unhappy with him later, he wants be alone with Alex. He needs some time with someone who isn't angry at him. 'Of course not. Are the boys okay?'

Alex gets comfortable, ignoring the dirty looks Pippa is giving him. 'They're good. Getting really good at rugby. I'm terrified they'll tackle me one day and take me down.'

Luke smiles, then winces when Pippa squeezes his hand a little too hard.

'Hey, Pip,' Alex says, using the nickname Pippa hates. 'How about you get your hubby a fresh water.'

'Why don't you, Alex?'

'Ah come on, Pip. I just want to talk about my kids for a few minutes. You'll be bored.'

Luke rubs her hand. 'It'll just be for a few minutes.'

Pippa glares over at Alex again, then stands up and grabs her bag. She leans over and kisses him on the side of the face. 'Don't disappoint me, Luke.'

The words are whispered, but he hears the threat.

As soon as she leaves, Alex closes the door to his room, then pulls out his phone and makes a call. 'Andy, hey it's Alex. Luke would like a break from all visitors except immediate family. Yep. Even her. Yeah. Good luck with that.'

He ends the call and nods to the door.

'Andy will keep her away until we talk.' He drags the chair right up to Luke's bed. 'So, we got to make this quick. Dillon has been arrested for assaulting you, Luke. Max took him away in handcuffs last night while you were in theatre.'

'What? Dillon would never hurt me!'

'I know that. He's an ass at times, but he's decent. The thing is, Pippa was the one who called Max. She's letting on Dillon attacked you.'

Luke looks up at the ceiling, blinking the tears back. This is so much worse than he could have imagined. His best friend has spent the night in prison because of his stupidity.

Alex grabs his hand, forcing Luke to look back over at him. 'I love you, Luke. I know you, and I trust you. I tell you everything and I hope you know you can do the same to me. There is nothing you can't tell me. Nothing. You hear me?'

Luke nods.

'Now I'm going to ask you a question and I want you to answer it honestly. Can you do that?'

He nods again.

Alex pauses and licks his lips. When he looks back at Luke, he could swear his brother is crying. 'Is Pippa hurting you?'

Luke nods, without thinking about it. He can't lie to Alex. Never has been able to.

'I'm sorry.'

Alex leans over and hugs him. 'I never want to hear you apologise for that.' He pushes back and looks at him again. 'Do you want my help, Luke?'

'Dillon didn't do anything, Alex. He would never hurt me. He's in love with me. He told me a few days ago. I don't love him like that, but he's never—'

Alex grips his hands. 'Hey. I know, okay. But I can't help him. Only you can do that.'

'How?'

'You need to tell Max what happened.'

The thought has Luke trying to push himself up the bed. 'I can't—'

'Yes, Luke. You can. I promise I will protect you. I swear to God I will. The guys will too. You know that. All you have to do is say that's what you want.'

'But it was my fault all this happened. She doesn't mean to. I just push her too far.'

Alex stares at him for a minute without saying anything. 'No, Luke. No one has the right to lay a fucking hand on you. No one. Your best friend is looking at a long time inside because of this. You are the only one who can put that right. If I call Max, will you tell him what really happened?'

He wants to. Desperately wants to help his friend. But if he does that, Pippa will get into trouble. It's such a mess.

He jumps when he hears Pippa's voice outside the door. 'Alex! Let me in. Tell Andy to back off!'

Alex leans over and rests his head against Luke's. 'It's just you and me, Luke. Remember when you got scared when you were a kid? You'd always come to me and I'd look out for you. Try to make things better.'

He remembers. Alex has never, ever, let him down.

'Trust me. Let me make things better for you. I'm begging you.'

'I'm scared.'

Alex sniffs as the tears fall down his cheeks. 'You don't have to be. I've got you.'

Luke loves Pippa. Really does, but this problem between them has nothing to do with Dillon. He did nothing wrong and, if Alex can make sure this wrong is put right, he has to try. Even if it angers her.

'Call Max.'

Alex kisses his forehead and stands up again. 'Why don't you get some rest. I'll call Max and stay with you.'

Luke nods then closes his eyes, exhaustion suddenly taking hold. He's done the right thing. He knows he has. He needs to save Dillon. Once his friend is safe, he'll work on how he can make things right with his wife.

He falls asleep quickly, his brother's reassuring presence helping to comfort him as it did all those years ago.

Dillon

Dillon wakes with a jump, as a loud clang sounds from somewhere nearby. It takes him a few seconds to remember where he is.

When he sees the grey wall and steel door, he closes his eyes, burying his face in the thin pillow. He barely manages to hold back the shout of frustration. How the hell has he ended up locked away again?

It's been a long time since he's lost his temper like that. Years since he was so filled with rage, that it consumed him as much as it did yesterday. Now he's got a raging headache, his throat is fucking killing him, and his arms are bruised to fuck.

His temper had kicked in yet again, when they tried to put him in the cell. As soon as that door shut, he knew she'd be getting her way. He knew Pippa would win and Luke would lose. And lose big.

Not that his struggles had helped him get out. Deep down he knew it was a waste of time, but tell that to his temper. His shouting, kicking, screaming, and general meltdown hadn't done him any favours.

Unable to calm him down, they'd left the handcuffs on him until he passed out. He doesn't know how long he spent throwing himself against the door. He's just damn lucky he didn't dislocate his shoulders when he rammed them against the metal door, again and again.

He's paying for it now. No doubt he's going to be black and blue. Not that he cares. All he cares about is that Pippa is still by Luke's side.

He promised Luke he wouldn't let anyone hurt him again. He swore he'd protect him. Instead that cow had hurt him time and time again, and now it looks like she is going to get away with it. Worse still, Luke will probably go home with her, and the whole fucking thing will begin again.

The door to his cell unlocks, but he can't be bothered looking up to see who is coming in. Someone sits on the end of the cot and clears their throat.

'How are you doing?'

Dillon ignores Max. He's done talking. It's not like it does him any good. With Pippa holding the reins, he's going to be well and truly screwed. Better get used to it.

'That was quite a display last night. I guess Gregg was right. You were emotional. And I know why.'

Dillon frowns and peers up at Max.

'You love Luke, don't you?'

Dillon looks back at the far wall. That's one topic he's not going to discuss with anyone.

Clearly realising he's not going to get anywhere, Max pushes to his feet and walks over to the door. 'Come on. I want to show you something. Hey! Quit glaring at the wall and get up. Trust me, you'll want to see this.'

What the fuck. It's not like he has anything better to do. His body protests as he slowly pushes himself to his feet, using the wall as a support.

'The after effects of your meltdown hitting, huh?'

Dillon glares at him, but doesn't bother replying. Max shakes his head and leads Dillon outside. He opens the door of a cell down from his and calls him forward. Maybe he's getting a new cell.

But the cell Max shows him is already occupied.

Dillon comes to a stop, his mouth dropping open, as he tries to process the scene in front of him.

Pippa's perfect make up is smudged, black mascara running down her face, and her hair is in a state. It's also the first time he's seen her without her signature expensive stilettos. Pippa's face turns to stone when she sees him.

Max steps between them, as Pippa launches to her feet. 'You

fucking bastard! This is your fault. All your fucking fault, Dillon! I hate you! You ruined everything! You ruined my life, you dick!'

Max quietly holds her back as she spits, screams, and generally goes fucking nuts. Dillon honestly doesn't think he's ever seen anything more satisfying. She struggles against Max, desperate to get her hands on Dillon.

'I'm going to kill you! As soon as I get out of here, you're dead, Dillon! Dead! You keep away from Luke. He's mine! I'll get out of here and take him away from you. You'll never see him again you cock sucking bastard!'

At that point, Max pushes her off him and leaves the cell, slamming the door behind him, cutting off her screams.

Max grins at Dillon as he straightens his shirt. 'Now wasn't that interesting? She's a little intense, isn't she?'

'What? I mean how? I thought... What the fuck is going on?'

Max drapes his arm across Dillon's shoulder and leads him away from the still screaming Pippa. 'She's been arrested for assaulting Luke. You're off the hook.'

'But how? What the hell happened?'

He shows Dillon into a small room with a couch and a coffee machine. 'Coffee? You look like you need it.'

Dillon nods absently. He's still back in the cell, watching Pippa lose it. He just wishes he had recorded it. It was so good to see.

Max passes him the paper cup of coffee, before grabbing a cup for himself. 'So, I believe you filled Alex Daly in on some troubling information you managed to get from Luke?'

'Did Luke tell Alex what happened?'

'He did. Alex decided to go back to Luke's house first. He was worried Pippa might try to clear up after herself. He found a pair of her shoes in the bins outside. One was broken, blood all over the heel. She kicked him, Dillon.

'That's what caused those strange holes on his leg. There was also a hairbrush with blood on it. Matches the wound on his head. We

333

found his car keys, wallet, and phone in her handbag... along with the key to the bedroom door.'

'Fuck! Hold on. She locked him in the room?'

Max nods. 'She assaulted him, took his things, and left him in there injured.'

Dillon knew she was a vile bitch, but what he just heard leaves his skin cold. He can't imagine what would have been going through Luke's mind, trapped in their bedroom like that.

'Alex called us in, then he went back to talk to his brother. Alex interrupted a fairly intense chat Pippa was having with Luke. While she was gone, he asked his brother some yes or no questions. Luke corroborated what you had told Alex.'

Max sips his coffee and licks his lips.

'He told me everything, Dillon. About how she's been treating him. And I agree with what you told Alex. I suspect she raped him too, but I don't think he fully understands what happened to him. He was disconnected as he was he telling me. Not really seeing that what she has been doing to him, was wrong. He was more concerned that you were in trouble for something you didn't do.'

'Is he pressing charges against her?'

Max shakes his head. 'Like I said, he's not fully processing what he's been living with. We can pin his current injuries on Pippa, but as for the years of abuse... well that'll be a little more tricky.'

'Personally, I think the priority is getting Luke's head sorted. He needs to process and accept what he's been living through. After that...' he shrugs and takes another drink of his coffee. 'He's going to need a lot of help.'

Dillon nods. That's an understatement.

'We've called someone to come and pick you up. Luke wants to see you. He's going to be admitted to a hospital down the country, for longer term treatment. I think it's the same place Tate is staying at the moment. He can get the help he needs.'

'I hope so.'

'Oh and for the record, can you please, please, not leave threatening messages on voicemails.' Max goes quiet for a few minutes. 'I am sorry for arresting you. You just don't help yourself.'

'I know. I just couldn't handle leaving her with Luke.'

'I get that. I like you, Dillon. Don't know why, but I do. But I would really love not to see you again for a while. Do you understand?'

'Yeah. Got it. Thanks, Max.'

'You know, I've heard some colourful language working here, but what she just unleashed on you, takes the award. She's got one hell of a mouth. I particularly liked the cock-sucker comment. Sounded amazing in her posh accent!'

Dillon can't help but laugh. 'Just shows what she knows.'

'What do you mean?'

'I'm the one who's cock is sucked. Not the other way around.'

Max laughs, nearly chocking on his coffee. 'Thanks for that image. Really appreciate it.'

Gregg gets out of his car when Max appears at the back door of the station with Dillon beside him. 'Hey gorgeous.'

Dillon shakes his head, but doesn't respond with his usual *fuck you*. The poor guy looks terrible. Even though he's rarely hugged Dillon, he can't stop himself. It's as much for personal reasons as anything.

Watching Dillon being dragged kicking and screaming from the hospital was traumatic. He's done watching his friends going through hell. The whole night was spent worrying about the three of them and he's worn out.

He returns the hug, hanging on to Gregg a lot longer than he thought he would. 'You okay?'

Dillon shakes his head, refusing to let Gregg go, so he holds him until he's got himself together. Dillon unlocks himself from around Gregg and wipes his face. 'Fuck, I'm sorry.'

'What for? I've been a mess all night. What happened yesterday was a nightmare.'

Dillon nods and wraps his arms around his chest. 'Can we just go. I need to put some distance between me and that bitch.'

Gregg gestures to his car. 'Your wish is my command.' He passes Dillon the coffee he picked up on the way, and waves at Max as he pulls out of the car park. 'I know what the coffee is like in there. That's the real stuff.'

'Thanks.'

'So, I was thinking it might be a good idea to bring you home first, so you can have a shower and grab a change of clothes. Then we can head over to see Luke.'

Dillon nods, but doesn't say anything as he stares out the window. Gregg leaves him to his thoughts. Max had filled him in on Dillon's behaviour in the cell, after he was taken in. He's seen Dillon lose it like that a handful of times before, and it was always intense. Gregg noticed the bruises around his wrists and up his arms. He must have been frantic to get out.

'How is he?'

'Confused mainly. Max tell you he'll be joining Tate?'

'Yeah, he said. Is he okay about it?'

Gregg nods. 'I reckon so. From what Alex said, he didn't take a lot of convincing. But who knows if that's just part of what she did to him, or if he really genuinely believes he needs help.'

'When is he going?'

'Another few days. They just want to make sure his leg is healing first. He's had an assessment and he's going to remain on the high-risk list for the moment.'

'Shit. I hate that he has to go away. Two mates in the same fucking facility. How messed up is that?'

'It's shite, I know. But it's where they need to be right now. And you know it's the best thing for Luke. None of us want him to go, but we can't help him.

'He's been mentally, physically, and sexually abused by his wife for years. It's going to take more than a few days in hospital to get him right. He has no idea what she was really doing to him. The only reason he said anything against her, was because you were arrested. But, that centre is the best of the best. They can help him.'

'For how long?'

Gregg hates the total devastation on Dillon's face. 'I don't know. It won't be a quick fix. You know that Dillon.'

He nods and focuses his attention on the landscape again. He's done talking, so Gregg leaves him alone.

Luke

For the first few minutes after he wakes up, Luke could almost imagine he's away with the band on tour, worn out after an amazing night on stage, playing to their fans, laughing, and joking until early into the morning.

Then the pain registers and the fantasy fades. He doesn't want to open his eyes until he knows who has drawn the short straw to sit with him. To make sure she wasn't allowed near him. To make sure he didn't try to hurt himself again.

This isn't what he wanted. He didn't want to worry his family and his friends, and he didn't want to make it sound like he is blaming Pippa for anything.

But, more than anything else, he didn't want Dillon getting the blame for his stupidity.

All he had wanted was to stop causing problems. All he wanted was for the pain to stop. Instead he'd done the exact opposite.

He can hear someone moving in the chair beside his bed. He freezes, until he picks up on the cologne, mixed with the recognisable scent of sour apple.

Luke opens his eyes and smiles with relief when he sees Dillon stretched out in the chair beside his bed, fast asleep with his arms crossed and his head down.

Both wrists are torn, and there are bruises on his hands. He looks tired too. Deep black rings surround each eye, and his hair is dishevelled.

He had heard the nurses talking about Dillon's loud and violent arrest, when they thought he was asleep. Dillon had a good hold on his temper most of the time. He must have been furious with Luke for him to lose it that badly.

Dillon opens his eyes and smiles at him. 'Hey.'

'Are you okay?'

He stretches then sits up. 'Me? Yeah. I'm fine. Thanks to you.'

'It's my fault you were in there in the first place. I'm sorry, Dillon. I never wanted you to get the blame. I'd never do that to you. I promise.' He looks angry. Probably at him.

Dillon clenches his jaw and looks at the floor for a minute. It takes him a little time to get himself together. He finally looks up and drags his chair closer. He grips Luke's hand, squeezing it so tight it hurts.

'Now you listen to me. I never want to hear you apologising for what happened. Never. You didn't do anything to me. All you did was save my neck.'

He pauses and looks away, quickly wiping his face on his arm. Is he crying? Dillon never cries.

When he looks back, Luke feels the loose grip on his own emotions crumble, when he sees the tears clearly tracing down Dillon's cheeks.

'I don't want you to think or worry about my arrest. You hear me? It's in the past. I'm fine. All you need to do is focus on you. Be selfish. For the first time in your life concentrate on yourself, okay? Your family are here for you. The guys are. I am. Always. Day or fucking night, you come to us. Talk. Cry. Shout. I don't care.'

'I'm sorry I did this.'

'No apologising, remember? You asked for help the only way you could. We're listening to you, Luke. Just promise me something?'

'What?'

'Promise me you'll never scare me like that again. Promise me. I can't lose you. Please.'

He nods. He'd do anything to make Dillon's pain go away. He thought by killing himself, he would bring them all peace. Seeing their reactions over the last few days made him realise how wrong he had been - about a lot of things.

'I'm going to miss you, Luke.'

'I'll miss you too.' He'll miss all his friends. Miss talking to them and laughing with them. Miss getting on stage with them. The tears come out and, embarrassed, he buries his face under his hands. Dillon gathers him in his arms and holds him.

'We'll all be here for you when you come home. We're all here for you Luke.'

Luke doesn't know how long he hangs on to Dillon as they both cry, but he's still wrapped in Dillon's arms when he eventually falls asleep.

Chloe

Two weeks later...

Chloe sits on the tailgate of Tate's truck, and straightens her jumper for the hundredth time since she arrived ten minutes ago. She's nervous. Excited too, but mainly nervous. Tate is getting out of rehab in a few minutes. He's clean... again. Or at least he's in a place where they're happy he can deal with it, without their constant support.

But she's still anxious.

She'd visited him a few times during the month he was in rehab, but it was far from normal. Being in the centre instead of their home, had added a level of awkwardness.

Tate had also been withdrawn, and she was on edge, overly polite in case she did or said the wrong thing. While a little easier than the last time, his treatment had taken a toll on him again. The first visit in particular, was one she wishes she could forget.

Tate had been barely recognisable, agitated and hostile. Not that she blames him. For someone who hates talking about what's going on in his head, having to open up about all the horrific things he endured as a child, was traumatic all over again.

But there's no way they'd be releasing him today, unless they were happy with his progress, so she has to believe that.

She looks up as the front door opens and a tall, imposing man steps out into the sun. Whatever nervousness she had, dissipates, as Tate walks down the path towards the car park, bag slung over his shoulder.

That's her Tate. Tall, confident, gorgeous, truly a sight for sore eyes. When he spots her, his face breaks into a huge grin.

'Mr. Archer.'

He walks over to her and dumps his bag on the ground. 'Ms. Quinn.'

They take a second to look at each other then, as if timed to perfection, their hands are all over each other. Tate kisses her and Chloe groans against his mouth, her tongue exploring and tasting. 'I missed you,' she mumbles as she hungrily kisses him.

'Mmm, missed you too. God you feel so good.'

'You taste so good.' She nibbles the side of his neck, sending a shiver through his body, which does nothing to calm the situation. 'Maybe not here?'

He nods, but keeps kissing and touching her. 'Maybe not. We probably should go home.'

She sucks on his earlobe. 'Stop on three?'

He nods. 'One.'

'Two.'

On three, he pushes away from her and smiles. 'Sorry about that. I was planning on talking to you first, not doing that.'

'Me too. Guess we both missed each other.'

She loves the smile he gives her. 'I wasn't expecting you to pick me up.'

'I needed to.'

Tate looks at her, really looks at her, just like he used to, before things went so wrong for them. She's never met anyone who can say so much by just looking at her. He loves her. She can see it in his eyes. And she loves him so much.

'You look incredible, Chloe.'

'You too. How about we get you home.' He helps her off the back of the truck and she holds out the keys. 'I'll let you drive.'

'Thanks.' He gets behind the wheel, as she climbs into the passenger seat.

'So, how are you?' she asks, as he pulls out of the car park, pausing to glance over his shoulder at the facility one last time.

'I'm much better. I wasn't allowed out until I'd filled my calendar with appointments.' He shrugs and smiles at her. 'Loads and loads of talking.'

She reaches across and takes his hand. 'I'm proud of you.'

'Thanks, but it's still early days. As long as I keep talking, I should be okay. I just took the drugs to stop myself from having to think about everything. If I keep letting it out, I should be able to steer clear of heroin.' He shrugs and falls silent for a minute. 'I don't want to be an addict, Chloe. I really don't.'

'I know.'

'I got to see Luke before I left.'

'That's great.' They had only told Tate about Luke a few days ago. It had hit him hard, but it was always bound to. It hit all of them hard. Luke is the single most decent, sweet guy she's ever met. It breaks her heart to think of what he'd been going through the last few years. 'How is he?'

'Quiet. He didn't say much. Didn't say anything really.' He pauses and smiles sadly. 'I hated seeing him like that. Hated seeing what she did to him.'

'He's in the best place with people who can help him. Just like you were for the last few weeks. He's got a long way to go, but he'll get there.'

'I hope so. Is it okay if I drop you to your Gran's place? I have to go to lunch with my family.' He grumbles a curse, as he scrubs his hand over his face. 'Released from rehab lunch, part two. Should be fun!' he adds with a grin.

'What do you mean part two?'

'I had to do the awkward lunch the last time too. It's a new tradition apparently. Get out of rehab and sit through a painful lunch. I could seriously do without this.'

'Do you...' she stops herself from asking if he wants her to come too. She's not sure where they are, relationship wise. Are they dating again? Are they friends? Until they actually have the conversation, she's in limbo.

'Would you?'

'Would I what?'

'You were going to ask if I want you to come with me, right?'

'I wasn't sure if I should.'

'I'd really like you to come, if you can. Maybe with you there, my folks won't be tempted to ground me again.'

She laughs at the look on his face. 'Yeah, Bria told me about that too.'

'I'll bet she did. I'm never going to live that part down.'

They talk about random things as he drives. There's a very noticeable politeness, and slight awkwardness to their conversation, but it's to be expected. They have a lot to talk about, and until they do, their relationship is on unstable footing.

She's deeply in love with him, and always attracted to him. But is that really enough?

As they get to the Wicklow mountains, Tate veers off the main road and pulls into a car park at the top of the valley. 'What are you doing?'

'Humour me for a sec. I promise it'll be worth it.' He grabs their jackets from the back seat and gets out of the car. He hands Chloe her coat, and silently takes her hand, leading her down the side of the valley and pointing to a rock. 'Will you sit for a sec?'

She does, and he joins her, as she looks down over the spectacular Lough Tay. She's driven this road too many times to count, but can't remember stopping here more than maybe once or twice. 'The view is stunning.'

'Gregg brought me up here after I got out of rehab, the last time. Gave me a few home truths.'

'About what?'

He turns to look at her. 'You, mainly. Convinced me to grow a set and ask you out. I didn't think it was the right thing to do. I thought I was too messed up. Too much of a basket case.' He takes a long breath and looks out over the lake again. 'But the irritating fucker wouldn't let it go. You know what he's like. When I called around and asked you to join me for the picnic, he was in my truck down the road making sure I didn't bottle it.'

'I'm glad he pushed you.'

Tate looks at her again and smiles. 'Me too. No question. I've never been more thankful that he got on my case about you. I guess I just couldn't see beyond what was going on in my head. I needed the kick.

'I know I let my head get the better of me again. And I know there's a strong chance I've lost you because of that. Fuck, I deserve to have lost you.'

'Tate—'

'This is part of my therapy, so button it,' he says with a small grin.

'Sorry.'

'Thanks. When you told me you were pregnant, I freaked out. I know you probably got that part. I thought that because my dad was a dick, I'd automatically be the same. That I'd be a lousy father, and that I'd seriously fuck up the kid by having anything to do with it. And, I'd just hit you. An accident, I know that,' he says, before she can interrupt. 'But it happened. I just got hit with all this crap from my past with him dying and... I let it win. Let my father win.

'I'll never forgive myself for not being there for you. I should have held you. Should have been able to support you. I let you deal with losing our baby alone and I'm so sorry Chloe. Sorry for not giving you what you needed from me. Sorry for falling back to drugs when I couldn't deal with everything. But I'm mostly sorry for not being there for our baby.'

He takes her hand in his, holding it firmly.

'All I ever wanted when I was a kid, was someone to love me and protect me, when I needed it the most. And then I go and treat my own child the same way. I didn't give them the love and protection they deserved. Never again, Chloe. If you can forgive me, and if we ever have a family, I will do everything I can to be the best partner, and the best father I can be.'

Chloe doesn't realise she's crying, until Tate reaches up and wipes the tears from her cheeks.

'You want a family?'

He smiles and nods. 'Yeah. I really do. I spent a long time thinking over the last month. I was scared. I'm still scared, but I want to have children with you, Chloe.' He smiles and takes her hand. 'The thought of mini versions of you in my life is fucking awesome. I want that. Genuinely want that.'

'It could be mini versions of you.'

He raises his eyebrows. 'God help us all. Seriously though, I'm in love with you, Chloe Quinn, and I know you feel the same about me. But I also know you need more than that. I'm hoping you'll give me a chance to show you I can be the boyfriend you deserve.'

Chloe wipes her face then leans over to kiss Tate.

'Is that a yes or a no?' he asks when she releases him.

'That was a yes, Tate. I love you so much.'

'So we're together again? I mean like a couple?'

She laughs and smiles widely. 'Yes Tate. We're going steady. Is that better?'

He wrinkles his nose. 'Never liked that.' He lifts her up and places her on his lap. 'Whatever the fuck you want to call us, I'm yours Chloe.'

She rests her forehead against his. 'And I'm yours Tate.'

'I like the sound of that.'

'Would you mind if we didn't live together again yet. I love you. I really do, but I just think it would be a good idea to take things slow before we move in together again.'

'Of course I don't mind. It might not be a bad idea. I know I kept things from you the last time. I don't want to make that mistake again. I'll take things at the pace you're happy with. I just want you in my life, Chloe.'

'Thanks. Can you promise me something else, Tate?'

'What?'

'We go to couple sessions too. I know you have ones to go to alone, but I want us to go together too. I need to understand you. Understand your addiction, and I'd prefer to do that with you, if that's okay.'

He pauses for the briefest of moments. When they began dating he'd put her in touch with one of the therapists at the centre, so she could ask whatever questions she needed to. But after what just happened, Chloe would feel happier if she could be involved in his recovery.

There are still things in his head that he needs to keep away from her, and she understands that. He's entitled to his privacy, but there's so much he's dealing with, that she knows she can help with. She just doesn't know how.

Eventually he nods and smiles weakly. 'Yeah. Okay.'

'You're not keen, are you?'

'No, but I get what you're saying. I want to spend my life with you Chloe. It's only fair you know what you're getting into.'

'That's not why I want to go.'

'I know. I'm joking. Well, a bit,' he adds with a smirk. 'But thanks.

It was actually suggested during my rehab, but I didn't know how to bring it up with you. I'll give the centre a call when we get back.'

'Speaking of getting back, we probably should go. Your mum will be worried.'

'Yeah. I have to be on my best behaviour with her until... well, forever. She's seriously pissed with me.'

'Just give her time.'

He smiles sheepishly. 'Time, eh? I've heard nothing but *give it time* for the last month.'

'It solves a lot of problems.'

Tate sighs and nods. 'Apparently. Not so sure Mum will be jumping to forgive me any time soon. But I can begin making it up to her by not being late for lunch.' He takes her hand as they walk back to his truck. 'But please don't leave my side.'

She laughs and pokes him in the stomach. 'Big guy like you needs protection?'

'Too fucking right I do! You haven't seen my Mum when she's pissed. Silent and deadly. I'd nearly prefer shouting.'

'She was worried about you. Her reaction was perfectly normal.'

'I know. I need to spend some time with Bria too. Things are still off after the first time I put myself in rehab. I've a lot of making up to do with her too.' He pulls her to a stop as they reach his truck. 'You first though.'

'Me first what?'

'I want to spend time alone with you after lunch, if that's okay?'

'That sounds perfect.' She kisses him again then pushes him towards the driver's side of the truck. 'Let's go. Your family is waiting.'

Tate nods and climbs into the truck, fastening his seatbelt. It may be his family, but she knows he'd prefer to face a stadium of strangers. Time to own his mistakes though, and that starts with walking into his parents' house and facing them.

36

Bria

Bria is nervous, which makes no sense whatsoever. She's spending the day with Tate. She'd done that countless times, but this is different. It's the first time they're doing this since his overdose, which damaged their relationship last year.

She glances over at her brother. His hand is squeezing the steering wheel. He's uncomfortable too, which helps her feel a little better. She knows he wants to fix this as much as she does.

'So you going to tell me where we're going?'

'Nope. Told you it's a surprise, so quit asking.'

'You know, you can be so irritating.'

He smiles over at her and for the first time in months, it's like he's his old self again. 'It's my job.'

He pulls through a gate into a field and Bria instantly recognises where they are. She did a track day with Gregg while Tate was away, a few weeks ago.

The guys are bike crazy and usually head off on their motorbikes as soon as they get back from touring. It's their way of blowing off steam and relaxing. She's never done one with Tate though. But that's for a very good reason.

As far as he knows, she can't ride a motorbike. But, she had taken an intensive course a few years ago, and had kept up the hobby, without telling him. She'd wanted to do something like this with him, but then he'd ended up in hospital, and the whole thing lost its appeal.

Tate takes his truck across the field and waves at the steward who lets him through the next gate. He pulls up beside a trailer and turns off the engine. 'Ready?'

'For what?' she asks.

He opens the door and climbs out. 'I'll show you.'

Feeling totally confused, Bria gets out and walks over to the trailer. Tate unlocks the back and opens it. He disappears inside and wheels out a brand new dirt bike. 'You like it?'

Bria loves it. It's what she had hired when she was here with Gregg, but a much newer model. 'Of course I do, but what's going on?'

Tate rests it on its stand and stuffs his hands in his back pockets. 'I've been trying to buy you a car for years, but you won't let me, and I get why you keep refusing. I know you don't want handouts and I respect that, but I'm hoping you'll let me give this to you.'

Bria stares at the bike, then up at him. 'This is mine?'

He nods. 'That's the plan. You'll need a proper road bike too, if you're going to go out with me and the guys on runs, but I want to see how good you really are, before I get you one. And I will be getting you one, so you don't even think about arguing with me. There's two things I know about: bikes and guitars. You buy either without me with you, we're going to have a problem.'

'Hold on. You know I can ride?'

'Yes. Don't be mad at Gregg for telling me. He was just so proud of you.' Tate comes around the bike and stands in front of her. 'I am too.

Really fucking proud. And not just because you got your license. I'm always proud of you, Bria. And, I watched the fashion show Gregg was in.'

'You watched it?'

'Of course I did. I know I give you a hard time about the fashion thing and you wanting to sort us out, but it's got nothing to do with your style or the pieces you create. I hope you know that.'

'It's the glitter, right?'

He laughs at that. 'You have threatened me with it a few times. I just didn't want you to make something for us, and then for people to think you just got the job because I'm your brother. That's the only reason. I didn't want to take away from how talented you are.'

Bria feels herself tearing up at that. Deep down she had assumed he was embarrassed by her style, and didn't want the band to be associated with that.

'Anyway, I just wanted to get you something, and I thought you might like a bike of your own for messing around on, until I get you a road one. It's insured and ready to go. I got you some kit too. Gregg helped out with the sizing, so it should fit. It's all in the trailer.'

Bria looks over at her brother and lets the tears out. She was continuously on his back about not spoiling her or getting her things, but she's not about to refuse his gesture. It's his way of trying to fix things between them.

Bria steps up to him and hugs him tight. 'Thank you, Tate. I love it.'

He hesitates then hugs her back. 'I also hear you're not too bad on the track.'

She wipes her face and shrugs. 'Gregg thought I could hold my own. You're the expert. How about I show you what I can do?'

He pulls a set of keys from his pocket and holds them out to her. 'Let's go.'

One week later...

Tate, Gregg, and Dillon walk along the path to the beach and sit on the sand at the far end. Tate can't remember the last time they took time together like this, and he has missed it. The last year has been so busy, they hadn't had time to just be together as friends.

They all desperately miss Luke, but they'll have to get used to his absence for however long it takes their friend to get better. Tate may have hated rehab, but he can't knock the facility. Luke will come through this. They're all confident he will, but it will take time.

Tate looks over at Dillon when he nudges him in the arm.

'You're scratching again.'

'Sorry.'

Dillon nods then looks back at the sea. He'd surprised Tate by arriving on his doorstep when he was released from rehab. He told Tate he'd stay for a few nights every week to keep him company.

Tate couldn't have been more grateful. He didn't want to be alone, but couldn't go back to his parents. Not yet, and Gregg was trying to get back on track with Bria. At least with Dillon there, when a nightmare hit, he had support.

He knows Dillon is worried about Luke and probably needs the distraction too, but if it helps both of them, Tate isn't going to argue.

After letting the silence hang for a good few minutes, Tate decides to get things moving.

'So, what are we doing guys? Are we calling it quits? Is Broken finished?'

'That kind of depends on you, buddy,' Gregg says, looking across at him. 'No you, no band.'

'I'm not ready to give it up. Not yet. I love it, guys. Seriously love it.' He pauses, and watches the sea for a few minutes. 'You had to go on without me once. I fucking swear it will never happen again. I won't let you down.'

'I'm not done either,' Dillon says. 'I want to keep performing. Fuck, it's the only time I'm genuinely happy. My ego needs the attention,' he adds with a smile.

'What about Luke?' Gregg says. 'You going to be able to work with him?'

Dillon chews his lip ring as he stares out at the sea. 'I know he doesn't love me the way I love him. I get that, and I will get over it. I've worked with him for years without any problems.' Dillon picks at a piece of seaweed. 'Besides, he needs something to come back to.'

Tate turns to look at his best friend. He doesn't want to be in the band without him. 'Gregg?'

'Oh, right. Sorry. No, I'm in. No question.'

'What? Really? That easy?'

'Of course. I never wanted to leave the band. Not for a second. But with circumstances as they were at the time...' he smiles and shrugs. 'Not going over all that again. Besides, I can't walk away now. Not when I'm finally getting used to the mountains of screaming fans I've amassed! I couldn't do that to them. It would just be mean.'

Tate laughs and pulls Gregg's head down to scrub his hair.

'Oi! Watch the do. It takes a long time to get it looking like that.'

'You wake up with it looking like that,' Dillon counters.

'Unlike you who has to work at it, you mean.'

Dillon holds up his middle finger, but grins. It's the first time Tate has seen him smile in far too long. They haven't had a lot to smile about lately.

This is what they're usually like. They take the piss out of each other, which helps to keep everyone grounded. They were a family, long before the band took off. Lately, they had lost some of that connection. Each one had pulled away to deal with their own shit, and it nearly cost them their friendship, as well as their career.

'So Broken Chords is back?'

Dillon and Gregg nod at him at the same time. 'You may be forgetting one teeny fly in that ointment, buddy.' Gregg says. 'Ellen grounded us. As in semi permanently.'

'And you quit, you fucker.'

Gregg throws Dillon a withering look. 'Whatever. You went to prison, so you can't talk. Ever.'

'I'm in a relatively good mood, so I'll let that slide and not deck you.'

'Appreciated. Anyway. It's all well and good us saying we're in. We have to convince Ellen.'

'Yeah. Small detail.' Tate leans back on his elbows and watches the waves for a minute. 'There will be touring. There always is, after we screw up. We all on for that? We okay to leave Luke?'

Dillon licks his lip ring, and pokes the seaweed again with his finger. 'He's where he needs to be for now. If we have to use a standby until he's well enough to join us, that's what we have to do. But we make it known and fucking crystal clear, that Luke is part of the band long term. I'm not doing this, if he's not a part of it eventually.'

Gregg nods. 'Couldn't agree more. No Luke. No band.'

'I'm with you there.' Tate knows how important the band was to his recovery. As embarrassing and humiliating as it was, coming back after his epic and repeated falls, he could come back.

Luke is in hell at the moment. Hopefully it'll offer him some comfort to know his friends have his back and will do their best to keep the band going, until he can join them again.

'So, it sounds like we have a plan. So who's going to draw the short straw and ring Vox to book a meeting with Ellen?' Dillon and Gregg turn to face him and he curses. 'Why me?'

'You're the frontman, buddy.'

Tate is exhausted. Emotionally and physically drained. But he always is after therapy. Opening up about everything in his head seriously takes it out of him. It was even worse this time.

Chloe was there too.

He loves that she wants to support him like that. It means the fucking world to him, but knowing that she's sitting there beside him while his past is laid out on the fucking table, isn't ideal.

He wants her though. Wants a future with her. Wants her to come home. That's all going to take time. It's not something he can rush, no matter how much he wants to.

Chloe joins him on the beach and hands him a cup of coffee. 'I think it was a good idea sending me for the coffee. There's an impressive crowd up there. Do you want to go for a walk?'

They head down the beach, away from the crowds. It's been a month since he was released from rehab. Things are better... mostly.

His mother is finally speaking to him again, although their relationship is strained. He understands why. She's disappointed in him. Fuck, he's disappointed in himself. It will take time to put things right with her. Maybe years.

Deep down he's accepted the fact she probably won't trust him again until he's proved himself for longer than six months. He reset the dial when he stuck the needle in his arm again. Messed up too many relationships that can't be fixed overnight.

Like the most important one in his life.

His relationship with Chloe is going from strength to strength. Starting afresh was the best thing they could have done. She knew him better than most people in his life, but he hadn't been honest with her about a lot of things.

Until she mentioned it at therapy, he hadn't realised that she didn't know his original name. But how would she know if he didn't tell her? As much as he'd like to ignore it, James is part of his past. He was miserable as James. Scared, lonely, in pain. But James made him who he is today.

Those first six years of his life were downright terrifying, but without that time, he wouldn't have met his new amazing, loving family. He'd never have begun his new life as Tate. Broken Chords wouldn't exist. He'd never have met his friends.

Or Chloe.

He'd hidden so much about his past from everyone close to him and that's not right. There's nothing to be ashamed of. If he learned anything from Luke it's that, what happened to him wasn't his fault. Sometimes people who should love you, hurt you instead. Probably hurt you more than anyone else could.

But that doesn't mean the person being hurt is to blame.

Luke will have to learn that.

And so does he.

If he's to have a future, he needs to face that, instead of hiding or blaming himself. Everyone he is close to deserves him to be honest, no matter how painful.

He may miss living with Chloe, but in a way, it's nice to take a step back and just date each other. Just because you live with someone, doesn't mean you talk more or necessarily know each other better. By taking time out of their lives to just be together, he'd got to know her better.

They'd go for walks, take long drives into the mountains, he'd give her guitar lessons and, in turn, she'd try to test his drawing skills. So far he's a total disaster art wise, but that's not the point. It's just about spending that uncomplicated time together as a couple.

'You're quiet.'

He smiles at Chloe and nods. 'Sorry.'

She takes his hand in hers. 'That was a particularly tough session for you.'

'A bit.' He's continuing what he began in rehab, talking about his father. Talking about what he remembers him doing. More and more details are breaking out of wherever he'd buried them in the back of his mind. The nightmares are worse, but he knows in time, it will get better. He hopes.

'Is Dillon staying with you tonight?'

He takes a drink of his coffee and nods. 'Always does after a session.'

'Who knew he was such a softy.'

'He's not as tough as he likes to make out.' Tate pulls her to a stop and turns her to face him. 'Are you okay?'

Chloe smiles, but it's weak at best. 'I'm so glad you're letting me be there for you like this, but that doesn't make it easier to listen to. I just wish I could do something...anything to help you.'

'Hey, you are. Okay, so I might not have been thrilled about you joining in the sessions, but it was the right thing to do. For us. For me too. I don't want there to be any secrets between us, Chloe. Never again, and I know I'm completely to blame for that. I thought hiding all the shit and only letting you see certain parts of who I am would be the better option. I was wrong. I just wish it didn't take nearly losing you for me to realise how much of a selfish dick I was being.'

'You weren't being selfish, Tate. You were trying to protect yourself. After even knowing a small amount about what you've been through, I understand why you went that way.' She wraps her arm around him, pulling him close to her. 'I'm here now, and I don't plan on leaving, okay. It was a bump in the road and we're getting over it.'

'I can't believe I nearly lost you.'

'Well you didn't, so stop thinking about it. We're good, Tate.' She reaches up and kisses him. 'You hungry?'

'You're not trying to cheer me up by offering me chips, are you?'

Chloe smiles and shrugs. 'There's a chance I might be. Is it working?'

He turns around and points to the takeaway near the car park. 'I can smell the chips from here. I think you've convinced me.'

They walk back along the beach in silence, but it's far from awkward. Being in her company is more than just comforting, it's soothing. All the stress, the whirlwind of thoughts and memories are quietened when she's around. Talking to her helps. It's hard, and he hates it, but it's helping to bring the memories out of the darkness so he can face them head on.

It's what he should have done months ago, but pig-headed stubbornness had stopped him. Or fear.

Whatever the reason, it's different this time. He's not hiding - as much as he wants to sometimes. He's facing it all, but with Chloe by his side.

'I love you.'

'I love you too, Tate.'

He wraps his arm around her, pulling her close to his side.

This time will be different. He'll make damn sure of it.

Chloe

Chloe sips her lemonade as she leans on the railing surrounding the headland. The last time she was here was just after she met Tate. She didn't even know who he really was at that stage. As far as she was concerned, he was a gorgeous guy she met on the beach.

When he told her he was famous, she hadn't taken it well. In fact, she'd stormed away from here, leaving him to chase down the road after her. But that's in the past.

She glances over her shoulder towards the picnic blanket laid out on the grass in front of the summer house. The owner, Grace, is a friend of Tate's mother and lets him use the quiet location whenever he wants.

They'd come up here about two hours ago for lunch, then he'd given her a replay of what happened in the summer house last time. Twice. She didn't think it was possible, but sex with Tate just keeps getting better and better.

Even though he'd been eager to try for a hattrick, she'd begrudgingly refused. Part of the reason for coming up here was so he could work and, as much as she would have loved to oblige, this is more important.

Right now, he's sitting on a bench outside the wooden hut, guitar on his lap as he glares at a piece of paper beside him.

The new album is nearly finished. Or at least the writing part. Until Luke is well enough to join them, they won't record any of the songs. Once Tate got down to it, it hadn't taken him long. Without all the turmoil he was trying to deal with, his creativity came back. A week of steady writing and he's on the final song.

But judging by the frown, it's not going well.

'If you keep frowning at the page you're going to get wrinkles.'

He doesn't look up from the page, just lifts his hand, holding up his middle finger.

'Are you stuck?'

Tate curses loudly then grins at her. 'You could help you know.'

She joins him on the bench and takes the guitar from his hands. 'Let's see what you've got so far.'

He's been giving her guitar lessons every few days and she's picking it up reasonably fast. But it wasn't just about learning the instrument. It was about spending quality time with him. And she loves every minute of it.

She's seeing a different side to him. One she had no idea existed. With everything going on in his head since she met him, he's been guarded. He had been trying to keep so much to himself, he'd kept a part of himself from her too.

Now he's let his guard down, she's seeing more of the light-hearted side he hadn't shown her before. She was used to him being more serious and brooding, but he's not like that all the time. He's smiling more. Laughing more. And she loves seeing him like this.

She plays a few chords then points to the page. 'That's exactly the same as the previous song.'

'You saying I'm copying my own songs?'

'I'm saying that's the exact same as the last song. Just that part.'

He picks up the page and hums the notes to himself, before cursing and slapping the page back down. 'Fucking thing has been bugging me for an hour. I couldn't figure out what was wrong with it.' He leans over and kisses her on the cheek. 'Should have asked you to check it an hour ago.'

'So do I get royalties for these as a co-writer?'

Tate grins and takes the guitar back from her. 'You'll be appropriately compensated, I promise.' He places the guitar on the grass and leans over her, caging her in with his body. 'I could compensate you right now.'

'What about dessert?'

'I was planning on having you for dessert.'

She laughs and pushes him off her. 'Do you ever stop?'

He winks and goes over to the blanket. 'Not while you're around.' He takes a plate of cake from the basket and brings it over to her. 'There. Dessert. You go first, then me.'

'I honestly don't know how you win awards for your lyrics.'

'I just reckon you have high standards.' He grabs a piece of cake and devours it in one mouthful.

'You are such a gentleman.'

He grins at her. 'Too fucking right. So, you got anything planned tomorrow?'

'I have some work to prepare for Monday but I can do that in the morning. Why?'

'Fancy taking the bike out for a run? We could head... well, anywhere really. Might give you a few lessons too.'

She nearly chokes on the cake. 'On your motorbike?'

'Yep.'

'Nope. Your bike and your horse are in the same category. I'll drive your truck but have to draw the line there.'

'Wuss. I'll convince you.'

'Good luck. I'll come out on your bike with you if you finish that song.'

'Fuck you're tough. Fine. You go and sit over there somewhere. You're distracting me sitting so close.'

Chloe kisses him and takes her plate of cake back to the blanket. She lies on her stomach facing him, watching as he plays and sings to himself, stopping every now and again to scribble something on the paper.

She desperately misses living with him. They need this time apart, she knows that. But that doesn't make missing him any easier to deal with. It's too soon though. He's only been out of rehab a little over a month.

But when is the right time?

That's the part she's struggling with. How long do they give it before one or other of them decides? He absently scratches the inside of his left arm as he stares at the page. He's doing it less and less, but it's a habit he's struggling to break.

Tate glances up at her and smiles.

He's hers. That gorgeous man over there is in love with her and she's in love with him. She can wait. However long it takes, she'll wait for him. He's worth it.

Tate

Tate is well and truly fucked. Twice.

Chloe cuddles against his bare chest, her hand running in slow circles on his arm, tracing the lines of his tattoo. This feels right on so many levels. Being with her like this feels right.

He'd gone all out tonight, even managing to impress himself. Posh restaurant, suit, flowers. The works. It's kind of embarrassing to think he's been with Chloe for well over a year and that was the first time he'd taken her to a restaurant. Better late than never. He should have taken her ages ago.

Dinner hadn't been a complete disaster. He'd never been a fan of getting dressed up and going out for dinner. So much of his life is spent in front of other people, when he is off he always preferred to keep to himself.

Okay, so he had booked the entire top floor of the restaurant to give them some privacy, but she didn't seem to mind, and that's all that matters.

He'll take her out more. A lot more. Normal couples go out to dinner. They sort of bi-passed all the usual dating rituals and that's his fault.

'Tate?'

'Yeah?'

'Can I stay over?'

He pulls her closer and kisses the top of her head. 'You never have to ask.'

'I meant on more of a longer term basis.'

Tate shuffles back in the bed so he can look at her. 'Like move back in?'

Chloe nods, her smile making him go all warm inside. 'If you're happy to share your space with me again? I understand if it's too soon for you or if you—'

Tate rolls over, pinning her under him, silencing whatever else she was going to say when he kisses her. He doesn't need to think about it. Not for a second.

His life has been missing a huge piece since she moved out. They needed to take things slowly, get to know each other properly, but fuck he misses waking up next to her.

Chloe laughs when he finally releases her. 'I'll take that as a yes.'

'Oh it's a yes. Are you sure you're ready?'

'Are you?'

He rests his forehead against hers. 'I'm sure. I've missed you so fucking much. Missed you being here with me.'

Chloe runs her fingers through his hair as she smiles widely. 'I feel the same. I love you.'

'God, I love you so much Chloe. I really do.' He gets out of bed and grabs a pair of jeans from the chair where he dumped them before dinner.

'What are you doing?' she asks, sitting up in bed.

'Get dressed.'

'Why?'

'We need to go and get your stuff. Might as well move back in now.'

She laughs as she checks her watch. 'It's close to midnight.'

Tate pulls on a t-shirt and passes her the dress she was wearing to dinner. 'And?'

Chloe stares at him for a minute then laughs and climbs out of bed. 'You make a valid point.'

'I do?'

'Not really. But what the hell. Let's go.'

'I'll get the car started.'

She blows him a kiss before he heads downstairs and out to his truck. She's moving back in with him. He must look like a right idiot, a massive grin on his face, but he's so fucking happy he feels like he's about to burst.

He hurries over to her as soon as she closes the front door behind her, pushing her back against the door as he kisses her.

'What was that for?'

'I'm just happy.'

She takes his hand and walks over to the truck with him. 'How about we get my things, come back here, and I'll show you exactly how happy I am.'

Tate unlocks the truck and climbs in. 'And how happy are you?' he asks as she fastens her seat belt.

'Happy enough to possibly dig out that red corset you like.' She winks and clicks the remote, opening the gate.

'Fuck...really?'

'Oh really. Now drive.'

Tate manoeuvres the truck through the gateway and onto the main road, the stupid grin even bigger than before.

38

Chloe

Three weeks later…

Friday at last. This week seems to have dragged on, but it always feels that way when the weather improves. Most of the day had been spent outside with the children, but all she wants to do is go home, get changed, and lounge in the garden with her sexy boyfriend.

But he's put a hold on that. Before she left work, Tate had sent her a cryptic message, asking her to meet him outside Newcastle after work, and she has no idea why. Tate isn't a fan of giving away too much information. It's kind of his thing.

She pulls into the carpark at the beach and shuts off the engine. No sign of Tate yet so she gets out of her car and climbs onto the wall to look at the sea. The last three weeks back in his house have been incredible. Being apart had been painful for both of them, but it was needed to make them stronger. And it worked. Chloe thought what they had was solid before, but now it's so much more.

He's talking to her. Opening up about what's in his head. Hearing about his nightmares hurt so much, but it's bringing him closer to her. Instead of shutting off and pushing her away, he immediately turns to her. Looks to her for the support she'd been so desperate to give him all along.

Chloe turns and smiles when she hears a powerful engine heading her way down the track. Tate pulls his truck into the car park beside her car, and points to the passenger seat. She climbs into his truck and he leans across to kiss her. 'Good day?'

'Yeah. It wasn't too bad. How about you. You look... strangely upbeat.'

'I can do upbeat.'

'True, it's just nice to see it again. So what's with the secret meeting? Is everything okay?'

His smile is one of the first truly genuine ones she's seen for a long time. 'Oh yeah. Just bear with me for a sec and put this on.' He passes her a blindfold.

'You want sex in your car?'

'No. Of course not.' He pauses and grins as he glances around the car park. 'Well, unless you're seriously offering?'

'No.'

'Fuck! Fine. Just put on the damn blindfold and trust me. Please. It'll be worth it.'

She ties it around her head and Tate pulls out of the car park. He drives for less than ten minutes before coming to a stop, and getting out of the car. He helps her down and takes the blindfold from her eyes.

She blinks, then stares at the stunning farmhouse in front of them. Beyond the fields to the back of the house, she can hear the waves crashing on the beach.

'What's going on?'

'Well, Gregg, Dillon, and I had a meeting with Ellen and some of the management team at Vox earlier.'

'You did? Why didn't you tell me?'

'I didn't want to worry you, or to get your hopes up. The three of us were worried enough, without telling you and Bria.'

'And?'

'Well, it was a fucking tense meeting. We were in there for two long hours. There was a lot to talk about.'

'And...'

'We're back.'

She screeches and throws her arms around his neck. Tate lifts her off the ground as he hugs her back.

'I'm so happy for you, Tate.'

He grins as he puts her back on the ground. 'Yeah. Me too. We thought it was done, you know. But we weren't done. And we need to keep going for Luke.'

'Is his place in the band safe?'

'Part of our agreement. We'll use another guitarist to fill in for the moment, but he's still part of Broken.'

'I don't know what to say. It's incredible news. Are Gregg and Dillon buzzing too?'

'Fuck yes. She gave us the option to take another few months off, but we decided against it. We don't do sitting around. You know that. We've already been off for too long. We need to get back to work. We want to get on the road again.'

'But what about the new album?'

'It's all set to go, but everyone agreed we hang on until Luke is with us. Ellen is putting together some dates in the US. There are loads of venues we didn't get to last time. I don't think the fans will mind us sticking with our current material for another few months. I know going away again isn't great, but—'

She places her finger on his lips, cutting him off. 'Touring is part of it, so never apologise for that. Besides, I might be looking forward to seeing your sexy bod back on a stage again.'

He pulls her into his arms and smiles. 'Sexy bod, huh?'

'Oh you know you're sexy, so don't go all innocent on me.'

He wiggles his eyebrows, but she shoves him away, laughing. 'Not here you oaf. Wherever here is. Why are we here?'

'Well, now my career is safe, or as safe as it can be, I thought it might be time for a change.' Tate holds out a set of keys. 'It's for sale. Fancy a look around?'

'You want to look at a house?'

He stands behind her and wraps his arms around her shoulders. 'Well I was maybe thinking that we could do with a new house. Somewhere away from town, where we could get peace and quiet.'

She turns to face him. 'I didn't know you wanted to move.'

He shrugs. 'I've always had my eyes open in case the right place came on the market. I told you when we first met, that I'm not a city guy. I prefer open spaces. This has fifteen acres and stables. Plenty of room for Jove.' He frowns at her. 'Bad idea? Too soon?'

'What? No! Absolutely not. I'm just surprised. It's massive. I mean the house looks massive.'

'Six bedrooms like Blackrock, but not as fancy. I don't know. It was just an idea. How about we have a look around and see what we think. It could be a dump inside.'

An hour later Chloe stands in the back garden of the property, and closes her eyes. No cars. No noise. Nothing except the sounds of birds and the sea in the distance.

The house is stunning. More than stunning. It's so different to Tate's Blackrock house, but not in a bad way. Its age gives it more character, but that's what she loves about it the most. She can see herself here with Tate. See them bringing up a child here. See Tate riding Jove along the beach. It's them. Everything about it is right.

Well, except for the price tag. She can only hazard a guess how much it's on the market for. It may be old, but it's recently been renovated. That would come with a hefty price tag. Her teacher's salary would barely cover the fees to buy the house, let alone make any serious contribution to the house itself. It's very much down to Tate what happens next.

The man himself finishes the call he was on, and joins her on the grass. 'First impressions?'

'It's stunning, Tate. Really beautiful, but it must cost a fortune.'

He laughs and kisses her on the forehead. 'Don't worry about that bit. I can afford it.'

'But what about Blackrock? You haven't even listed it yet?'

'I might not sell it immediately. I mean I plan to, but if this is a goer, then I'll wait until we're in, before I make any decisions. Do you really like it? If you don't, just say. I'm not about to buy a house unless we're both happy with it.'

She turns around to look back at the farmhouse. 'I can see us here.'

'Yeah. Me too. It's a good thing the estate agent wasn't showing us around. Your massive grin would have given the game away.'

'I'm only human, Tate.'

'Well I'm really glad you like it, cause I just put in an offer.'

She stares at him, sure that he's joking with her. But he's not. He's deadly serious. 'You have?'

He nods. 'And it was accepted straight off the bat. Fingers crossed, if all goes to plan, we could be in here in a few months.'

Chloe squeals and throws her arms around his neck. 'This isn't a joke?'

'Nope. It's real. Don't get too excited though. Until we sign, it'll all up in the air. There's nothing to say the sale won't go through smoothly though.'

'I can't believe you just bought this. It's perfect, Tate.'

'It's our first home together. It needs to be.' He twists the ring on his thumb and shrugs. 'I thought it would be a good place to bring up a family.'

Chloe takes his hand in hers. 'You really thought that?'

He nods. 'That bedroom down the end would make a perfect

nursery.'

Chloe knows the smile on her face is heading towards epic proportions.

'What's with the weird smile?'

'I had the same thoughts.'

'You did?'

'Absolutely.'

He leads her over to the bench at the end of the garden, overlooking the sea. 'Please tell me to put the brakes on if this is too fast for you.'

'I love the house, Tate.'

'Not the house part. I was talking about what I'm going to say. Do you... have you thought about... I mean if you wanted to try... I don't know. I'm fucking this up. Why the fuck do my interview skills leave me when I have something important to say to you?'

Chloe turns to face him. She's nearly positive she knows what he's trying to say, and it couldn't make her happier. 'Do you want to have a baby Tate?'

He nods, the smile a little hesitant as he waits for her reaction. 'If it's too soon I totally get that.'

Chloe throws her arms around his neck, hugging him tight.

'Can't... breathe...'

'Sorry. I just didn't think you'd say that. I mean I hoped you would, but I just wasn't expecting it yet.'

'It just feels right, Chloe. All of this does. I want a family with you.' He runs his hand over the side of her face, brushing her hair back behind her ear. 'Are you sure you want... well, me. Like this. I mean really sure.'

'I've never been more sure of anything in my life.' She wipes the tears away. 'Are you really sure you're ready?'

'I'm far from ready to be a father, but who is? The difference is I *want* to be father. More than anything.' He picks her up, placing her on his knee. 'So we're going to do this? Have a baby?'

'Too fucking right we are!' she responds, earning a loud laugh from Tate.

'Fuck I love when you curse like that.'

39

Gregg

Six weeks later...

Gregg wheels Tate's bike up the ramp onto the back of the truck, and secures it to the load bed. Tate is still inside, making sure they haven't forgotten anything. The removal company had taken all the furniture over to the new house yesterday and his studio equipment will be following in a few days, once the new studio is ready. Then the old house will be ready to go on the market.

It's amazing what a cash offer on a house can do. The property sale had gone through in six weeks, a bloody miracle, but one Tate and Chloe were more than happy to accept.

Gregg is going to miss this place. He gets why Tate wanted something a bit more rural. His demon horse needed space, but they'd spent a lot of time here over the last few years. It kind of became a second home to him. If it wasn't for the astronomical price tag that would no doubt be attached to it, he'd be sorely tempted to buy it himself.

Tate loads a box into the back seat of his truck and shuts the door. 'It's just the studio left. Everything else is gone.'

Gregg pulls the strap tight, making sure it's going to hold the bike. Tate would be less than chuffed if his Kawasaki took a dive onto the road.

'You had any thoughts about when to put it on the market?'

Tate leans against the bonnet and crosses his arms. 'Funny you should mention that. I've been thinking. There's no rush to sell it. I might hang on to it for a bit.'

Gregg raises his eyebrows at that. Tate is clearly raking it in, if he can afford both places. 'Right. You going to rent it out?'

'Nope. I was kind of thinking you and Bria could live in it.'

'Oh ha ha.'

'I'm being serious, Gregg.'

He stops securing the bike, and examines his friend over the back of the tail bed. No grin. No weird smile. 'Okay. Now you're either getting really good at keeping a straight face...'

'Or I'm being fucking serious,' Tate says. 'I know you love this place and you need to move. You said so yourself. I'm not giving it to you like *here's a house*, but you live in it, stick your place on the market, then buy this if you want, or something else. Whatever. Just live here as long as you want and save up. This place is paid for, so you can stay here rent free. Just cover the utilities.'

Gregg silently stares at Tate. He wasn't expecting this. Not for one second. Tate is massively generous. He doesn't throw his cash around or flaunt what he has, but he'll step up and help out whenever he can. But giving Gregg and Bria his house rent free is a bit much. 'I appreciate the offer, Tate. I really do, but—'

'But what?' Tate comes around the side of the truck and stands beside him. 'You need to get away from the place where you were kidnapped. Where you were being watched.

'And you can't bunk out in Dillon's house forever. You'll never get your head straight while you still own that house. And I know you love your house. I get that. I really do. But this is bigger than a house. This is about your head space, Gregg. Being there won't help you move on. It won't stop the nightmares.'

Gregg smiles, but it falls short. Tate is right. He's not moving on from what Angel did to him. He's tried, really tried, but it's not getting any better. If he keeps going the way he is, there's a chance he could lose Bria.

Maybe Tate is offering him the answer to all his problems.

'Are you absolutely—'

'Yes! I'm sure. You'd be doing me a favour. It'll be sitting empty otherwise.'

Gregg peers up at the stunning three storey property, then back at Tate. 'This place is worth millions. Are you sure you want to just let me live here rent free?'

'Fine. Give me fifty quid a month. Will you shut up and take the fucking house now?'

Gregg pulls Tate into a hug, letting go when his friend shoves him away. 'Too much hugging?'

'Yeah. Too much. I'm taking that as a yes.'

'Thanks, Tate. Really. You don't know what this means to me.'

'I think I know. I'm still taking the studio equipment though. No way I'm leaving that behind.'

'Drat! Fair enough. Guess I can't complain.' He smiles as he looks up at his new home. 'I better go tell Bria.'

Gregg watches as Bria takes a minute to process what he just said. She turns around, looking at the massive living room in Tate's house - their house. 'Are you freaking kidding me?'

'Nope.' He holds up the set of keys and jiggles them. 'It's ours. The plan is to put my place on the market, find something new, then live happily ever after. Or, depending on how my royalties are going, maybe even buy this place.'

Her eyes widen at that. 'Oooh. You'd buy this place?'

He shrugs. 'Maybe. You know I love it, but I'm a long way from even considering that option. First thing to do is move in, and put my place up for sale.'

She wraps her arms around his waist and smiles up at him. 'How do you feel about that?'

'Honestly? Really good. I don't think it hit me until you mentioned it, how much being there was getting to me. She held me captive next door. How did I not see how messed up it was, even suggesting staying there?'

'You didn't want her to drive you away. There's nothing wrong with that. It's your home.'

'Nah. It was. The second she took me from there, it stopped being my home. Now it's just the place something bad happened to me.' He runs his hand through her hair, brushing it back from her face. 'Now the next question is, am I moving in here alone or...'

'Gregg Egan. Are you asking me to move in with you?'

'Might be. If I was, what would your answer be?'

'I think I'd say yes.'

Gregg takes her hand and leads her up to the master bedroom. It's easily the size of the whole top floor of his old house, and far more luxurious. 'My bed is going to look pathetic in here. I might have to invest in a new one.'

'Maybe we could change the carpet and blinds too? I'd prefer this didn't look like my big brother's room. Which right now, it kind of does.'

Gregg grimaces, then nods in agreement. 'Gotcha. Good point. So, no sexy time in here until we sort that out.' He pulls her into his arms. 'But after I deal with that one teeny issue, do you think you'll be happy here. I mean maybe put all that other stuff behind us?'

Bria slides her hand under his t-shirt and rubs along his back. 'Yes. This house has always been a home away from home for me. I can't think of anywhere better to move on and start our life together.'

'Excellent! Me too, Bria. And I'm sorry. I was being stubborn staying in my place. I thought I could deal with it. Guess I'm not done with therapy, huh?'

Bria kisses him, then pulls him closer to her body. 'One day at a time, Gregg. Let's get you in here, then see how you feel.'

'Yeah. That sounds like a plan. So, how about we head over to mine and start the whole moving process. We can use one of the spare rooms until we de-Tate this one.'

'I'd love that.'

He tries to move away from her, but she holds on to him. 'You okay?'

'I love you, Gregg.'

Gregg can't help but grin like an eejit at her words. He'll never get tired of hearing them from her. Even having been in love with Bria for years, isn't helping him accept this is actually happening. That he's in a real life, not-just-in-his-head, relationship with her. 'God, I love you too. I really do.'

'Right answer,' she says as she slaps him on the arse and walks away. 'C'mon sexy. Let's get you moved, so I can ravage you many, many, times.'

40

Chloe

Chloe pulls up outside their new house and stares up at the stunning property. She can't believe it's theirs. It already feels like home. Not that there was anything wrong with the house in Blackrock - far from it. It was stunning, but this is *their* house.

She parks in the garage and walks around to the back of the house, stopping in the garden to listen to the sea. At the moment, a pile of building equipment is stacked up against the side of the granny flat at the end of the garden. It's going to be Tate's new studio, or will be in a few weeks once the work is completed.

The three roomed building is being converted, soundproofed, alarmed and, once given the final seal of approval by Tate, will have all their recording equipment moved there from the old house. It will give them somewhere they can relax and practice in peace.

Her phone sounds just as she's walking towards the door. She reads the text from Tate and smiles.

On the beach. T x

She quickly changes out of her high heeled boots into a pair of trainers before wandering through the fields and on to the beach.

But that's as far as she gets. In front of her, just at the water's edge, she finds Tate. But it's a very different Tate to the one she was expecting.

He's standing beside a table and two chairs, wearing a perfectly fitting navy suit, which makes him look incredible. She slowly approaches him, not sure what's going on.

'Hey.'

He kisses her, then pulls out her seat. 'Hey. Hungry?'

'Well, yeah, but what's all this?'

'Happy anniversary.'

'I'm confused. It was our anniversary in May.'

'You would have to point that out. I was in rehab for our anniversary so this is our belated one. And we didn't get a chance to celebrate moving in so it's a joint celebration.'

'We already christened the bedroom, kitchen, living room, and staircase. I don't think that's bad, celebration wise.'

He grins as he sits down. 'Fucking impressive when you say it like that. But I meant celebrating with clothes on.'

'Oh. Bit of a difference. Well I for one have no problem with the *clothes on* part. You scrub up pretty well.' That's one understatement. His suit matches his dark blue eyes perfectly, the open neck shirt teasing her with glimpses of his neck and chest tattoo. She loves him in his everyday clothes, but Tate in a suit is a dangerous sight.

'You okay? You're a bit flushed.'

He grins, knowing full well what's wrong with her. She's told him enough times what the sight of him in a suit does to her. 'I'm fine,' she responds, trying to play it cool and failing miserably. 'This is incredible, Tate. Thank you.'

He shrugs and smiles at her. 'You're worth it.' He takes the covers off their food and Chloe laughs. Spaghetti bolognese. 'Yeah I know it's the same old spaghetti. But there is a hidden meaning behind the meal.'

'Go on.'

'Apart from the fact I can't cook anything else, it was the first meal I cooked for you. It's kind of our meal. Fuck, that sounds unbelievably corny.'

She reaches across the table and takes his hand, rubbing her thumb over the tattoo. 'Corny but lovely. Thank you.'

He licks his lips and pauses for a moment. 'I don't think I've ever told you how unbelievably lucky I feel to have you in my life.'

'Tate—'

'No, I need to say this. Part of my therapy,' he adds with a small smile. 'I mean it, Chloe.' He pauses for a moment then takes a breath. 'I nearly lost you, and I still don't have a fucking clue how I managed to hang on to you. But I have, and I swear I'm not going to hurt you again.'

He stands up and walks around the table, lifting her and her chair up, turning them around to face him. When Tate drops to his knee in front of her, Chloe swears her heart stops for a moment.

'I love you, Chloe Quinn. I can't imagine my life without you in it. I know what I want, Chloe. And it's you. And maybe, if we're lucky, we can have a family one day.'

She knows she's crying, but she can't stop the tears of happiness.

'I know I'm far from perfect. And I know I'm not easy to be with, but I promise you I will work my ass off every single day, to show you I'm worth taking a chance on. If you'll have me.'

Tate whistles, and Chloe laughs when Jove walks through the gate and up to Tate. He takes a box from a pouch on Jove's headcollar, then nudges Jove.

'Down.' Jove bends one of his front legs so he's kneeling beside Tate. When Tate opens the box and holds it out, Chloe nods enthusiastically before he's even asked her. 'Can you just hold on a sec! Don't go stealing my thunder. I've rehearsed this all day.'

She wipes her cheeks and nods. 'Sorry. Carry on.'

'Thank you. Anyway, right so, ah fuck it. Chloe, will you marry us?'

She throws her arms around his neck, knocking him to the ground. She laughs as they land in a heap beside Jove.

'Am I taking that as a yes?'

'Yes! Absolutely yes!'

Tate pushes onto his elbow and slips the stunning ring onto her finger. 'You're really going to marry me?'

'Marry both of you,' she says, nodding over to Jove who is watching them. 'Although, I think he's a one man horse. I'm not sure he'd be on for sharing you.'

'He'll have to get used to it,' Tate says, resting his forehead against hers. 'Because now I have you, there's no fucking way I'm going to let you go again.'

Tate

Tate packs away the last of the dinner things and looks over at his beautiful wife to be, standing in the moonlight staring out at the sea. God she's stunning. He thought he had lost her. He deserved to, but somehow, he managed to earn himself another lifeline. And this time he isn't going to mess it up.

He wants a future with her. Wants a family with her. The thought still terrifies him, but he can do it. He knows he can. As long as he's with her, he can do anything.

She glances over her shoulder at him and smiles.

Tate crooks a finger at her calling her over to him. Chloe walks up to him and takes his hand. 'You okay?'

'Oh yeah. Never better. You?'

'I'm great.' She traces her hand down the front of his suit jacket and grins. 'I do like you in a suit. There's something about the piercings and tattoos teamed with a suit that is... well, rather nice.'

'I know. Why do you think I got into it. It's all for you, Chloe. I hate the damn things.' He looks over to the sea and smiles. 'Fancy a swim?'

'What? Now?'

'Why not? No waves. Stunning summer night. C'mon.'

She looks at the sea then back at him. 'You're being serious?'

'Why wouldn't I be?' He slides off his jacket as he kicks off his shoes. 'You're not going to let me get in all alone, are you?'

'But what if someone sees us?'

'The only way to get anywhere near this beach is by boat. Can you see any around?'

'Well, no...'

'Exactly.' He slips off his trousers then hooks his fingers under the waistband of his boxers. 'What do you reckon? One more layer?'

Chloe stares at him for a second then laughs. 'Now I know you're joking. Leave them on. I wouldn't want you to have a fish related injury.'

He holds out his hand and gives her his best pleading look. Chloe sighs and unbuttons her blouse then takes off her skirt. 'I'm leaving my underwear on.'

'Spoil sport.'

She stands beside him and looks down the beach. 'Now what?'

'Oh that bit's easy,' Tate picks her up and throws her over his shoulder, then runs down the beach.

Chloe

She may not have been too enthusiastic about the late evening dip. Or the way in which he convinced her to actually get into the sea, but lazing in the sea as the gentle waves lap around them in the moonlight, she has to admit it was one of his better ideas.

It's so peaceful, just the two of them with no one else around for miles.

She floats in the water while he swims, contentedly watching his powerful body glide effortlessly through the water. She could never tire of watching him.

Tate rises from the water and gives her the kind of look he usually reserves for the bedroom. Or the kitchen. Or wherever he happens to be when he wants her.

His hand slides around her waist, pulling her towards him. The kiss confirms her suspicions. As does the rather impressive package digging into her stomach through his boxers.

'I get the impression you want something?'

'I always do when I'm touching you.' His hand slides under the waistband of her panties. 'There's no one around. I want you to scream as you come.'

It's not like she has any say in the matter. Tate slides a finger inside as his thumb massages her clit, faster and faster until she's gasping for breath. She clings on to his arm, keeping herself steady as he relentlessly fucks her with his fingers.

But she honestly couldn't give a damn who sees or hears her. It's just the two of them though, just them and his fingers which are driving her closer to orgasm.

She digs her fingers in to his biceps, her nails tearing at his skin as she desperately tries to hang on to something, anything. Being in the sea, the water swirling around them, is making her feel like she's floating, even more than usual.

'Look at me, Chloe.'

His blue eyes are focused on her, watching her fall apart under his touch. 'Oh Tate...'

'Don't hold back on me. Scream my name, Chloe. Scream my fucking name. Now.'

Tate

Hearing her scream his name in the open is such a fucking turn on. She collapses in his arms, while he holds her up against him as she comes apart. She's so fucking sexy when she comes. Her lips parted as her breathing quickens, the slight flush to her checks and chest, the glassy look in her eyes that means he's given her exactly what she wants. And more hopefully.

Before she's fully recovered he kisses her, his tongue slowly fucking her mouth. Her pussy is still tight around his fingers, the orgasm still rolling through her.

'Do you have any idea how stunning you look right now?'

He kisses down the side of her neck, before he brushes his lips against hers again, tasting the salty ocean on her skin.

'I'm addicted to you, Chloe.'

He lifts his hand out of the water, sucking her juices from his fingers. 'I have no problem with that in the slightest,' she replies with a satisfied smile. 'Watching you do that is a teeny bit of a turn on, you know that?'

Tate picks her up, wrapping her legs around his waist. 'Kiss me.'

'You taste of sea and me,' she says, when they come up for air again. 'Not too bad.'

'Too fucking right it's not. My favourite things all in one place. You getting cold?'

'Now I've come down yeah, a little.'

Tate keeps her in his arms as he walks out of the sea. He lowers her onto her feet then passes her his suit jacket to put on.

'I'll get it all wet?'

He shrugs and helps her put it on. 'It's just a jacket. I don't want you getting sick before I leave. Doubt you'd be impressed with me.'

He sits on the sand and pats his legs. Chloe sits on him and he wraps his arms around her, keeping her warm.

'You okay now?'

She lies against his chest and sighs contentedly. 'Never better. I can't believe we're engaged.'

'I know. I feels right though.'

'Yeah, it does.'

'When do you fancy?'

'Fancy what?'

He kisses her head and tucks his jacket around her. 'Getting hitched.'

'I don't know.'

He doesn't have a clue either. He's still trying to get his head around the fact he's engaged in the first place.

'I don't think there's any rush. It's not that I don't want to marry you,' she adds quickly. 'But I'm sure you want Luke there too. A lot will depend on when he's released.'

Tate takes a long breath then rests the side of his face against hers. He's so unbelievably relieved to hear her say that. 'Thank you. I didn't want to suggest delaying in case I upset you.'

'Why would it upset me? Luke is family. We can't get married without him being a part of it.'

'God, I love you. You sure you're happy to wait? Luke won't mind if...'

'No. We'll wait,' she says, moving back so she can look him in the eye. 'It's an all or nothing kind of deal. We will absolutely wait. It wouldn't feel right otherwise.'

'Fair enough. But that doesn't mean you just forget about it and get on with life. We can still plan, but just not decide on a date until he's back with us.'

'Do you want a big wedding?'

Tate shrugs. 'To be honest, until I decided to ask you to marry me, I'd never thought about a wedding at all. What I do know is that, I'd prefer it wasn't anything like the fucking circus Pippa had when she married Luke. The whole damn thing was suffocating.'

'Thank God for that!' Chloe says. 'I'm so relieved we're on the same page. That's absolutely not us.'

'Phew! I'm not a fussy kind of guy. I like things simple. To be honest, as long as you're there, and my family, and the band, I'll be happy. I'll go with what you want though. One hundred percent.'

What he would really love is a small wedding on a beach somewhere. He's not a fan of the stuffy traditional weddings. But he'll go with whatever she wants. Fuck the cost - she can have everything she asks for.

'What about here?'

Tate frowns, thinking he's hearing things. 'What? On the beach?'

'Well I meant more the house. It's got loads of room outside. We could get a marquee or something fancy like that.'

The bear hug she gets as a response, has her gasping for breath.

'Ease up! Are you trying to kill me?'

'Sorry. That just sounds too fucking perfect. That's exactly what I wanted. I thought you'd be going for something a bit more fancy though?'

'How better can you get, than at your own home, with all our family and friends? Sounds perfect to me too.'

'So that's a deal? Here it is?'

She nods against his chest. 'Deal.'

Chloe settles against his broad chest, curled up against him as they watch the sun set. For the first time in too long, he's excited about what's to come. Since meeting Chloe, things have been chaotic, unsettled. He feels like he's finally in control of his future. Or at least, as in control as most people are.

He'll leave in two days for a very long eight weeks on the road. Chloe and his family are worried about it, and he completely understands why. To help not only himself, but them too, he asked his sponsor to come on tour with them. The relief it gave them was so worth it. And, if he's being really honest with himself, it's given him the safety net he needs.

He's accepted the fact he's always going to be a drug addict. It's part of him and he needs to live with it. There will be times something random will get to him and he'll withdraw or brood. But he's put too much effort into controlling it. Too much work into knowing how to handle the pull.

But he's still scared. More than he'll ever admit to Chloe or his family. He's fallen twice. Falling again will kill him. No question.

He's got something to live for. Chloe, his family, the band, his career.

His future.

He wants to be here for all of them. And maybe, if he's really fucking lucky, he can get a second shot at being a father. And this time he'll step up. This time he'll be the father he wanted, when he was a kid.

Chloe

Chloe wakes to sunlight streaming through the enormous bay window, the sound of the sea in the distance completing the perfect way to wake up. She looks down at the beautiful solitaire on her finger and smiles. She's engaged to Tate Archer.

'You're thinking how lucky you are to be marrying me, right?'

A large, tattooed arm slides over her waist, pulling her close to the solid chest behind her.

'Wow! It's like you read my mind.'

His hand strays under her t-shirt, working its way up her body.

'You any good at reading my mind?'

Chloe moans quietly when his fingers graze against her nipple. 'I don't think I need to be a mind reader.'

He rolls over, trapping her under his body. 'It's your fault. There's no way I can keep my hands off you.' He kisses her, pushing her legs apart with his knee.

She groans as his bare leg presses against her underwear. 'Go for it. I'm not going to stop you.'

He smiles and makes quick work of her panties, then tugs the t-shirt she slept in over her head. 'I love that you sleep in my t-shirts.'

'I love, how you love, that I sleep in your t-shirts.'

Tate applies a little more pressure with his leg and groans, deep in his chest. 'You wet for me Chloe?'

She gasps when he moves down the bed, spreading her legs wider so he can place open-mouthed kisses along the inside of each thigh.

His fingers brush over her pussy, the gentlest whisper of a touch that makes her whimper.

Chloe lifts her hips off the bed, trying to close the gap between them, but Tate grips her thighs, holding her in place. 'I asked you a question, Chloe.'

His breath skirts across her clit and she moans loudly. 'Yes, Tate. I'm wet for you.'

She cries out, arching her back off the bed as he sucks her clit. Chloe digs her fingers into his dark hair, holding him against her, as she watches him licking and sucking her, like a man possessed.

He peers up at her as he slips a finger inside, curling it around until he finds her G-spot.

'That's it, Tate. More... please.'

The tip of his tongue swirls around her clit, a second finger joining the first to stretch her.

'Fuck, you're so tight, Chloe.'

She moves her hips, grinding her pussy against his face as the orgasm builds. 'I'm close.'

'I know,' he growls, before flicking his tongue against her clit. Tate keeps up the rhythm, all the while keeping his dark blue eyes on her, watching her.

'Oh fuck! Tate. Yes, Tate!' she cries out as the orgasm pulses through her body. Tate doesn't stop, keeping the orgasm going, his tongue and fingers drawing it out until she's breathless.

Tate crawls up the bed, caging her with his body. She groans as he slowly slides his fingers into his mouth, licking them clean before kissing her.

He tastes of her, his tongue slowly swiping over hers. 'I could lick you out all day. You taste so fucking good, Chloe.'

Her hand wraps around his length, her thumb rubbing over the ring piercing the crown.

'I'd let you do that to me all day, but now it's my turn.'

Tate

Chloe's hand wraps around his stiff cock instantly making him groan aloud. Her thumb grazes against the piercing again. He sucks in a breath. 'Fuck, Chloe. Do that again. Harder.'

She does it again, harder this time, sending a spasm through him.

She runs her thumb over the piercing again, applying just the right amount of pressure before moving down to the barbell in the base, doing the same. That fine line between pain and pleasure, drives him crazy. It was part of the reason he got the piercings in the first place. 'You hard for me, Tate?'

'Too fucking right I am.'

Her tongue replaces her thumb, slowly sliding over the piercing, taking her time to lick every drop of precum, swallowing it before wrapping her lips around the head.

She sucks him to the back of her throat, her tongue pressing firmly against his dick adding more pressure.

'Fuck, Chloe...'

She releases him slowly, the sensation on the piercing going straight to his balls. As if reading his mind, she licks his cock, giving the piercings a little extra attention, then sucks on his balls.

He's not going to last long. The pressure is already building, his balls tightening as she swirls her tongue around the sensitive flesh.

He reaches over his head, gripping the headboard. Chloe slides his dick back into her mouth, her tongue brushing off the piercing in the base.

She speeds up, sucking him harder. Her hand, tongue, and mouth lavish attention on his dick and balls, the sensation blowing his fucking mind.

His balls tighten as she pushes him over the edge. The headboard creaks as he pulls against it. She takes him as deep as she can, swallowing everything he gives her. Chloe meets his eyes, looking fucking hot, as she cleans his dick, her tongue slowly moving from his balls to his tip.

'You look so fucking hot when you do that.'

She slowly draws her tongue along his dick, sucking the ring in the tip into her mouth, pulling on it before she releases him. 'What? That?'

Tate flips her onto her back, pinning her to the bed under him, caging her under his body. He pushes his hips forward, sliding the pierced tip of his dick into her warm pussy before pulling out again.

'Stop teasing me.'

He does it again, slower this time. 'What? Is this teasing you?'

She rakes her nails over his chest, brushing against his nipple piercings and sending a jolt right down his body to his dick. 'Is that teasing you?' she counters.

'Nope. No reaction at all.'

She knows full well even looking at his nipples can send him into a frenzy. She flicks her nail against one of the piercings and he gasps.

'Who's teasing who here?'

Chloe smiles at him as she gently pulls on his nipple again. 'How about we both stop teasing. I want my fiancé to fuck me. Now.'

Chloe sips her coffee, listening to Tate singing to himself while he showers. Her gorgeous man had made her a lavish breakfast in bed, insisting she stay put for as long as she wants. He's got a few things to do with the band in an hour, but promised they can spend the rest of the day together, once he gets back.

Loads of people sing in the shower, but this is on a whole new level. This is a multi award winning, front man for an internationally famous band, singing in the shower.

Whether he's on stage with the guys in front of thousands of screaming fans, or in the shower singing to himself, his voice gets her every single time. It's deep, and rich, and without a doubt, sexy as hell.

She looks down at the ring on her finger, a wide smile spreading on her face. And he's all hers. Tate Archer is going to be her husband, and she honestly couldn't be happier.

Then she sees his bag on the ground by his side of the bed and her happiness diminishes a little. It's part of his job, and she has no problem with it, but she really wishes he wasn't leaving for so long. Two months is a long time without him.

It's not ideal timing, but they want to fight for the band. Want to make sure Luke has something to come back to, when he's better. And she absolutely understands and supports that.

Broken Chords needs to get back to what they do best, but unfortunately, for the moment, with someone else standing in for Luke. Hopefully it will only be temporary, but a lot of that will depend on Luke.

At least it's term time so she'll be busy. And she has a wedding to plan. Once they discovered they want the same thing, wedding-wise, he'd told her she can take the lead with the plans. He won't be able to do much while he's away, and it will help occupy her in the evenings.

The singing stops and Tate appears in the doorway, a towel wrapped around his waist. 'Recharged and ready for me?' he asks with a wink.

'As tempting as that is, you'll be late if you don't get a wriggle on.'

'I'm the singer. Nothing starts until I get there.'

She squeals as he launches himself at the bed. 'Ugh, you're all wet.'

'The question is, are you?'

She shoves him off her, laughing when he grabs her again. 'Get off me!'

He kisses her, then sets her free. 'Spoil sport.'

Chloe covers his groin with the towel, hiding temptation. 'You have to go to work.'

'Fuck that! I'll be working for the next two months straight. Right now, I want sex.'

'You are truly a sweet talker. Get. Up!'

He sticks out his tongue then pulls himself off the bed, throwing the wet towel at her as he walks into the wardrobe. 'I want you the second I come home.'

'How could I possibly resist.'

He winks at her over his shoulder, then disappears into the walk-in wardrobe. 'You sure you'll be okay with Jove?' he asks, as he searches for some clothes.

'Of course. As long as I don't have to ride him, I'll be just fine.'

'I'll give you lessons when I get back from touring.'

'Eh, no thank you. Gregg warned me about him. I'm not getting on Jove's back.'

'Gregg is a wuss. You'll be grand, don't worry. I could always get you your own horse if you want?'

She nearly laughs at his suggestion, but stops when she realises he's being serious. 'Tate. No. Don't even go there.'

He reappears in his usual jeans, t-shirt, and boots, grinning widely. 'Oh I promise. I forgot to say, the builders should be here on

Monday to finish the studio.'

'No problem.'

'And they'll be converting one of the bedrooms at the end into an art studio for you.'

'They'll what?'

He slips on his belt and watch, then sits on the bed beside her to fasten his boots. 'I asked them to fit it out as a studio for you. They'll finish my one first. I want to get the equipment set up while we're away, then they'll work on yours. I've arranged for a designer to pop around after I go tomorrow, so you can work out some ideas.'

'Tate... seriously?'

'Is that okay?'

'Of course it is. But you don't need to do anything to the room. I can just use it as it is.'

'Why should you?'

'Because...'

He kisses her on the forehead then grabs his keys from the bedside table. 'Stellar argument. Put your thinking cap on. I'll be back in a few hours and I fully plan on spending the rest of the day butt naked, in bed with you.'

42

Tate

Two months. Eight weeks. Fifty six long days.

Tate groans to himself as he counts the time down on the calendar on his phone. That's too long to be away from Chloe. Away from his fiancée.

She's his fiancée. Fuck, he loves the sound of that. He doesn't want to leave her, but he's excited about going on the road again. After his meeting yesterday, he'd spent the rest of the day as planned – butt naked with Chloe. He lost count of the number of times they'd made love, but it wasn't enough. It can never be enough.

Tate smiles as his stunning wife-to-be steps out of the bathroom, a towel wrapped around her.

'You really think a towel is going to stop me?'

She smiles and shakes her head at him. 'There's no time for that. We have to leave in half an hour and you're still in bed.'

'I'm fucked.'

She throws her wet towel at him. 'That's entirely your fault. Now get out of bed, have a shower, and get dressed.'

He does the first one, but gets a little distracted on his way to the shower. 'You honestly expect me to leave you for two months?'

'Yes because that's what's going to happen. Your adoring public are desperate to see you all again. Get off me!'

Her struggles aren't in any way meant to shove him off, but he lets go anyway. As much as he doesn't want to leave, he does need to get ready.

'Fine. Spoil sport.'

She laughs as she pushes him into the bathroom and closes the door in his face.

Ten minutes later he joins her in the kitchen and gathers her in his arms again. 'I hate this bit.'

'Yeah. Me too. I wish I could join you this time, but we're right in the middle of term time.'

He brushes her hair back from her face. 'I know. It's grand. This whole tour is going to be a bit different. No Luke. Dillon out of prison. Me out of rehab. Gregg watching over his shoulder all the time. I think we just need to do this, to prove to ourselves that we can.'

'You can. I know you all can, but don't put any extra pressure on yourselves. Like you said, you are all recovering. Don't push yourselves too hard.'

'I promise.'

She nods towards his phone in his hand. 'You have all your appointments in your calendar?'

'Yes. I've got my scheduled call saved, I'm booked in for a few video chats too, and I'll have my sponsor with me.' He tilts her head back and smiles at her. 'I've got a handle on it. I promise. There isn't a hope in hell I'm going to fuck up again.'

'I know. Let me worry about you though. It's my job.' She grabs her handbag from the counter and checks her watch. 'Right. You'd better say goodbye to Jove, then we have to head. I'll meet you out front in five.'

He goes out the door to the yard around the back of the house. Beyond the hedge he can hear the sea, and it instantly brings a smile to his face. Moving from town was absolutely the best thing they could have done. This is exactly where he wants to be, and Gregg is right at home in Blackrock with Bria. His friend is sleeping better and even managed a walk on the beach, when he called over yesterday.

It's funny how things had worked out for the two couples.

If only things could be as promising for Luke and Dillon. They were keeping Luke's visitors to just his family, for the moment. Alex had been amazing though, keeping them up to date with his progress. And he is making progress. It's slow but that's to be expected. The abuse had been going on for years.

And Dillon...

Well, Dillon is being Dillon as usual. He hasn't spoken of his feelings for Luke since they decided to give the band a go again, a few weeks ago. Gregg and Tate had tried to get him to open up about it, but he stuck firm, changing the subject every single time.

On the plus side he doesn't appear to be drinking as much, he hasn't missed any rehearsals, and he even seemed to be drug free, but you never can tell with Dillon.

He smiles at Jove as he approaches the stable. His horse had settled straight in to his new home and Tate loves having him so close. 'See you in a few weeks.'

Jove snorts at him as Tate strokes along the side of his neck. 'You behave for Chloe and no biting. Please.'

He takes the next snort as a yes, then turns around and walks back to the house. The car is waiting outside for him, with Chloe standing beside it.

'All set?'

'Yep. You don't have to come with me.'

'Shut up. I won't see you for two very long months. I am coming with you to the airport.'

He gives up arguing. To be honest, he doesn't want to argue. Bria and Chloe will join them later in the tour for a weekend, and he's already counting down the days.

As they pull out of the driveway, Tate looks back at his... their, new house and smiles. For the first time ever, he actually feels like he's leaving his home, instead of just a house.

Dillon

Dillon paces his hotel room, the tension rolling off him in waves. He'd gone to the hotel gym and worked out for a good two hours, not that it did fuck all to relax him. In five hours, he'll be getting back on stage in front of the world for his first proper concert. TV performances were different. The crowds were smaller, more mixed.

Concerts are a whole different animal. Everyone in the audience is a true fan of Broken. They'd paid hard earned money to see the band in person. The energy, the excitement, the rush, is so different.

Normally he'd be hyped up, eager to get out there and soak up the attention that came with his job. But when he gets on stage this time, it'll be as a convicted criminal. Not a badge of honour he's thrilled about owning.

And they're going on as a threesome.

That's probably the part that's hitting him the hardest. They'd had to do it before the odd time, if one of them came down with something just before a show.

But Luke isn't sick.

He'd been crushed, ground into pieces by the woman he loves - or loved. Dillon has no idea how his mate feels about the bitch now after what she did. Fuck, he's not even sure Luke comprehends *what* she did to him.

That'll take time.

A lot of time, and a lot of help.

Walking away from him, had been the single most gut-wrenching thing he's had to do. Since they started the band, the four of them hadn't gone a week without seeing each other, well apart from when Tate went to rehab and he was arrested.

He had to leave him, even though he would have preferred to ditch the whole fucking tour and call it quits. He's doing this for Luke. That's the only fucking reason he hasn't walked away from all of this. The only reason he's not drowning in a bottle of whiskey in some dive bar.

He ignores the tears pouring down his face. Fuckers keep coming no matter how hard he fights. Since Luke admitted what Pippa did to him, Dillon can't keep a hold on his emotions.

And he's trying so fucking hard.

Hearing what Luke had been going through broke him and he doesn't know how to fix himself. Or even if he can.

He needs to get over this or he's going to be no fucking use to anyone. Luke is safe. He's getting help and he's safe.

But that doesn't mean Dillon's feelings have lessened even a fraction. He told the guys he's fine. But he's not. He can never be with Luke. He accepts that, but that doesn't mean he can just turn it off. Stop loving him.

He'd written to Luke every day. Actually put pen to paper and sent a letter by post. Luke wasn't allowed any phones or computers while he was there. Dillon gets why. Luke needs to focus on his mental and physical health. He can't do that while scrolling through all the shite that floods social media.

Especially about him.

They'd made a statement about Luke's health. He was taking time off for stress or something like that. If he wants to tell the truth when he's better, that's up to him. But it didn't stop the rumour mills from making shit up.

It's part of the fun that comes with their fame, but Luke doesn't need that kind of attention. Not now.

His stand-in, Tom, had been with the band since their tours moved from small back street venues in Ireland, to stadiums all over the world. He's an incredible guitarist and a genuinely decent guy. He'll fill the gap for the moment and is happy to do so. It also helps that he's not a blow in. He knows Luke, knows the band. He's not going to try and muscle in and take over.

Still feels wrong though.

He drops onto the bed for a grand total of two minutes, before he's on his feet again.

Fuck he's wound up. Dillon opens the fridge with a little more force than necessary. Fucking thing is filled with food as always. It's the lack of alcohol that pisses him off.

Blanket rule the four of them brought in.

No drinking before performing.

Tell that to his brain right now. He could easily take on a full bottle of whiskey, and that would just be for starters. After slamming the fridge door closed again, he flops back on the bed and glares at the ceiling. No drink. No drugs. No way to unwind, to loosen the vice around his chest, that's there from the second he wakes up every day, until he eases it with drink or drugs.

He closes his eyes, and tries some of that deep breathing shit Tate had to do whenever he was stressed. Seemed to work for him, so anything is worth a shot.

But then his mind takes over and that's the worst thing that can ever happen to him. It's full of seriously messed up shit he'd prefer not to think about.

Like his parents.

Like Luke.

Like her.

Apart from Luke, she was the one person he's ever really genuinely loved. But it all went wrong, and to this day he still has no idea why.

Their whirlwind romance had developed while he was working as a truck driver in the UK for a few months. He hadn't even had a chance to introduce her to the guys yet. It was one of those *instantly fall in love* things you read about in romance books or see in cheesy movies. But it was real. So fucking real.

To him anyway.

He had been due to go away with the band for the weekend. It was one of their very first tours. Nothing major - just a small Irish tour to some small venues. He'd stayed up all night with her before he left. She'd taken her time saying goodbye to him, refusing to let him go until the last minute. Everything was pretty fucking amazing.

He'd left, stupidly thinking he would be coming back to a life with her and a future he was so excited about. Instead he came back to an empty apartment, an *it's not you, it's me* letter that gave no answers, and an engagement ring that had been on her finger for less than a few days.

Her choice. Fuck her!

'Stop it!' he shouts, startling himself. He's not going there. Not again. It had taken him a long time to stop thinking about her, every single minute, of every fucking day. If he drops his guard now, he's done for.

He grabs his phone from his pocket and hits the first name that comes up on his recent calls list. Jason answers after the first ring. 'You okay, Dillon?'

'You want to hit the gym? I need to blow off some steam.'

'Sure thing. Give me five minutes.'

Dillon ends the calls and sighs. Okay, so maybe working out again isn't his best plan, but he's fucked otherwise. It's either sit here thinking about Luke and the woman who kicked the living shite out of his heart, before stamping on it, or pace the room for the next five hours getting deeper in his head.

Both options could, and have, ended in him hitting some inanimate object he shouldn't. And that never ends well for him.

Chloe

Eight weeks later...

Bria leans over Chloe to peer out the window as the airplane comes in to land. 'This is ridiculous, but I'm so excited!'

'About the concert, or seeing Gregg?'

'Gregg of course! Maybe the concert?' She rests her chin on Chloe's shoulder. 'You looking forward to seeing my grumpy brother again?'

'So much. It's weird. I'm excited but really nervous too.'

'It is kind of a big deal. First time seeing our boys back on stage this year. It's been a long year.'

She couldn't agree more. Thankfully, the latter part of the year had been a little less eventful than the first part. No kidnappings. No stalkers. No prison. No rehab.

Gregg, Tate, and Dillon seem to be on the right track. Everything they're doing the last few weeks is for Luke. He may not be touring with them, but they've been keeping him up to date, making sure he was as involved as he could be.

It's still not the same for any of them, but hopefully, he'll be back where he belongs soon.

After a short wait, they step off the aircraft, the hulking forms of two bodyguards behind them, as they make their way to pick up their bags. They were told the protection was organised by Vox, but they're positive Gregg and Tate were a major factor in that decision.

They pick up their bags and walk through arrivals, easily spotting Liam and Andy standing heads above the crowd.

'How is he?' Chloe asks Liam as he loads their bags into the back of the SUV.

'He's great, love,' he answers with a smirk. 'Seriously. I think performing really helps him. He's sleeping, eating, talking, doing everything he should by the book.' He nudges her in the arm. 'He's super excited about seeing you.'

The bodyguards fill them in on the news from the last few weeks as they drive them to the hotel. Apart from the usual band antics, it seems to have been uneventful for the most part. And that's a relief. They could all do with a healthy serving of uneventful for the next while, at least.

Twenty minutes later, they step out of the elevator in the hotel. Chloe hugs Bria when Liam stops outside the first hotel door in the corridor. 'I'll see you in a few hours. Have fun.'

'You too,' Bria says, winking, as she follows Andy down the corridor.

Liam knocks, then steps back as Tate opens the hotel room door, instantly pulling Chloe into his arms before she can say a word. Liam brings her bags into the room and leaves them to it, closing the door behind him.

Tate tilts her chin back so he can look in her eyes. 'Fuck, I missed you so much.'

'I love that you have such a way with words.'

When he smiles, it sends goosebumps up her arms. She hasn't seen him smile like that for too long. 'Award winning song writer, remember?'

'How could I forget, when you spout out sweet nothings like that?'

He kisses her, nudging her mouth open so he can slip his tongue inside. She wraps her arms around his neck, returning his kiss with as much passion.

He places his hands on her face and holds her a few inches from him as he looks at her. His dark blue eyes lock on her lips, then her nose, finally meeting her eyes. 'You look fucking incredible, Chloe.'

'Again with the sweet talking.'

He runs his thumb across her lip, bringing her back to the first time he did that, all those months ago. A gorgeous man had asked her out on a date and she'd said yes, only to find out during that picnic, she was eating sausage rolls with a major celebrity.

'What are you thinking about?'

'The picnic you took me on when we first met.'

He winces and rubs the back of his neck. 'Wow. Talk about a mood killer.'

'What do you mean?'

'You stormed off on me when you found out who I was.'

'Okay, so that part wasn't the best. I was thinking about before that happened. When you ran your thumb across my lips like you just did.'

His smile comes back and it's utterly wicked. 'Now you're talking. From what I remember, it got rather heated between us.' He pulls her against his chest again, wrapping his arm around her waist to hold her close. He nuzzles against the side of her neck, his beard tickling her skin. 'It was the first time I tasted you.'

'Oh I remember.'

'The first time you were laid out naked for me to kiss, and lick.' He sucks her earlobe and she moans. 'And suck.' His fingers comb through her hair, gripping the back of her head to hold her in place. 'Chloe?'

'Yeah?'

'I'm going to fuck you now.' She laughs, as he picks her up and carries her over to the bed.

'Tate. Hang on a second.'

He puts her back on the ground by the bed. 'You okay?'

'Yes. I mean, I think so. I'm not sure.'

He frowns down at her. 'What's wrong?'

'It's not that there's something wrong, as such.'

'Jesus Chloe. Tell me.'

'I'm pregnant.'

He freezes, like someone pressed pause on the scene. She can't even see him breathing.

'Tate?'

His eyes rise to meet hers, and he takes a long time to just look at her. Then he smiles, and it's the most beautiful thing she's seen. He crushes his lips to hers, as he grabs her ass so he can pick her up and spin her around.

He takes a step back from her. 'Are you sure? I mean that in a good way. Not that I don't want it to be true. Cause I really do, but I'm just checking. And this isn't me freaking out. I promise. I just... you know are you sure? Not about me not freaking out. I mean are you really sure you're pregnant? Fuck, I'm screwing this up again.'

She presses her finger to his lips, silencing him. 'Hey. Take a breath. You're not screwing anything up. And yes, I'm sure. I did six tests. Also, you're allowed to freak out. There's nothing wrong with that. I'm freaking out a little. It's a big deal.' His Adam's apple bobs as he swallows. 'You going to take a breath and calm down?'

He nods, so she takes her finger away. Tate swallows again, but doesn't say anything as he gives her a strange look.

'You're freaking me out now. Are you okay? Are you happy about this?'

'Are you fucking kidding me? Yes, Chloe. A million times yes. Are you okay? I mean are you happy? Are you feeling okay? Do you want anything. Can I—'

She presses her finger to his lips again. 'Slow down. I'm fine. I'm happy. I'm healthy. Everything is perfect.'

'Really?'

She laughs and cups the side of his face, running her thumb along his cheek. 'Really, really.' She takes a step closer, pressing herself against him. 'Well there is something you can do for me? I'd be extremely grateful if my gorgeous fiancé got naked right now.'

'Are you okay to—'

'Just fuck me, Tate!' she shouts, startling him. 'I've been sex free for eight weeks and I'm horny as hell.' She grabs his dick through his jeans and squeezes him gently. 'Don't make me beg.'

If she wasn't so turned on by even being close to him, she'd probably laugh at the look on his face.

'I don't know,' he says. 'I kind of like the idea of you begging me to fuck you.'

'Why does that not surprise me. When are you on stage?'

He frowns then checks his watch. 'Five hours.'

'That should be enough time.'

'For what?'

'For my unbelievably sexy rock star fiancé to fuck me at least three times. Please.'

He blinks once then smirks. 'Three times? You know I need to hold a little in reserve for the show.'

She drags her nails down his chest, brushing off the bar in his nipple. 'Are you really telling me you can't handle that? Big strapping man like you.'

'Fuck it! I'll collapse on stage.' He takes her hand to bring her over to the bed, but she stops him. 'How about the couch? You strip and sit down.'

'I love it when you get all bossy with me.'

He takes off his clothes and she feels the heat building in her. His body is a sight for sore eyes after eight long weeks. He is absolutely built for sex. The tattoos, the piercings, the muscles, it all adds up to create her stunning fiancé.

'You need a minute?' he asks, smirking at her.

'Shut up and sit down.'

'Yes Ma'am.' He sits on the couch and slouches back, patting his bare leg. 'C'mon then, sexy.'

Chloe takes off her clothes, the heat of his gaze sending pulses through her pussy. She's so wet and he hasn't laid a hand on her yet. His dark blue eyes are full of lust and need, as he rakes his gaze over every inch of her body as she undresses.

'You are so unbelievably stunning, Chloe.'

She straddles his legs, holding her hips off him, just hovering over his dick. 'Beg for it.'

Tate narrows his gaze then smirks at her. 'Oh like that, is it?'

She brushes her pussy against him, loving the way his dick twitches against her. 'Yeah. I think it is.'

Tate never took well to being held back. He's a control freak through and through. And that's why she loves turning the tables on him.

He licks his lips then meets her eyes. 'Please Chloe. Fuck me!'

Having this giant of a man beg her, nearly sends her over the edge. She holds him upright, sliding the pierced tip into her, groaning as she slowly stretches to accommodate him.

'Fuck Chloe. You're so tight.'

'It's been two months without you inside me. What do you expect. So, you ready to get banned from another hotel?'

He rests his head back on the couch, his thick neck rippling as he swallows. 'So fucking ready.'

She settles back on him, his dick stretching her to her limit. 'Hands over your head. Make it loud, Tate.'

He lifts his arms, gripping the back of the couch firmly in his hands. 'Just fuck me. Please...'

With her hands on his shoulders, Chloe does exactly as he wants. The barbell in the base of his cock brushes against her as she moves. She missed this so much. Missed Tate inside her like this.

The muscles in his arms strain as he nears orgasm. She knows his body well enough by now. 'Not yet.'

He nods. 'I know. It's just so fucking good, Chloe.' He turns his head, his eyes glossed over and sexy as hell. 'Harder, Chloe.'

She rests her hands over his nipples, pressing down on the piercings. Tate arches back, grinding out a low, guttural curse. 'Hold it back.'

His entire body is trembling now, the effort of holding himself back, adding a fine sheen of sweat to his skin.

The only sound in the room is their damp skin, slapping together, and his heavy breathing. She's so close herself, but she wants to hold him back a little longer. It'll be so much more intense once she finally releases him.

'Chloe...'

His broad chest is rising and falling rapidly, each breath rasping out of him as he fights against what his body needs.

'Now, Tate!'

Before she's even finished saying his name, his hands are on her hips, holding her against his groin. Then his hips move and Chloe gasps as he pushes deep into her.

'Piercings. Now!'

She gently tugs against his nipples, pulling on the barbells. His thrusts increase, his grip on her hips keeping her from being thrown off him. Chloe comes, the orgasm stealing the air from her lungs. She collapses against his chest, her hands still on his nipples, twisting them the way he likes, as she mutters his name.

'Fuck, Chloe!' His entire body tenses, as his hot cum shoots inside her and it feels so damn good. He keeps thrusting into her, his head back on the couch as he rides it out, before finally stilling.

Chloe lies on his chest, listening to the sound of his rapid heartbeat. His dick pulses inside her, the spasms sending waves of pleasure through her.

'I think you might have pulled one of my nipples off.'

She laughs against his skin. 'Sorry.'

'Don't be,' he says, running his hand over her hair. 'So worth it. Loud enough for you?'

'Oh yeah. You might be banned.'

He shrugs. 'There are worse reasons to get kicked out of a hotel.' He takes a deep breath. 'Fuck, Chloe. You fucked me.'

She lifts her head, resting her chin on his chest. 'I think you did that to me at the end. I can't move.'

Tate laughs, then lifts her off his lap and carries her over to the bed. He covers them with the duvet and faces her, stroking her hair back from her face. 'We're going to have a baby.'

Chloe doesn't think she's ever seen Tate so happy before. He's been happy, she knows that. But this is a different type of happy. He's got something he thought he'd lost. They both have. 'We're going to have a baby.'

He rests his hand against her stomach and falls quiet. When he wipes his face on the pillow, Chloe gathers him in her arms. 'Hey, what's wrong?'

'Nothing. Just happy. Ignore me. It's just hitting me.'

She kisses the tears from his cheeks and holds his face in her hands. 'We've got this Tate. We're going to be the best parents to this little guy or girl. I know it.'

'Too fucking right we are.' He rolls onto his back and smiles up at the ceiling. 'And I can't wait.' He turns his head and grins at her. 'So, ready for number two fuck session yet?'

'You're ready?'

He wiggles his eyebrows at her. 'I think I could be persuaded.'

Tate

He's grinning like a fucking idiot, but he can't stop. The sound technician working on his earpiece keeps giving him funny looks, but he couldn't care less. Chloe winks at him from the other side of the room and his grin just grows.

He's going to be a father. Him! It's the second chance he was too afraid to wish for. All he wants to do is pick her up and tuck her into bed with him. But there are a few thousand fans waiting a few metres away, who would probably have a problem with that.

Gregg lifts his arms and turns as another technician works on him. 'What the fuck are you so happy about?'

'Just looking forward to going out there.'

'We've done this for the last few weeks and you haven't been so smiley. Stop it please - you're freaking me out.'

Tate holds up his middle finger. 'I'm allowed to smile.'

'You're the grumpy one. I'm the smiley one. Don't go muscling in on my thing.'

Dillon appears, chewing on an apple lace. 'Why the fuck are you smiling like that?'

'Oh would you both lay off? I can smile.'

Dillon shrugs. 'It's not really your thing.'

'I'm actually going to hit you both.'

Dillon grins, then lifts up his t-shirt so another technician can attach the sound pack to his belt. 'Just had a quick chat with Luke. He said to say hi and good luck for tonight.'

'How's he doing?' Tate asks, nodding his thanks to the tech when he finishes and stops poking him.

'Quiet, but okay I guess.' Dillon frowns and chews his lip ring.

'Hey, he'll be with us again soon.'

Dillon nods. 'Yeah, I know. So we ready to put on one hell of a show?'

Tate grins again and joins Gregg and Dillon when they hold one hand out in front of them. Tom hangs back, refusing to join in their pre-show ritual. They tried to tell him to stop being stupid, but he leaves the three of them to it. Tate gets it. Luke is the fourth member. Tom doesn't want to get in the way of that.

Tate places his hand on top of theirs.

'For Luke.'

'For Luke.'

He looks over Dillon's shoulder and nods at Chloe and Bria. 'Get your asses over here.'

They glance at each other, then slip in beside Gregg and Tate, adding their hands to the top of the pile. Tate looks at Chloe and raises his eyebrows. She nods and smiles at him.

'This has to stay between us,' Tate says.

'What does?' Gregg asks.

'I'm pregnant,' Chloe says, smiling up at Tate. 'We're going to have a baby.'

The stunned silence hangs for a few seconds, then the screams and hugs start. Tate is rugby tackled by Gregg and Dillon at the same time, which fucking hurts, but he doesn't complain. It's been too long since the band had something they could celebrate.

'I knew you weren't just grinning for the sake of grinning,' Gregg says, punching him in the shoulder.

'Yes. You're a genius.'

Dillon drapes his arm around Chloe's shoulder and hugs her. 'Congratulations. It's fucking brilliant news.'

'We know,' Chloe says, hugging him back. 'Thanks, Dillon.'

'Time guys.' Sam and her clipboard join them and she looks around the group. 'Okay. Why are you all smiling like that?'

'Just looking forward to getting out there,' Dillon says.

She hugs her clipboard to her chest as she examines each of them. 'Right. Sorry, just not used to seeing you all... smiling. It's not a complaint. You should do it more often.'

Tate takes Chloe's hand and leads her to the side of the back stage area. The sound of the crowd waiting for them makes talking difficult. They're loud, buzzing just like he is. It's going to be one hell of a show tonight. 'I love you.'

'I love you too.' She looks him up and down and gives him a grin that hits him below the waist. 'You look really sexy.'

'Stop giving me that look. I don't want to go out there with a hard on. Save that for later.'

She runs her hand down his chest but stops at his waistband, hooking her fingers under his belt and pulling him close for a kiss. 'I want you all to myself when you're finished. You walk off stage and take me back to the hotel room immediately. You understand?'

'Oh I think I can do that.' He kisses her again then waves as someone calls him. 'Gotta go. I want you to stay at the side of the stage. I need to see you while I play.'

'Wouldn't dream of being anywhere else.'

Tate kisses her, then joins Dillon, Gregg, and Tom at the edge of the stage. Their logo appears on the screen behind the stage, and the crowd go crazy.

'Ready?' Tate asks.

'Oh yeah,' Gregg says, twirling his drumsticks in his hand.

Dillon nods. 'Always.'

'Better get out there then.'

They step onto the stage and the roar is deafening. As Tate takes up position at the front of the stage, he looks over at Chloe and winks. She smiles and winks back.

He's one lucky bastard.

Epilogue

Luke

One week later...

Luke sits on the bench in the garden and tries not to fidget. He's constantly on edge, and no amount of deep breathing or relaxation exercises are doing anything to help. He twists the wedding ring on his finger. Another part of his fidgeting. He'll wear a groove in his finger if he doesn't stop.

He should take the ring off. But he's still married. Legally anyway. Emotionally... he's still trying to figure that part out.

The facility he was sent to is massively expensive, reserved for those with enough funding to help clean up their messes. Everyone is nice, but he misses his old life. Not that his old life was all that great either.

Something he's still trying to get his head around. Still trying to process. But he's seriously struggling.

Pippa hit him.

She hit him a lot, but it doesn't matter how many times he's been told her actions weren't his fault, he knows it was. He's spent so long talking about it. Listening to others giving him advice. Listening as they tried to tell him he's done nothing wrong. Pippa was the one with the problem. Not him. He did nothing to deserve the treatment she gave him. He did nothing to deserve the verbal abuse. The physical abuse. The sexual abuse.

He runs his tongue over the back of the stud under his lip as he tries to process that. He'd been sexually abused by his girlfriend for years. His girlfriend, his wife, had raped him so many times.

It took a group of strangers to make him see that. To make him realise what she was doing to him was rape.

The more he talks with the counsellors about his life with Pippa, the more he realises how much she controlled him. How much she hurt him. How scared he actually was.

He thought he was messing everything up. That he was a terrible boyfriend. He thought by taking his life, he'd spare her and the guys. He keeps messing up, and they all have to deal with picking up the pieces. He can't even kill himself without screwing that up too.

Luke turns when he feels someone looking at him. Dillon is standing at the entrance to the garden, dressed in head to toe black, as usual. He hadn't been allowed visitors until today, and Dillon had put himself on the list ahead of everyone else. Something Luke is *mostly* happy about.

He hadn't really had a proper talk with Dillon since well before his wedding. He can't remember the last time he actually sat down and talked to him like they used to, before Pippa came along.

But that's his fault too. He turned his back on his best friend, just because Pippa didn't like Dillon. Maybe she felt threatened by him. Maybe she had a reason to feel that way. Dillon had admitted he loves him.

Past tense.

There's no way he still feels that way. Luke would be lucky if Dillon even liked him anymore. But he is here to see him, so hopefully there's a chance he can fix the most important relationship in his life.

Dillon sits beside him and stretches his legs out, crossing them at the ankle. They both let the silence continue for a few minutes, but Luke likes it. He missed just being in his company.

Dillon isn't a big talker and neither is he. Maybe that's why they get along so well. They're so similar in some things, but polar opposites in others. Luke had always been shy, painfully so at times. He hated drawing attention to himself, which makes no sense for someone who performs on a stage in front of thousands. Dillon, however thrived on attention. It was like he needed it to survive.

But Luke knows a lot of it is an act. Luke knows Dillon. Really knows him. He knows things about him, that Tate and Gregg don't, and probably never will.

'Thanks for coming.'

Dillon nods and offers him some apple liquorice from a paper bag.

'You know I hate that stuff.'

Dillon grins and pulls one of the laces from the bag. 'Everyone does, thank fuck. So, how are you holding up?'

'I'm okay.'

'How's the food?'

Luke smiles and nods. 'Yeah. Decent enough. Better than what you cook.'

For the first time, Dillon pulls off his sunglasses and looks sideways at him. 'Fuck you!' He grins and winks at Luke.

'I need to say something to you, and I don't want you to interrupt me.'

Dillon nods.

'I owe you a big apology.' Dillon opens his mouth to speak, but closes it again, remembering what Luke just said to him about interrupting.

'Remember the night when I brought you home from the pub and stayed with you. Well, before you passed out, you told me you were in love with me.'

Dillon's face drops. 'Shit.'

'At the time, I didn't know if it was just the drink talking, or if you were serious. But then I came to see you again. Pippa had just told me I couldn't see you anymore. I had to leave the band too.'

Dillon's green eyes harden and he clenches his jaw.

'I was low and confused. And I was cruel to push you to tell me how you felt. But when you did... I reacted. I shouldn't have kissed you. Not because kissing you was wrong. I shouldn't have done it, because you have feelings, and while I do love you, it's not in that way.

'And I am so, so, sorry for saying what I did. I should never have used the word *wrong*. I know that's what your mother said to you when you came out, and I never, ever, meant to hurt you like that. I'm so sorry, Dillon. You're one of the most important people in my life. I don't want to lose you.'

Dillon turns around and tucks one leg under the other. 'My go?'

Luke nods, dreading what his friend is about to say.

'You have nothing to apologise for. I know you're straight. I should have handled the situation better than I did. And I shouldn't have kissed you back. No way. I guess I got carried away in the moment, and I owe you an apology for that. I admit I was a bit pissed off when you called the kiss *wrong* like that. I guess it brought me back to that fun time in my life, but I know you didn't mean it like that.'

Dillon takes his hand in his and Luke doesn't pull away. It feels nice to have the contact.

'I promise you'll never lose me as a friend. And my feelings are my problem. Not yours. It was a fucked up time and we both did things we wish we didn't. I will say something though,' he adds with a sly grin. 'It was a fucking great kiss.'

Luke laughs at that. 'I don't have as much experience kissing blokes as you do, but yeah, it wasn't bad.'

'You're right. I have extensive experience. It was the best kiss I've ever had. I mean that.' Dillon drapes his arm around Luke's shoulder and pulls him against his side. 'I still love you, Luke, but I'm not going to be weird about it. I promise. And, as irresistible as I think you are, I will get over you. Eventually.'

'I know.' He turns to look at Dillon. 'I really wish I could give you what you want.'

Dillon smirks, then looks out over the garden. 'Who the fuck knows what I want? Probably need to figure that part out for myself. Or I could go after Tate next.'

Luke laughs. He can't remember the last time he laughed. It feels strange. 'Can you please take a video if you do? I want to see him deck you!'

'Charming. But yeah, he'd flatten me. Think I'll stick to guys who aren't in the band.'

'Might be best.'

'Luke.'

'Yeah?'

'Are you sure I didn't fuck things up between us? You're my best mate. I'd hate—'

'What happened is on me. And that's not me blaming myself, or beating myself up. It's the truth. I made the move on you. I know you Dillon. You'd never have done anything, unless I told you I was okay with it. We're good... well, as long as you think so too?'

'Of course I do! I miss you, Luke. I miss talking to you. Miss being a rude, opinionated, self-absorbed dick with you. I just miss you.'

'I miss you too.'

Dillon pulls him closer, which isn't normal for him. He doesn't do touchy feely like this. But Luke isn't complaining. It feels nice to be held like this by him. Dillon is safe. Always has been.

'So when do you get out of here?' Dillon asks after a short silence.

'I don't know. Not for a while.' He doesn't want to go into details with his friend. Taking all those pills hadn't been a cry for help.

And now?

He's not sure.

He's got Dillon, Tate, and Gregg. He's got his amazing family - especially Alex who has been incredible. But everything else is a terrifying blur. He's scared of what's facing him. Scared of seeing Pippa. Scared of going back to that house. Scared of the looks, the comments, the pity. But more than anything, he's scared he'll never find himself again.

He's thirty-seven years old and has no idea who he really is, or what he wants. He's completely lost. Living from hour to hour, trying to come to grips with just making it to the next hour.

Luke rests his head against Dillon's shoulder, taking comfort from his friend, from someone who loves him without question. It's what he needs right now. He needs to know someone out there cares about him, and that he's not a complete failure.

'Will you visit me again?'

'I'll be here every day. I promise. Do you need anything?'

Luke considers that for a moment, then smiles. 'A guitar. I miss playing.'

'That I can absolutely do. Any one in particular?'

'No. You pick. Not one of the expensive ones though.'

'Leave it with me. I'll bring it in tomorrow.'

'Thanks.'

'It'll be okay, Luke. I promise.'

Luke desperately wants to believe Dillon. But right now, he can't see how his life will ever be okay again.

Thank you for reading **Split Rock**.

I hope you enjoyed catching up with the band again. There's plenty more to come!

The next book, **Crushed Rock**, is coming soon.

Do you fancy staying updated with news about my books?

• Join my mailing list at: www.kafinn.com/

• Like me on Facebook: www.facebook.com/kafinnauthor

• Follow me on Instagram: www.instagram.com/kafinnauthor/

• Keep up to date with new releases: https://books2read.com/ap/nE2Kdj/KA-Finn

Also, if you have a moment, I'd appreciate if you could review **Split Rock** at the store where you purchased it. The band and I would love to know what you thought of the book.

Thanks for your support!

K.A. Finn

Coming next...

Broken Chords #4

K.A. FINN

Broken Rock

Broken Chords # 1

A dark history. An uncertain future. With the press, rumours, and saboteurs against them, will these lovers ever find their melody?

Irish rockstar Tate Archer thought his ugly past was behind him. So when an anonymous tormentor sends him cryptic messages about his forgotten childhood, the haunted frontman turns to hard drugs to cope with the residual trauma. But after his release from rehab, he can't help but wonder if the perfect prescription is the beautiful stranger he meets on the beach.

Chloe Quinn prefers things uncomplicated. So she isn't looking for anything serious when she draws close to a handsome guy who helps fix her car. But just as she's falling for her new seaside squeeze, she feels betrayed when she learns he's actually a troubled famous singer.

As the messages draw him deeper into his past, Tate finds the siren call of booze and narcotics nearly impossible to resist. And with his reputation spiraling downward, Chloe fears she'll lose him to old habits as someone seems intent on not only destroying his career, but his life too.

Will Tate and Chloe hit their harmony, or is this duet just not meant to be?

Fractured Rock

Broken Chords # 2

Irish rockstar Gregg Egan is new to the celebrity lifestyle. As the latest member of the band, he's still finding his feet. Being secretly in love with his lead singer's younger sister, isn't helping. For the sake of the band and his friendship she has to remain off limits.

Bria Archer grew up surrounded by the members of the band. She never expected to develop feelings for the drummer. Especially when he's her brother's best friend. But when her life takes an unexpected turn, he's there to help her pick up the pieces.

But someone finds out about their secret. Someone intent on keeping Gregg and Bria apart no matter the cost. Their stalker knows far too much about them. Knows things Gregg has kept to himself for years. Things he doesn't want the public to know about.

With the pressure mounting and too much to lose, Gregg and Bria have to make a decision about their relationship before it tears the band, their friendships, and their lives apart.

www.ingramcontent.com/pod-product-compliance
Lightning Source LLC
Chambersburg PA
CBHW020504020726
47493CB00001B/175